# Praise for Kar(

This was a thoroughly enjoyable story. I found the characters quite engaging and you could tell the author has a true understanding of Native American culture.

D. G.

This book is everything a reader could wish for. It has mystery, suspense, hot passion with a brazen love. It has perfect descriptions of the beauty of this native country. You feel as if your there. Evil doers and brave medicine men.

L.J.C.

A delightful and action packed novel.

J.

I'm absolutely amazed at this story line. It was beautifully written and touched my heart to the very depths of my being.

Cinderella 7

Look for these titles by
Karen Kay

*Lakota Series*
Lakota Surrender
Lakota Princess
Proud Wolf's Woman

*Blackfoot Warriors*
Gray Hawk's Lady
White Eagle's Touch
Night Thunder's Bride

*Legendary Warriors*
War Cloud's Passion
Lone Arrow's Pride
Soaring Eagle's Embrace
Wolf Shadow's Promise

*The Warriors of the Iroquois*
Black Eagle
Seneca Surrender

*The Lost Clan*
The Angel and the Warrior
The Spirit of the Wolf
Red Hawk's Woman
The Last Warrior

*The Clan of the Wolf*
The Princess and the Wolf
Brave Wolf and the Lady

*The Wild West*
The Eagle and the Flame
Iron Wolf's Bride
Blue Thunder and the Flower

*The Medicine Men*
She Steals My Breath
She Captures My Heart
She Paints My Soul

# She Brings Beauty To Me

By

KAREN KAY

The Medicine Man Series

Book Four

PK&J Publishing

1 Lakeview Trail

Danbury, CT 06811

She Brings Beauty To Me

Copyright © June 2024 by Karen Kay

Print ISBN: 979 8 32749 3 599

Cover by Darleen Dixon

Blurb created by BlurbWriter.com and Karen Kay

This book is a work of fiction. The names, characters, places, and incidents are products of the writer's imagination or have been used fictitiously and are not to be construed as real. Any resemblance to persons, living or dead, actual events, locale or organizations is entirely coincidental.

All Rights Are Reserved. No part of this book may be used or reproduced in any manner whatsoever without written permission, except in the case of brief quotations embodied in critical articles and reviews.

For avoidance of doubt, the Author reserves the rights to this work and does not grant to any person any rights to reproduce and/or otherwise use the work in any manner for the purposes of training artificial intelligence technology to generate text, including without limitation, technologies that are capable of generating works in the same style or genre as this work.

Artificial Intelligence, in any form, was not used in the writing of this work.

# Contents

| | |
|---|---|
| Dedication | page 9 |
| Special Recognition | page 10 |
| A Note about the word "Indian" | page 12 |
| Prologue | page 14 |
| Chapter One | page 24 |
| Chapter Two | page 42 |
| Chapter Three | page 59 |
| Chapter Four | page 71 |
| Chapter Five | page 86 |
| Chapter Six | page 97 |
| Chapter Seven | page 108 |
| Chapter Eight | page 120 |
| Chapter Nine | page 130 |
| ChapterTen | page 153 |
| Chapter Eleven | page 172 |
| Chapter Twelve | page 188 |
| Chapter Thirteen | page 204 |
| Chapter Fourteen | page 212 |
| Chapter Fifteen | page 228 |
| Chapter Sixteen | page 235 |
| Chapter Seventeen | page 247 |
| Chapter Eighteen | page 262 |
| Chapter Nineteen | page 273 |
| Chapter Twenty | page 286 |
| Chapter Twenty One | page 297 |
| Epilogue | page 301 |
| Glossary | page 305 |
| Author Bio | page 307 |
| Preview 'She Belongs To Me' | page 308 |

**Dedicated to:**

**My husband Paul**

My Inspiration

**Kirstie Alley**

Who helped all those years ago

**Patricia Janečkovou**

The beautiful voice who was taken away too soon

**Patricia Running Crane Devereaux**

**Toni Running Fisher**

**Harold Dusty Bull**

**Maria Ferrara**

Founders In Part of the Blackfeet Nation Help Learning Center All Those Years Ago

# SPECIAL RECOGNITION

There are so many authors, artists and friends who inspire me, and I would like to mention a few of them.

**Thomas E. Mails**

Author of the book:

*FOOLS CROW*

**John G. Neihardt**

Author of the book:

*BLACK ELK SPEAKS*

**John Trudell**

Lakota poet, songwriter, actor, activist and writer.

His poems/songs: "My Heart Doesn't Hurt Anymore"

and

"Paint Yourself, Protect Your Spirit"

are truly inspiring.

**James Willard Schultz**

Author of the books:

*MY LIFE AS AN INDIAN;*

*WHY GONE THOSE TIMES? Blackfoot Tales*

*RISING WOLF, THE WHITE BLACKFOOT;* and

*AN INDIAN WINTER OR, WITH THE INDIANS IN THE ROCKIES*

**Jeffrey Prather**

Author of *INITIATION, Boys Are Born, Men Are Trained*

**Frank B. Linderman**

Author of *PRETTY-SHIELD*, *Medicine Woman of the Crows*

**David Foster & Jackie Evancho**

**HIT MAN RETURNS, David Foster & Friends**

*Pie Jesu (Andrew Lloyd Webber)*

"*Pie Jesu Domine, Dona eis requiem*" *from the Latin Sequence,* "**Dies irae**"

**Linda Crews Sheffield & Starr Miller**

Who Have Helped

# A NOTE ABOUT THE WORD "INDIAN"

At this time in history, the term "Native American" did not exist. The Indians were called simply "Indians," although within their own culture they were more usually known by their tribal name. Also, even in the present day, depending upon the tribe, American Indians often call themselves "Indians" and are proud of it (as an example, the Blackfeet "Indian Days Pow-wow"). This is true of the Blackfeet, the Lakota and many of the other northern tribes. There are, however, several tribes I know of who prefer to be called "Native American" or, in some cases, "First American." But, once again, these are modern terms and simply did not exist at the time period of this novel.

Additionally, Russell Means, one of the founders of the American Indian Movement, has stated that the commonly held history of this word "Indian" is not accurate.

In the words of Russell Means:

"There is a mistaken belief that [the word Indian] refers somehow to the country, India. When Columbus washed up on the beach in the Caribbean, he was not looking for a country called India. Europeans were calling that country Hindustan in 1492.... Columbus called the tribal people he met "Indio," from the Italian in dio, meaning ' in God." Source: https://www.azquotes.com/author/9927-Russell_Mean

# PROLOGUE
Pest, Hungary
The Estate of József and Mária Fehér
Spring 1855

"Czanna, hurry. There is no time to waste!"

"What is it, Frederic?" Eighteen-year-old Czanna Fehér stepped from her bedroom into the grand hallway on the upper level of her family's ancestral mansion. By closing the heavy wooden door against her maid, who still lingered in the room, Czanna ensured her conversation with her brother would remain private. It was important in these days after the Grand Revolution of 1848. Even the walls had "ears." Indeed, since the revolution for independence had failed, their entire family was constantly on guard against spies.

Taking her brother's outstretched hand, Czanna rushed with him down the hall, noticing details about the corridor she had always taken for granted: the white, gold-flecked marble flooring; the gold, woolen curtains and the gold hardware holding them in place; the white and gold tiles of the arched ceiling and the white columns with gold trim that supported them.

At the end of the passage loomed her favorite feature, though it stood more exactly outside the hallway. There at the very end of the pathway stood a heavy gold-flecked glass door, opening up onto a balcony that supported a three-tiered fountain from which water fell down in every direction and at every hour of the day. At the very top of the white fountain stood the statue of Dacso Fehér, one her noble ancestors. And, there he reposed, captured in time, ever alert and ready to take action to defend his home, should there be a need.

Yet, she had only a moment to admire the grand walkway and its balcony because Frederic was ushering her toward the third-floor study, a room where they had often played in their youth. He opened the door, closing it as they both hurried past the large rectangular desk that stood so stately upon a wall-to-wall woolen rug of blue and gold. Her brother didn't hesitate in his movements, ignoring the alcove overlooking the estate and guiding her into a corner of the room. There he paused, and, since Frederic was acting in so clandestine a manner, Czanna prayed the acoustics of the spot would keep their conversation from being overheard.

As soon as they were both seated in the blue-and-gold chairs and were facing one another, she asked, "What has happened?"

Frederic looked cautiously around the room before he murmured, "Our parents have been arrested and are awaiting trial."

"Arrested? Awaiting trial? Surely you jest!"

"I do not," he said. "Indeed, it is true. There is even talk of hanging them both for their part in the rebellion of 1848."

"No! It cannot be true! The new government would never go so far as to arrest a nobleman and his wife."

Frederic reached out and took Czanna's hand into his own as though to comfort her. But, such consolation lasted only a moment before his gaze bore into her own, and he said, "I fear it is no lie. Now, listen to me carefully. Someone—and we don't know who—has reported our parents as part of the noblemen who helped Lajos Kossuth when he was in power in 1848. As you know, his followers, save some who escaped, have either been imprisoned or executed."

"No!" Czanna let out a scream.

"Sh-h-h. Do not cry out again, Czanna. Now, listen and hear me well. I am working with others who supported the Kossuth revolution; we are planning to make an appeal to Emperor Franz Joseph to free our parents. I believe we will be successful. But, you must remain strong as I tell you this next part: our entire family, including you and me as well as our little brother and sister, could be hung along with our parents if the appeal does not go well."

Czanna gasped. "But, I thought the new government had proclaimed they would support the idea of freedom for all, including all those who supported the 1848 Revolution."

"Although there is talk of this, it is not true," replied Fredric. "Listen carefully. I was able to speak briefly to our father today, and we both agree you and the rest of the family must flee. It is for your own safety and the preservation of our family. You must leave here this very night, and you must take our younger brother and sister with you."

"Tonight? Leave Hungary? Leave the only home I've ever known?"

"I fear you must," answered Frederic. "Neither I nor our father can envision any other way to keep you and the rest of our family safe."

Czanna looked away, forcing herself to become calm. Then, after a moment, she said softly, "Yes, of course. I am sorry I am so shocked; it is only that—" Her voice broke. Then, looking up at her brother, she asked, "And you? You have mentioned our brother and sister, but what about you? You are coming with us, are you not?"

Frederic glanced away from her, his composure hard, although a muscle twitched in his cheek. At last, he said, "No. I am staying here. I fear I cannot escape with you. There are people I am working with who also wish to free our parents, and if I am not here to help these people, our parents' freedom is not assured."

"Oh, I see. You are to stay here and help our parents. And, of course there is no one else who will work harder than you to free them. Still, if I must leave tonight, how will I ever be able to go away unseen? Where would I go?"

"To America. You must go to America."

"To America? But, America is so far away, and I hear it is a savage land."

"Yes, I have been given rumors to believe the same as you," said Frederic. "But, there are reasons why America is the only country where our father and I believe you and the rest of the family will be safe. It is there where you will be able to hide yourself from any Hungarian spies. I have already spoken to our father's manservant, Henrik, and I have asked him to accompany you. He, however, refused the coin I offered him to do it. He said it is his duty to ensure you and our brother and sister are kept as safe as possible. He will guide you and shelter you as much as he is able. He also understands why I must stay here to try to free our father and our mother, and he agrees with our father and me. He has also given me his solemn word of honor to help you and our brother and sister to reach the American frontier with as little incident as possible. Henrik will, of course, be bringing his own daughter with him."

"Yes, of course. Since she is his only family, she, too, must embark upon this journey. Although she is barely ten years and four, I believe I shall welcome her assistance very much, especially since our younger sister is still a babe."

"Yes. Now, listen well to me. You and the others are to sail north on the Danube this very night, and once you are out of the city of Pest, you and the others will go by coach to the coast, there to set sail for America. I have purchased the boarding tickets for you all on a ship sailing from the port there tomorrow. The name of the ship is on the tickets. I will now give them to you and not to Henrik. Count them and ensure there are five." Frederic handed her the tickets.

"Yes. There are five tickets here."

"Good. Now, come, I have a private box in this study where I have stored the papers you will need as well as enough gold and silver so you will be able to buy lodging and food. Keep the money on your person at all times. I have two strong, but light bags to serve this purpose. Do not store the coin in a trunk or any other convenience that is separate from you, nor are you to tell anyone, including Henrik, about the treasure you will be carrying on your person. I'm sorry. I know this is a heavy burden I am forced to place upon you, but there is no other manner in which to ensure you will be safe from harm. Never show what I am to give to you to another soul either—not to our younger brother and certainly not to Henrik. I will give Henrik other monies so he will not suspect that you also carry a treasure with you. Please bend close for what I am about to show you and tell you. These very walls may well have ears. I fear I am placing you now as the head of our family from this day forward. This family now extends to both Henrik and his daughter."

"But...about the gold and silver. I understand what you say about showing it to no one, including Henrik. However, Henrik has been with our family for his entire life, and he wouldn't—"

"I trust no one," interrupted Frederic. "Someone reported our parents for their part in the revolution—someone who knows us and has access to our parents' secret papers. Because this spy is within our midst, we are all in danger. Do you understand? We could all be tried for treason and hung."

"But, Frederic, since our youngest sister, Béla, is only three years old, surely it is possible for her to stay here. After all, it will be a hard journey for her. Is there no other way?"

"There is none. It will be worse for her if she stays, and this is another reason why I spoke long and ardently to Henrik about the need to bring his daughter with him. I could not have rightly placed you into the position as the head of our family if you also had to act as a nanny for Béla. Henrik's daughter, Lilike, will care for Béla, which will leave you free to think clearly about what is best for our family. Do you have any other questions?"

"I…I—"

"You all must flee…and tonight. I do not know how much time we have until the palace guards come here to arrest our entire family."

"I…I can hardly believe it."

"I know."

Glancing up at Frederic's solemn face, Czanna was startled to realize this might be the last time she would ever see her brother, unless… "Brother, if we are all in danger, then you must come with us. I beg you. Come with us."

"I cannot," Frederic replied. "You know I cannot. I have it in my power to free our parents and clear our family's name. This means more to me than my life. Please understand, I must stay here and fight. But, you must go. You must find safety in America. Lose yourself in the wild western frontier of America. Do not use our family name. Trust no one. And, under no circumstances are you to return to Hungary."

"Never?"

"Never," Frederic confirmed, shaking his head. "I believe it must be so. There seems to be no empathy in the new government towards those who strove to free the people. But, do not fear. There is yet a ray of light in all of this."

"Yes?"

"Do you remember our cousin Alfred?"

Czanna nodded. "I do. He is about ten years older than you, I think."

"Yes, he is older than I. Do you remember him being a part of the Revolution, also?"

"Yes, I do," said Czanna. "But, he became a Hungarian forty-eighter and escaped into the American West, didn't he? I assume he must have changed his name in order to evade capture."

19

"Yes, he did," replied Frederic. "But, he and I have been writing to one another these last seven years. I wish I knew where he is located exactly in the American West. I know only the following: he uses the English name of Old Tom Johnson and he lives within the Glacier Mountains located in the far corner of the Northwest Indian Country. I have written to him, informing him of what is happening here to our entire family, and I have told him to watch for you and our siblings in the next few years. But, since I do not know exactly where he makes his home in the Glacier Mountains, I am trusting you — not Henrik — to hire a guide to take you to him."

"But, why not Henrik?"

"Let me say this one more time: someone who knows us and who has access to our papers betrayed us. I like Henrik, same as you. But, I trust no one except you to take our family to safety."

Czanna nodded.

"Now, I have also written a letter that I will give to you to take to our cousin, whom you may call Tom Johnson. I am putting this letter into your care to present to him once you locate him; plus, there is one more of our family's possessions which is, perhaps, the most important of all I have to give you. Our father begs you to find our cousin and give him this." Frederic reached inside his coat to draw out an object carefully wrapped in the finest linen. Looking around the room, inspecting its nooks and crannies in detail, he then gave the package his attention and unwrapped the linen.

Czanna gasped. "Why, it's our…our—"

"Coat of arms, our Crest. It is worth a treasure, not only because it is made of bronze, gold and silver, but because it is also a seal we must preserve. Our father instructed me to caution you to hide it well, and, to this end, I have personally created a trap in your trunk where you may hide our seal. When you at last find our cousin, you are to give our family's crest to him. It is important. The seal must be preserved, even if our country falls. It will also identify you to our cousin. Our father wishes you to give our cousin the seal because, if my plea to Emperor Franz Joseph fails, our cousin would then be the oldest living member of our family. As you well know, it is always the eldest of our family who must bear the responsibility for preserving it. Seek out our cousin. He will help you. Give him my letter and the seal and ask him to help you all to disappear into the rugged country of the American West. I fear there may well be Hungarian agents who will try to follow you. Do you understand?"

"I do. But, Frederic. How can I go there and leave you here knowing...knowing...?"

Frederic again shook his head. "I cannot go with you. Please understand this: my duty is here. When you arrive in America, send me word of your arrival but say nothing more. I believe you will need to hire a coach to take you to a settlement called St. Louis. From there, you can book passage aboard a steamboat that will take you into the depths of the American West. Our cousin has written to me telling me he has become a fur trapper. I admit I think it is a terrible occupation, but it is, perhaps, the only livelihood for a man in the ruggedness of America. At least where he is now, he is not in the line of fire. Join him there, and once you are safe from harm, use the money I have given you to buy property, if you can. I will do my best to free our parents. I cannot emphasize this enough: do not let anyone know you carry with you a treasure in gold and silver, nor tell another living soul about the family crest; you are not even to say a word about this to our siblings, and certainly not to Henrik."

"But, I must have some money I can easily show and use to buy necessities. If I am to hire a man to take us to our cousin, I must—"

"Of course you will have to carry some coin with you. But, what I am giving you to carry on your person is more than mere coin."

"Oh, yes, of course. Yes. I understand now."

"Hear me well, and do not forget what I am about to tell you: until this is over, you can trust no one who is Hungarian, except, of course, our cousin. Someone has betrayed us. Now, remember these words I say to you: do not ever come back to Hungary for any reason."

"But, Frederic, not ever?"

"Not ever. Swear this to me now: you are never to return to Hungary."

"But, what if—?"

"Do you swear?"

Gazing up into her brother's solemn expression, Czanna nodded and whispered, "I swear."

"Good. As you know, our family is one of the noble families who sided with the Revolution. I do not have the knowledge of what the future holds here. But, whatever our future is to be, I and our father and mother wish you and our siblings to survive. Make a new life for yourself, as well as for our brother and sister. Do you understand?"

Czanna nodded.

"Good. Now, grab your cloak, gather our siblings together and go! Outside of what I've given you, take nothing else with you."

"But, my clothes, my shoes, my—"

"They are all Hungarian made. You must disappear. You and our brother and sister are to have nothing with you or on you that can identity you as to whom you really are. Now, Henrik waits outside with a coach."

Czanna's brother, who was probably her best friend in all the world as well as being her brother, took both her hands into his own. Breathing in deeply, he said, "Farewell, Czanna. I will miss you and the others. I am sorry to burden you with so much responsibility. If there were a way to do it, I would take the cares of the world away from you, our sister and our brother. I, alone, would carry this weight if I could. But, there is not a manner by which to do it. I must free our parents. I will write. Look for my letters, but do not write back to me except to inform me of your journey and that you have reached America. Know this: I will never ask where you are and you are never to tell me. Nor will I ever ask you to go against your word and return to Hungary. Again, I am sorry I have to burden you with this, but upon your shoulders rests the future life of our family."

Czanna nodded, looking down and hiding, if only for a moment, the shock as well as the tears in her eyes. It was at some length when, at last, clearing her throat, she said, "I know and I understand the burden I carry. Farewell, Frederic. We will see one another again. I am certain of it."

"Let us hope your words will hold true."

Standing up, Frederic reached out a hand to pull Czanna to her feet. He hugged her, and, as was tradition, he kissed her gently on each side of her face. Then, Czanna stood to her tiptoes and, reaching up, returned the endearment.

Shaking a little, Czanna stepped back and, turning away, hurried from the study, rushing toward her younger siblings' rooms.

"Farewell," she called as she reached the door.

"Farewell, Czanna," answered Frederic. "Godspeed."

\*\*\*\*

**Cherokee Proverb**

"A woman's highest calling is to lead a man to his soul to unite him with source.

"A Man's highest calling is to protect the woman so she is free to walk the earth unharmed."

# CHAPTER ONE
## Northwest Indian Country
## Territory of the Blackfeet
## The Month of High Water, June 1856

*Was this the wind singing over the dry prairie cliffs?*

He-stands-strong-against-the-enemy paused and listened. Scouting ahead of his party and intent on saying his morning prayers, he had been in the act of climbing up the steep rock-hardened bluff overlooking the sweeping, spring-green prairie. But now, hearing the distinctive melodic tones of a woman's voice, he halted, listening.

Looking outward at the pinkish sun rising up in the east, he hesitated for a moment to admire its beauty, there where it sat within the gray-, blue- and pink-painted sky. The air here was dry, as usual, though it was slightly cool. As he gazed eastward, listening to the woman's song and admiring the stark beauty of this northern landscape, a feeling of peace fell over him. He smiled, for it was a welcome sensation.

Although the words of her song were in a language he didn't understand, it little mattered. The wind carried the clear notes of the feminine voice to him, and he stood for a moment, transfixed in place. Then, with as little noise as possible, he pushed himself into an indentation in the face of the cliff that shot up from the prairie. Layers of rock jutting outward would cause a man to carefully place a foot when scaling it, but it also provided a means to "disappear," a skill essential to the scout.

He knew this place well, for the Pikuni people had often used this very cliff in the long ago past. The first time he had stood upon this bluff, he had imagined it looked as though the hillside had been cleaved through by a child's gigantic hand rather than the passage of time.

His people called this place a *pisskan*—a buffalo jump. In the days before the horse, this was one of the many places in Pikuni country where the people had lured a herd of buffalo into falling off a cliff. The event, though filled with danger, was one of the greatest means by which to obtain enough meat for the tribe to last through the long, northern winters.

However, the people rarely used the *pisskan* now. Those days were now relegated to the long ago past—a period referred to as the "dog days," a time before the horse. But, the memory remained, and even today, when game was scarce, the *pisskan* could be called into practice and used for the benefit of the people.

Again, the wind whispered to Stands Strong, bringing the lilting quality of the woman's voice to his ears. He didn't move. He couldn't. He didn't even think; it seemed he could do little more than listen.

The song ended, leaving him with the desire to hear more of her lyrical voice. He didn't have to wait long, however, and the pleasant feeling that swept through him when she began another song startled him. That he should be so enraptured by a woman's singing was not a pleasant state of mind for him.

He was here to say his early morning prayers, true, but he and another scout were also performing a scouting duty requested by the chiefs of his tribe. And, because the lives of the Pikuni people depended upon his accurate information and evaluation of the environment, for Stands Strong to become entranced by a woman's voice was against all scouting protocols.

Yet, when she began the next melody, he recognized the sadness in her voice. Sadness—this, he understood. The woman was grieving.

Even though he could not look upon her person because of his current position below her, he knew she was white. Although Indian women often sang as they went about their daily routines, the notes, scale and rhythm of this woman's song were arranged in a way usually foreign to the American Indian's ear. No drum accompanied her singing...only the wind.

*But, what is a white woman doing here? Alone upon a deserted windswept bluff?*

Although he was acquainted with several white trappers in this, the Blackfoot country, he was only aware of three white women in all the regions of Indian Country. His almost-mother was one of those women; her two friends, who were sisters, were the other white women. All three lived with the Pikuni people and were each one married to an esteemed medicine man.

Was this woman a friend of these other white women? It seemed a reasonable assumption. This was especially so since he could think of no other reason for a white woman to be here alone, standing upon a desolate bluff and singing about the sorrow in her heart.

*Is she lost? Is this why she is grieving?*

Could she be related to the three white women he knew? Perhaps. Yet, his almost-mother had mentioned nothing of a friend traveling into Blackfoot country. And, she would have spoken of it, if only to ensure the person arrived safely.

Given these facts, it seemed unlikely the woman was distressed because of her inability to find her friends. However, reaching this conclusion brought more questions about her to mind, and because his duty as a scout demanded he investigate any matter which seemed out of the ordinary, scouting rules alone required him to discover what this was all about.

And so, although a sense of empathy demanded he should leave this woman alone to her anguish, he could not. Her being here was too unusual a circumstance. And, if he were wrong and she were actually looking for the three white women who lived amongst the Pikuni, he could take her there upon completion of his scouting obligation.

Yet, he was also aware of another reason to learn more about this woman: within him burned an urge to look upon this feminine person who sang with so much beauty in her voice. But, how was he to make his presence known without frightening her?

There was not a way to continue his climb to the top of the ledge without making noise. And, this alone would surely startle her. Yet, he had to do it.

Quietly, as soundlessly as possible, he stood away from the rock face which, up until now, had hid him. He looked upward toward the flat ledge.

Because she stood so closely to the edge of the precipice, he could see no more than the bottom of her dark-blue dress. But, the color of her clothing was of no importance to him since it told him nothing about her nor why she was here. He would have to announce himself in a manner that would least frighten her, and, if possible, he would talk to her since it was the only means available to him to discover why she was here.

Negotiating the footholds of the surrounding rocks, he climbed upward until he could at last pull himself up onto the ledge behind her. And, once he was positioned on the ridge, he squatted down behind her.

From this particular angle, Stands Strong could only see the back side of her, and yet he determined from this alone that she looked to be young and, most likely, pretty. Her figure was slight, yet rounded in its girlish splendor. Her dark hair hung loose down her back in waves and curls, and nothing adorned her head, which seemed odd for a white woman. His almost-mother had once related a story of the many hats a "proper woman" was expected to have in her possession.

The color of her hair was a deep, dark brown, almost black. Yet, now and again, as a beam of the early morning sun encompassed her, the dark color appeared reddish where the sun highlighted it.

He sat on the edge of the shelf, unwilling to stand to his full height; he did not wish to shock her, and he was certain his appearance behind her would alarm her. However, knowing she would come to feel his presence eventually, he remained seated, his legs under him as he sat on his heels.

At last, it happened, and he watched her beautiful profile as she gazed over her shoulder. Her scream as she spun around to confront him sounded unusually loud, and he was certain it could be heard by all living creatures in this part of the world. He continued to watch as she took a pace backward toward the edge of the ridge.

"Careful there," Stands Strong called out in distinct English as he stood up. But, he took no action to step forward. "You are close to the edge of this cliff, and I fear if you step farther backwards, you might fall to your death."

She caught her breath, then she gasped out, "You…you…are Indian!"

He nodded.

She screamed again and brought her hands up to cover her mouth.

In response, he held up both of his hands, this being the Plains sign for "I have no weapons and my intentions are to parley with you."

Again she screamed, but this shriek wasn't as loud as her others had been. Then, the two of them did little more than look at one another as each one tried, though perhaps in vain, to determine the true intent of the other.

At length, he said, "If I meant you harm, it would have been done by now, and so fast would I have done it, you would not even know what had happened."

She swallowed hard before saying, "Excuse me, but these words you speak to me do not help your cause about your peaceful intent. And, why are you talking to me in English? I...I thought there were not any Indians in this country who spoke English."

He laughed, but only a little.

"Sir, are you mocking me?"

He shook his head and forced his countenance to appear blank, before saying, "I am not mocking you, and I mean you no insult. It is only that many of my people, the Pikuni, speak English."

"Many?"

"It is so," he responded. "I know of several of my people who know and use this language, and three of them are white women."

"White women? In this country? In your camp? Living with your people? Are they captives?"

He shook his head. "They are not captives. They are there of their own free will and have become part of the Pikuni people. Also, one of those white women is my almost-mother."

"Your almost-mother?"

He nodded, then explained, "She is my almost-mother because, although she took me as her son, we are not of the same blood."

"I...I..." The beautiful woman caught her breath, but remained silent. Whatever she had been about to say was lost to the wind.

He asked, "Are you looking for these three white women? My almost-mother's name in English is Sharon. And, her two friends are sisters, Laylah and Amelia. Is this the reason you are here alone? If so and you are looking for your friends, I will take you to them as soon as I accomplish my mission."

"Your...your mission?"

Fright swept over her facial features, and she took another step backward, prompting him to say, "I fear I might have to rescue you if you move back any farther."

"Oh," was all she said as she looked over her shoulder. "Yes, you are right. I am very close to the edge of this place." She took a few paces forward. "But, sir, you mentioned I am here alone, and this is not true."

Grabbing hold of the rifle slung over his shoulder, Stands Strong bent at the knees, turned around in a three-hundred-and-sixty-degree circle. And, quick though it had been, his gaze was thorough. But, his scan of the environment did not show another human being in the vicinity of this place; he did not even sense the presence of another person, which he would have been able to feel in the spiritual world.

"Sir, forgive me, please. I did not mean to alarm you; it is simply I, and no one else, who is in this place. I have come here as part of a wagon train, and I do not know your friends or your…almost-mother."

He frowned. "You are part of a white man's wagon train? How many white people are with you?"

She looked away. "Yes, to your first question. I am not alone because I am with the wagon train. Indeed, there are many men there."

Turning slightly, he scrutinized his surroundings once more, expanding his reach out into the environment with his mind. But, he detected nothing except the natural order of the prairie world. Glancing back at her, he said, "I do not sense the presence of a white man's wagon train."

"And yet, they are there. I have simply walked a great distance to get to where I am now."

"You walked a vast way, and alone? In the dark hours of the morning? You, a woman?"

She caught her breath and glanced away from him.

"You have much courage to have done this."

"No, sir," she said. "You are wrong. I am not courageous. I am simply troubled, and I walked here to pray. I wished to be away from the wagon train when I spoke to God."

He nodded. Yet, he repeated his observation and said, "I understand what you say, and yet, I disagree with what you have told me about your bravery. What you did took courage."

"Or, perhaps I was too deeply grieved and so gave no notice to what was in the environment around me."

He nodded. "From your song, I have come to understand your heart is burdened. Have you lost someone? A husband, perhaps, or a child?"

She bit her lip before saying, "Sir, I do not have to answer your questions. Know simply that I tell you the truth. I have not come into this country alone."

He nodded. "When you are ready, I will take you back to your people."

He watched as she bit her lip yet again. But, at length she said, "Sir, I fear to tell you this, but I do not wish you to accompany me to the others. It could turn out in a bad way for you. But, also, I am frightened of you."

He didn't acknowledge her in any way. Instead, he simply looked at her quickly before withdrawing his gaze. But, within his glance, quick as it had been, he noticed the element of sadness again within her dark eyes. With this woman's wavy dark hair blowing in the wind and because she was wearing a feminine, flattering blue dress, she looked beautiful almost beyond description.

At last, he said, "A woman like you should not be alone in this country. At this time of year, there are always war parties about, and you could come upon one. If this were to happen, it might not go well for you. It would depend upon the war party's opinion of the white man."

"And yet," she replied, "I have come here on this cliff without incident, until now. Sir, what do you intend doing with me or to me? You say you mean me no harm, yet you are standing in the way of me leaving here, unless, that is, you wish me to jump off this cliff."

"*Pisskan.*"

"Pardon?"

"*Pisskan.* It means a buffalo jump. In the long ago days before the horse, my people used places like this to lure the buffalo here to jump off this cliff."

She paused, then said, "It is a rather cruel practice, isn't it?"

"Cruel? Is it heartless to use a place like this to obtain enough meat to see the people through the long winters? Without this, the people would starve and die, for the winters are long and dangerous in this part of the country, and sometimes even our best men are lost in the blizzards during the great snows. This makes hunting difficult and food scarce."

"Oh." She looked down. "I am sorry. You are right. I do not know this country well enough to place values on it that are foreign to it."

He nodded and smiled a little.

"Why do you grin, sir?"

"Your words were kindhearted and wise, and I smiled because your kindness brought joy to my heart."

"Joy? To your heart? But, sir, I thought…"

He waited a moment, then encouraged her to explain by asking, "You thought…?"

She looked away from him. "Sir, truly, how can this be so?"

He frowned, then repeated, "How can this be so? Say what you mean."

She turned slightly away from him, her gaze seemingly lost somewhere in the distance. At length, however, she murmured, "I fear to speak further."

"Fear? I understand fear. And yet, if I am to help you, it might be wise to say your thoughts aloud. I believe I am man enough to hear an insult without wishing to harm you, if it is an insult which causes you distress."

"Will you give me your word of honor to do me no harm if I tell you a description of the Indians, one that is commonly told by the men in this country?"

"I can and I do."

She looked down and away, changed her position so she once again faced him, then murmured, "Sir, I…I thought… I have been told Indians are humorless creatures and never take joy in anything but war and torture. I have been told this by those who know about the savage nature of the Indians—that the ideas of kindness and empathy are foreign to an Indian's heart. And, I have been told they treat their women as slaves."

Stands Strong couldn't help himself: he laughed aloud. "Who told you this?"

"The books I've read and the stories told by men and women around a campfire."

As was his tradition, Stands Strong paused a moment before speaking. Then, at length he asked, "Have you never thought to question the character and intent of those who would tell you such stories? Or wonder if the white man perhaps embellishes them? Has the white man never observed that those men who carry these bad tales are, in truth, speaking of themselves?"

"Sir!"

He couldn't help chuckling, though he supposed his frowning at the same time might seem odd to her. But, to correct her further seemed pointless. After a moment, he asked, "Would you sing again before you leave?"

"You heard me singing?"

"I did. It is one of the reasons I am here. I wanted to see the woman with the sad voice."

Once again, she looked away from him, and several moments of silence passed between them before she replied, "Yes, I will sing for you, but my songs are sad this morning. I cannot help it. Indeed, I have come here to pray."

"Then, we share this in common. It is my intention to pray, also. This is why I was climbing up these rocks in this early morning hour."

"Excuse me, sir, but I thought... I have been told... No, I read in a newspaper back East about Indians and praying and..." She hesitated, then continued, saying, "Never mind. It isn't important now. "

He simply smiled at her again. "Is this another 'fact' you learned from the white men who lie?"

She looked down and away from him. Then, quietly, slowly, she began to sing:

*Jesu, Deus Filius, Dona eis requiem.*
(Jesus, Son of God, Give them rest.)

*Pie Jesu Domine, Requiescat in Pace.*
(Pious Lord Jesus, May they rest in peace.)

*Pie Jesu Domine, Requiescat in Pace.*
(Pious Lord Jesus, May they rest in peace.)

*Jesu, Deus Filius, Dona eis requiem.*
(Jesus, Son of God, Give them rest.)

When she had finished the song, she took a step forward and, looking down, sang, "*Amen.*"

Only the wind answered her prayer as her voice echoed over the prairie.

He didn't speak; neither did she. However, when it became apparent she would not be treating him to another song, he spoke quietly to her and said, "I am of the Pikuni tribe, although I think you might call us the Blackfeet. By birth, however, I am Lakota, or as the white man calls us, the Sioux."

She nodded. "Thank you."

He responded in kind, bobbing his head.

"Sir, I cannot help but ask why, if you truly mean me no harm, have you come here this morning?"

He smiled a little. "This is my country and has been used and taken care of by my people for thousands of years. Would you take offense if I asked you the same question?"

She looked away as she answered, "I meant you no offense, though I realize now it sounded this way. I guess what I meant to say is why have you bothered to come here and speak to me? Truly, you could have continued on your journey without appearing before me." She paused, then, looking up at him in what might have been a speculative manner, she said, "Still, although perhaps you don't wish to answer my question, I wonder why you took the trouble to come here and have words with me."

He answered her honestly and said, "The beauty of your voice captured my attention. And, when I realized you were singing a white man's song, there were other questions I needed answered."

"Other questions?"

"*Hau, hau,* yes. But, I have already asked them of you. I will repeat them if you wish."

She glanced away from him, presenting him once more with the beauty of her profile. "I… No, it isn't necessary. The morning, however, is becoming late, and I fear I will be missed if I do not return to the wagon train. I must go. I just came here to…"

As she glanced down, Stands Strong couldn't help but see the tear that trickled down over her cheek. He didn't say a word, nor did he move. Instead, he barely breathed, waiting for her to continue.

And, at last she carried on, though her voice was no more than a whisper when she said, "To say goodbye."

He understood, and a feeling of compassion embraced him. His nod at her was almost imperceptible as he quietly murmured, "There is danger for a woman alone on the prairie, and someone should ensure you are able to return to your people unharmed. I would be that someone."

She smiled slightly, though weakly, before she softly said, "Thank you, but no. I...I fear you would scare the others in the wagon train, and there might be trouble."

Stands Strong frowned before asking, "Do I look to you as though I am the kind of man to run from trouble?"

"No, sir. You appear to me to be a man who would defend those he loves to the very end. But, sir, I don't wish to be the cause of any trouble. Please, I beg you to understand why I do not wish you to be with me when I rejoin the others. There are people with me on the wagon train whom I love dearly, and sometimes the innocent get harmed when there is fighting."

He nodded before saying, "Then, I will not take you there, but instead I will watch you from afar to ensure you return there safely."

"I...I thank you, sir. But, it is unnecessary."

"I disagree," he responded. "It is very necessary. A real man must ensure the women in his life are protected. But, ease your mind. You will not see me; they will not see me. Yet, you should know I will be there if there is a threat to you."

He watched as she gulped. Then, without looking up at him, she asked, "Sir, did you tell me this very moment that I am a woman in your life?"

Stands Strong couldn't help but smile a little before answering. But, without pausing too greatly, he said, "Of course you are a woman in my life. Have we not been speaking to one another? And, are you not here alone? No true man would leave you to possible harm when he could keep you safe."

"But, you know nothing about me."

"Does it matter? You are alone; it is not safe here for you. I will watch over you until you return to your own people."

He gazed at her as tears suddenly burst from her eyes to land upon her breast, and his heart beat fiercely in his chest in response. What had happened to this woman to cause her to not even expect a man to defend her?

She said, though her voice broke, "Sir, I am sorry for what I said to you earlier. I was wrong to say what I did."

Stands Strong nodded.

"Sir, I fear it is getting later and later, and I must be going. But, before I go, may I ask your name?"

"Yes, you may ask, but I should not tell it to you because, to my people, when a man says his own name, it is as though he is boasting."

"Oh, I think I understand. And yet, sir, I would like to know it. I promise I shall not think you are bragging. Please, won't you tell me?"

He hesitated, but, after a few moments, said, "I am called Stands Strong. And, what may I call you?"

"Czanna."

"Zaanna?"

"Yes."

"It is a beautiful name given to this woman whom I will always think of as *O'tsipohioo Matsowá'p Aakíí*."

"Oh my. You said this name so beautifully. Mr. Stands Strong, what does it mean?"

He grinned. "Do you really wish to know?"

"I fear I do."

He took a deep breath, feeling suddenly at a loss. The name would tell her of his admiration for her, and he might embarrass her. But, at last he said, "It means Brings Beauty Woman in the Blackfoot language."

"Thank you. It is a grand name, although I am uncertain I deserve it. But, sir, didn't you say you were Lakota by birth?"

"*Hau, hau.* I am. "

"Then, could you please say my name in Lakota, also?"

He paused only a moment, then said, "*Wiŋyaŋ Gopa Aya.*"

"Thank you for telling me who you are and for giving me such an exquisite name, although I fear I do not deserve such an excellent description. And, thank you for including me as one of the women in your life. I...I am now ashamed for what I said to you earlier."

He shrugged. "Do not be. How could you have known the truth? Besides, my tongue is not lying to you; there is much danger for you alone in this country. Your actions were good and defensive."

She looked away from him before repeating, "Thank you. I must be going. But, before I go, please tell me, Mr. Stands Strong, is there a reason for your name? I have heard Indian names mean something."

He nodded.

"Will you tell it to me?"

He frowned before answering. In due time, however, he said, "Again, it is not done for a man to say his name because of the fear of boasting, and if I tell you it all, it might seem as if I am, in truth, conceited."

"And yet," she said, "I would very much like to know what caused you to deserve this warrior's name. Won't you please tell me?"

He sighed, but said nonetheless, "It means He-stands-strong-against-the-enemy."

"And, did you do this? Stand strong against an enemy?"

He didn't answer.

"Please, will you tell it to me? You see, I'd like to remember our meeting here today. If you will disclose to me a little about your name, it might perhaps aid me in understanding you a little better so in all the years to come I will always remember the man who came to aid me, even though I still think it isn't necessary. Please?"

When her gaze pleaded with him, he sighed, yet explained, "I was young. My almost-mother and my almost-father were under attack by Cree warriors. When a Cree warrior came forward to kill my almost-mother, I used my child's arrows against him, though they did him little harm. I was only seven winters then."

"What is seven winters?"

"Seven years old," he clarified.

"Thank you, Mr. Stands Strong. No wonder you bear such a strong name. I know it took ignoring your pride to tell me, and I am grateful for your doing this for me. Know this, Mr. Stands Strong, I shall always remember you."

Then she stepped forward as if to skirt around him, but, in doing so, she tripped on the hem of her dress and lost her balance, falling backward.

But, Stands Strong had been anticipating such a move, if only because she stood so close to the edge of the cliff. With a few quick steps toward her, he caught and righted her. And, though he wished to let his hands linger upon her curves for a while longer, he knew it was wrong to do so. And so, without her having to say a word to him, he let her go after ensuring she was again secure on her feet.

"Thank you, Mr. Stands Strong. I am glad you came to me this morning. I have learned something quite important because of our speaking to one another today."

"Important?"

"Indians are people, same as my people. Your ideas about how to live might be different from mine, yet these stories I have heard from the traders and others are either wrong and highly embellished, or are outright lies. I wish you well, Mr. Stands Strong. And, I thank you for presenting yourself to me today. Perhaps there might come a time when we shall meet again."

He simply nodded. "I will always remember the woman who brought beauty to me."

He wasn't certain, but it appeared to him as if his words caused another bout of tears to form in her eyes. Yet, whether she was crying or not, she spun away from him, and he watched after her as she ran over the flat surface of prairie and away from him. And, so quickly did she run, he thought there might be a spirit wind chasing her.

He thought back over their conversation. Indeed, he would have no trouble remembering her. She, with her beauty and her quiet way of speaking, had touched his heart this day.

He waited for a moment before following her. As he had promised, he would keep out of sight, though on this flat treeless prairie, it was difficult to remain unseen, but not impossible.

At least, because he was walking instead of riding his pony, he could hang back until he was a mere dot on the horizon. And, crouching low, he could watch her until he was assured she reached the safety of the wagon train and her own people.

He had not lied to her about the dangers for a lone woman on the prairie at this time of year: war parties often dared to travel during the early morning hours when they least expected to encounter an enemy.

But, although he had not told her, there was another purpose behind following her to the white man's wagon train: there was intelligence he must gather about these white men who dared to come into Pikuni country without permission. Could this be the start of the trouble his almost-father had foreseen and had warned him about?

Stands Strong's almost-father, Strikes Fast, had counselled him before Stands Strong and his friend had left the Pikuni camp on their quest to gather intelligence for the chiefs.

"My almost-son," Strikes Fast had said, "be on your guard as you and your friend, First Rider, travel into the realm of the white man's fort. I see danger there. Discover what it is, yes. But, live to come back and tell us what it is."

Stands Strong had nodded. "I will remember your words. I will also tell my friend your advice so we will be alert to any danger."

Perhaps Stands Strong's conversation with the white woman, Czanna, would aid the Pikuni people by bringing his attention to the wagon train. What were these people doing here?

Regardless, he would watch over her as she returned to her loved ones, and he would also gather as much intelligence as he could, reporting it back to his chiefs.

## CHAPTER TWO

The early morning sun shone down its warmth upon the back of her head as Czanna strode north and west across the treeless prairie, returning to the site of the wagon train. Gazing forward, she studied the brown grassy hill as it rose up gently from the flat plains and stretched out for many kilometers in front of her. Just over the knoll there, she knew she would find the wagon train.

A scent of smoke still lingered in the dry morning air, even at this distance of perhaps a mere kilometer, around a half of a mile. Czanna grimaced and pinched herself; she had to remember to calculate distances in miles instead of kilometers here in the American West.

She rolled her shoulders, relieving some of the stress in her muscles, if only a little. What, in the name of the good Lord, was she to tell the others?

Carefully, she retrieved the letter she had tucked within the bodice of her gown last night. Was it only the previous evening when a man, recently come up from the fort, had given it to her? For a reason she didn't understand, it seemed as if a lifetime had passed since then and now.

Sighing, she glanced down and scanned the letter's contents again before bringing it in close to her and holding it against her chest, handling the paper as though it were a person. Gently, she folded the letter and placed it back into its position against her heart.

The letter—written by her brother's manservant, Mr. Sebestyn—represented her only contact with the world she had once known. But, oh, what terrible news it brought.

Climbing up to the top of the hill, she looked forward, expecting to see the wagon train lazily positioned in a circle, there under the early morning sunlight. But, where was it?

Czanna felt a rush of anxiety flood over her as she quickly scanned the horizon in every direction. It was as though by her look alone she willed the caravan to suddenly appear.

But, it was not to be.

Fear engulfed her as she gazed down upon only one wagon, it appearing to be alone and vulnerable as it stood upon the vast, green-and-brown grassland. At least it was her wagon, thank the good Lord. But, where were the other seven prairie schooners?

*What has happened here, and where is my family?* Czanna thought.

As alarm swept through her, she picked up her skirts and ran down the hill. As she came in closer to her own coach, she could at last see her two siblings as well as Lilike, Mr. Henrik's daughter, who had become Czanna's maid. Lilike was holding Czanna's baby sister, Béla, on her right hip and was standing next to György, Czanna's brother, who had only recently turned twelve years old.

Oddly, Czanna noted how tall György had become since beginning this journey. Why, he was almost as tall as Lilike.

At present, they were huddled in the back of the wagon's shadow; this would account for why Czanna hadn't been able to see them at a quick glance. But, at least she could see them now, thank the good Lord.

But, what had happened? And, where was Lilike's father, Mr. Henrik?

As if her thoughts alone had produced him, big and bulky Mr. Henrik jumped down from the seat of the wagon and trod away from the front of it. As he looked up at Czanna, he lifted his hat and greeted her, saying, "Mistress Czanna, happy I am to see thee. I have been worried about what might have happened to thee."

"Thank you, Mr. Henrik," replied Czanna. "I am sorry if I caused you any grief. I...I simply needed to be alone for a while. But, where are the other wagons? Why are they not here?"

"They all be gone, Mistress. Thine own family and me-self are the only folk left here, alone upon this vast land, and, afeared though I be to tell it to thee, ye and me have some trouble."

"Trouble? Please, Mr. Henrik, come walk with me for a moment and tell me what has happened in my absence." Quickly, Czanna glanced at her siblings and her maidservant, greeting them, too, by saying, "I am happy to see you all, but please allow Mr. Henrik and me to speak to one another."

György and Lilike nodded. It was Lilike who whispered, "I am so very happy to see you, Mistress."

"And I, you. Please give your father and me a moment so he might tell me what has happened here."

Lilike nodded.

Czanna felt as though she were spinning in all directions at once, though, of course, she stood up straight and without moving.

*How did this happen so quickly?* Czanna thought. *I left upon my lonely walk last evening – only hours ago.*

Once she and Mr. Henrik were out of earshot, Czanna said, "Now, please tell me what has occurred here."

"'Tis the gold seekers, Mistress. They came up from the fort late in the evening last night and joined us; they were carrin' tales of gold and were braggin' of goin' to the gold mining fields. 'Twould not be so bad exceptin' for the scout, Mr. Hanson, the man I had hired to take us north into the Glacier Mountains. He has gone with them gold seekers now and has left us stranded; but, worse, he has taken with him all the silver I gave him when he agreed to the task."

Czanna frowned, momentarily speechless. Briefly, she recalled Frederic's words to her before she and the rest of their siblings had been forced to flee Hungary:

"*I am trusting you — not Henrik — to hire a guide to take you to our cousin in the mountains.*"

But, she had met Hanson, had talked with him and had even approved of Mr. Henrik's choice. It was, therefore, as much her fault as it was Mr. Henrik's.

Straightening her shoulders, Czanna glanced up at Mr. Henrik's sunburned face and murmured, "I heard it said, when we were at Fort Benton, that the gold fever is a fearsome disease."

"'Tis true, Mistress Fehér, and worse. 'Twould appear the fervor came upon all our companions last night. Whiskey flowed freely, and I became afeared at what might happen. I set me sights on guardin' me own daughter and thine own brother and sister. Ne'er did I sleep until the camp became quiet in the wee hours of the mornin'; only then did I rest. But, when I awoke, the other wagons were gone. I failed thee, Mistress. I have failed me own master, also."

"You have not failed us, so set your mind at ease, Mr. Henrik. Though this is bad news, indeed, we can overcome it. After all, we never expected to stay with the entire wagon train for very long, since they are going farther south and west while we are bound to travel north and west. We should be able to go on alone, should we not?"

"Be that not the case, Mistress. I do not know the way into the Glacier Mountains. That rascal, Hanson, knew not only the trails and passes into the mountains, he knew thine own cousin, Mr. Tom Johnson, and where he lives in the mountains."

"Oh, yes, I remember this detail about it now. But, take heart, we shall hire another scout. We can return to Fort Benton — we are not so far away from it—and, once there, we will be able to seek out and hire another."

"We cannot, Mistress. I fear that no-good scoundrel took all the silver I paid him, amountin' to two hundred Yankee dollars."

"Oh no!"

"The rascal was gone with them before daylight."

"Do you have more coin? I fear we will need it if we are to return to the fort and hire another man who knows the trails."

"I do not have more coin, Mistress. 'Tis what is worryin' me own self. Thine own elder brother ensured me-self and ye would have enough silver to hire coaches and ships and scouts. He has trusted me-self to safely see thee to thine own cousin, and I fear me own self has failed me master's eldest son. Been waitin' for thee, Mistress. Indeed, 'tis no choice for me-self but to go after the rascal and get back me own silver. I beg thee to understand; I must go after the ne'er-do-well. There be no other choice. I must needs apprehend him, for I dare not fail thy brother."

"No! Mr. Henrik! Surely you must see that if you do this, you will leave us here alone! Please do not leave us."

"And, the silver, Mistress? What will ye and me use for coin to hire another? Forgive me, Mistress Fehér. I must go after him. I have been given no other choice. Gave me own word to thine brother, I did. While thou was gone, I got to thinkin'. Four horses ye have and the wagon. Thou must take the wagon and three of the horses back to Fort Benton and there wait for me own self to return to thee; the fourth horse shall carry me to the thief, where I shall retrieve the stolen silver from him. Ye and me will then hire another scout, but I shall, from this day forward, be careful about whom I trust."

"Mr. Henrik, I hear what you say, but you must consider, too, what will happen to us without you. I do not know the way back to Fort Benton. Please, we are all alone here in this, the wild American prairie land. Please do not leave us."

"I am sorry, Mistress, but I must. 'Tis a matter of honor. Here," said Henrik, "take me own compass with thee and the meager silver coin I have left. I do not need either. Tha' scoundrel cannot be too far ahead and, indeed, what need have I of a compass in this land where 'tis sun, mountains and wind enough to guide a man?"

"But, Mr. Henrik, no. I beg you, do not do this."

"Nay, Mistress. I must. 'Tis my honorable duty. Here"—Henrik pushed the compass into her hand—"ye need to go north and east to the Missouri River. Once thou comes to the Missouri, follow it north and east as best ye can. The fort be on the Missouri River. Stay there. Wait for me own self. I should be only a few days. If I be longer than a few days gettin' back to ye, believe I have met me own fate and hire thine own scout to take ye to thy cousin." Handing her the bag he carried, Henrik continued, "I freely give thee all the coin I have—little though it be—to see thee on thy way. Godspeed."

"But—"

"I must go, Mistress. Forgive me own self for hirin' that no good rogue. But, I must be on me way. Have already saddled the mare. Thou must take the wagon and these three horses back to the fort." Henrik gestured toward the roans. "Wait for me own self there."

Stunned into silence, Czanna felt utterly helpless as she watched Henrik turn away from her. Short of running after him, what could she do to stop him?

She watched, as if in shock, as Mr. Henrik took the few steps necessary to bring him to his roan, and, placing his foot into the saddle's stirrup, he mounted up to take his seat. Feeling as though she were living a nightmare, Czanna murmured, "I do not wish you to go, Mr. Henrik, but if you insist you must, Godspeed. I will return to Fort Benton, and there I shall wait for you."

Henrik nodded. "I will be back for thee, Mistress." And, with these few words, he reined in his mount, turned from her and headed farther west and south, where the snow-capped mountains rising up from the prairie floor looked to be little more than a giant child's toy.

Czanna watched Mr. Henrik until he was a mere speck on the horizon. Then, realizing he would not be turning around and coming back to them, she gazed away.

So lost was she in her own thoughts, she jumped when a feminine voice asked, "Why has me own father left thee and me?"

It was Mr. Henrik's daughter, Lilike, who had asked the question; she had come to stand beside Czanna. Three-year-old Béla was still clinging to Lilike's hip when the child suddenly cried, "Zanna!"

As Czanna looked down upon the babe, she nearly cried. What was to become of them all?

"Here," muttered Czanna, "I'll take the baby."

Lilike seemed happy to give the child over to her mistress.

Positioning the baby onto her own hip, Czanna mustered up a clear voice and said, "The scout, Hanson, whom your father and I hired to help us, has betrayed us all and has left with some gold seekers, who, it seems, left in the early morning hours. The terrible part—and why your father left us—is that the scout took every bit of coin Mr. Henrik had given him to act as our guide into the Glacier Mountains. Because this represents all the coin we have, your father has gone to retrieve the silver and return to us in a few days."

"A few days, Mistress?"

"I fear it is true."

"But, me own father? Won't he be in danger by followin' after the gold seekers?"

"He will, indeed, be in danger. But, Mr. Henrik is, after all, strong of body, and, when determined, he can be a terrible force to contend with. Please try to ease your mind about it; I believe he will return to us."

"But, Mistress, ye and me own self cannot remain here for two days.  I fear 'tis not enough water left to drink were ye to have to stay here for even one day and a night.  And, 'tis not a bit of water in sight."

"I know," replied Czanna.

"Hast thou a plan, Mistress Fehér?"

Czanna drew in a deep breath before at length replying, "We will return to Fort Benton, which is only a few days away from us.  And, once we are there, we will await you father's return."

"Ah, 'tis a good plan, Mistress."

"Please, Lilike, because we are in a foreign land, I beg you to address me as Czanna.  If we are to do as the people in this foreign country do, we should refer to one another by our first names.  It may take some practice, but I think it will be well worth the effort.  We must—at least for the moment—hide our identity."

"I will do me best, Mistress Czanna."

Czanna nodded.  "Now, as far as the plan goes, returning to Fort Benton is the only sensible action to take in a circumstance such as this."  Czanna couldn't say more; indeed, she was close to tears.

"They were awful," Lilike said without any coaxing as she glanced outward in the same direction where her father had gone.

"Who was awful?" asked Czanna.

"The gold thieves," replied Lilike.  "I feared for all of us, and we went without our supper last night because they frightened us so.  Thy brother, sister an' me own self hid in the wagon."

"I'm very sorry I wasn't here," murmured Czanna.

"'Twas nothing ye could have done.  The gold robbers were dirty, smelly, loud and were cursing somethin' most awful all the night through.  Gamblin', they were.  Me own self could hear them," said Lilike.  "Come morning, it seemed even the good-hearted men in our wagon train had caught the 'golden fever.'  Even their own wives had gone with them.  Me own father was sleeping and could not be easily woke.  To his credit, once he awakened, me own father tried to stop them and ran after them. But, they would not listen. And, now they be gone. Mine own father, too."

"Yes," said Czanna. "Now they are gone. And, as you say, it is done. But, come, we must eat a little of the food we have with us in the wagon, and then we must be on our way. Fort Benton lies east and north of here in that direction." She pointed. "We will travel to the Missouri River, which, if my memory serves me correctly, is not too far away. And, once we reach the river, we shall head up north until we reach Fort Benton, there to await your father rejoining us. Also, once there, we shall have plenty of water to drink and food to eat."

"Yes, Mistress Czanna," said Lilike. "Saints be praised, me own self will help thee with preparing breakfast."

"That would be most welcome," said Czanna. "And, then we must hitch up two of the remaining horses to the wagon and be on our way for as long as we have light. Master György should probably ride the best of our horses, I think, while I shall drive the wagon."

Lilike nodded. "'Tis a good plan, Mistress. Does thou wish meself to take the babe?"

"Yes, please. I will need both hands to prepare the meal, and later to hitch up the horses to the wagon."

"Aye, Mistress," said Lilike, and, reaching out, she took hold of the baby, bringing three-year-old Béla into her arms. "It will be no trouble for the babe and me own self to put some breakfast together, and perhaps with thy brother Master György's help, we can be on our way."

"Yes," said Czanna. Then, again, "Yes."

****

"Where did you go last night, Czanna?" asked György as soon as she and her brother were alone.

Czanna glanced away from György. She didn't speak; she was afraid she couldn't. Indeed, she felt as though her tongue might never be able to voice the words she knew she had to say. After all, young though he was, he had a right to know what had taken place all the way across the vast ocean. At the moment, however, all she could think was this: what else was going to befall them?

"Czanna?"

Czanna gave her brother a quick, though sad look before saying, "Because we now number only four, including my maid, I fear I have news I must tell you even though, if we were back in Hungary, your youth would prevent me from relating it to you."

"My youth? I am *not* so young. With Henrik gone, I am now the man of the family."

"Yes, you are," Czanna replied. "And, so I shall tell you what happened last night that caused me to leave here. In truth, my heart was so low after receiving some news from home that I had to go away to think and to pray."

"There is bad news from home?" asked György.

"Truly, there is, and I will tell it to you," answered Czanna. "But, do not say any of what I am about to tell you to Mr. Henrik when he returns, nor to Lilike."

György stuck out his chin, raising it into the air. He said, "I may be young, but I am not as unaware as you seem to think I am."

"I do not believe you to be unaware, my brother. Rather, I fear the news is very bad." Czanna swallowed once, then again, before saying, "I received word that our parents and our brother, Frederic, are alive no longer. They were hung a few months ago."

György said not a word even as the color drained from his face. Then, without warning, he burst into tears. Taking hold of the letter Czanna had placed into the bodice of her gown, she drew it out and offered her brother the post from Sebestyn. "Here," she said, "you can read it yourself, if you wish."

Quickly, György took hold of the letter and read it through. Upon completion, his face drained of even more color, causing him to appear as though he had washed his face in wet, white clay instead of water. Glancing up at Czanna, even his brown eyes looked pale as he asked, "Are we going back to Hungary, then?"

"We cannot," answered Czanna. "I promised Frederic we would never return to Hungary. He was insistent about this...very insistent. He even demanded I give him my word on it, and I did. Under no circumstance, he told me, were we to return to Hungary. Besides, if our parents and Frederic are no longer alive, there is no safe harbor there for us. Frederic's last instruction to me was to take you and Béla away and bring you both here to America; he entrusted me to make a new life for us all in the American West. He begged me to speak to no one about who we are, not even telling others we are Hungarian. It is why we have no clothes with us, and it is because the manner in which we would be dressed might cause another to learn what our true nationality is. This includes never speaking in our native tongue, not even to one another. Indeed, I have been considering that we should change our names. And now, with Frederic and our parents gone, I am convinced of one other detail I had not considered until now: we must have American names."

György nodded. "You are right, Sister."

Czanna inhaled deeply, then said, "Let us do it now. I think my name is American sounding enough that it could remain the same. Do you agree?"

"I do," replied György.

"Good. Then, we might Americanize your name to George instead of György. It is almost the same, but with a little different pronunciation. Also, we must change our last name from Fehér to..." She hesitated, frowning. Their family name would be, perhaps, the most important aspect about them to require a change. "What do you think of the surname, Finley? Or perhaps Farrell?"

"They are both good. But, I think I like Farrell best," said George.

"Then, it shall be Farrell."

"And Béla?" asked George. "What should our baby sister's name be?"

"Let me think for a moment. Béla is much too European sounding. I believe Briella is an American name, and its sound is much like Béla's own. What do you think of calling her Briella?"

"I like it," answered George. "But, we must also change Lilike's name. Perhaps we could keep it the same, only pronounce it differently. I believe the name Liliann is American."

"I think you are right. Then, Liliann it is. We shall tell her about the different pronunciation at once. But, we must not say anything to her about what has taken place back home. Are we agreed about what our actions must and must not be?"

"Yes," said George.

"Good. Then come, let us eat what food we have with us for breakfast. Then we shall hitch the horses up to the wagon, saddle your horse and be on our way. In this manner, we might be able to take advantage of the remaining daylight to get us as close to Fort Benton as possible. I simply wish we did not have to face making the journey alone."

As Czanna looked behind her toward the direction of the cliff where she had met Stands Strong, she wondered if he had, indeed, followed her. And, if he had done so, and if she could make him aware of their troubles, would he offer to help them?

He had said he would follow her without himself being seen. At the time, she had told him it was unnecessary. But, now she could only hope he had not taken her advice too seriously and had, indeed, trailed her, perhaps becoming aware of her plight.

Silently, she said a prayer, asking the Lord to please make it be so.

\*\*\*

From the rim of the treeless rise in the land, Stands Strong lay flat on his stomach and watched the white woman, Czanna, trod back toward what was clearly a white man's wagon. But, there was only one of the prairie wagons, not the many she had described to him.  Had she lied?  Or was this an indication of trouble of a different sort?

He dismissed the lie, however, if it had been one.  She had been alone with no one to protect her against him if she had found him to be an enemy.  Only a fool would have told the truth in such a circumstance.

Still, he wondered about her plight; she had been close to tears more than once during the short interval when they had spoken to one another.  What had been the cause of her grief?

He recalled now how difficult it had been to follow her and remain unseen.  The reason for this was, of course, because the wide prairie provided few places to conceal oneself.

But, a well-trained scout could always use the environment to fade into it, and Stands Strong had used his rifle to dig a trench in the dry dirt and sand.  When done, he had set several patches of grass around the pit as a shield.  In this manner, he'd been able to look out upon his surroundings without himself being detected.

As he gazed down upon the flat plains extending out in all directions, he could clearly see the one, lone wagon with its white, cloud-like covering blowing in the constant winds of the prairie. But, assuming Czanna had been honest with him and there had been more wagons the previous evening, where were they now? And, most importantly, if they were gone, why had they left without her and her family?

From his position, he watched as an older man strode around the front of the wagon to greet Czanna.  Stands Strong waited for the inevitable hug between the man and the woman, assuming the white man to be her husband or perhaps her father.

But, there was no hug, nor could Stands Strong detect there was even a moment of cheerfulness in their greeting.  Instead, the manner in which they spoke to each other suggested they might share no special relationship; there was too much distance between them to believe they held a unique relationship.  Even their hand motions did not suggest any particular affection or intimacy.

Why did these two people, who obviously knew one another, show so little emotion to each other? This seemed especially odd because Stands Strong had observed that the white men within the fort—and even his almost-mother—tended to greet one another with great enthusiasm, as did the Blackfeet upon greeting one another.

Because Stands Strong was watching their mouths and lips closely, he could discern a few of their words. Nothing seemed out of the ordinary until he saw the white man's lips utter the word "gold."

*Gold!* That could mean trouble.

What was it his almost-mother had told him about the sparkling golden rock? *"There is always trouble in the white man's world when gold is involved."*

Indeed, the Pikuni people had long looked upon the white man's lust for gold as unreasonable. And, as clearly as the white man didn't understand the tensions and war between the Plains tribes, the Indian did not comprehend how this golden rock could cause the white man to forget all else except obtaining it.

Even family.

As his almost-father had once told him, *"There is no common sense to be found from one white man to another when there is gold to be fought for and won."*

So, his almost-father was right: there was trouble coming into Pikuni country…and it was in the form of the golden rock.

Because Stands Strong had not come alone into this part of the prairie, he reached out into the environment to locate the position of his friend and fellow scout, First Rider. Using the time-honored form of communication between scouts—the mind-to-mind speak—he said silently, "There are white men upon the prairie."

"I know," answered First Rider, who was Stands Strong's almost-cousin. Although First Rider was the adopted son of Pikuni Chief Chases-the-enemy, First Rider's real father had been

Crow, as was his mother. And so, because neither Stands Strong nor First Rider were blood relatives of the Pikuni, their friendship with one another was, perhaps, natural. Indeed, they had spent their early years playing boys' games together, and growing up into their adult years, they had chosen similar paths to follow in life.

"Where are you?" asked First Rider in the same mind-speak.

"I am in a trench I have dug on the hill leading to the long-ago used *pisskan*," answered Stands Strong, using the same manner of communication. "I am looking at a single white man's prairie wagon, and I have seen the word 'gold' upon the lips of the man who appears to be the owner of the wagon."

"You have done well to have discovered this, Almost-cousin. I will join you there shortly."

The communication ended.

His almost-cousin must have been close by because First Rider came belly crawling into the trench after very little time had elapsed. Quickly, utilizing the language of sign, Stands Strong told First Rider of his encounter with Czanna; he spoke of his shock when, having followed her, he had seen only the one wagon. Lastly, he went on to describe the older man who had uttered the word "gold" and who had then ridden away, leaving his family alone upon the prairie.

First Rider signed, "What kind of man is this who deserts his women, the boy and a babe alone on the vast prairie? He is either touched in the head or evil. Do you know which he is?"

"I do not. But, because the woman, Czanna, mentioned several wagons were a part of her group, this man might have left to find and bring the others to justice," replied Stands Strong, again utilizing the sign language. "The men from the other wagons have, after all, left this one of their own behind, when all know one wagon alone could invite all manner of evil upon it."

"Your ideas are reasonable," said First Rider in sign. "But, I still think the man has none of his wits about him."

"Maybe," signed Stands Strong. "But, I also watched as the man gave the woman a purse and another object. Perhaps he believes these small objects will protect her and the rest of his family from a misplaced arrow. Also, I saw his lips say he would meet up with her at Fort Benton."

First Rider remained silent.

"As you know," continued Stands Strong through the language of sign, "our chiefs have bid you and me to join our cousins Medicine Fox, Howling Wolf and Snow, who are heading south to obtain the wild ponies. But, although you and I were to be part of their party, the chiefs first asked us to discover what the danger is that my almost-father dreamed about. And, upon discovering what might be the danger, we agreed to report anything we find back to the chiefs.

"And now," continued Stands Strong in sign, "after witnessing the word 'gold' spoken on the tongue of the white man, I believe we may have found the threat to our people. And, if this be the case, we must learn more and then report what we find back to the chiefs."

"Yes," First Rider signed.

"Yet, there are now two parties we must follow. One is the white man who has left his family. We are tasked to discover what danger this man has experienced, and if the threat be gold, we must return to the chiefs with haste. There is also the family he has deserted, who, being a small party, will likely come to harm if left undefended. Because I have already met and spoken with one of the women traveling in the prairie wagon, I believe she might influence the others to allow me to join them. In this way, I will do what I can to ensure they arrive at Fort Benton unharmed."

First Rider nodded. "I will, then, follow the trail of the man. I will watch these gold seekers and determine who these people are and what they plan to do. I will then bring the news to you, and together we shall leave our cousins who are traveling south in search of the wild ponies while we report our discoveries back to our chiefs."

Stands Strong nodded and signed, "Good. Let us now do as we have agreed before the white men, who are seeking gold, get too far away."

"Yes," agreed First Rider in sign, and, with each man placing his hand upon the other's shoulder, they parted. Stands Strong watched his cousin for a moment, but then returned his attention to the family and their single conveyance. A lone wagon upon the trail was a dangerous position for the white man to have put upon his family, since any war party in the vicinity would look upon the wagon as fair game and an easy target.

However, as serious as it was, Stands Strong couldn't help smiling a little as he watched the two women and the young boy try to harness two of their horses onto the white man's transport.

He debated whether he should approach the family now and give them the aid they needed. However, glancing toward the north, he saw several black clouds gathering there, and, realizing a storm would soon be upon them, he surmised Czanna's family would not be in a position to hunt. *Hánnia*, they would require food.

The storm, while it would release its fury upon these people, was not necessarily harmful. And, it would act as a shield against any wandering war party, giving Stands Strong the chance to hunt. Since a food offering had a way of easing another's fear, it might, perhaps, act as a peace offering to Czanna and her family.

Climbing out of the dugout, Stands Strong took the time needed to fill it in again with the earth nearby, adding some landscaping around the place in case another scout were in the vicinity. Then, on belly and forearms, he scooted up and over the hill and disappeared from view.

## CHAPTER THREE

Really, she ought not to be blamed for the mistake. After all, no one had ever told her what would happen to a compass if she were to hold it next to a pistol.

It had been an honest, if time-consuming, error. After Mr. Henrik's departure from them, Czanna had panicked and, after a frenzied search through her clothing, had found her pistol. She had tucked the weapon neatly into the waistline of her skirt, not realizing what would happen to the compass' directions if she held it too closely to her gun.

She, however, knew it now. Problem was, where were they?

Hitching up the two horses to their wagon had proved to be a lesson in humility. Having grown up with stable hands to do the task, neither she nor her brother had ever performed the chore without the aid of another. So, it had taken hours before the horses were properly harnessed to the wagon and ready to go, and even then she was certain their two horses had practically accomplished the chore for her and George. At least, Czanna was aware the two animals thought it was so.

They had, indeed, told her so. Not with words, of course. But, having completed the chore, Czanna had petted first one of the geldings and then the other. It was then when each animal had informed her about the task, certain the chore would not have been accomplished without their assistance.

She had almost laughed but had been able to keep any mirth from showing upon her countenance, afraid the horses would take offense. It was strange, this knack she enjoyed. She couldn't remember a time when she hadn't delighted in her gift of gab with animals—horses in particular—though she had never spoken of this to anyone. Indeed, she was certain she would be looked upon as an oddity instead of what she really was: a young aristocratic lady who enjoyed having conversations with horses.

And so, they had begun their journey back to Fort Benton at last. However, no sooner had they started on their trek than the sudden appearance of black clouds had all but blocked out the sun, temporarily obscuring any direction. Worse, a fine rain had begun to fall, creating a fog and shrouding any landmarks which might have helped give her the direction she needed.

By sunset, the clouds had lifted, and at last Czanna could correctly discern the right direction to go. However, any joy she might have felt in the discovery was soon whisked away; she had been traveling due south, and it was the completely wrong way. Instead of bringing her family closer to Fort Benton, she had taken them farther away from it.

"Anyone could have made the same mistake, Czanna," said twelve-year-old György, whom they were now calling George. He had reined in his horse so the animal stood next to the wagon.

"I doubt if you would have done the same," answered Czanna. "Sometimes boys seem to have a better sense of direction than we females." She sighed. "Trouble is, we are far off course and evening is fast approaching. We have a little food with us but no water, and I was so hoping our trek might take us to the Missouri River before nightfall, thus preventing our becoming too thirsty. Now all we have for water are the puddles left behind from the rain."

"But, do not despair, Mistress," offered Liliann, who was sitting beside Czanna up front. "We will certainly come to the Missouri River eventually."

"Yes," responded Czanna. "However, I have this day carried us even farther away from Fort Benton and the river. Still, seeing the reason for my mistake, I shall now place my pistol elsewhere than at my waist since I have seen the metal, set next to the compass, influences its direction."

"Czanna," said George with a note of urgency in his voice, "we must stop soon and give our horses a rest. They cannot travel much farther without water."

"Yes, you are right," uttered Czanna. "What I think we shall do is unhitch the horses and hobble them so they may eat their fill of the prairie grass and where they can also take advantage of any puddles of water they might find upon the ground. But, I dare to think we may not find relief for our thirst in those same puddles.

"Then," continued Czanna, "there is the matter of supper. We must eat something. Yet, I fear what food we have in our wagon for supper is not enough. It is a problem I had not anticipated."

"Mistress, are thou saying ye and me might go hungry, as well as thirsty?" asked Liliann.

"Yes," answered Czanna simply. "Forgive me. I fear I did not realize how reliant we had become upon the men in the wagon train who hunted for game each day. And so, we consumed the food we had brought with us without thought, not realizing how dependent we have been upon the hunters. It was silly of me not to know this. But, I didn't. And, to add to matters, I do not possess the skill nor the knowledge of how to hunt to supplement the remaining hard bread we have in our wagon. Do you know how to hunt, George?"

"I know a little about it," replied George. "Our father used to take me duck hunting. If we encounter any ducks or other game, I, at least, know how to aim and shoot."

"Well, I daresay your expertise in the sport is better than mine," said Czanna, wiping her brow and squinting her eyes as she looked east. "Here, since it is becoming dark, let us find a good place to spend the night. At least, because we now know which way to go, we can put some distance behind us tomorrow. There!"—she pointed—"I see a lone tree up ahead. Perhaps we might pull the horses and the wagon in next to it and spend the night there."

"Yes, Mistress, and me own self shall help thee," agreed Liliann.

"Thank you, Liliann," replied Czanna as she picked up the reins and raised her whip. But, remembering how much better the horses seemed to know what to do than she, she set the whip down and instead shouted out, "Ay, ye horses! Move out!"

And, slowly their lone wagon headed toward the lone tree, which stood proudly upon this vast and, except for the mountains outlining the distant horizon, unending prairie.

\*\*\*\*

Stands Strong shook his head and grinned as he beheld the solitary wagon heading due south instead of north and east.

*White people. Has no one ever taught them how to obtain the correct direction?* he thought.

His almost-mother was an exception, but even she sometimes lost her way even when there were many signs in nature to guide her.

Having left the wagon party to fend for itself at the first hint of rain, Stands Strong returned to the narrow valley where he had hobbled Holy Dog, his spotted faithful and fast buffalo-running pony—a Paint. He had then planned to spend the majority of the day hunting buffalo, elk or deer…whatever was plentiful. Luckily, he found a small herd of buffalo at a well-known water hole, and, having killed two fat cows, he had first prayed over the cows, then had skinned the kill and had cut up the meat for easy carrying. Loading it upon his pony, he had set out on foot to find Czanna, her family and the prairie wagon.

It was dusk when he at last tracked down the white man's covered wagon, and, making as much noise as possible to ensure the family knew someone approached, he trod toward the white people, leading his pony which was burdened down with meat.

"Mistress Czanna! An Indian comes!" It was the other woman and not Czanna, who, shouting loudly, scurried fast around the single tree that rose up bravely upon this vast prairie. On the woman's hip sat the baby who jiggled up and down with the woman's movements.

Perhaps he might enlighten these people as to the advantages of carrying a babe upon the back. But, for now there were other worries: the boy and Czanna were rushing toward him. In the boy's arms was a rifle, and even Czanna looked to be armed with a small pistol. Within a single moment, they pointed both rifle and gun at him.

"Come no farther!" shouted the boy, although his voice broke on the words, announcing his age.

"It is I, Stands Strong, who comes to visit. Czanna, I bring your family food and water."

"Stands Strong? Is it truly you? And, did you say you have brought us food?"

"And water," he answered. "Yes, it is I. I saw your problems and determined I should help you and your family."

"Put down your rifle, George. It is all right," said the beautiful woman, Czanna. "I know this man."

"You *know* him? How is this possible, Sister?"

"I met him this morning while I was praying. His almost-mother is white, which is how he comes to speak English. Welcome, welcome, Mr. Stands Strong," said Czanna as she pushed her pistol into the pocket of her skirt. "George you might safely put away your rifle."

"I will not! I will only stop aiming at him, Sister, when I am assured he is friendly. If this be a trick…"

"He could have harmed me this morning at any time since I forgot to bring my pistol with me. Nothing happened. We simply talked, and he promised me he would guard me from harm as I returned to what I thought was the wagon train. He could even have harmed us now. But, he hasn't. Instead, it does look as if he has brought us food."

"He is a stranger bearing gifts, and I do not trust him," said the youngster. Yet, George pulled his rifle back to hold it crisscrossed over his chest.

Stands Strong recognized the boy's action as a sign of a temporary truce. Without mentioning it, Stands Strong admired the boy. No real man surrendered his only means of defense until he was completely certain there was no danger to be had from a stranger.

"Come," said Stands Strong. "Let us unload this meat and the hides from my pony. We shall have a feast tonight before we are obliged to darken the fire."

With emphasis, George declared, "We will not darken the fire for any reason while you are with us! What? So you can scalp us in our sleep?"

"Would you rather bring a war party upon you?" Stands Strong answered. "The smoke from the fire alone will carry on the wind to any warriors on the trail, and a war party travels only at night in this, my country. Do you wish to fight off men of war instead of one single Indian?"

The boy didn't answer.

"George," said Czanna, "please be polite to our guest. I, for one, will welcome the food and the water he brings, as well as his knowledge of this land. If a war party does come upon us, wouldn't you like to have another man at your side instead of a sister who has never shot at a target, let alone at a man?"

George frowned. However, he didn't utter a word. Instead, he spun around and stamped toward the back of the wagon, his rifle held steadily in his hands.

But, Stands Strong barely noticed, except to glance at the boy with even greater admiration. However, a moment of high regard was all he had to spare; there was work to be done. Bringing his pony to stand next to their fire, Stands Strong began unpacking the meat and the hides.

He asked of Czanna, "Have you sticks to hold the ribs over the fire?"

"I do. I shall fetch them."

As she turned quickly away, Stands Strong watched her for an instant, noticing the movement of her skirt as it swayed to and fro while she walked away from him. Captivated, he gazed at her feminine figure for another moment or two…longer than he knew was right. Her beauty was such that he would dare any man to resist looking at her. And, though his gaze was discreet, he filled his mind with her image, wishing he had the right to look at her as much as he desired, which could—if she were free and unmarried—be a lifetime.

****

The fire and its smoky scent had long ago ceased to be, and the black of night had fallen over the prairie. The moon was only now rising in the east, and the sky looked as if a child had fallen, scattering a million pieces of light onto the "land" above. A little south and west of the wagon, a nighthawk screeched. Glancing up, Stands Strong recognized its long dark wings only because of the horizontal white stripe on each of its wings.

Stands Strong smiled. The nighthawk was a good sign. Were a war party close by, the nighthawk would not be singing as it went about its nightly hunting of moths and insects.

He had seen that the younger woman—a blonde, who appeared to be a girl instead of a fully grown woman—as well as the baby slept inside the prairie wagon, perhaps for protection since the overhead canopy of white sheltered them against the elements. Much like the travois of his own people, the wagon was stuffed full of household items: clothing, food, blankets and other needed equipment.

As Stands Strong sat his nightly watch, leaning back against the trunk of the sturdy, but small prairie tree, he directed a discreet glance at the beautiful white woman, Czanna. There she sat upon her bed of blankets which she had positioned next to the wagon. Placed beside her and lying on the blanket within easy reaching distance was her white man's firearm.

This was good. This was wise and smart.

However, there was one oddity about her and her family he did not understand: none of them changed into sleeping clothes for the night as his almost-mother usually did. But, perhaps it was because *he* was here, causing Czanna and the rest of the family to be uneasy and on guard.

But, there she sat, the picture of feminine beauty with her long dark hair falling over her shoulders. Its rich color looked black under the dim, yet sparkling lights from the stars. Truly, some of those tiny lights twinkled against her dark tresses, and the effect reminded him of the "wolf road"—the Milky Way. The beauty of her hair was exquisite, and his glance remained upon her, though he knew he should look away.

He didn't, however, look away. Instead, he warmed to his subject. Although he knew she wore the same dark-blue dress from earlier in the day, he could not distinguish its exact color now because the lighting was too shadowy and dim.

Still, her choice of dress did not hide the curves of her figure from his perusal, and he appreciated every rounded hill and valley within her silhouette. And, though his gaze at her was not hidden and might have been detectable to another, he didn't care at present, and he watched her as she sat still, her gaze not upon him but out into the night where all four horses were grazing—her own three mounts and his own pony.

"Mr. Stands Strong?" It was the voice of the boy. "May I sit with you?"

Stands Strong nodded and padded a place next to him.

"Will you be on watch through the entire night?" asked the youth.

"I shall," replied Stands Strong.

"But, if this be so, and if you intend leading us back to Fort Benton, do you not need some sleep?"

"I will obtain the rest I need once we reach the fort and I have ensured you are all safe," answered Stands Strong.

"But, how will you be able to remain alert if you do not get some sleep now? And, without enough rest, you might doze off even while in the saddle. What will become of us then?"

Stands Strong grinned a little as he gazed at the boy. He took his time answering—as a man should—but at last he said, "A man who must guard women and children does not doze off nor does he wrap his sleeping robes around him until any danger is passed. A man is expected to endure through the urge to sleep. It is his duty to those he loves."

"But, you don't love us."

Stands Strong shrugged.

"That's true, isn't it?"

Again, Stands Strong said nothing; he merely lifted his shoulders.

"So, if you don't love us and we are not your family, why have you decided to help us?"

Stands Strong paused for a moment in thought. Because of his almost-mother's teachings, he was well aware of what were the white man's ideas of love and family. He was also cognizant of another fact: the white man held little regard for his Pikuni people's custom of extending their family to include others unrelated by blood.

At length, however, he said, "After talking with your sister this morning, I took her pain upon my shoulders, and, in doing so, came to regard her as one of the women in my life. I told her this, which is the same as a vow. And, since I have decided to make her one of the women in my life, I must protect her and her family…you."

"But," said the boy, "she is not really a woman in your life. That's all made up."

Stands Strong shrugged. Yet, realizing he needed to help the boy to understand, he said, "My almost-mother is white, and I hold her here" — he pointed to his chest — "within my heart. Perhaps this is why I could feel your sister's pain and decided to take on her sorrow as my own. By doing so, I extended my strength to help her. Besides, a man is expected to defend and help women and children. It is his duty."

"His duty? Why?"

"Because women and children are innocent in the wars of their men. And so, they need protection against enemies who would seek to bring war to them. A woman's gifts are many, and a man without a woman is an object of pity. Never forget, without women, there would be no race. *Áa*, a real man protects his women and his children...you."

"I am not a child!"

"*Saa*, you are not. When I said 'you', I meant all of you...your family. Though you are not yet a man in strength, you must now put away your childhood dreams and become a real man. No longer may games take your fancy. Instead, your attention must go to the environment so you can protect your sister and the other girls. Be aware, there are many dangers for your family on the prairie, and, without the force of the white men's powerful guns, you are all in danger from the war parties who roam the prairie at this time of year."

"Are there really war parties on the prairie? And, do they truly travel at night? Or are you making all this up?"

Stands Strong grinned, but only a little. In due time, he replied, "I tell this to you true; I am not making this up, and war parties are plentiful at this time of year. It is also true about war parties: they usually wait until nightfall to ride through this, my country. This is a common and usual practice amongst our people. However, if there are many men in the war party and all are well-armed, then the warriors might ride out upon the prairie during the day when all eyes can see them. Most men, however, travel only at night when they go to war."

"Oh," said the boy, looking away. "Sir, I...I was wrong to distrust you in the beginning, and I apologize. I see now how it is and that you came here to help us, not betray us."

"There is not the need to apologize, young George. This is what you are called, is it not?"

George nodded. "It is," he said.

"Good. Now, listen well to me when I tell you how greatly I admired your stand against me. It was good and it was right. *Nitákkaawa*, my friend, what did you know of me? *Áa*, you were right to question my intentions, and you are still right to continue to be leery of me."

"But, I am not suspicious of you now. Is this wrong, then?"

Stands Strong smiled at the lad. "You must trust your heart in these matters. If you have looked into my heart, and, having witnessed what is there, you now feel you might trust me, do not question what it is you sense, because this goes beyond the physical. But, do not trust another man too quickly. Wait, watch and be on your guard always, because a man can hide behind sweet words and many gestures of friendliness that are not meant."

George was quiet for a long while. At last, however, he asked, "Mr. Stands Strong, will you teach me how to survive here? And, also will you help me to learn how to protect my family?"

"*Áa*, I am glad you have asked this of me, and I will agree to do it, but only if you give me your promise about one other matter," said Stands Strong.

"Oh? What is it you wish me to vow?" The youngster pulled away from him and frowned.

"Only this," answered Stands Strong. "You must be patient with yourself in the learning. I am twenty-three snows old, and I have lived in this land all my life. I have been taught about life on the prairie first by my own father and grandfather, and then by my almost-father and my almost-uncles and -cousins. Truly, I have been learning about this world and about the secrets our mother, the earth, holds since I was six winters old. Remember, once you begin this journey, take pride in each new skill you learn."

"Oh, I think I understand. All right. I can do what you ask. Is this all?"

"Almost. There is one more promise I would seek from you before I begin to teach you."

Stands Strong watched as George lifted up one eyebrow and slanted him a wary glance. The look amused him, if only because the young man appeared to be so serious. But, Stands Strong knew he didn't dare laugh. Instead, he calmly stated, "You must vow to me that you will practice every skill I show you, and you must further vow to never give up trying until you have conquered the skill you seek."

"Never?" asked George.

"Never," answered Stands Strong.

"Then, I shall give you my word of honor. I will practice those skills you teach me, and I shall not stop practicing them until I have learned them so well I know I can do them," promised George. "I swear it."

## CHAPTER FOUR

Czanna glanced toward the wooden wagon wheel on her left and sighed. There were streaks of mud within its cracks, and she knew the markings should be washed off to ensure the wheel would remain strong and serviceable. Perhaps she would do the task when they reached the Missouri River. But, not tonight; it was a job best done in broad daylight.

Briefly, she looked up at the bed of the wagon and its white covering, listening for any signs of a problem with her young sister. But, there was nothing to be heard, only the sound of the deep breathing from both the babe and her maid, Liliann.

Czanna's gaze traveled then toward the four horses grazing steadily upon the spring-green, prairie grasses. She noted they were all four hobbled and that they were also easily seen by Stands Strong. Briefly, she listened to their quiet horse-talk before gazing away.

Only a few days had passed since she and her family had left Fort Benton, and, during that time, Czanna had taken to sleeping in the open unless there was bad weather. However, she always made her bed next to the wagon, and as she slept she kept her pistol primed and ready to shoot, if the need were to arise. It had become a habit to keep her gun with her as she slept, and this was especially true now, since Mr. Henrik was no longer with them.

Mr. Henrik. Where was he? Would he really come back to them soon? Or would he be confronted with problems she could not even conceive of? And, if there *were* problems—serious ones—would they be of the kind that could result in injury to him or even cause his death?

She gasped at the thought and determined to not think of it again. Instead, she would pray for Mr. Henrik's safe return, and she did so now, bowing her head and asking the Lord to keep Mr. Henrik safe.

Opening her eyes, she looked straight ahead but could only see shadowy images of her brother and Mr. Stands Strong. Oddly, they appeared to be deep in conversation.

Looking away from them, she stared out onto the prairie, it appearing endless beneath the starlight overhead. But, she had experienced so many losses within such a short period of time that these seemed to cause the night's beauty to appear a drab sight, bringing on the unpleasant feeling of being alone…and frightened.

How could she *not* be frightened? Truth was, she felt haunted by her worries, her most problematic anxiety being how to keep her family safe.

Indeed, if considered in the light of how much knowledge she possessed of this country, it was an alarming task Mr. Henrik had left upon her not-so-broad shoulders. At present, not only was she, and she alone, responsible for ensuring her family did not suffer from the elements, but she was also charged with bringing them, one and all, safe and secure, to their cousin in the Glacier Mountains. Once there, she would give her cousin the treasure entrusted to her by her brother. Her cousin would then recognize her and would help her and the rest of her family. But, until then…

*Am I strong-willed enough and smart enough to accomplish this?*

She had to be. She simply had to be, although if she were to be honest, she would admit to fearing the assignment given her was beyond her.  What did she know of this Western world?  And, most importantly, what did she know of surviving in it?

Czanna gazed down into her lap, suppressing the inclination to cry.  Briefly, she reached up to dry the single tear that had dared to escape her eyes.

If, indeed, Mr. Henrik did not return, it would be her responsibility alone to complete the task her brother had given her, though the mere thought of what would be required of her overwhelmed her.  Breathing in on a sigh, she coughed once, but not because of nerves, rather, it was due to the dry air's effect on her throat.

Looking up, she gazed into the night's sky with all its twinkling stars, hoping their glittering light would dispel any doubts of her inability.  But, even the beauty displayed in the heavens didn't relieve her mind.

It didn't help, either, when a strong wind blew up behind her, blowing her hair every which way, tickling her face and covering her eyes.  Reaching up, she took hold of the whole of her mane and forced it to fall down over her back where its length reached almost to her waist.  If only it would stay in place.  But, as delicate wisps of her hair blew continuously forward, she gave up trying to tame it and let her mane go wherever it would.

*No wonder the Indians commonly wear braids,* she thought.

Perhaps she might make use of the American Indian hairstyle, if only to train her locks to stay put.  Or maybe she might find a different manner in which to wear a hat—one that would keep her hair from becoming a nuisance.

She sighed.  She should try to get some rest.  Tomorrow was an important day, and, since being alert was crucial, she had best greet the first rays of the sun with a full night's sleep.

Briefly she lay down, covering herself with a blanket, but it wasn't long before she sat up again.  Nervously, she glanced around the campsite; brown dried grass was surrendering in patches to the fresh green of spring.  Even the hard ground beneath her was softened by the gentler new grass sprouting up here and there.

How strange was this land. Until reaching the Mississippi River, she had traveled by coach amongst a society not too different from her own. After all, the eastern part of this country was quite civilized, its society and culture extending all the way to the town of St. Louis.

But, there it had all changed, and the trappings of civilization were more and more becoming hard to find. And, for the first time, she had been in the company of Indians.

She had known, of course, that the farther west they were to travel, the more she would see of the native population of this land. What she hadn't realized, however, was the beauty of these people and their attire, complete with tanned buckskin cloth for shirts, dresses, leggings and moccasins.

Equally startling to her was the loveliness of the women in both face and figure, as well as the utter masculinity of the men, their height and size overwhelming to her. She had been surprised and intrigued at first.

Then had come the stories of their ungodly savagery upon the "peaceful" newcomers to this land. She had gasped at the cruelty revealed in these tales. But, was it only this to blame for the negative opinion she had held of the native peoples?

How odd it had been when, recently, those first ideas had faded away, and simply because of meeting and speaking with Stands Strong. For the first time, she had realized there was, indeed, another viewpoint about the native people of this land and about the people coming newly into it.

But, she cautioned herself, she shouldn't be too quick to trust, whether it be the American Indian or the white man, alike. After all, it was no Indian who had betrayed both her and Henrik, and it was no white man who had come to her aid this day.

And yet, despite Stands Strong's offer to help, he was an American Indian, and, having no conception of his culture or what he held to be true, could she, indeed, trust him?  Or, would he, as had the scout whom Henrik had hired, betray them in the end?

Perhaps.  Perhaps not.

Certainly, he was the only person in this strange land who had befriended her, even though she hadn't sought his friendship.

Czanna breathed in deeply, fearing sleep would not be found this night.  Indeed, now that her stomach was full and her mind was free to think of other problems besides hunger, she revisited the many loving memories of the people she admired most—her father, her mother, her brother and Mr. Henrik, too.

As she began to cry anew, she realized her life was going to change drastically from what she had known so far in this lifetime.  Would it be a good change, or would it not?  Would she be able to find happiness here?  Or would the untamed and dangerous quality of this land eventually wear her down?

Gazing forward, Czanna stared at her brother George, who was still sitting next to Stands Strong.  Their obvious camaraderie looked appealing.

Yet, she wouldn't go there.  Not only did her younger brother often become cross when she joined into his conversations with others, but he also appeared to be listening intently to whatever Mr. Stands Strong was telling him.

Watching their shadows in the dim light of the stars, she became aware of one simple fact: somehow Stands Strong had won George's cooperation.  Perhaps it was because they were all well fed for the first time in days; the fire-roasted buffalo ribs had been so delicious and satisfying, that maybe George had been given no choice but to drop his guard.  Although, perhaps George had changed his mind because young men—and George was a young man—found it easier to relate to another male rather than to a female…namely her.

Whatever the cause of the two men conversing, Czanna was happy to not be included in their talk.  Or was she?

After all, in addition to the devastating knowledge of the demise of her family, as well as her fear of losing Henrik's support, were her present worries. How was her family to remain alive and safe in this land? And, how was she to ever find her cousin in a land so vast and uncharted?

It was daunting to think of the responsibilities fate had thrown her, nor would her duties change whether or not Henrik remained alive and returned to them. One of these duties was urgent and was now hers and hers alone: she had to find and hire another scout—one who would not betray them and one who would help them to find their cousin who lived in the Glacier Mountains.

But, where was she to find such a scout?

With all this talk of gold—especially in light of Mr. Henrik's recent experience—how was she to know who to trust and who not to? Moreover, because of her own inexperience, would she be thrust into a similar position as Mr. Henrik?

Indeed, her mistake today was only an example of what could be forced upon them unless she quickly learned about this land and its dangers, as well as its rewards—if there were any. She had her own example, certainly, to draw upon to convince herself of her inability to remain alive in this environment. Without Mr. Stands Strong's insistence on putting out the fire after supper, she, George, Liliann and the baby might even now be facing a war party instead of a restful sleep.

*But, how could I have possibly known about war parties and what might attract them?*

Glancing again at Stands Strong and George, Czanna frowned. Stands Strong possessed skills and familiarity with this environment—skills and familiarity she didn't have—and he had been willing to come to their aid today. Might he possibly extend his goodwill further and help her locate her cousin? If she asked him nicely and offered him enough silver or gold, would he agree to further help them?

True, he had mentioned he was duty bound to complete a mission for his chiefs, but couldn't she be convincing enough to cause him to put his chiefs' requests aside for a little while?

Czanna frowned again. Of all the men she had met so far in this American wilderness, if she were to trust any of them, it would be Stands Strong.

Why? Was it because he had helped her and her family today? Or was it because he had promised to stay with them and lead them all the way to the fort?

Or was it more than any of this? After all, hadn't he told her that he now considered her to be one of his "women"?

Upon this thought came another recently discovered fact about these native peoples: Indian men were allowed to marry more than one woman. Exactly how many "women" did this man have in his life? Was he even now married to several winsome beauties?

Gazing upon him now, Czanna studied him as well as she was able, given the darkness of night. American Indian or not, there was no denying he was a handsome man and one who seemed to be strong enough and manly enough to protect and care for others. Wouldn't these qualities alone attract several young women?

Glancing away from him, a stray thought crossed her mind, and she knew it was most likely true: he was not a man to stray from his woman's side. Therefore, if he were married, her chances of hiring him would be nearly impossible regardless of her offers of gold and silver. Instead, he would complete his mission for his chiefs — whatever it was — and would hurry home. But, as the Lord God was her witness, she would ask for his support anyway. She would at least try.

Arising from the warmth of the blankets and buffalo robe that made up her bed, she paced toward George and Stands Strong, and, bending down near to but outside the invisible circle they made, she sat down on her calf muscles and spread the skirt of her dress out around her.

"When we leave in the morning," Stands Strong was saying to George, "I will show you how to leave a campsite so hidden to the eye it would be almost impossible for a war party to discover the traces of the camp. This is one way to elude an enemy whose numbers are greater than yours."

"You promise you will teach me?" asked George, his young voice breaking over his words.

Stands Strong pointed to himself and said, "This one will show you how it is done."

George smiled. "May I help you to stand watch now?"

"*Áa*, yes, you may," answered Stands Strong. "Your desire to do this is honorable and right, and I would not think to tell you no. "But, consider this for a moment," continued Stands Strong. "There is much to learn and many lives depend upon a man staying alert on the trail, as you have reminded me. I will not relax my guard despite my lack of sleep, and it is because when there are many lives to be defended, a man must then be the man he is supposed to be. Now, though I agree you are man enough, consider this: I am accustomed to the rigors of this land. Are you?"

"I...I... No, I am not, but I would still like to help."

"And, so it will be. But, I still think you should seek your sleeping robes soon, if you agree. Do you?"

"I...I..." Suddenly, George became aware of Czanna at his side and made a face at her, clearly showing his annoyance. Then, in a whining voice, he asked, "Ah, Czanna, why are you here? What do you want?"

"I'm sorry to interrupt, George, but I have a question I would like to ask Mr. Stands Strong."

"Can't you ask it later? Or tomorrow?"

Czanna was about to answer her brother when Stands Strong spoke up and said, "Mr. George, you are young and so perhaps do not know what I am about to tell you. I ask you only to listen well to me when I say this: a real man never speaks in the way you have to a woman.  But, especially he does not speak in this manner to his *sister*."

"But, why did she have to come here and spoil it all?" George complained.

"Careful, young warrior," advised Stands Strong.  "Remember, we men are taught to be kind and tolerant toward our women. *Hánnia*, without women, there would be no life to continue our tribe, and perhaps no beauty nor meaning to life either, for what man would dress himself well or even train himself to be strong, if not for a woman?  A man might fight off intruders or enemies; he might even go to war from time to time, but without a woman, a man's life is meaningless.  The Pikuni have a saying, 'Not found is happiness without woman.'  Know this: a real man—one who is able to put away his boyhood prejudice—speaks kindly to the girls and the women in his life and tribe, and if he cannot do so because of some argument or a differing opinion, he must leave for a while until he knows he can return soon and speak to his woman kindly and without anger."

George looked down.  He nodded.  But, as though shamed, he didn't say a word.

"Perhaps you are tired, my friend.  It has been a day filled with many problems.  And, you are young—"

"I am not so young!"

Stands Strong smiled at George.  "You speak true.  But, I have been hoping to have words with your sister.  There is much she and I should discuss.  Do you object to seeking your bed while she and I talk to one another?"

"What do you want to talk to my sister for?"

If Stands Strong was at all annoyed by the question, he didn't show it.  Instead, he calmly explained, "Your sister is now the eldest member of your family.  There are many possible dangers on the prairie at this time of year, and I must discuss them with her.  However, if you do not wish to sleep yet this night, you may stay and listen as we talk to one another. But, I ask you to listen only. What I am about to say to her is for her only."

George seemed to consider this for a moment, then said, "Because *I* am the man of the family now, I will stay. I'd like to know what the dangers are anyway."

Stands Strong nodded. "So be it." Glancing at Czanna, who was sitting toward the outside of the invisible circle he and George made, Stands Strong said to her directly, "As I have just said, I have need to talk to you about the perils the prairie holds at this time of year and what you must instruct the others to do, if you are to survive."

Then he stood up and, with only a few steps, came to sit down in front of her, crossing his legs at his knees.

Glancing forward, Czanna gazed up and across the short distance to look at Stands Strong. Silently, she gasped. A gentle half-moon had at last arisen on his left, and beneath its gentle silvery cast, Stands Strong looked handsome almost beyond belief.

At present, he wore his hair in two neat braids, one on each side of his face, but she remembered he also wore one single braid at the back of his head. Parting his hair slightly to the right, he had attached a white feather to his hair on that particular side, allowing the feather to fall down over the braid. A long string of silver-colored beads were also attached to his hair in a similar manner as the feather, and the string dropped down beside the feather over the same braid.

He wore round white shell earrings. And, although she thought the province of earring wearing was strictly feminine, on this man the earrings looked manly and proper. In addition, a long looping shell-beaded necklace fell down over a white, hide shirt. While she couldn't see it now, she remembered his shirt ended at about his mid-thigh in an uneven hem, perhaps mimicking the shape of whatever animal it was made from.

Now that she was closer to him, she could clearly see his breechcloth was different from his other clothing; perhaps it being made from another animal than the rest. But, whatever its material, this masculine piece of clothing was dyed blue and had a white stripe running down its center. Even his leggings, as he sat before her crossed at the knees, were of a whitish color, though she could see painted symmetrical shapes of blue, yellow and white upon them. On his feet looked to be a tougher kind of buckskin moccasin, and both moccasins had the same geometrical shapes painted on them in identical hues to the colors on his leggings.

He was tall, even as he sat before her; he was somewhat thinly built, although muscular; and his posture was straight with no slumping shoulders, a condition a little unusual for a man of his height. His skin color was tan, perhaps only a few shades darker than her own. His eyes were a very dark color of brown, appearing to be almost black. His cheekbones were high and prominent, his nose was not long and was aquiline—but only slightly so—while his lips were full and well-shaped for a man.

And, as the moonlight flattered each and every part of Stands Strong's physical demeanor, Czanna wondered why no one who knew anything about this land and these people had warned her about the looks and charisma of these young Indian men. She had heard many men on the steamship and at Fort Benton describe Indian warriors as ugly fiends, devils, even as Satan, himself. But, as she had decided earlier this morning and was still inclined to think now: it simply wasn't so.

Swallowing hard, she gazed away from him. She had to, if only because the raw strength and virility of this man was too much to realize so quickly. Besides, a woman of the gentry class did not stare at a man.

But, he was speaking, and, looking up, she gave him her full attention as he said, "Before I tell you of the dangers we will face even before the sun first rises, I would hear what it is you have to ask me."

"I...I..." Czanna couldn't quite meet his regard, and so she glanced away from him and gulped, not yet comfortable with her observations of his utter male beauty.

He didn't say a word, however. Instead, when she dared to gaze back at him, he was looking down, appearing to be calmly awaiting whatever it was she had to say.

Because the wind was strong this night and blowing in her direction, his clean manly scent wafted toward her. It was not unpleasant. Indeed, it was the opposite, and something within her stirred to life.

She swallowed as a feeling of complete femininity made her hesitate to speak. Naturally, he being larger and stronger than she, a notion of being his inferior caused her to hesitate. But, this would never do.

Lifting her chin, she reminded herself of who she was, and also who he was. She was of the dominant, aristocratic class in her homeland. Therefore, he was not her equal, regardless of how good-looking or how helpful he might be. In particular, she had every right to employ him, to ask him to leave off his duty to his chiefs and to help her family instead.

Still, she hesitated. But, when he remained aloof and quiet, and it appeared he would calmly wait for her to begin, she murmured, "I... Mr. Stands Strong, I have come here to ask if you might please be our guide into the Glacier Mountains."

He looked up at her and asked, "The Glacier Mountains? Are you speaking of the Backbone-of-the-World Mountains?"

"I...I do not know."

"If you are referring to the mountains farther north and west of here, they are one and the same. The Backbone-of-the-World Mountains is what the Pikuni people call this particular mountain range."

"Oh."

"Where in those mountains would you wish me to take you?"

"I...I don't know exactly."

Glancing up at him, she saw him frown before he asked, "For what purpose are you seeking to go into the Backbone-of-the-World Mountains?"

"I…we…as a family…have a cousin who left our country many years ago and journeyed into the northern reaches of Indian Country. I am told he is a fur trader and that he lives in the Glacier Mountains. This is all I know."

"What is your white cousin called by his own people?"

"Do you mean his name?" she asked.

"I do."

"Oh," she responded. "Tom Johnson is the name he goes by."

"Old Tom Johnson? Long Rifle?" Stands Strong smiled at her. "This man is your cousin?"

"He is, indeed. Do you know him?"

"I do. He is married to a Pikuni woman. And, he often comes to our tribe to trade. I will take you to my people where you will be safe while you wait for him to visit our tribe."

"Will you? I would greatly appreciate this. When do you think he might visit your people?"

"Perhaps by this same time next year. Maybe sooner. Maybe later."

Czanna swallowed. This was not acceptable. After all, she had promised her brother to find their cousin as quickly as she possibly could. It was important, therefore, to not be too ready to agree with what Stands Strong was suggesting. She said, "I have a great need to find my cousin before this next year comes, and this is because I have important news for him. Therefore, I must see him as soon as possible. Please, Mr. Stands Strong, if you would take us to him sooner than this, I would pay you well for your trouble."

"Pay me?"

"Yes," Czanna responded, feeling as though she were on solid ground with this man at last. He was, after all, little more than a servant and, therefore, hers to command. "I am prepared to give you many silver coins if you will only take us to him before next year."

"Silver? Silver coins?"

"Yes, or...do you wish to have gold coins instead?"

Oddly, his look at her appeared to change from curiosity to hostility, all in the space of a few seconds. But, Czanna chose to ignore the warning; she was certain she could convince him to be their guide now, even if he were married and had the need to return home. She was preparing to make another even better offer to him, indeed, when Stands Strong stood up to his feet and stepped back away from her. And, although his voice was not harsh when he asked, "Is it your wish to insult me?" Czanna began to sense all was not well.

What had she said?

She didn't come to her feet, however, to confront him. She could only replay her words in her mind. Somehow, in some way, she had said something wrong.

But, what?

After hesitating a moment, she glanced up at him and replied, "No, sir, I do not mean to insult you. I have urgent business with my cousin which is why I cannot wait a year or more in your camp hoping he will come there visiting. I have traveled far from my home to arrive here and to be in a position where I can seek out and speak with my cousin. A year and many months have I been traveling away from my home with my younger brother and sister with me, and only because it is urgent for us to find our cousin. This is why am I seeking your aid. If you doubt my ability to pay you, I will be most happy to show you the coins I carry. I could give you these in advance, also. Truly, I am certain I have enough gold to make your time spent with us worthwhile."

She had barely spoken the words when suddenly Stands Strong spun around, turned his back on her and, without another word to her, strode quickly away from their camp. She watched his retreating figure as he disappeared into the dark of the night.

Even now, she could feel the shock of his sudden departure deepen her already crushing gloom.

It was, perhaps, an understatement to think it had not gone well. And, it was unpleasant, indeed, when George exploded with laughter.

"Why are you laughing?" Czanna asked. "There is nothing funny about this."

"Sister, isn't it obvious? Didn't you listen to him scolding me?"

"He didn't scold you."

"Yes, he did," said George. "It's only that he spoke so kindly to me, it didn't sound like scolding. He is obviously angry with you. I don't understand why. But, he is angry with you, and, rather than say any unpleasant words to you, he left." Again, George laughed.

"Oh dear," whispered Czanna. "I don't know what to do, and I don't understand what I have said to upset him. But, this I do know: we need him. He is the only man in this vast land whom I feel I can trust with the duty to bring us to our cousin. Oh, what am I to do?"

"I don't know, Czanna."

A black cloud of her own making seemed to hover over Czanna, and she felt like crying. Indeed, her lower lip was trembling, and she could feel the tears at the back of her eyes threaten to fall down her cheeks. It was a bad habit, this breaking into grief when she and her family were in trouble, but what was she to do? Her world and all she had ever known was crumbling down around her.

Gazing at George, she said, "I don't understand this country, George. Truly, I don't understand it at all. And, I fear my not knowing the mores of this people and the dangers of their land could cause us great harm. Forgive me, George, but I do not have the knowledge, nor do I possess the strength, to keep us safe here. Indeed, I fear we need Stands Strong."

## CHAPTER FIVE

*The spirit-killer golden rock...*

As Stands Strong trod out of their camp and into the blackness of the night, he scolded himself for aligning himself with this woman and her family. *Áa*, it was true: a man was duty-bound to help a woman in trouble, but he had gone so far as to extend his commitment to her by making her "one of his women."

He was now alarmed at himself for doing so. Assuming Czanna to be similar to his almost-mother in moralities, he had gladly welcomed her into the fold of his life. He could see now he had been mistaken to do so.

*Ha'ayaa,* it appeared she was the same as all other white people. They came here without permission; they brought with them whiskey, the wicked spirit water, which drove his people crazy; they carried sicknesses into Indian Country which the medicine men of the tribes had never before experienced; and these people stole from and murdered one another in their mad rush to find the golden rock.

*And she has, this night, offered the spirit-killer rock to me. Is it her intention to drive me into acting in a manner as crazy as the white man?*

Through his Lakota father, Stands Strong had been taught to respect the medicine ways even though he wasn't a true medicine man. Indeed, all his life he'd had familial ties to and experience with the traditional approaches to healing. And, although his Lakota family was now gone, those traditions of the medicine men had been carried on by his almost-family's ties.

Indeed, his almost-father, Strikes Fast, was a great medicine man, and Strikes Fast, along with his friends Eagle Heart and Gray Falcon, could cure most of the ailments presented to them. But, the crazy spirit within the white man's whiskey, as well as the madness brought on by the golden rock, eluded all three of them, their "cure" being to simply never indulge in them and their mind-altering ways, and to keep them far away from those who could not resist their temptation.

And yet, here was this white woman attempting to lure him into the white man's sickness by offering him the golden rock. And why? To lead her and her family to their cousin in the Backbone-of-the-World Mountains? It was a journey he would gladly do for her simply because she asked it of him.

But, perhaps he should not blame himself for trusting her, since his mistake was a natural oversight. After all, his almost-mother was white, as were his two aunties who had married into the Pikuni tribe. Not only was his mother, as well as these white aunties, beautiful in both spirit and body, they had showered him with motherly love over these many years of living with the Pikuni people. There was nothing, indeed, he would not do for these women; without hesitation, he would die for them.

Thinking back, within his memory was no incident of these women indulging in the madness of whiskey, although the white man stocked the dangerous brew within his forts. Truth be told, these beautiful women upheld the Pikuni ideal of what a woman should be, and they blended so well into the life of the Pikuni, he often forgot they were white.

His error was this: upon first meeting and speaking with the woman Czanna, he had extended to her the same allegiance he upheld for his mother and his aunties. He could see now this woman, Czanna, didn't deserve it.

Or did she? Was he certain she meant to lure him into losing all sense?

*Ha'ayaa,* in this he must be truthful, and the truth was he was not completely certain this was her intent. Yet, she had offered the evil spirit rock to him as "pay" for a thing he would do simply because he wished to know her better.

But, could his assumption about her faults be in error? Should he, perhaps, ensure he knew all the particulars before he became even more infuriated? Instead, rather than spit angry words at her, he had left.

He sighed. Because he had already vowed his aid to this woman, his sense of honor gave him no choice but to return to where she was and speak to her as calmly as he was able, perhaps discovering why — in her own mind — she had offered the evil rock to him.

Glancing up into the star-drenched sky overhead, he called upon what had once been his medicine helper, the white bear, asking her for her aid in calming his anger enough to keep his tongue and his mind straight.

But, truth be told, he would rather face a raging buffalo than talk to the white woman.

****

He did not find her where he had left her. Instead, he discovered Czanna had returned to her sleeping robes, there beside the wheel of the white man's wagon.

Perhaps this was good. In this way, their conversation would be private.

He trod right up to her and sat down in a position where he and she would be forced to face one another — the best pose in which to council together. As he sat down, he took note of the warmth and the softness of the buffalo robe upon which both he and she sat. Idly, he wondered where she had obtained the robe.

But, her head was down, her face in her hands, and she appeared to be so deeply steeped in her thoughts that she had not yet taken notice of him. He cleared his throat as a means of bringing her attention to him without startling her.

Immediately, she gazed up at him and gasped, perhaps because of the shock of seeing him. Maybe she, like many of the other white men Stands Strong had known, closed all her other senses when her eyes were shut. If this were so, she had probably not been aware of his silent approach.

Although the night was dark, it was not black enough to hide the paths of the many tears that were streaking downward over her lovely face, some of those tears so recent they were still wet. But, although his heart went out to her, he set his mind against the allure of her beauty. He had to do so; he had to be firm in his resolve against her until he learned more about her.

In a low voice, he uttered, "I have returned here with the hope of speaking to you with good words upon my tongue. Is this agreeable to you?"

She merely nodded.

"*Soka'pii*, good. If I ask it of you, will you tell me why you have an urgent need to make this journey into the Backbone-of-the-World Mountains?"

She nodded and said in a soft voice, "I will tell you what I can. But, first, may I please ask why you left? I don't understand. All I did was bid you to help us. Did I not offer you enough of the gold or silver coins as the price for your services? I could give you more if this be your upset."

Stands Strong calmed his urge to shoot back angry words in answer to her question, amazed and disconcerted at how she continued to tempt him into evildoing. At length, he said, "There is a madness the white man brings into my country, and the Indian, who must defend his family and his tribe, seeks to keep his distance from the white man's evildoing. This is why I left."

"Evildoing? Are you telling me you think I am evil because I have asked for your help?"

He inhaled deeply and sorted through his thoughts before uttering, "Not you, nor what you have asked of me. It is what you have offered me as the pay you would give me if I help you. This pay is evil."

"Pay? Evil?" She cried out the words before she burst into fresh tears, then she spread her hands again over her face as though she didn't wish him to see the effect his words had upon her.

Her actions caused Stands Strong's heart to open up a little to her, and he offered her an explanation, whispering, "Since my people have known the white man, he has brought us friendship and many beautiful goods we value. But, he has also brought with him a wicked thing, and we have stood horrified at the white man's attempt to exchange this evil for the quality of hides and furs he obtains from us."

"I do not understand. What did I offer you that you find evil?"

"I will tell you, though it is not my place to utter these words to a woman who is also a white person. But, so as to understand you better, and you, me, I will say to you what many of my people speak of to one another about certain white traders. What I tell you is true; the white man brings whiskey into this country and steals the Indian's mind and spirit by means of this brew, causing the Indian warrior to commit war on his friends, as well as his family. A man whose mind has been stolen by the white man's brew cannot be long without it, and such a man has been known to kill his wife and his own children when his spirit and his mind have been taken by this whiskey."

With her lips shaking, she uttered softly, "I am sorry to hear about this, Mr. Stands Strong. Believe me, I am sorry, indeed. But, please, I have not offered you whiskey in exchange for acting as a scout for us."

"Your tongue speaks true. This you have not done."

"Then, why are you angry with me?"

He paused as he tried to keep control over his mind and the urge to still utter bad words to her. At last, he felt he could speak with only a little resentment, and he said, "There are stories brought to us by Indians west of the Backbone-of-the-World Mountains, those who once lived close to the Everywhere-water. A few of those Indians were able to escape from either death or enslavement brought to them by the white invaders. They have told us stories of these trespassers to their land, who, when they first arrived, said they brought peace, yet who begot death to the Indian people or made slaves of those they did not kill. The scatterings of those few who were able to get away have made their home with us or with a few of the tribes on the west side of the mountains. And, from those few people we have learned of the terrible golden rock and how, because of desire for this rock, the invaders' spirits have been stolen. This white aggressor acts like a man under a spell—one cast by a demon spirit. And, if the captured Everywhere-water-people do not willingly work in the underground caves owned by their attackers, the white man either kills them with his deadly weapons or he enslaves them by forcing them to dig in these caves that he calls 'mines,' where the evil rock lives. Because of this golden rock, whole tribes who once lived next to the Everywhere-water have been wiped away by this spiritless invader and his guns. Real Indian men of those tribes fought these intruders. But, because Indians had not the guns nor the means to fight back equally, they lost these battles. And, as they had known would happen, they were killed.

"Of course," Stands Strong continued, "we have seen the golden coins the traders carry and which they value, but we did not know of the demon's spell which has been cast upon the rock. It is from the tribes who once lived close to the Everywhere-water that we have learned of this rock and its immoral power over a human being. Those Everywhere-water people have told us to beware of the invaders who carry this spirit-killing and evil rock. And, Miss Czanna, you offered this rock to me tonight."

Looking at her, he saw her eyes were opened wide, and she gasped before she said, "I am very, very sorry to hear these stories, Mr. Stands Strong. I have not known of these Indian people, nor have I had any knowledge of the white invaders of their homeland. But, please, I must ask you, do you think I am like these trespassers you speak of who are trying to steal your spirit?"

Stands Strong hesitated to respond, since the truth might cause her more grief. However, at last he answered, but with a question, and he asked, "What else can I think?"

No sooner had he uttered the words than she again broke into tears, hiding her face once more within the folds of her hands. He waited patiently for her to regain her composure, and, as the night sank deeper and deeper into the shadows and still she wept, his heart softened for her plight and a thought took hold of him. Could her reaction to his words, if it had been a true response, offer him proof of her innocent and genuine intentions? Indeed, could he have been wrong to decide her actions were meant to lure him into evildoing?

But, contrarily, couldn't she be using her tears to soften his heart while hers remained hard?

At last, she calmed herself enough to say, "Mr. Stands Strong, I don't know what to do. I…I don't understand this country or its people and their moralities."

As though she hadn't cried enough, she broke anew into tears, and this time in response to her, Stands Strong leaned forward, stretching out his arm to her and taking her hand into his own. *Ha'ayaa*, be her tears real or not, he could not sit in front of her and do nothing.

He said, "Maybe I have been wrong."

She placed her other hand over her face and hiccupped.

As softly as he could, he asked, "Will you tell me about what is in your heart? I fear I do not understand your wishes concerning me, and I do not know why you so urgently need my help."

It took much time for her to compose herself. However, he patiently waited until at last she murmured, "Where I come from, no one gives service to another without coin being exchanged. This is why I offered it to you."

Using the hem of her dress, she wiped the tears from her face and brought up her head as the dark brown of her eyes met his. She sniffed a little before she continued, whispering, "In my country, service performed for another is never given without some pay being exchanged. You see, in my homeland, nothing is free and available for general use. Indeed, one must have coin to obtain shelter and to obtain food and clothing. Sometimes food is given in exchange for service performed, but it is more common to offer another person the silver or gold coin. Some men accumulate more of these silver and golden coins than others, and they live very well. But, some men do not have the means to accumulate the pay they need to provide food and shelter for their families, and so they fight amongst themselves for what they must have. Perhaps this explains why the white man wars so greatly with one another: so he might obtain the golden coin.

"You see," she went on to say, "in this country of yours, the gold and all else is free, and if a man can find what he needs, he can live well. But, in my country, the gold and even the silver coins are not free, nor is anything else free, save the air and water. I don't know if this be true, but it seems to me it has always been this way.

"But, please, Mr. Stands Strong, I have only offered you the gold or silver coins because I need your help and I know of no other way to obtain your assistance other than by asking you to take what I have to give, which is coin. Do you see? It is important that I give you something of worth for what I ask of you. The truth is, I have nothing to offer you but coin."

For a moment, Stands Strong sat stunned into silence. Could it be true? In the world where she came from, was nothing free for all to use? Did not the Creator make the world and his creation for all peoples to have and to use?

Quicker than the flash of an instant, he understood — not the complexity she spoke of — but rather, he recognized her innocence.

93

She had offered him what she had to give—something she felt was valuable.

*Áa*, he had been in error to condemn her without speaking to her first. But, was there any wonder he and she hadn't understood one another? His people were as different from hers as the mountains were to air.

At last, Stands Strong muttered under his breath, "*Wáíai'taki tsaahtao'.*"

"I beg your pardon? I did not properly hear you."

Stands Strong shook his head as if to dispel the thought. In truth, he had no words to speak in response to the concepts she proffered, and so his mind had turned toward a quality she *did* have to give.

However, before they talked further, he would be certain he understood her correctly, and he asked, "Is it this way, then? Did you believe you were doing as well as you could by presenting me with the gold coin?"

She simply nodded.

Because her hand still remained within his own, he squeezed it before he said, "I see now I have been wrong about this and about you. I freely admit it to you, and I hope by telling you of my mistake, your concerns will be eased. Know this: I will help you with what you have asked simply because, as I once told you, you are now one of my women. *Noohk*, you owe me nothing, except perhaps your friendship."

"But, Mr. Stands Strong, I fear you already have my friendship. I have freely given it to you. Indeed, you might be my only friend in this country. Were it not so, I would never have been able to ask for your service, coin or not. Please forgive me for giving you the impression I did not value your friendship." Again, she sniffled. "I am sorry I angered you. Truly, I am. I...I didn't know what your people have suffered because of the greed of others."

"Greed?"

"Yes, have you no one in your society who selfishly believes he may steal or kill so as to obtain what he must have, yet who cannot obtain what he needs by honest means? Or perhaps you are aware of evil men, who, parasite-like, can only live off the backs of other men?"

"We do have such men," answered Stands Strong. "But, their counsel is never sought. A true man overcomes the urge to steal from or kill others in his tribe who might stand in the way of attaining glory. Only a boy in a man's body does this."

"Yes. But, I cannot possibly ask you to endure the hardships involved in helping us without my giving you something in return. I am well aware that by aiding us, you could lose your life, same as us. And, Mr. Stands Strong, I have nothing else to offer you in exchange for your help, except the coin. Indeed, if you will not take it, I know not what to do."

"*Wáíai'taki tsaahtao'*," he repeated.

"I am sorry, sir, but I do not understand your language."

"I know."

"Please, won't you translate it for me?"

What was wrong with him? Could he not control his tongue while he was in the presence of this beautiful woman? Once again, the words had slipped out of his mouth without first thinking the thought through.

He shrugged in response to her question, pretending his statement meant little to him. But, in truth, he would rather face an enemy warrior than translate what he had said.

"Please?" she asked again. And, when he didn't answer, she repeated, "Please?"

He was going to have to tell her. He would not lie to her nor would he refuse to answer, since only a coward would seek to avoid the truth. And, he was no coward.

Stands Strong took a deep breath, summoning up his stamina before saying, "Become my woman. Marry me. Then it is my duty to do as you ask."

She Brings Beauty To Me

## CHAPTER SIX

"Marry you?" Czanna jerked up her head. She had been staring down into her lap, ashamed of herself; she had tried to use what she knew about hiring servants as a means by which to gain this proud man's cooperation. She had done this without first acquiring the knowledge of what he considered valuable.

But, marriage?

How could she ever marry him? He was Indian, while she… She was of the aristocratic, gentry class in Hungary. Indeed, though he was quite handsome, as well as heroic in coming to her family's aid, he was obviously not her equal. Indeed, they were worlds apart.

Yet, as she gazed at Stands Strong across the short distance between them, she was reminded of where she was: she was no longer in Hungary, and whatever had been accepted there was not necessarily so here. Indeed, she had to put her considerations and prejudices behind her. That is, she would have to do so if she were to make a new life here.

Still, marriage…?

She had always thought she would marry a man from her own culture, or at least from a society closely related to it. Indeed, if she were to marry a man so utterly foreign to her, mightn't she be in danger of losing the essence of who she was?

She, who had thus far lived her life in luxury, would be reduced to a mere circumference of a tepee, or worse, as her living quarters. To be sure, she would be required to do the work expected of a woman within his tribe, and she knew these to be demeaning jobs, tasks only fit for a servant. She might even be required to convert to his religion, a circumstance she could never agree to.

Make no mistake, to marry him would require her to put the noble way of life forever behind her. True, her brother had forced her to vow to never return to Hungary. Plus, he had instructed her to make a new life for herself in the American West. But, she doubted he would have ever considered she should willingly become an Indian man's wife.

As she gazed at Stands Strong, this man who was truly her only friend in a world of unknown fears, she was presented with an acute and terrible problem: she could not marry him, if for no other reason than their situations in life were so different. Yet, if this be what he required of her in order to give his allegiance to her, dare she not marry him?

Czanna gazed up at this man again but found she was staring at the top of his head; his eyes were centered downward. Indeed, he appeared to be patiently awaiting her response.

However, instead of answering him directly, she asked, "Mr. Stands Strong, I know you like me well enough, or you wouldn't have made me one of the women in your life. But, why marriage? Do you love me?"

Raising his head, Stands Strong stared directly into her eyes as he said, "I desire to have you as my wife."

"Yes, I understand this," said Czanna. "But, this is not an answer to my question: do you love me?"

She thought he might again back away from answering her directly, but instead he surprised her when he said, "I would like to make love to you. No true man will continue to pretend friendship with a woman when he desires to take her to his sleeping couch."

Stunned at his open honesty, Czanna couldn't account for the instantaneous and powerful flames of carnal sensation that rushed through her. Moreover, an image of her being held in Stands Strong's arms and accepting his kisses flitted through her mind.

And, without willing it to happen, a cascade of fire was even now surging through her bloodstream, creating a desire within her to come in close to him...very close to him.

Did she secretly wish for this man's embrace?

Surely not. But, if this were not true, why did every sense within her so unexpectedly yearn to scoot in close to him, and there to urge him to hold her, to touch her?

Clearing her throat, she tried to put these thoughts out of her mind and contemplate, instead, what could possibly be her response to his declaration. At length, however, she decided she had not a single idea of what to say, and so she remained silent.

But, her silence was not going to aid her cause in securing this man's cooperation for his assistance, especially when he wasn't helping her with the dilemma of how to respond to his proposal. Indeed, he didn't utter another word. Looking downward, he was clearly awaiting her answer.

Knowing she would have to give him a reply, and soon, she first needed to discover an important fact of Indian life, a detail which might give her the means to gently say no.

"Mr. Stands Strong," she began, "I am told Indian men might take more than one wife. Are you already married?"

"I am not," he answered without hesitation. But, then he asked, "Are you?"

"I...I am not," she replied. "But, my God and my religion do not allow a man to have more than one wife, and I could never marry you if you already have or might intend taking another wife besides me. Knowing this, do you still wish to marry me?"

He inhaled deeply, glanced up at her and said, "My almost-mother is white, as are two of my aunties. I know well their beliefs. I know also their husbands honor their religion and their God, as I would, too. If we were to marry, I would take no other woman as my wife."

She sighed. Oh dear, there was to be no easy way out of declining his proposal. But, decline it she must, if only because their positions in life were so very ill-matched.

And so, she said, "Mr. Stands Strong, of all the men I have ever known in this country, I like you best of all. But, your proposal comes at a difficult time in my life. Please let me explain: on this very day when we met one another, there at the cliffs, I had only learned of the deaths of my beloved elder brother, my father and my mother. They were killed in a terrible manner back in my homeland of Hungary; they were hanged by the neck, though they were innocent of the charges made against them."

Swallowing down the instant urge to tears, she continued and said, "The morning when you found me, I was singing and praying to God. I felt then, and still do, so deeply grieved, I knew I could not go on with what my brother had charged me to do for my family. And yet, I had to keep on, for my younger brother's sake and for my little sister's. This was why I had walked so far in the dark of the early morning. I didn't know what to do; I was only aware of the need to try to let go of my pain by saying goodbye to my brother, my mother and my father. And so, I sang as best I could, using the song as a means to ask the Lord to keep them safe. Forgive me, but I am not yet over their loss."

He inclined his head. "It is hard to lose those one loves."

"Yes, it is, and thank you. But, my situation grows worse. I now fear we may have lost Mr. Henrik, too. He was my father's manservant, and my brother charged him with the duty to take us to our cousin here in Indian Country. But, the man he had hired whom we had met at Fort Benton—a Mr. Hanson—to scout for us, and who was to lead us into the mountains, robbed us by stealing all the coin Mr. Henrik had given him. And, I am told this robber left us in the middle of the night while I was gone. Mr. Henrik then went after this scout who is now part of the gold seekers' circle of friends.

"And so you see," she continued, "I am still deeply grieved by my situation. And, I fear it is too soon for me to consider marrying a man I have not known for even a full day."

He made no response to her words, not even by making a faint motion toward her.

Encouraged, Czanna cleared her throat and then continued. "Please, I am sorry to give you this answer to your proposal, but I fear it must be my response, at least until my grieving has come to an end. Yet, when one considers what has happened between us tonight, isn't it fair to believe we are quite different in our viewpoints?"

"Perhaps," he replied. "But, although I understand your words and my heart is heavy because of your loss, I do not yet know what is in your heart about what I have suggested. Can you tell it to me?"

She gulped. Indeed, she didn't quite have the courage to look at him and speak the words she knew had to be her response. And so, she stared off to the side when she said, "Well, it is this way: if we have so quickly argued over a matter that has been misunderstood between us, what would we face if we were to join together as man and wife?"

She looked back at him and saw he had raised his head to stare at her, and her stomach dropped as though a storm of butterflies had been awakened there, and for a moment—if a moment only—she wished this man would simply take her in his arms and kiss her, giving her the sympathy she seemed to require.

At length, he said, "All newly married people face these same or similar problems. Perhaps not the same, but there are many difficulties they must meet as one...if they are to be happy. But, come, you have answered a different question than the one I asked. And, although I understand your loss and the terrible thought of keeping going, I think time will not likely change your feelings about the matter of our marrying one another; although, of course, I will wait until your spirit is cleansed of the hurt you now bear.

Or, are you trying to tell me no, you do not wish to become my woman, but are saying it in as kind a manner as you can?"

"Well, I...I..." Czanna shut her eyes and paused, if only to collect her thoughts. Despite what had been thrust upon her by circumstance, she needed to answer this man with what truthfully had to be her answer, but she had to do it without alienating or insulting him. At last, opening her eyes and gazing back at him, she continued, saying, "Mr. Stands Strong, I like you very much, and were our cultures not so different, my answer might be the opposite of what it must be. The truth is, I cannot marry you, because you and I have been raised so differently. And so, my answer must be no."

His response was merely one of silence.

"Forgive me, but please let me explain why this must be my answer. Whether this is right or wrong, marriage is done differently where I come from. Indeed, I have always known I would not marry for deep fondness, nor for love or passion. The manner of my upbringing has been to emphasize a woman's duty to marry in order to extend and to enrich the fortunes of both families. Marriage is not, then, a matter of the heart, but is done for the good of the family's wealth it holds in land and in coin. Please understand, I am not free to say yes to what you ask because it will not enrich the coffers of my family's wealth."

He nodded, then asked, "By fortune and wealth, do you mean the golden rock?"

"Yes."

"*Soka'pii,*" he said in the Pikuni tongue. "As I understand your words, marriage in your tribe is usually loveless? And it is done, not because of a bond between the man and the woman, but because the family wishes to attain more riches?"

"Yes."

He didn't answer at once. In truth, he didn't speak for several minutes. At last, however, he said, "This would mean neither the woman nor the man would ever come to know or experience the deep commitment they would usually share in a marriage."

"Well, actually, that is not always true," she said. "Sometimes a woman and a man begin to love one another with each passing year. But, if not, because the marriage was made for the reason of wealth and not because of the heart, both a man and a woman may have love affairs. Indeed, it is even expected."

"Love affairs?"

"Yes, not marriage, but love and passion can be experienced with someone other than one's wife or husband, if one is discreet about it. Indeed, it is accepted for a man to keep a love partner, or perhaps two, if the family fortune allows it. Women may also fall in love with a man who is not her husband. But, such affairs are always to be so discreetly accomplished, no one would ever know."

For a moment, it appeared Stands Strong had become incapable of speaking whatever was on his mind, because he was silent for so long. In due time, however, he asked, "When you tell me of the love between a man and a woman who are not married to each other, do you mean the love of the body or simply the admiration one might feel for the other?"

She cleared her throat before saying, "It would be the former, as well as the other."

Again, it appeared to her as if he were stunned. At length, he muttered, "Let me ensure I understand this completely: you, a woman, would be allowed to make physical love to a man who is not your husband?"

"Yes, if it is done in secret."

Again, he appeared to be struck silent. But, in due time, he asked, "You tell me true about this? Women are allowed to have love affairs in your country?"

"Yes."

He had been looking downward, but when he brought up his head, he was frowning, and he swallowed hard before asking, "Are there penalties if the unmarried couple is discovered?"

"Sometimes," she said as she watched him closely, feeling as though she were explaining the deeds of a devil to a saint. But, whatever surprise he might have experienced at first, he appeared to quickly suppress the reaction, and his thoughts were no longer visible for her to witness upon his countenance.

Unexpectedly, an idea took hold of her, and though she tried to make the wayward thought go away, now that it was there, she could not shake the concept from her mind. It was an exotic notion, true; it was quite a sensual inspiration, too. Yet, if he were agreeable, it might be a means she could employ to repay this man for any of the hardships he would face because of agreeing to lead her family into the mountains. And, wasn't her family's safety the most important duty she carried?

Still, she hesitated, if only because it was a bold idea. And, it was also one she would have never thought to offer Stands Strong had she not already found him to be handsome, dependable and, indeed, utterly masculine. But, did she have a choice? If she were to say yes to this man's proposal of marriage, it would be as though she were destroying her former life. Although, perhaps if tides did not change in her homeland, she might have to consider turning her back completely on creating a similar life to the one she had once known and loved there.

But, at present, the idea of making her life here in America similar to the one she had known in Hungary was a concept she did not wish to destroy. Besides, hadn't she always known her married life might include an affair of the heart?

Nevertheless…

She knew, but tried to ignore, the words used for a woman who was considering the possible pact she was considering making with Stands Strong. And, she didn't wish to be regarded in this manner, especially by him. But, did she really have an option?

No. There was no easy way out of this. Without Stands Strong's help, she and all her family would surely perish. She needed a man—a man who knew this country and who could give them the support and the aid they would require.

Stands Strong was such a man.

Still, she wondered: if he did agree to her terms, would she ever outlive the shame of even asking him? Quickly, in less time than it takes to think it, she reflected on the lives of her younger brother, her baby sister and even Liliann. If she didn't act to secure their futures when she at least had the chance to do so and something terrible happened to any one of them, would she ever outlive the knowledge of having once had the opportunity to keep them safe?

Deciding it was better to act than to remain silent and ineffective, she realized there was only one action to take, and, mustering up her nerve, she inquired, "Perhaps now is not the time to ask this of you, Mr. Stands Strong, since we have not known each other very long, but considering your question to me and in light of my upbringing, if I were to agree to expand our friendship to include love, but not marriage, would this be enough for you to agree to stay with us and guide us to my cousin?"

Without even a moment of hesitation, he asked, "'Love' meaning of the heart or of the body?"

She, however, hesitated answering his question because she wasn't certain she could say the words she knew she must. But, also there was a note of unpleasantness in his tone. Nevertheless, at last she said, "I suppose this would be up to you."

"Then, let us do them both," he said at once. "But, you must give me an example of what I might expect if I accept your offer of expanded friendship as a means of pay for my taking you into the Backbone-of-the-World Mountains."

"What? What is it you are saying?"

"I mean this: if this is to be the pay you are willing to give me, then do it. Let me decide if it is good enough for the trouble of taking you to your cousin. Come here where I will allow you to kiss me, and we shall see how you do."

"What? Did you say 'allow'?"

"I did. I am asking you to give me a sample of this...'love' you have spoken about to me."

"A sample? Would just a kiss be what you're asking me to give you?"

He nodded. "For now," he added.

"I see." She shot him a quick glance, but he looked about as helpful as a bull in heat. She asked, "Perhaps you could help me?"

"Is this to be part of the agreement, too? Must I do all the work?"

"But, Mr. Stands Strong, even in your society, isn't it the man who kisses the woman first?"

"Not always," he answered. "Now, come here, and let's have your best kiss." He crossed his arms over his chest, looking as if he were as approachable as the stars overhead.

"Oh, very well. But, it will only be one kiss."

He didn't answer, and not even by way of a gesture did he offer her any assistance. Worse, as Czanna scooted toward him, he looked to be as kissable as a skunk.

But, she was going to do it anyway. She had made the offer; she wouldn't take it back. Coming up onto her knees, she leaned forward and gave him a gentle peck on his cheek, noting how smooth his skin was and how clean and alluring was his scent.

Oddly, in reaction to him, a sensation much like an explosion flooded through her bloodstream, and she felt an overpowering—and sexual—excitement take hold of her. For a moment, she wished she possessed the courage to ask him to do more than share a sweet, simple kiss.

Would he say yes to broadening the kiss into love making tonight?

She was, however, confused when his reaction to her kiss was to say "And, this is the best you can do?"

"You said only a kiss, sir. And, I have kissed you. What do you say now to our agreement?"

"Humph!" He held up a hand and snapped his fingers. "You expect me to be moved by little more than your lips against my cheek?"

"What? What was wrong with the kiss?"

"*Ha'*! Heap big work! That's what is wrong."

"Sir! I don't understand."

"I mean this," he said, his arms still crossed over his chest. "The man who would take you to his sleeping couch would need big and much patience because he would have to do all the work of teaching you about love. Much work. Too much work for nothing except a few moments spent under the sleeping robes. No treaty. No agreement."

And, with this said, he came up onto his feet and walked away from her as though she weren't this moment aching for him to touch her.

*Much work? Oh my, what I have done? I have offered him the best I have to give, and he has refused it. Will he now cease to even be my friend?*

As though he were privy to her thoughts, he turned back slightly toward her and, looking over his shoulder, said, "You may try again tomorrow, and we shall see how you do then."

"See how I do then? Sir!"

But, if he heard her, she didn't know it. He was already gone

# CHAPTER SEVEN

Stands Strong grinned as he walked away from the beauty. So, she liked him well enough to present him with the gift of her body. But, he realized another pertinent fact: she would never have made the offer to him if she didn't already sense he might be a good mate for her. Women possessed instincts about this, and it was known to him that a wise man paid attention to a female's primeval senses.

A man was also much the same, he figured: he might desire and lie with many women—and without consequence—but he, too, could primordially sense his equal in a woman. And, in this regard, they had much in common.

Still, for Czanna, he assumed there must be some feeling of love for him, or at least passion, for her to even entertain the idea of offering him the gift of her body. *Áa,* although it might appear she had proffered the suggestion out of the need for his guidance, he knew she would never have suggested it without also desiring to keep him near her.

However, it was now apparent to him why she hadn't said yes to marriage, but had asked him to agree, instead, to love without marriage.

Maybe he should rejoice in her proposition since, in defining her concept of the state of marriage, and seen from her viewpoint, she had paid him a compliment. Marriage, to her, was a loveless cause, not the realization of the spiritual enlightenment that came from two people becoming united. She also thought love was not necessarily a part of marriage, but, rather, it was a precious gift to be bestowed to another man she desired bodily—a man other than her husband.

And, if this were so, why then should he strive to marry her when she thought real love was to be given not to her husband, but to a stranger?

However, there was a negative concept he had gleaned from her body movements and her facial expressions, and he should give some attention to this, too: not only did she consider him to be unequal to her because of their differences in culture, she also thought him to be lacking in wisdom, perhaps even intellect. It had been there in her eyes, a form of disrespect, as though she considered herself to be superior to him. It was an error—one perhaps garnered from her upbringing.

But, only a strong man, one quick in thought and in action, could protect her in this land of unpredictable weather, war parties and other dangers, where the elements could be as deadly as an enemy. Most likely she would come to realize this…if she were to remain here.

But, perhaps she hoped to return to her homeland. If she did return there, she would take a part of him with her whether he wished it to be this way or not.

What she didn't know and what he was *not* going to tell her was this: he would take her into the mountains regardless of desire, love affairs or marriage. He would do it simply because of his male sense of duty to the female of the species. However, he also liked her. Maybe he liked her too much. Indeed, if it were left up to him, he would have already bedded her and, by doing so, would have made her his woman.

Truth was, he didn't care what her ethic was or was not as regards marriage and love, or lack of love. To the Pikuni, as well as the Lakota way of thinking, if a man desired to bed a woman, he married her and stayed married to her.

But, he wouldn't tell her this either; it might scare her away from him when, even now, thinking as he was about her, his blood was pooling toward the center of his body, creating quite a masculine response. *Áa*, it was true: he wished to keep her with him, at least for now. But, despite her negative response to his proposal, if he were to be honest, he would admit he might like to keep her with him for a long, long time—perhaps for the rest of his life.

****

On bended knee, Stands Strong leaned over the top of Czanna's head and placed his hand upon her shoulder.

"Wake up, *O'tsipi Matsowá'p*. Though the sky is still dark, dawn is nearing and we must be on our way."

He had positioned himself on the ground above her head, the best position in which to resist her allure. However, Czanna's high-pitched groan almost caused Stands Strong to throw away all caution and take her in his arms right now and make love to her.

But, it wasn't right. There were others here, and his actions might cause her family—if they were to awaken—to think of her in a bad way. Besides, he didn't wish her to know how much he truly desired her.

Still, when she stretched out her arms and the material of her dress pulled at her breasts, perfectly outlining each lovely mound, he experienced an instant and utterly virile response.

He shouldn't do it, he knew he shouldn't, and yet he found it almost impossible to resist leaning down over her face where he could inhale her luscious feminine scent. His senses reeled, and, positioning his face over hers, he kissed her, gently tracing her lips with his tongue. When her groan—high and feminine—reached his ears and when she raised up her arms to bring him in a little closer, he almost lost control.

Without moving away from her, however, he whispered, "Dawn is coming swiftly, and we must be on our way. Your beauty might cause me to wish to stay with you and make love to you regardless of the others in our camp, but perhaps now is not the time to teach you about lovemaking."

Again she groaned, and Stands Strong knew he had best end this while he could still maintain control over his lust. As it was, an overpowering urge to take her in his arms and have his way with her was goading him on, telling him no one would know if they made love now. And, when she brought back her head to rain kisses upon his neck, he almost consented to the urge.

Instead, he took her arms from around his neck and sat back upon his heels. Then he murmured, "Imagine, if you were my woman, with every movement of the sun, we could awaken each other as we have done this morning...and we might enjoy more than simply admiring the looks of the other."

Again she moaned, then whispered, "So, my knight, you agree to an expanded friendship with me?"

Coming once more over her, his face above her face, he murmured, "I said 'if you were my woman,' which you are not. As for agreeing to your pact, I am still wondering whether it is worth the trouble to teach you about lovemaking only to have you leave and give your knowledge about love to another." Once again, he brought his lips down to hers and kissed her, only this time he rained kisses not only upon her lips, but on the tip of her nose, her chin, her cheeks. Then, he barely breathed, "Awaken, my beauty. We must prepare to leave before the sun is up and a war party comes upon us when we are unaware."

Changing his position, he came to squat at her side and, once settled, reached down and helped her to sit up, admiring the wayward sway of her long, dark curls and the dizzying scent of her body. When she again moaned, his body reacted in a purely male way, as if he needed reminding that he was attracted to her.

He ignored his body's response, however, and, gently taking ahold of her, he turned her so her back was facing him. Then, lifting up her hair, he massaged her shoulders, following the action with wet kisses all along the breadth of her shoulders and neck, basking in the feminine scent of her.

## She Brings Beauty To Me

She moaned, and he answered her in return with pure male readiness. He, however, ignored his response—at least for now.

Even though she wore layers of clothing, he could feel the texture of her skin—soft, pliant and utterly feminine—beneath his fingertips. And, her clean, alluring scent was urging him to make love to her now.

Upon this thought came another: if he were to make love to her, their agreement would be set. Strangely, he found he was unwilling to give in to her offer so easily...yet.

He expanded his massage up and down her back, cherishing each gentle curve of her figure, and when her high-pitched sigh reached his ears, he couldn't help himself: he pulled her back into his arms.

Immediately, he found the pressure point on her neck and kissed it, then made a trail up to her ear, massaging it with his lips. She squirmed and tried to turn around so she was facing him, but he knew if he let her do this, he would make love to her despite the others, despite war parties and despite even himself.

Instead, he kissed his way across her back to the other side of her neck where he caressed her from the top of her collarbone up to her other ear. She sighed again, and he knew he had best stop now while he still could.

But, she didn't appear to be in any hurry to let the embrace end, and, reaching her arms up, she brought them together around his neck and leaned back against him. But, it was her question which alarmed him when she asked, "Do you love me?"

"I wish to make love to you," he responded easily.

"You know, of course, that's not an answer to my question."

"All right," he said. "Then, let me ask you the same question: do you love me?"

"I do, Mr. Stands Strong. Even on such short acquaintance, I can honestly tell you I love you very much. I just can't marry you."

He almost surrendered to her right then. But, caution caused him to hesitate. If he made love to her now, not only would a marriage between them be unlikely, but he would also, in the eyes of his people as well in his own eyes, ruin her. He whispered, "Ah, but this isn't bad, is it? To not marry me? After all, don't you look upon the union of a man and a woman as loveless?"

"I do."

"Then," he responded, "I would rather we engage in a love affair and cease to discuss marriage at all."

"Oh, yes. Then, you agree to my suggestion?"

He laughed. "I am not so lacking in wisdom as to be quick in leaving my thumbprint on your white man's truce paper. We will see how much trouble it will be to properly show you how to love a man."

"Hmmmm," was all she replied. "But, Mr. Stands Strong, wouldn't it be worth your time? After all, what if I might possess some quality about me to add to your knowledge of lovemaking?"

He laughed. Truly, his reaction was honest, if only because she had surprised him. He had never imagined she might be privy to a bit of wisdom concerning lovemaking, perhaps bringing with her a form of knowledge over and above what he already knew concerning the topic.

After a moment, he kissed her neck once more and sat back on his heels, though he kept his arms around her, resting his head against the back of hers, aware that even the scent of her hair enticed him to do more. He murmured, "Come, awaken the others. I have started a fire and have two of your kettles filled with warm water for your women's bathing. Then, we will begin our journey. But, our time on the trail will be short. We are in a part of this country and at a time of year when many war parties are out upon the prairie. And, we have little defense against them. In truth, if a war party should discover us, they would kill both me and your brother. And, since you and your sister—"

"Liliann is not my sister. She is my maid."

"Sister." He emphasized the word. "In this country, she would be considered your almost-sister, since the two of you must remain together for the safety of you both. Now, a war party, if they were to come upon us, would take you captive, and since the both of you are beautiful, one, maybe two of them, would take you both as a wife."

"Do you really think Liliann is beautiful?"

He laughed aloud and heartily. Leave it to a woman to single out this detail from all the other cautions he had told her.

He asked, "Do I have eyes to see?"

"Then, you do?"

"Of course she is beautiful. But, I am not wishing to make love to her, nor is she as pretty as you."

"Then, you think I am prettier than she?"

"I do."

"But, you still think she is pretty?"

He smiled and murmured in Czanna's ear, "When a man desires a woman, it is she and only she who is in his thoughts. Besides, your almost-sister is young and not yet a woman. I desire to have a woman in my arms, and this she is not."

"Then, you do not desire her?"

"I do not," he confessed. "Only you."

She sighed. "I guess this is good enough. And so, you are in love with me?"

He grinned. Here they were again at the question of his love for her. Obviously, he was going to have to tell her the truth, though disguised, and he said, "Of course I love you. We are friends."

"Friends? But, I thought you said you could no longer consider me a friend when you wished to bed me."

"I did, and for good reason. I asked you to be my woman for your sake and for your reputation within my tribe. I should not mislead you. Desiring a woman and caring for her in friendship is a part of a man's nature in loving a woman. But, let me explain further: if we make love and are *not* married, in my tribe there is a disgrace which paints a woman in a bad way.  And, it could go bad for you."

"And, you?  Would you be painted, too?"

"I fear not," he replied.  "I would be congratulated on my good judgment and good luck, while you would be shunned, perhaps worse.  Further, no good woman would speak to you.  This is why I suggested we should marry.  I will, however, be happy with being no more than your lover if I decide it is worth teaching you about lovemaking.  But, whatever you and I decide, we will be friends anyway."

Because they were sitting so closely together, he felt her sigh, and holding her as he was he could feel her breasts rise and fall with her breathing.  Meanwhile, his body answered hers in the age-old manful way.

"But," Czanna said after a while, "it isn't fair to judge a woman and not the man, though I must admit it is much the same in my society."

Perhaps it was because they were sitting so closely together, but he felt her frustration, and he said, "I agree.  It is not fair.  However, I cannot change the ideas and thoughts of each man and woman in the tribe.  It has been this way for hundreds, perhaps thousands of years.  And, this, my beautiful friend, is why I asked you to be my woman."

"Then, you didn't propose this to me because you have come to love me?"

He groaned, wishing he were not involved in this conversation with her.  But, common courtesy demanded he answer her, and he said, "I desire to make love to you.  For me, if I feel this way about a woman, I should propose to make her my woman."

She was quiet for so long he was about to rise to his feet and begin the chores needed for their journey, when she asked, "Have you ever asked another woman to marry you?"

115

He let out his breath in a gasp, wondering how she had managed to pull him into a conversation so taboo.  But, he answered her politely and said, "I have."

"You have?  And, did she agree?"

"She did not, though she told me she wished to be my woman."

"But, why did she not marry you if she wanted to?"

Again he paused, while he considered rising up to his feet and walking away.  But, then again, it was he who had originally spoken of marriage to her, and he understood the bad effect it might have on her were he to refuse to discuss the matter now at hand with her.  And so, he said, "Because I am Lakota, and she is Pikuni."

"I do not understand," Czanna said.  "Aren't the Lakota and the Pikuni tribes?"

"They are."

"I still do not understand."

Stands Strong sighed before seeking to enlighten her, and he paused for a moment, realizing there was to be no backing away from having this talk with her, though it was a subject he had not ever discussed with another living being.  It was at some length when he said, "The grandparents of the girl I sought to marry were killed by a Lakota warrior.  Indeed, her father's own brother was killed in war with the Lakota.  Because of this, the father of the girl I sought to marry swore he would never have me as a son-in-law, stating he would kill me first."

"Oh dear," she said.  "But, couldn't you both have stolen away?"

"We could have, but instead she chose the peaceful way to bring the matter to a close, and in the end, she chose to marry another.  The man she married is a good man, and they are happy together.  She is now with child."

"Oh.  What is her name?"

"Good Shield Woman."

"And, did you love her?"

He slanted Czanna a smile, one he hoped was lopsided, as though he didn't care about what had happened. But, at length he confessed, "I did."

"And, do you love her still?"

He deliberately refrained from answering her question directly, saying only, "A man never stops loving a woman. He merely moves on."

"Oh," was all she said. Then, she asked, "Are you courting another woman in your tribe now?"

"What means this word 'courting'?"

"It means to show a woman you are interested in marrying her."

"*Saa.*"

"And, the word '*saa*' means…?"

"No."

She didn't seem to have an answer to his simple admission, and so he came up to his feet quickly so as to get on with the day as well as to put the topic of discussion behind him, when she said, "I am glad."

Caught off guard by her admission, he further astonished himself when he replied, "So am I. Now, awaken your little sister and your almost-sister, before dawn comes upon the land. We must be on our way."

"I will do as you say. But, sir, if you have prepared our baths, as you said earlier, and we women are to bathe, I must have your word that neither you nor my brother will be anywhere near us as we attend to our bath. Do you promise you will not look at us?"

"I will not promise this to you. What man can resist looking?"

"Then, I will require one of your buffalo robes to place around us while we bathe."

He chuckled. "You would deny me the pleasure of a simple look?"

"Indeed I would, sir."

Again he laughed. "Then, I shall engage myself in scouting duties so I will not be tempted to see what you look like without clothing."

"And, the buffalo robe? Will you give me yours to place around us for privacy...in case your duties cause you to be situated within looking distance of where we must bathe?"

He sighed. "I will. But, I will also ask you women to attend to your bathing quickly. We must be on our way."

"And so, we will do it as quickly as possible. Do you think we will reach the fort today?"

"Not today," he said. "Maybe one, maybe two suns. Come, we have spent a pleasant morning, but we must now hurry. We will only be able to travel upon the open plains until the sun rises. So, we will break camp quickly and travel as far as we can while it is still dark and the war parties have made or are making their day camps."

"Day camps?"

"This is Pikuni territory. Enemy war parties do not dare to appear on the open prairie during the hours of Sun's light."

"But," she said, "if this be true and they make camp during the day, why can we only travel during the darkness of early morning?"

"Because some young warriors are anxious to prove themselves and do not care for the safety of the war party. Your wagon, being only one, tempts such men. We will not provide the temptation so long as there is only me and your brother to defend us."

"And me, too. I could help in our defense."

He grinned at her. "And you, too. Come, you must hurry." With this said, he turned and stepped away from her, his back to her, allowing him to hide the evidence of his sturdy response to her, which was still in evidence. He only wondered how long it might take her to recognize the urgency of his body to make love to her.

At least he could control it...for now.

## CHAPTER EIGHT

"*My* friend comes."

"What friend?" asked Czanna.

"*Istisitsa Ohkitópii,* First Rider," Stands Strong responded. "We have been scouting together for our chiefs. He went to discover what had happened to your man. He brings the man with him."

"The man?"

"This man who was with you and your family, but who left you to seek revenge. He is greatly injured. My friend has made a travois for him."

"A travois? What is a travois?"

Stands Strong nodded, but his attention was not upon her and he didn't answer her questions. Instead, he was gazing forward, though occasionally he glanced both right and left.

The crisp scent of dawn had, at last, arrived, although only blue and pink shadows from the sun fell upon the land. And, at the present moment, Czanna was at the helm of the prairie schooner, while Liliann walked beside the wagon on her right, Liliann carrying Briella on her hip. Stands Strong, who was on Czanna's left, was keeping his pony down to a walk, his pony matching the steps of the other horses.

"How badly injured is Mr. Henrik?" asked Czanna.

"I do not know," answered Stands Strong. "My friend only tells me they are coming."

"Tells you?"

He nodded.

"Are he and Mr. Henrik here, then?"

"Not yet," said Stands Strong. "They will, however, be here soon."

"But, how can he find you?" asked Czanna. "And, how do you know he comes with Mr. Henrik?"

"Scout talk," he answered.

"I beg your pardon?" she asked. "What is scout talk?"

"Silent talk. Mind-to-mind speak."

"Mind-to-mind speak?" Czanna gulped. Was this man's mind perhaps touched by the sun? Or could he really speak to people in perhaps a similar way she could talk to animals? "What is this you are telling me? I have never heard of this mind-to-mind talk."

"I have not the time to explain," he answered. "Know only they will be here soon. My friend did not tell me the condition of your Mr. Henrik."

"He is not my Mr. Henrik," Czanna said. "He was…is my father's manservant. Oh dear, if Mr. Henrik is badly injured, will he be able to recover?"

"I do not know. We will have to discover this once they join us. I must go now."

"But—"

She stopped speaking since she was now talking to the wind. Stands Strong was already galloping away.

What, in the name of the Good Lord, was "scout talk"? And, what was a "travois"? Czanna closed her eyes for a moment. What else was she going to discover in this strange and foreign land? In truth, the concept of two people "speaking" to one another over a great distance…this "scout talk"—whatever it was—only served to strengthen the conclusion she had already made: she did not belong here.

However, she reminded herself of her own similar experience with silently speaking to horses. Didn't she talk to them, and they back to her?

But, similar though the concept might be, it was still different. She had talked to horses that had been standing next to her; she had never "talked" mind to mind with another human being, and especially not one who was at some distant point away from her.

Yet, if Stands Strong's news were true and Mr. Henrik were coming back to them, wasn't the news hopeful? If Mr. Henrik were injured but still alive, could it not follow that, once recovered, he could take back the reins of leading her family to their cousin?

And, if he were to recover, there might not be a need to urge Stands Strong into having a clandestine affair with her. Or would there be?

Wasn't it true that Mr. Henrik, much like her, was unfamiliar with this country? It was why he had hired Hanson, the scout who had betrayed them. But, if Mr. Henrik chose not to hire Stands Strong — or if Stands Strong refused the position due to there being no "pact" between himself and her — Mr. Henrik would have no choice but to hire another man, perhaps another Indian who might be willing to accept gold in payment for his services.

At the thought, a strong feeling of disappointment swept over her, and Czanna knew the reason why: she wasn't being fair to Stands Strong. She had offered him a pact. If he accepted her suggestion, she was bound to it, same as he.

But, there was now another, though different, predicament. Earlier, on this very morning, she had spoken the truth to Stands Strong when she had told him she was in love with him.

After all, how could she *not* love the man? He was intelligent, handsome and he knew his way around the mountains and the prairies of this land. Plus, he had come to her aid without a moment's thought given to his own comfort...perhaps even to his life.

There was also this morning to consider: only a short while ago she had melted in his arms, wishing he would do more than merely kiss her. Indeed, so strong was her desire to bring him in close to her, she almost ached with the need.

Truth was, were he on a par with her socially, she might very well be inclined to accept his proposal of marriage.

But, he was not her equal, and a union between them could never happen; their differences were too numerous. She knew she would never make a suitable wife for him—one who would be subservient to him and who would submit to the drudgery of whatever were the wifely chores of an Indian man's wife. Nor could he ever be the sort of husband she was expected and required to find and to marry—one who would be of a similar circumstance as she and who would accumulate the wealth required for her family's needs.

In truth, she and Stands Strong were worlds apart, and to ask either of them to change the manner of their lifestyle was simply unthinkable and unfair to them both, as well as to their families.

Yet, she craved his touch. And, obviously, he must also enjoy hers.

Maybe, given time, he might consent to engage in an affair of the heart—one that would ultimately allow them both to walk away without damaging one another.

She closed her eyes as a feeling of remorse overtook her. Would a mere love affair ultimately hurt him? This she did not wish to do.

But, it was unlikely she would hurt him. Indeed, he didn't love her. It was evident in the way he avoided answering her questions about love, stating instead how he wished to make love to her.

But, loving someone and making love to that someone were different. Even she, as unschooled as she was in the endeavor, knew this.

Well, it was useless to think about it. Her future life with a husband of a similar social status as hers seemed a long way off into the future. Truly, there was no sense in worrying about it now.

But, if Mr. Henrik survived — and she prayed he would — there was one matter she would ensure: only Stands Strong would be their guide. It would be he, indeed, and no other who would take them to her cousin's home in the Glacier Mountains. And, Stands Strong would be well paid for his efforts. She would ensure it.

****

The sun was high and the day was becoming quite warm when Czanna espied an Indian man standing atop a gentle rise upon the surrounding green and brown grasses of the prairie. The man was engaged in waving his robe in an extremely odd manner, and he made the gesture over and over before he then began walking his horse down the slope of the hill.

Placing a hand above her eyes, Czanna could see the horse — and it was dragging an odd-looking contraption behind it. Even from a distance, Czanna could discern two — or was it four? — long, strong poles attached to the animal on both sides of its body, their attachment utilizing some means of ropes to secure them, and in between the two poles were several shorter branches of wood stretched together to form a kind of bed. And, on the bed was...

Was it a man? Was it Mr. Henrik? Further, was the setup being pulled behind the horse called a "travois"? And, putting the facts all in order, if Stands Strong had been right about his friend bringing Mr. Henrik to them, was the concept of mind-talk actually real?

Czanna felt as though her thoughts were spinning out of her control. If this were true, then it would follow that this mind-to-mind speak was real, indeed. And if this were so — and looking at the lone Indian, his horse and the travois which she could see were quite solid and of this world — she knew she did not belong here in this strange world of prairie, grasslands and mountains. Nothing of the society she had left behind had ever prepared her to learn of a people who could speak to one another through a mind connection — and at a distance.

As she pondered upon her thoughts, the heat from the sun overhead seemed to pound down upon her, causing Czanna to feel unusually warm and headachy. In response, she slid her woolen shawl off her shoulders and placed it next to her on the wooden seat.

Because of her uncertainty and confusion, she made a decision: she wouldn't think about this "scout talk" until she had a chance to question Stands Strong a little more about it. Placing her hand over her eyes again to block out the early morning sun, she watched as Stands Strong and George rode out to converge with the other Indian and his horse-pulled travois. She then saw Stands Strong—who, upon reaching them first, had jumped from his pony and stepped toward the travois—gaze down at the one who was lying stretched out upon it. The other Indian—the fellow scout who must be Stands Strong's friend—and George followed. And, as the three of them stood around the person on the travois, Czanna saw George reach out to take the injured one's hand.

The man—it had to be Henrik—did not respond.

"What is happening, Mistress Czanna?" asked Liliann.

"I think," answered Czanna, "the poor fellow on the travois over there"—she pointed—"might be your father. A day or two ago, Stands Strong told me his friend was journeying to find your father. And, this morning he also told me his friend was bringing your father here. I am sorry to tell you this, but your father is greatly injured."

Liliann gasped. "Greatly injured? I must go to him at once."

"Of course you must," said Czanna. "Here, give me the baby, and please feel free to go to your father and be with him as long as you wish. I will keep my little sister with me."

Czanna had barely spoken the words, when Liliann took hold of the baby and, giving Briella a quick kiss, handed the child up to Czanna. Liliann's hands were shaking.

Briefly, Liliann gazed up at Czanna and said, "Thank you Mistress. I shall go to him now."

Czanna nodded. Liliann's lips had twitched with every word she'd spoken, and Czanna watched as the young girl raced over the prairie toward the men. From a distance, Czanna heard the girl's scream and watched as Liliann threw herself upon her father.

Oddly, it was Stands Strong's friend who bent down toward Liliann, and took her hand into his own. Meanwhile, Czanna looked on as Stands Strong squatted next to his friend, and the two men conversed in both words and a few hand motions, and, had she been able to leave the wagon, she would have joined them there, too.

"Liliann," said Briella in perfect English, her index finger pointing to the maid. "Gone."

"Yes," said Czanna, "but Liliann is not gone for very long. She will be coming back. You see, she is only visiting her father, who is ill. We are lucky that Mr. Stands Strong and his friend decided to help us. I will be grateful to them both, and I shan't forget their kindness toward us. No, indeed, I shan't forget."

"Go there!"

"No, not now," said Czanna. "We must remain here with the prairie wagon and the horses. But, I think there are some of your toys in the back of the wagon, if you would like to play with them. I think Dolly is back there."

"Yes," said Briella. "Dolly. Needs nap."

Czanna smiled as she released her sister and guided her to crawl into the back. Czanna murmured softly, "I only wish I could take a nap with Dolly."

"I nap, too," said Briella as she picked up her doll and, holding Dolly close, laid down, keeping the doll firmly held within her small arms.

****

It wasn't long before Czanna saw Stands Strong rise to his feet and jump up onto his pony's back. Then, taking his seat, he pressed the animal into a run down the slope, his direction toward her and the wagon. He reined in just short of them. But, he didn't speak. Instead, he gazed at Czanna, and it was she who took the lead and asked, "How is Mr. Henrik?"

Stands Strong dismounted, and, holding onto his pony's reins, he climbed up onto the seat next to her. Quickly settling himself, he said, "He is injured…bad. He is dead to the world, although his body still lives."

"He is dead?!"

"His body lives on, but his shadow is gone."

"What do you mean, 'his shadow is gone'? And, what is a 'shadow'?"

"The essence of who he is, his spirit or soul, as you call it. It is not with him now."

"Then, he is as good as dead? Is it this you mean to say?"

"*Saa*, it is not. Often when a warrior goes out alone to find his medicine, he fasts for several days and nights. After a time, his shadow leaves his body to have adventures upon the plains and to find, if he can, his medicine and his medicine helper. But, this man you call Henrik, is close to death. First Rider and I have decided that if we are to help him we must take him to Grass Woman Springs. The water there is healing, though it smells"—he made a face—"bad. But, if he is to live another day, we must take him there. It will delay you going to the fort."

"Then, it must be. In truth, I was only going back there to await Mr. Henrik's return to us."

"*Soka'pii*, good. Tonight I will go to the springs and shall scout there to ensure no war party has come there to heal their own."

"I will go with you," she said, her response surprising even her.

"You will not go with me." He turned his head around to stare at her. "Do you know how to scout, how to creep into an enemy camp without being seen or heard?"

"Of course I don't."

"Then, you will stay here."

"I shall not stay here while you go there," she insisted.

His reaction to her words seemed odd to her because he grinned. Then he said, "I will sneak out of camp tonight, and so stealthy will I leave, you won't even know I am gone."

"Very well. But, if this be your intention, I shall sleep next to you."

He laughed. "And, I will welcome you, if this is to be your plan, though I doubt either of us would sleep. But, come now. You are needed here to help defend this wagon and the others."

"Nonsense. Your friend and my brother can defend our wagon. If you are going, then I am coming along with you."

"Why?" he asked. "Surely you know your duty is to stay behind and guard your almost-sister and baby sister."

"Yes, it's true. But, I have another obligation, too. And, the task I speak of is to learn as much as I can about this land so I and my family can survive in it. If I stay here, I will miss the opportunity to learn how to scout and what it even means to 'scout.'"

Although instinct might have appeared to be dictating her tongue, she knew exactly why she was being so insistent. It was simple, really. She would keep this man with her, and she would keep him safe if she had to.

True, she had spoken honestly when she had told him she wished for the opportunity to learn more about this land, but there was another reason she was demanding to go with him. And, it was one she would not voice to him, though it was not very hard to understand: she was still grieving for loved ones now gone. Added to the loss of her brother, as well as her father and mother, was now Mr. Henrik's plight. She was not going to lose Stands Strong—her only friend—too. She would take her gun, and she would defend him with her life if need be.

*My life?*

The truth startled her. She had only known this man for two days…two short days. Did she really care about Stands Strong so much as to come to his defense, even risking her own life?

*Yes, I do and I would.*

But, she had no intention of dying; especially now, when the responsibility to secure her family's welfare lay squarely upon her shoulders. But, if her family's welfare depended on her, then she would learn how to care for each one of them here in this strange and hostile land.

When she raised her eyes to his, she found him staring at her. He didn't utter a sound, though. He simply looked at her. Yet, so intense was his regard, Czanna felt as though she were melting under it.

"*Ánniayi.* So be it," he said after a time. "But, if you go with me, I would caution you—and I would have your word on it. You will do exactly as I say. This is important since you do not know how to scout. And, if this is to be your attitude toward me when I must perform a scouting mission, then I will have your word, also, that you will submit to learning the skill. Otherwise, you will not go out with me again when I am required to scout. Do you agree?"

"I..." Did she have a choice? "Oh, all right. But, I agree only in this way. Yes, I will learn as quickly as I can about what you do and how you scout. But, I will only do as you command so long as you are not in any danger. There. That is what I will agree to. But, you should know this: I will keep an eye on you, and if I see you are trying to sneak away tonight, I will dog your steps. I promise I will."

Suddenly, he laughed, the sound of it deep and virile. He said, "I fear I will have to rename you, and it shall be Stubborn Woman. Yes, I think I shall call you by your new name, Stubborn Woman."

"I am not stubborn!"

He merely grinned.

## CHAPTER NINE

Czanna paid heed to every little thing in the environment around her, vowing she would come to know as much about this northern land as she possibly could, given such short acquaintance with the prairie.

Before the sun had even risen up into the eastern sky, Stands Strong, with George's help, had navigated their wagon down a gentle slope, taking the wagon into a nearby coulee. There, the two of them had hidden the wagon amongst a grove of huge cottonwood and willow trees that grew up next to the shoreline of a swift mountain stream. The coulee was not as deep as it was wide, and it was hoped that the covering of the tall grasses and trees there would hide the wagon from the eyes of an enemy war party.

As Czanna kept pace alongside the wagon, she had to step up high in order to walk down into the coulee, so tall were the grasses leading down into it. Because she was also balancing her young sister, Briella, on her hip, it wasn't the easiest activity to perform.

Looking behind her, she saw Stands Strong's friend, First Rider, following them into the coulee, leading his horse and the travois behind him. Liliann was walking alongside the travois, her hand holding her father's, though the man had yet to regain consciousness.

Once at the bottom of the coulee, the two Indian men, along with George's help, raised up a temporary shelter for Mr. Henrik. In truth, Czanna was amazed at how little time it took to erect it.

Because the refuge was constructed with the wood, grasses, mud and bushes to hand, it took on the look of the environment and faded into it. Indeed, had she not known it was there, she would have overlooked it.

The structure was small and round, but was sufficiently large enough to allow Mr. Henrik to lie down full-length within it, and, being as wide as it was long, it allowed Liliann to remain with her father.

No sooner had the poles and branches for the shelter been put into place than the three men—she was beginning to think of her brother as a man instead of a boy—were strategically placing more branches, bushes, grasses and mud onto or next to the shelter, further deepening its disappearance into the environment.

The wagon was the last to require the men's attention, and they were soon maneuvering branches, bushes, grasses and mud on top of and down the sides of the wagon until its white covering no longer stood out like a beacon. But, would the white canvas ever come clean?

Soon Stands Strong approached her and whispered, "We may not speak openly in case there are enemy warriors nearby. You need to change your clothes if you are to accompany me this day."

"But, why?" she asked.

He smiled. "Your dress, though it is a dark blue, will stand out upon the prairie under the sun. And, its material will snag on the prairie grasses, the vines and bushes, and, besides giving an enemy a clue as to who you are, your dress alone could lead them to us. I fear you will be required to clothe yourself in buckskin if you are still desirous of coming with me. I have extra clothing. You may use it and may also cut it to fit you, if you wish."

"Well, although I am still…'desirous' of going with you, I do not like this idea. No men's clothing for me. I'd rather look like a woman, not some skinny man. Besides, I refuse to wear some poor animal's skin."

"I understand, but I must also advise you again to keep your voice to a whisper. Remember, we are not in a camp with many warriors to protect and keep you safe from enemies. Besides"—he grinned at her—"the manner of your clothing will not hide your feminine figure from me. But, if you do not wish to dress yourself in what clothing I have with me, you have my permission to stay here."

She frowned at him. Was he serious? Was she now required to dress so as to look like a shorter, skinnier version of him?

He was continuing to speak, and he said, "I go now to prepare my weapons, as well as food for us so we may scout ahead of the others. But, be quick to decide what you will do. Either you go with me or stay here. I care not which you choose to do." And, with these words, he grinned at her again, but his smile was lopsided, pulling up only one corner of his lips. To her chagrin, it caused him to look endearingly handsome.

"But, I protest!" she murmured. "Look how much taller you are than I am. Your clothing will not fit me. Indeed, do you not see how much longer your legs are than mine? Why, having to wear your leggings will cause the bottoms of them to drag over the ground, leaving a trail. Besides, I would be required to wear a breechcloth, as well as a shirt that will hang on me probably to my ankles."

"Do not worry," he soothed. "I will help you to cut the clothing to fit you, but if the shirt is big and falls well down your legs, you would not have to wear a breechcloth."

"Sir, I will not go naked under the clothing."

He smirked, looking much too highly amused. And, he said in a whisper, "I beg you, do not give me reason to imagine you naked." He laughed then. "Wear some of your own clothing beneath it if you must, but ensure you have the means to easily answer nature's call. We will be traveling as fast as we safely can, and there will not be the opportunity for you to remove your clothing in order to simply relieve nature's demand. Nor do I think you would be too willing to undress when I am watching you, which I would have to do if you insist on wearing clothing that cannot be easily taken off when your body requires this of you."

"Sir!" Though the word was said as softly as possible, it was still meant as a real objection.

"If you decide to accompany me, I will be over there." He pointed. "I have brought with me an extra pair of leggings and a shirt. We can fit them to you if you agree to learn to scout."

She let out her breath on a snort. However, after a moment, she said, "Very well. Lead the way, O master."

Again, he laughed, and when he said "That's better," she raised her chin into the air, earning herself another snicker from him.

\*\*\*\*

The sun was high in the sky, and the deep blue above them was filled with cottony clouds. Those puffs were mostly a pearly white, Czanna observed, although a few of the cheerful white fluffs held a slightly gray color on their underside, threatening an afternoon shower. But, otherwise there was no hint of rain, the prairie air being clean and dry. The ground beneath them was hard, but at least it wasn't as muddy as it had been when they had been forced to wade through a small mountain stream. Also, and sadly, here on the high prairie above the Missouri River there were no trees to hide them properly.

Now since they had come closer to the springs, the land—and the requirement of remaining concealed—required them to twist in a rough and torturous manner over and through the long green grasses, the large bushes and the rocks—and to do it on their bellies and forearms.

So far, their journey had been agonizing for her. They had set out the previous evening, leaving when the stars had become visible in the night sky. Then they had traveled north and east toward the springs.

Although it had seemed to her as though they'd ridden too far and too fast on this unknown—to her—terrain, she hadn't been about to complain. Still, she had feared that at any moment her horse might step into a gopher hole or some other obstacle and she would be thrown from the saddle. Luckily, it hadn't happened.

It had been during the first rising of the moon when they had guided their horses into a coulee a little south of their present location. There they had left their horses, the coulee being populated with cottonwoods, pines and numerous stretches of short dense patches of willow trees. They had hobbled their horses deep within the concealment of the many cottonwood trees, the height of these providing some protection against the sharp eyes of an enemy war party. It had been there, also, where the prairie grasses grew abundantly, providing food for their ponies.

"Do you not worry about someone finding the horses while we are gone?" Czanna had asked, her voice no louder than a whisper.

Stands Strong had merely shrugged before responding to her in a like manner, saying, "Only if the horses of an enemy speak to them."

"Speak to them?"

"Ponies talk to one another in many ways: by scent and by horse talk."

"Well, if it happens, perhaps I might help. Since childhood, I have often talked to my horses, and I think sometimes we understand each other."

"Do you now?" he'd asked, eyeing her mysteriously. He'd then smiled before saying, "You continue to surprise me, and I wonder what else I will discover about you besides your beauty and your willfulness."

"Thank you for saying I'm beautiful, but I am not willful."

"Stubborn, then."

"Sir, I am not stubborn either, but if you will only agree to my pact with you, perhaps you will discover much more about me."

His grin at her had been wide and oddly sensual before he'd replied, "I intend to discover all your secrets and secret places without having to place my thumbprint upon your treaty paper."

She had wanted to question him further about what he'd meant by "secret places," but he had already turned his back on her and was moving away. She'd had to run to catch up to him, but if he'd noticed her difficulty in keeping abreast of him, he hadn't mentioned it.

She had been utterly dismayed to learn they would go the rest of the way on foot, or rather on their forearms and outstretched bodies. Why?

As though she had asked the question aloud, he had answered her in a whisper, murmuring, "To walk upright is to invite any wandering warrior to seek us out and kill us. To be a scout means to use concealment as a means to remain alive, and a scout must be, at all times, unseen regardless of the environment. We will be traveling the rest of the way over the tops of these hills—"

"You mean mountains, don't you?"

"*Hills.*" He'd emphasized the word. "We must travel in this way so we will be able to look down into the land and the coulees below. We must observe everything in the environment without ourselves being seen, because we are looking for any sign of an enemy."

"A sign?"

"*Áa.* Any smoke or its scent, waves of motion in the air, plants moving without wind or game startling suddenly. We are looking for anything out of the ordinary. If we see or smell or detect any of these, it means there is life nearby, and it is probably an enemy war party."

"Why an enemy? Couldn't it be a bear instead?"

"And so, you would consider a bear to be no enemy?"

"Oh. I see your point. But, couldn't it be a friend who starts a fire or who causes the animals to suddenly run?"

135

"Perhaps. But, if they be friends, why try to remain concealed when they are in Pikuni country? And, not always are 'friends' friendly." He grinned at her. "A scout does not assume that warriors from an allied tribe are always peaceful. He does not take chances. He sees, he inspects and he reports his findings to his chief when next he is in camp."

And so they had crawled, scooted and bellycrawled across the prairie and its hilly apexes. Sometimes they'd been required to descend or ascend a hill to get to the other side, and then, happily, they had walked upright, yet bent over at the hip. Always, they were looking down, looking down, trying to see if there were any indications of a war party.

At present, the sun was still shining down upon the land from its high place almost directly above them. Below them stretched one coulee after another where, at their lower edges, stood a few trees. Much farther in the distance were mountains, some still showing white at their peaks. But, those might have been hundreds of kilometers away. Yet, whether there were enemy warriors roaming about in the deep coulees or not, it was a beautiful sight to feel the warmth of the sun. Low green buttes rose up here and there on the ground below them, some closer to hand and showing off a tall bush or two.

Although it seemed to her that they had ridden or crawled well over fifty kilometers in the night, she knew it wasn't true. Perhaps they had ridden ten kilometers at the most.

According to Stands Strong, they were now close to Grass Woman Springs, and even though he pointed toward it, she still couldn't see it. It was a famous place, and Stands Strong had regaled her with stories of it when they had rested, those short breaks being too few in Czanna's opinion.

But, Stands Strong had kept her entertained, regaling her with many of the tales and legends of Grass Woman—his almost-uncle, Eagle Heart, having heard the stories from his father, who had known Grass Woman personally. It was at this particular sulfur spring where Grass Woman— known to Czanna as Sacagawea— had cured an illness which had threatened her life while she had been journeying with her husband, her baby and the white men. Czanna had found it fascinating to hear the stories as related to her by Stands Strong, if only because the tales had been told by Sacagawea personally.

But, these little respites for rest were quite few since she and Stands Strong were on a mission to determine if the spring were free of enemy warriors. So far, they had not seen any sign of an enemy.

Oddly, since beginning this adventure with Stands Strong, Czanna had begun think of herself as "Stands Strong's woman," though she didn't really merit the status since they were not married and since she did not intend to marry him. Although Stands Strong had made references to her becoming his woman many times during their rests, they were yet to tie the knot in any way, be it a mere romance or marriage. Indeed, there had not been the opportunity to do more than ride hard in the beginning of their expedition, and then, having secured their horses, to sneak over the grassy and rocky landscape.

Though her arms were protesting the uncomfortable position of crawling through numerous bushes and over uncomfortable rocks, there was another aspect about this journey she hadn't expected: she felt happy.

Indeed, there was much to be said about the freedom of movement this land presented. In truth, the journey through this terrain reminded Czanna, if only a little, of her childhood. Though her homeland was distinctly different, here and there were the characteristic scents of nature, of grasses and of flowers common to both—all of it adding to the thrill of the simple beauty and awareness of being alive. And though she didn't know how it had happened, it yet seemed to her as though she was able to put the shock of her terrible losses to sleep, at least temporarily. Of course, she was helped in her newfound joy because of the great deal of teasing she endured from Stands Strong, who seemed to delight in pointing out her lack of knowledge of the prairie, its buttes and coulees, even the flora she didn't recognize, like the tiny cacti now in bloom and dotting the land.

Strangely, she was even beginning to savor the feel of the "poor animal skins" she was wearing. They were both comfortable, free of easily tearing and they dried soft even when wetted.

True to his word, Stands Strong had helped Czanna cut his clothing down to fit her. Upon her first donning the unfamiliar garments, the skins had been full of his scent, and if she were to be truthful, she would admit to basking in it, his pleasant aroma imparting a feeling of well-being to her. With a deep sigh, she was starting to realize she not only loved this man—as she had already told him—she was, indeed, falling in love with him…as unlikely as this might have been.

At present, as she crawled over the green grass beneath her belly and her arms, it smelled fresh, and as she passed by the yellow and white prairie flowers, their sweet fragrance spoke to her of their joy in being able to bloom under the warmth of the sun. Funny, instead of feeling tired and plagued by the hardship of their crawl, the earth and the life around her imparted a feeling of being a part of all this. Never, ever would she have imagined she could be subjected to such physical hardship and yet feel so pleasant about it.

As she crawled up beside Stands Strong where he waited for her, he turned, took off his quiver filled with arrows and his bow, and rolled over onto his back; she, too, lay down beside him, the sweet-smelling, hard ground cradling them both. He took her hand in his and, turning his head toward her, said, "I will tell you a truth about me, if you wish to hear it. I admit I have not desired to lay bare my private thoughts to you, but after seeing what you have endured this night, and without complaint, I am feeling more kindly toward you and so would like to tell you a secret. Would you like to hear what I have to say?"

"Indeed, I would, Mr. Stands Strong."

He inhaled deeply, then said, "You have now asked me many times if I love you, and always I have tried to avoid answering you. But, I believe the time has come when I should answer your question as truthfully as I can."

When he paused significantly, she asked, "Yes? What is your answer?"

"It is this: I love you as the friend I have told you I would be to you, though I have also been honest about my desire to make love to you. But, because I know you a little better now, I admit I have come to not only desire to make love to you, but to love you as the woman I would choose to spend the rest of my life with. When I first spoke of marriage to you, it was because my feelings about you required me to ask you to be my woman. But now, before Sun, the Creator of all, I tell this to you true. I love you, and I give my love to you freely and for all my life if you would only have me."

Czanna paused, uncharacteristically at a loss for words. Although she had suspected his true feelings for her—since Stands Strong had often suggested a marriage between them—to hear his words spoken so sincerely touched some deep and hidden part of her, a secret longing which had, perhaps, been lying dormant until this moment. "I...I..." she whispered, gulping down a constriction in her throat. "I, too, love you very dearly. And, were I not who I am... But, please understand, it is not you I have said no to. I have said no to the idea of having to change who I am in order to become your woman."

Stands Strong didn't speak up at once. But, after a while, he said, "I understand what you say. However, I would not have you change who you are, nor would I demand it of you."

"Yes," she answered, "but what you might not understand is that I would have to change." She inhaled deeply, giving herself a moment to collect her thoughts. Then she continued, "Please consider this: until coming into this country, I had never camped outside, not even for a single minute of my life. Yet, if I were to agree to marry you, I would be required to camp as a way of life. Truly, though you tell me you would like to have me as your woman, consider this: I know nothing of cooking or sewing or skinning an animal, and I have never lived in a place as small as a tepee. Truly, do you really wish to have such a woman as I am in your life?"

When he didn't answer her question at once, she continued and said, "Not only can I not envision myself doing the work of the women in your camp, but, indeed, I fear you would be sadly disappointed in me."

He grinned at her before he answered, saying, "Yet, here you are with me now, scouting through a rough terrain which demands great discipline and a heap big more than would be required of you were you to live with my people."

"But," she countered, "I am only doing it because I have to if I am to learn how to survive in this land. Besides, there is more. Somehow, in some way, I must keep alive the memory of my parents and my brother. It's up to me, after all, to carry on our way of life and to be true to the manner and the life I was raised in. Because of their deaths, I have been entrusted with this duty, and I must remain as I am if only to honor their lives. Though I have been honest with you when I have told you I love you, to marry you would be as to turn my back on the memory of my parents and my brother."

When again he was not quick in answering, she added, speaking softly, "I cannot do this; not and remain true to myself."

He breathed in and out, his sigh oddly strained, before he said, "I do understand, and yet here we are, and perhaps it is here, too, where you will have to make your home, and I think you would encounter these same problems regardless of living with either the white man or the Indian."

"Perhaps," she replied. "However, I must try to hold on to what I am and remain true to my family and to what is expected of me."

"So it seems. But now," he continued, "as you have asked for my understanding, I must ask for yours. Though we have only known one another for a few days, already my love for you has grown into being a great admiration. Never could I have ever believed I might meet a woman so beautiful who would willingly follow me and do as I do when I scout. And you, who are a white woman, are accomplishing this without much complaint, though I know it is hard for you. But, hear me on this: my reasons for refusing to engage in an affair with you are as meaningful to me as yours are for refusing marriage. I tell you this now with a full heart, I would happily agree to this 'sharing a romance' with you if the consequences were not so grim for you were we to be discovered to be lovers without being married."

"Grim?"

"*Áa*, harsh they are. There is a terrible price for a woman to pay amongst my people, both Lakota and Pikuni, if she, whom others believe to be married, is discovered in the arms of a man other than her Indian husband."

"Oh? What price is it you speak of?"

He didn't answer; he merely looked away from her.

"But, Mr. Stands Strong," she continued, "how would this 'terrible price' affect me since we would not be husband and wife? We would be merely lovers."

He turned his head toward her, glanced at her and simply smiled before saying, "To my people it is the same. If we make love to one another, we are married. Even if you tell others we are not married, the price for a woman is the same as if she be married to the man she has made love to."

Shocked again, she could only ask, "Truly?"

He didn't answer.

"But, sir you have yet to tell me what this awful price is a woman would have to pay."

He pointed to the tip of his nose. "I would have no say in it, you understand."

"No, I...I don't understand. You would have no say in what?"

"It is an old custom amongst the Pikuni, as well as the Lakota. If it is decided all the facts are true by the Pikuni All Friends Society, they can take action against a woman who has strayed away from her husband, and, since your custom about love with another is different from ours, there very well might come a time when you could be found in the arms of another besides your 'husband,' as you have already told me."

"I understand, but what is this custom?"

"It is an ancient practice, and one I think should be put aside forever."

"All right. But, please tell me what this gruesome tradition is you seem to be unwilling to tell me."

He sighed. "Amongst my people there are several women whose noses are cut here." He put a finger to the end of his nose and made motions of slicing through it. "These women strayed from their husband's side and had 'love affairs'—as you call them—with another."

Czanna gasped aloud. "How cruel! If true, this is worse than being merely horrible or grim."

"I fear it is true."

"And, is the man subjected to the same?"

"*Saa*, he is not. He is free to marry another."

"How utterly barbaric! How inhuman!"

"It is, indeed. Still, it happens. And, so it is that I can never have this affair with you, nor can I engage in an act my people consider is marriage, knowing you feel it is your right to simply be with me in body, but to marry another."

"But...but, there would be little danger of any of this happening to me now, since we are at this moment not married, nor are we lovers.  Would they do the same to a woman, like me, who merely asked to have an affair with you, but who has not yet done it?"

"Questions of the heart are never punished," he answered.  "Only the act."

"Oh.  And so, if you agree to the pact I have suggested and we have an affair only—no marriage—would they try to find me and cut off the end of my nose?"

"*Saa.*"

"Again, that word means what?"

"No.  It means no, they would not seek you out to commit the deed, but you would be in danger were you to come into my camp after having made love to me and then marrying another."

She sat for a moment in thought.  At length, she said, "Then, really, I don't see the problem, since I do not intend to ever go into your camp."

"And yet, it is in my camp where you might likely find your cousin.  Do you think others would not see, would not know what we do or have done if we make this pact between us?  Think you that we might fool even the wise men?  If we love each other and have this affair, they will know."

"Mr. Stands Strong, I think I might safely say this to you: I do not think I will ever be required to go into your camp.  I am asking you to take me to where my cousin lives in the mountains, not into the encampment of your people.  I think your fear of this is for naught.  Indeed, you have only to agree to the pact, and I will uphold my end of the bargain without ever putting forward a single toe into your camp."

"But, you forget, I cannot agree to it, nor will I."

"So, does this mean you will walk away from me, never to help me to find my cousin?  Or do you simply mean you will never agree to the conditions of ,my offer to you?"

"I will not agree to the treaty you seek with me," he answered.

"But, Mr. Stands Strong, if you love me as you say you do, and if I am determined to never go into your camp, why can you not agree? Please understand, I fear that if you do not look more favorably upon my offer, I...well, I don't know what I will do. I must find my cousin somehow. So much depends on me finding him. My entire family relies on my—" She broke off.

He squeezed her hand. "There is more to this than I am telling you. And now, as you have been honest with me, I must be so with you."

"Oh? There is even more you haven't said to me?"

"I fear there is," he responded. "Tell me, beautiful woman, does your God sanction your stepping outside your marriage to make love to another? Or, if you were to meet my people, as I think you will surely do even if I take you into the mountains, will your God look the other way if you are only pretending to be my woman and have no intention of marrying me?"

She paused and cleared her throat before saying, "All my life, I have been told He will forgive."

"This may be so for you, but I will tell you this: Sun, the Creator, who is my God, does not look the other way, and it is hard for me to understand your God is so different from mine. But, perhaps He is. And, now I must say to you what I have withheld from you: what you ask of me is impossible for me, since I am one of Sun's children. If I were to stray away from Him and make love to you, I would be severing my ties with Sun, and since I do not believe it is good or right for a woman to make love to a man other than her husband, I, too, would pay a penalty, though perhaps not the physical one you might have to face.

"But, maybe the fault is mine," he continued, "since I have been reluctant to discuss this with you, so let me tell you this in another way. If I make love to you, I would ruin you for another, and since you do not believe you could ever become my woman, it would taint me in a spiritual way, since I would be engaging in an act I know is harmful to you. My God does not look favorably on this."

"But, you do not understand. I—"

He held up his hand for silence.

"And so," he carried on, "this is why I cannot agree to your treaty. If I make love to you, you become my woman in my eyes, in the eyes of my people and my God. If you then find another whom you decide would more favor you in keeping the memory of your parents alive, and if you walk away from me, you might have to pay a penalty whether we are married in your mind or not. You would not escape my people as you seem to think you might. And, since your cousin is married to a Pikuni woman, sometime, even if many moons away from this moment, there could be a price to pay, for me as well as for you, since it is within my knowledge that you have not wished to marry me. Still, though I understand there are many reasons why you would do as you must, Sun, the Creator, sees all, and from Sun I cannot hide my thoughts or actions.

"Now," he persisted, "since it is a custom in your land to seek pleasure outside of marriage, I think, perhaps, as you say, your God might not disfavor you. But, this trait in your God is not in mine."

Stunned, Czanna lay perfectly still. "Then," she said at last, "what you are telling me is that, regardless of what my ideas are of no marriage being created between us, there would still be harm created?"

"It is so."

Startled, recognizing for the first time the harm her request might cause herself, and perhaps this man too, she found she couldn't speak. And, as she lay beside him, neither of them spoke a word, until at last Czanna burst out, saying, "Oh dear! What am I to do? I trust no one else in this land but you to keep us safe. But, because I now understand why you have been so hesitant to agree with what I proposed and because I need to be true to…" Czanna didn't finish the thought.

Stands Strong didn't speak for several moments. However, at length he said, "Take heart, beautiful woman. Perhaps your cousin might be intent on joining my people for trade. If so, there would be no reason to make the treaty between us. I fear we must wait until we join my people. However, if your cousin has not come down from the mountains to trade with the Pikuni, then we would be required to talk about the treaty again. But, it is useless to speak of it now when we do not know yet the movements or intentions of your cousin.

"Besides," he went on to say, "having no treaty between us is likely the only manner by which we might safely remain with one another and retain our honor."

Czanna cleared her throat, then said, "I am not certain I understand what you are saying. Why would having no 'treaty,' as you call it, make any difference?"

"Because it is this way: by having no agreement between us, I might be freed from the problem of my mind envisioning ways I could make love to you."

"But—"

Again he held up a hand. "My devotion to Sun does not allow me to make love to you, and having you near me and thinking of what could be were I to agree to your suggestion makes my being with you difficult for me. Perhaps it is the same for you, too."

"All right," she said. "I guess I understand. However, I should say this to you: I do not find it difficult to be with you since I won't make love with you unless there is a pact between us."

He grinned at her before saying, "Think you that I could not convince you? Recall again what happened between us during the early morning hours of a time not long ago."

She didn't answer. Of course, he was right. How could she have discounted so easily how she had practically melted in his arms? It wasn't that long ago when he had held her so closely to him, although it seemed as if a lifetime had passed since then.

However, though what he said was true, she would never openly admit to how passionately she had hoped he would make love to her. At length, she said, "But, I believe this is so unnecessary. After all, I am the one offering this deal to you. In a way you are innocent. And, in view of this, is it not inconceivable to think your God might look the other way? Besides, truly, I do not ever intend to meet your people."

"Can you be certain this will never happen?" he asked. "My plans are to go to my chiefs and tell them what I have observed as a scout. This requires my taking you and your family with me. And, even if your cousin is not in my camp and would require us to seek him out in the mountains, because he is married to a Pikuni woman, he will have to come into the Pikuni camp from time to time. He would also need to bring you with him."

"Yes, I understand," she said. "However, consider this: what if you and I fulfill the terms of the treaty *after* you return to your camp? I could stay in the fort and wait for you, and when your business is concluded with your chiefs, you could return to the fort and only then lead me and my family into the mountains."

"And, you would patiently await my return? Or would you ask another man—who might be of the same ilk as your former scout—to lead you there?"

"I...I would wait for you."

He shook his head. "You are speaking without knowing the Indian character. What if we did as you say, and I return to my people without you, and my chief has another even more important scouting mission for me? I cannot say no."

"Yes, you could. You could simply tell him you have made arrangements elsewhere."

"I would not. Not when our land is being invaded by gold seekers who are a different kind of white man than the white traders who are friends to us. These new men coming into my country are without morals or good sense, and, by their acts, they bring danger to my people. I would not be able to say no to my chief."

Czanna didn't speak, and, after a moment, Stands Strong continued, saying, "I believe there is no other way but to take you and your family with me into the Pikuni camp. Besides, when you speak of Sun perhaps overlooking my actions with you because of my innocence, you forget that even if Sun were to forgive me...I cannot. A man must not abandon his own ideas of what is right and what is wrong. And, if I agree to your suggestion and make love to you, I see danger for you. Therefore, I cannot agree to this treaty."

"But, Mr. Stands Strong, I promise you that if you would only change your mind and agree to my offer, I would do most anything to stay away from your people so there would be no trouble."

Stands Strong responded to her suggestion at once and said, "Beautiful woman, do not forget my words to you so easily. Now, though I have not seen into the future and do not know what it holds for you or for me, I must again say this to you: I will not risk the loss of your beauty or ruin you for another by having this affair with you. And, since you believe it is not in the best interest of your family to become my woman, there is little else we can do but to remain as we are now."

"But, what are we now, Mr. Stands Strong?"

"We are friends who also share a similar desire, one for the other. But also, because we are friends, we must always act for the best interests of one another, and never should we indulge the passion between us by carrying our love and friendship into lovemaking. There must be a limit, and we must not cross it."

"Yes," Czanna agreed, but then remained quiet for several moments, uncannily experiencing a feeling of having lost something of great value. But, why?

And, then it struck her—a thought so quick, it appeared to have no time: she wanted, she needed to be close to this man. But, there was more to it. She *craved* the feeling.

Yes, she had been truthful with herself and with him earlier when she had told him she needed to keep him close to her because of the terrible losses fate had thrown her. But, what she hadn't known then, but knew now, was there was more to it: she wished for a closeness with this man so intense that it felt akin to desiring to crawl under his skin in order to attain the "oneness" she seemed to need.

 She gulped, not understanding what this was really about, and she found herself asking, "By your saying we should only be friends, does this mean you are never going to kiss me again?"

He turned his head to look at her, and she saw he was smiling broadly at her. He said, "A man has a right to tempt a woman with what might be were our minds more agreeable." And, having delivered these mischievous words, he came up onto his forearms and leaned into a position over her, there to place a wet, sensuous and delicious kiss upon her lips.

Perhaps he'd meant the kiss to be little more than a tease instead of a real kiss, but almost at once the caress became more passionate until he had positioned his body over hers, and, for a moment, she lost herself to the feel of his hard masculine chest as it pressed in against the softness of her breasts. Using his tongue, he opened her mouth to his, and as he deepened the kiss, she became lost to the musky masculine taste of him. Liquid fire rushed through her in response, and she answered him back with her own raw desire, giving back to him as much as she was being given.

Then his tongue swept in and out and around her mouth as though he were making love to her with a kiss alone. And, when he groaned deep in his throat, she lost all sense of time and place, feeling free—at least for a little while—of her duties to the memory of her parents and the life she had once known and craved. Her only awareness at the moment was the erotic scent of him and the invigorating sweet-salty taste of his kiss.

Without thought of where they were or the problems they faced, she felt herself open up to him as his lips caressed her eyes, her cheeks, her nose and even her ears. Truly, she felt on fire, and she couldn't have stopped him even if she had wanted to, which she didn't. Beside herself from the exotic thrills racing through her system, she couldn't help sighing, the sound high-pitched and urgent. And, when he scooted down lower over her still, kissing a path up to her neck and upper chest, his every caress caused an explosion of carnal hunger to release within her, and she wished him to never stop.

It wasn't until he appeared to encounter some difficulty in removing her shirt — his own shirt that she was wearing — when the reality of what was happening between them seemed to elicit a sharp change in him.

She protested at once and murmured, "Oh, please don't stop!"

But, stop he did, though he didn't move away from her at once. Instead, he lay atop her, placing his head to the side of her and resting his face within the full spread of her hair. His breathing was quick and heavy, and she gloried in the feel of his chest against hers and the sound of his breath. His gasps were deep, and he was taking many of them, and because he was so closely entwined with her, she became aware of the vast differences between his muscular strength and her softer femininity.

She moved her hips a little, if only to experience more fully the thrill of being so close to this man who appeared to be quite ready to make love to her.

"*Saa,*" he whispered. "Do not move in such a way."

She didn't answer; she also didn't repeat the motion.

At last, with another deep breath, he rolled over to the side of her and did little more than take several more deep breaths. He didn't speak; neither did she. Indeed, she felt quite happy simply listening to his strained breathing, knowing she was the cause of it.

Still, he didn't say a word to her. Indeed, it was she who first spoke what was in her heart and in her mind, and she whispered, "If I did not believe you at first, I do so now. Sir, had you not ceased kissing me, I would have let you do whatever you wanted, marriage or not, pact or not. You were wise to observe this and say it to me."

He didn't answer her confession. In truth, what could he have said? It was more than apparent he could have made love to her here, now, regardless of where they were and the possible dangers there might have been in the environment.

"Perhaps," he murmured at last, "we should not touch each other too much when we are alone. Until I at last get back to my chiefs with my observations, we might be wise to keep a little distance between us."

No! His suggestion tore at her heart, and she murmured, "But, sir, I do not wish to be distant from you."

"I know," he said. "I do not wish it, either. Yet, I fear it must be. I thought I would have more control, but—"

"More control?"

"*Áa,* more control.

"I still do not understand."

He merely chuckled a little, reminding her of the teasing man she had come to know over the course of these last couple of days.

At last, he reached out and took her hand in his and said, "Come, we are close to the springs. Let us continue our scouting, and let us hope we have not alerted a war party of our being here. We forgot, for a very pleasant moment, why we are here. There is a man's life we are trying to save. Come, we must complete our scouting quickly. The life of your man is at stake."

"He is not my man."

"I know," he whispered. "I only say it to try to regain my scout's discipline."

"I...I am afraid I do not understand."

His response was another low chuckle, and, turning away from her, he sat up, picked up his quiver full of arrows as well as his bow and repositioned them over his back. Coming back down onto his forearms, with his body stretched out over the prairie, he gazed at her briefly and said, "Let us finish our scouting quickly and return to the others."

"But, I..." She broke off her protest. What could she say? Henrik's life could, indeed, depend upon the swiftness of their scouting. And, so she found herself saying, "Yes, you are right again."

Looking at her from over his shoulder, she saw a light in his eye when he said, "This time. Only this time."

## CHAPTER TEN

A few days later, Stands Strong found himself lying belly down upon one of the highest points surrounding Grass Woman Springs, his duty being to keep a constant vigil in order to ensure the safety of them all. Luckily, the spring grasses provided a cushion against the hard ground of this high prairie, for he dared not stand up nor even sit up as he cast a glance in every direction, looking for signs of a war party.

He had instructed George to do much the same as he, but George's position was from a different rise in the land and his attention was centered in an opposite direction.

It was a day-and-night watch they were forced to keep, and between Stands Strong, George and First Rider, they managed to keep a constant guard. Stands Strong's plan was to remain as invisible as possible to any wandering war party and, if necessary, to act as a decoy away from the springs, thus allowing the man Henrik to use the healing waters to recover, if a recovery were even possible.

Stands Strong let his mind wander a little while yet keeping his attention on the environment. True to his word, he was avoiding *Ótsipi Matsowá'p*, meaning Brings Beauty, or simply *Matsowá'p*, meaning Beauty in the Blackfeet tongue. And, he thought she was doing the same with him. It was hard to remain away from her, however, when he desired to be with her constantly. But, he could think of no other solution for them. Truly, their worlds did not meet, and perhaps they never would.

And so, more times than not, he found himself staying away from their encampment at the sulfur springs.

It was odd to think how similar his relationship with Matsowá'p was to his liaison with Good Shield Woman, the woman he had once asked to be his wife. Good Shield Woman, too, had let her devotion to her father be the reason to marry another. Stands Strong had truly loved Good Shield Woman, and she had loved him in return and had admitted she would have accepted his proposal but for her devotion to her father and the rest of her family.

Was it only a year ago when Good Shield Woman had made her choice? At the time, Stands Strong had thought he might never repair the damage to his heart. But, over time, and upon seeing how happy she was with her new husband, Stands Strong had at last put the loss behind him.

Could he do the same with Matsowá'p? Of course he could and he would. After all, he and Matsowá'p had only known one another for a short time. It should be easy to stay away from her and to let her go as soon as he had guided her to meet with her cousin.

Yet, it wasn't easy to stop thinking about her and wishing it could be different. Since his first encounter with her, she had weaved a place into his heart and into his mind until she was now almost always in his thoughts. Indeed, she was even invading his dreams, allowing him to recall again the softness of her skin, the luxurious taste of her and the enticing aroma of her femininity.

But, this alone wasn't the full extent of his problem with her; she was being helped by other forces. *Niitá'p,* indeed, he felt as if the spirits were pushing him toward her also, since Windmaker, himself, brought her delicate and particular scent to him within the gusts and drafts of the prairie winds. And, at such times, Stands Strong begged Windmaker to have pity on him and stop reminding him of her.

But, it was not to be.  The very force of nature seemed to conspire against him.  Was he wrong, or did Windmaker know some wisdom he, being a mere mortal, didn't?  After all, why else would the power of nature try to persuade him to make love to Matsowá'p?

He already knew she would fall into his arms.  And, perhaps it was this remembrance which was the most maddening.

Still, he wondered if Windmaker were aiding the Creator in testing his fortitude.  Was this merely an ordeal to determine if he would really keep his scruples and remain aloof from her, especially when every impulse within him begged him to give in to her and make love to her?

Perhaps.  But, it little mattered.  He would keep his honor, yes, but he would also not watch her walk away from him without mustering a fight to keep her.  But, his weapons to do this were not the same as the armaments of lance or gun.  Instead, his offense was simply to tease her, to cause her to laugh and to touch her now and again, inviting her to become accustomed to him—at least he would do these actions if he felt himself up to the challenge of controlling his impulses.  But, there was another factor in a relationship between a man and a woman, and if a man were wise, it was one he would never forget: that element being kindness.  Many were the times when Stands Strong had watched his almost-father win, without really winning, an argument, simply by acts of kindness.  The truth was no one had really 'won' the argument.  Instead, his almost-father and -mother had both merely agreed on taking a different path.

*Niitá'p*, as the wise men had always known, it takes a strong man to be kind, especially when a man's first instinct is to simply conquer.

*Áa*, he would fight for her, but he would not force her against her will to marry him, which was really the problem.  He knew he could easily kiss her and caress her and beckon her to fall into his arms. But, because of his lack of control over his own passion, he dared not do it.

After all, it was only a few days ago when he had almost lost control and made love to her and, had he done it, it would have sealed their pact, a deed he knew was wrong. But, contrarily, he wasn't certain he would ever win her, especially when duty to her family and its memory haunted her.

Would she, in the end, decide the same as had Good Shield Woman?

Enough! With a force of will, he forced himself to think of something else, and he set his attention back to where it should have been—on the environment, as well as on the others in Matsowá'p's family.

From the start, he had noticed Liliann was almost always to be found with her father, barely leaving the man for longer than the time it took to eat or to attend to personal matters. Because Henrik still lay within the springs and because the girl stood continually at her father's side, her dress was always wet and burdensome. Stands Strong's friend First Rider had apparently noticed this and so had taken pity on her. Only yesterday, Stands Strong had observed Liliann now wore an extra pair of First Rider's leggings as well as his shirt, both having been cut down to fit her.

Recalling this, Stands Strong smiled, since he had done the same for Matsowá'p. He sighed, his attention once again taken up by Matsowá'p. She was not happy with him at present because he had required her to take over Liliann's duty in caring for the baby.

Of course, Matsowá'p had objected to the task since she had wished to take a shift as lookout. But, Stands Strong had been adamant in denying her the duty.

"Why?" she had asked him a few days earlier.

"Because," he had answered, "your almost-sister, Liliann, is needed to stay at her father's side. Or would you rather I watch your baby sister in your place?"

Her response had been to frown at him, but in the end she had relented. Indeed, she'd had no choice.

Besides, if he had allowed her to take a turn at standing guard, it would have added another worry to his many problems. For one, it would have required Matsowá'p to be alone in a world she didn't know or understand. For another, she wasn't yet skilled in scouting, and certainly she had no knowledge of Plains Indian warfare. After all, what would she do if a war party were to come upon her unaware?

He didn't wish to think about it. Indeed, he would remain firm in disallowing her to stand watch. But, George was another matter. Though he was much younger than his sister, he was still a man, and he certainly considered himself to be the man of the family. And, having instructed George carefully in what he was to do, Stands Strong took some comfort in seeing that George was keen and alert to doing his duty, young though he was. Truth be told, the circumstance of George's family had caused the boy to set aside his boyhood ways as he took on more and more of the duties usually restricted to men. But, George was not alone in this endeavor; so, too, was Matsowá'p.

Matsowá'p. Beautiful Matsowá'p. Stands Strong's mind went back to their mutual scouting expedition only a few days ago. Their careful watch had found no indication of a war party, allowing them to return to the others without incident. Then, informing the others of the spring's safety, they had all worked on the task of taking down their temporary encampment.

It had been a short journey to the springs, the man Henrik having been placed upon a bed within the wagon. This had allowed one man to lead the procession across the prairie while another pulled up the rear, guarding it from behind. One of the three men had been needed to stay with the wagon so as to defend it; this man had been George. Matsowá'p had taken over the steering of the wagon, while Liliann and the babe had been settled in next to Henrik in the wagon.

They had traveled at night since there was no timber or other cover to hide their movements over the prairie, and they had delayed going anywhere until the moon had risen up into the dark sky...around midnight.

Once at the springs, they had set up a camp within a patch of willow trees and had been ensconced there since. They were not far away, however, from Fort Benton. But, none of them were in a rush to go there. Rather, they had all agreed to allow as much time as possible for Henrik to recover, knowing this was needed if he were to live.

Stands Strong heard a sound and looked down toward where it had originated, seeing First Rider climbing up to this rise above the prairie.

As soon as his friend was level with him and had come down to rest upon his belly beside him, Stands Strong asked, "How is the man?"

"He has only awakened once. But, he is breathing more easily now."

"*Soka'pi*, good," said Stands Strong. "Has dripping the healing water onto his lips aided him?"

"Perhaps," answered First Rider. "But, he is weak, and I begin to fear he may not recover."

Stands Strong nodded, then said, "The injury to his leg will heal whether the bullet is removed or not, but the damage done from the slug lodged in his breastbone may not heal without taking it out. We might consider moving along to the fort because it is said the white man has ways of taking bullets from a man without killing him. Although, I fear the journey to the white man's fort might cause the man's death. Have you tried your touch upon him to see if the bullet might be drawn out using your special medicine?"

"I have not," answered First Rider. "I fear his daughter will not leave his side and, as you know, I cannot perform the task while she is near."

Stands Strong nodded, his brows drawn together in a frown. "This is to be understood, and it is good we answered her plea to help her father. Still, if you cannot perform the medicine power you have, he might not live. Perhaps I should ask Matsowá'p to speak with her almost-sister and try to persuade the girl to let you be alone with him. All our people know you have the healing touch, and I think you should at least be given the chance to try to extract the bullet without the need to use the white man's butchery. If, even after your ministering to him, he remains as he is, do you agree we should take him to the white people at Fort Benton?"

"*Áa*, I, too, agree with all you have said."

"*Soka'pi.* Then, I will try to speak to Matsowá'p yet this night." Stands Strong sat up, ready to give the watch over to First Rider, but before he left, Stands Strong said, "I have not seen nor heard an enemy. But, be on your guard, my friend."

"I will. However, before you go into camp, I would ask if you might try to work your own medicine upon the ill man?"

Stands Strong did not reply. Instead, he frowned. Then he said, "As you know, I am no longer the owner of the medicine I once thought was to be mine."

"I do not know this," said First Rider. "Once a man has been given his medicine by his animal helper, it is his to use."

"You speak truth, my friend, and it would be so if my animal helper, the white bear, had given me her power. But, she did not. There were no ceremonies given to me, no special songs she taught me, nor did she share any of her bear medicine with me. And, as you know, my shadow never found her in the spirit world despite my going on several quests to find my medicine. She aided me once when I was little, but she has never come to me again. Nor has any other animal answered my plea to become my helper."

First Rider didn't speak for several moments. After a time, he said, "And yet, you have great medicine. I see it in you; I feel it is there within you."

"You honor me, my friend," responded Stands Strong. "Perhaps what you see or feel in me is the medicine I should have gained from my father, who was the inheritor of the medicine ways from his father before him, and so on. There is a long line of medicine men in my Lakota family so old no one knows who was the first to bring it into our bloodline. But, whatever should have been passed along to me was not. And so, I have set aside my desire to be welcomed into the same profession as my father.

"However, there is hope," Stands Strong went on to say. "Perhaps one day, my son—if I sire one—will be the possessor of this, my Lakota inheritance. But, as for my own quest to become a medicine man, I have put it aside. The duty of scouting is, for me, a happy and worthy obligation. It is enough."

"And, you are the best scout we have."

Stands Strong nodded, then before he crawled down the bluff, he said, "Be on your guard. There may yet be an enemy war party close to us, and one who is looking for a fight with the Pikuni."

"*Áa*, I will do so."

\*\*\*\*

It wasn't until the next evening when First Rider considered he might try to remove the bullet from the man Henrik. But first, he would have to take the man's young daughter in hand and locate her elsewhere. Stands Strong had, indeed, asked Matsowá'p to speak with her friend.

Yet, the girl continued to remain where she was.

Glancing briefly at the girl, First Rider hesitated to approach her. He already knew from experience that she didn't speak the sign language, nor did she understand the Pikuni tongue. And, his own knowledge of English was poor, at best.

Returning his regard back to the girl's father, First Rider observed the man hadn't moved since early morning. Grass Woman Springs was shallow at this time of year, which had allowed them to lay the man Henrik down with most of his body in the water while his head rested upon the pool's grassy shoreline.

A few days earlier, First Rider had placed his own buffalo robe beneath the white man's head to aid in his comfort.

But, the young girl needed to leave him to his work, and, because of her, First Rider had not been able to use his medicine upon the man. Yet, respecting her rights, he hadn't approached her to try to communicate, fearing it might be an impossible task. Yet, the time was now when he needed to test his medicine and see if he could remove the bullet from the man without the need of poking him or letting the white man cut him open. He would try to speak to the girl.

To this end, he found himself wading into the small pool, and, coming up behind the yellow-haired girl and tapping her lightly on the shoulder, he tried to communicate by means of sign language what he required of her.

But, she didn't understand, and she merely shook her head, a sign First Rider had seen the white man was fond of when he meant to say no.

However, since First Rider required the girl to give up her vigil for a while, he tried to communicate once more, his hand motions a little slower. He had to bring her to understand she must leave and allow him to work his skills as a medicine man upon her father. The young girl, however, merely shrugged her shoulders.

He smiled at her and tried to communicate with her in a different way, adding a little of the English language he knew, and as he signed, he said, "I…medicine man. Bullet…out…must…come. You…leave. Medicine man…try…heal."

"I cannot leave me own father," she murmured softly. "How do I know thee will not try to kill him?"

It took First Rider a little time to understand her words, but at last he did, and he said, "He…live. Not…kill. Try…heal."

She began to cry. Again she shook her head.

However, First Rider didn't give up, at least not yet. He offered his hand to the girl, palm up. When she didn't take it, he slowly took her hand and placed it in his own. Then, looking down into her eyes, he said, "Must...try...bullet...to get. You"—he pointed with his finger to a place close to the springs, yet far enough away so he might do his work—"there...sit. You...watch."

She bit her lip. "Thou will not cut him open?"

"I...not," First Rider answered. Still holding her hand, he said, "Here, come. I...take you...good...sitting...place."

She nodded.

At last, gaining her agreement, First Rider helped her up onto the edge of the springs and, patting her hand, again grinned at her. He said, "No...talk...no...come...between. Watch...only."

Again she nodded.

And, seeing it, First Rider turned back toward the girl's father.

****

Since First Rider had returned from his duty to stand guard the previous night, he had been praying to Sun, the Creator, having taken on the duty as a medicine man because the white man's daughter had begged him to save her father's life.

As First Rider prayed, he offered up the smoke from the sacred pipe and asked for the Creator's help, begging Sun, the Creator, to have pity upon him, as well as upon the man Henrik. Once his prayers were done, he left his best eagle's feather as a gift for the Creator. Indeed, First Rider had personally beaded the feather's hollow shaft, and it was an item he treasured. It was now given to and belonged to the Creator.

Though he had only attained the age of twenty and three snows, First Rider had long been known to be a healer to his people. Even as a child he had possessed the "power."

It was said he had attained this healing touch from the Big People. He had been told by his mother and his almost-father, Chief Chases-the-enemy, about how, when only three winters in age, he had been taken by a Big Person and had been in company with her for many moons before his almost-father and his mother had been able to rescue him.

Because the Big People—in particular, the women of this tribe—were sacred to the Creator, these people had long been recognized as being endowed with a power to heal. So, all the chiefs of his tribe, as well as the older medicine men, had assumed the Big Person, a female, had somehow given some of her power to him.

First Rider didn't remember. He only knew it was he who, even as a child, had often been called upon by the medicine men to heal others when all else had failed. He had so far in his young life been successful and thus had garnered a reputation for himself as a medicine man. And, although he had the "gift" of being able to take objects from within a person's body, he rarely used the skill. It wasn't usually required of him to call it into practice. And, indeed, he wasn't certain exactly how he was able to do it.

But, the man Henrik required he use this faculty tonight because the bullet was lodged into the man's breastbone, thus it was situated too close to his heart, and if not removed, the man would likely die. This, First Rider knew, having set his hands upon the man to "see" the wound in the white man's body.

However, First Rider wished the girl would go away instead of remaining where she was at the shoreline, so that he could work upon the man without an audience. Indeed, he might fail, and if he did, her father, Henrik, would eventually die from the wound.

If they took the man Henrik to Fort Benton, the white men there would surely seek to cut Henrik open in order to remove the bullet. But, First Rider was certain that if done, this man, because of his weakness, would perish under the knife.

Although First Rider made it a practice to not attend to an injured person while another looked on, and though he wished it were different, this one time he would allow the girl to remain. Upon touching the white girl's hand, he had become convinced she not only would not interfere, but she would aid him in some way, though he was uncertain how she might bring this about.

And so he began. Beating his sacred drum, he sang the medicine song given to him in his long ago past…most likely the source of it being the female from the tribe of Big People. Again he didn't remember. He only knew the song had come to him upon his first attempt to heal another.

It was different from other Pikuni songs. Its rhythm was similar to the regular beat of other medicine men's songs, but this chant was particularly different and strange. The notes, though in rhythm, were misaligned, were high and then low, and even the words First Rider used he didn't understand. He only knew whatever they meant, they were sacred.

He sang and he sang, always beating his drum. The song went on and on until, at last, he felt ready to try to remove the bullet, and he stopped his song. But, upon ceasing his song, he heard it still, and it was then when he realized someone else had been singing along with him, only at a higher pitch.

*It is the girl, still vocalizing the medicine song.*

Glancing up at her, he smiled, then waded to the shoreline where she sat. Facing her, he took up the rhythm again and beat his drum as his voice joined hers, amazed to hear the girl reciting the strange words to the song, also.

His attention was so caught up in the need to heal this man, he didn't stop to wonder how this young, white girl knew these strange words well enough to sing them with him. He only considered how her voice, added to his, aided him in healing the man.

Then, without fanfare or any warning at all, he felt his shadow, his very being, touch hers. There it was. For a moment set out of time, he understood her, and he knew she understood him. Indeed, he could see clearly how alike they were to each other.

*Does she know she could be a healer?*

At last, they both stopped their chanting, and they gazed at one another, neither acknowledging nor saying any words at all. And, had he the means to speak her language, he would have told her how precious her help had been this night. As it was, he gave his drum and mallet to her, saying only, "Safe…keep…them…for me."

It was an honor he was bestowing upon her, but he didn't know how to convey the meaning of what he'd said, and so he merely smiled at her.

When she nodded, he gave her another grin, then turned around and waded through the water back to the white man. He began his song once again, hearing her sacred echo of it, and then he placed his hand palm down over the injury, but not touching it, and, using a circular and pulling motion, he sang and he sang to Sun, the Creator.

Because his eyes were closed, he didn't see how it happened; he only knew what had taken place because the object jumped suddenly up into his palm as though it were attracted there. Quickly, he placed his fingers around the bullet, and, in relief, he sighed. Then, bringing up his hand, he spread his palm open.

There it sat: the bullet. It was bloody and black, as would be expected, but it was now in *his* palm, not within the white man's body.

But, the wound was now openly bleeding, and, taking handfuls of the healing water, First Rider let the water take away the "evil spirit" of the bullet, as well as the "bad wishes" of the one who had shot the man, Henrik.

Turning slightly around, First Rider motioned to the girl to come forward. She did so, and as soon as she had come in close to him, he asked, "Strip…of…skin…deer. Need…now. You…can get?"

"I will try. Could thee use my petticoat as a bandage instead?" she asked, raising her skirt slightly to show him.

He shook his head. Only now did he see she wasn't wearing his shirt and leggings. "Skin...only." He was about to turn back toward the white man when a thought occurred to him, and, stretching out his arm toward the girl, he opened his palm and showed her the bullet.

"Yes, sir," she said. "I saw what thee did. It was as if thy palm pulled up the bullet." And, then she cried.

Reaching out, First Rider caught hold of her hand and, turning his palm upside down, let the bullet fall into her hand. He said, "You...keep. You...helped. Good...omen...this. You keep."

"I will," she said, her lips shaking as she spoke. "I will get thee a skin of the deer, also. Thank thee." And, then she cried again and was gone.

First Rider watched the young girl as she stood up to her feet and sprinted toward the only other woman in camp—Matsowá'p. Because he knew Matsowá'p was wise in many ways, he felt assured he would soon have the skin he required to help stop the flow of blood.

She was a pretty girl, this daughter of the white man, and someday, he thought, she might make some man a good wife. He, however, did not include himself in the role. He was already in love with the beautiful daughter of Chief Flying Hawk.

Turning back to the white man, First Rider continued his vigil to cleanse the wound, and, using pressure, he brought the two sides of the wound closer and closer together. And, all the while, he sang the healing songs, the ones he had heard so long ago.

****

"What do you mean, your people are on the move to come here?" asked Czanna of Stands Strong.

"Did you not see the scout on the hill waving his blanket?"

"Ah...no, I did not," she answered him. "There was a scout, other than you or my brother, on a hill?"

"Áa, over there"—he pointed—"and he was waving his blanket, telling me our people are on their way to Fort Benton to engage in trade. A fireboat is expected there in less than a few movements of the sun, bringing many new trade items to the people. My people are, perhaps, two, maybe three suns south of us."

"He said all of this with his blanket?"

"He did."

"Oh" was her only response. But, after a moment, she asked, "By 'sun,' I assume you mean a day?"

"Áa, I do."

"And, by 'fireboat' you must be talking about a steamship?"

"Áa."

"So, I will be meeting your people after all." She paused for a moment in thought. "I must remember to thank the good Lord about your having the wisdom to not enter into our treaty yet. Otherwise, I fear I would be inclined to take the same steamboat away from here, and then, I fear, all I have been charged to do here would be lost. I bow again to your good sense."

He smiled at her. "I know my people, and I know this, my country. Were I in your own country, you would be wise, while I would be unknowing."

"Yes, perhaps, though I doubt it." She sighed. "You are wise in so many ways I do not understand. Even if we were in my country, I think you would still be sensible and aware of many aspects about the environment that would have escaped my notice. And, this is another reason why I seek to have your alliance."

His response to her words was to merely smile at her.

They were standing a little away from the band of willow trees where two different shelters had been erected—one for the men and one for the women. At present, they were both looking out upon the beauty of the sunrise, where the sun's rays were shooting up their vibrant morning colors, there in the east. In admiration, they both became silent. Although the sun had yet to peek up from behind the horizon of numerous hills, already the sky was afire with the different hues of red and pink, as well as various shades of blue and orange, while the steel gray of the sky overhead was surrendering to the light, icy blue of an early morning sky.

"How did this other scout know you were here?" asked Czanna quietly. "Until only a moment ago, we were both concealed within the shelter of the willow trees."

"Your man Henrik, as well as his daughter and my friend, First Rider, are clearly visible. First Rider, with only a few signs, told the scout what is happening here."

"And so, First Rider also saw the scout?"

"Of course. He, too, is a good scout, though he is more well-known as a medicine man amongst my people. Within a few days, three other medicine men will join us here to help us with the further healing of your man's wounds."

"He is not my man."

"I know," was Stands Strong's response as he turned in full toward her. "Perhaps I should call him your father's man? I have not done so because I have not wished to bring sadness back to your mind."

Tears stung Czanna's eyes, reminding her of the thousands of reasons why she was falling so deeply in love with this man. Not only was he more virile than any man she had ever known—being broad in the shoulder, as well as strong and muscular in all the right places—Stands Strong also possessed a kind heart. How could she not love him?

A cry sounded from within their shelter, nestled as it was deeply within the cluster of willows, and Czanna looked back toward the trees. She said, "I believe my sister has awakened, and I must go to her before she cries out too loudly. Are you staying in camp for breakfast this morning? Or are you bound to return to your post?"

"I will be here for our first meal. Our people, pushing onward toward us, will give us the safety we require to build a good fire. We might, I think, have some good, real food, since I am certain the scout will tell my own and First Rider's families where our present location is. Between them all, they will wish to hunt and bring us fresh game so we might all eat some good, real Pikuni food."

"Oh," she muttered. "What do you mean by 'real Pikuni food'?"

"Fresh game, a deer or elk meat, perhaps. Its ribs roasted over an open fire is the best food I ever tasted. No longer will we be required to eat only the dried meat we have in store. We shall have some real food instead."

"Yes, it will be a pleasant change. And so, you think your mother and father, as well as First Rider's family, might join us?"

"*Áa*, they will. My almost-mother worries about me when I am not in camp, and so I am certain both she and my almost-father will join us here. My almost-brothers and -sisters will come, too, unless called elsewhere. First Rider's parents will do the same, since they, too, worry about him. From now until we reach the fort, we will be under the protection of my people."

"Oh, this is good, I suppose, although I am not certain I am anxious to meet your family."

He laughed. "You will love them and they, you. Do not worry. My almost-mother will dote on you, since she is white, too. I fear she might ask you many questions, though. Prepare yourself to talk a great deal."

Although Czanna wasn't certain she was happy at the prospect of meeting the members of his family, another cry and loud shouts from within their tiny shelter had her glancing back in the direction of the willow trees.

Returning her regard back to Stands Strong, she said, "Please, before I go and see to my sister's needs, I must bid you to tell me if you think your family will be inclined to believe you and I… I mean to say… Will they think we are…? What I am trying to say, or to ask, is do you think they might believe we are…lovers? Am I in danger?"

169

He smiled at her. "They will see the truth at once. Fear not, they will know we are not lovers. If it were so, there would be three small lodges pitched within the thicket of willow trees, not two... Although..."

She jerked her head up to stare at him and asked, "What do you mean, 'although'?"

Again, screams from within the little group of willows caught Czanna's attention, and she said, "I must go. Please, I beg you, do not give them any reason for them to think we are... Oh, also, before I go, let me ask you if there is anything I should prepare for your family?"

Reaching up his right hand, Stands Strong drew his fingers through the locks of her hair, causing Czanna to sigh in response and causing him to groan in turn, the sound low and much too masculine; unfortunately for her, it stirred a passionate reaction to him from deep within her heart.

After a while, he said, "You need do nothing. It is they who will bring gifts. Now, I must go and alert George so he may join us here for the first meal of the day."

As though he were reluctant to do so, he dropped his hand. He said, "Go now to your sister and see if you can quiet her."

"Yes, yes, of course I will."

But, Czanna's mind wasn't eased at all when, before she turned away, Stands Strong's index finger came up to tap his nose. And, when his parting words were, "Besides, I will never tell them how you have begged me to make love to you," Czanna's breath caught in her throat.

"But, I never begged..."

It was pointless to continue, especially because there might be other ears in the camp to hear, and since she would be required to raise her voice to be heard by him. Stands Strong was already striding away from her, his gait fast and his laughter on the air.

*Oh dear. What if his family comes to discover what I have asked of this man? Will they demand I submit to the ultimate disfigurement?*

*Please, dear Lord, help me.*

# CHAPTER ELEVEN

$\mathscr{A}$ few days later—and early in the morning—Stands Strong's and First Rider's families came riding in close to their camp at Sacagawea Springs. Czanna heard their laughter and gaiety first, then both she and Briella stepped out from their shelter hidden in the willows to watch them.

Although there were only the two families coming to visit, there were many people in the procession. The prairie was flat between the hills and the numerous coulees surrounding Sacagawea Springs. And, from where Czanna stood, she had an easy view of the numerous, colorful and happy people forming a line across the flat land.

What she hadn't expected to hear from this group was their laughter and gaiety. It caught Czanna off guard; these were not a somber and moody people. So, once again, the truth was set before her to see. Indeed, the Europeans telling their stories about these people had lied.

There was noise: the talking and laughter, the giggling of children at their play, the neighing of ponies. And, there was color, lots of color in the beading and the delicate painting of their clothing; there were reds and blues and whites as well as yellows and oranges and greens. Even the ponies upon which they rode were painted with the same hues and designs of their owners. Added to the colors, those ponies were each carrying what had to be the families' numerous possessions in bags painted red, blue, yellow, orange, green and white, some of the parfleches being large and some were small.

Never had she seen a procession such as this. Placing her hand over her eyes, she saw there were four men in all; two were leading the procession and two were following in back of it. All four of these men—who looked to be in their late thirties or early-to-mid forties—all appeared to be rugged, yet handsome at the same time.

The two men who were in the lead were each one sitting upon a handsome pony, one of those steeds in the lead being a white stallion. Behind them came a complete entourage of women, children, dogs and horses followed behind. Of the two men who pulled up the rear of the entire party, one sat astride a white stallion, while the other rode a black-and-white spotted Appaloosa. Seeing them, Czanna now understood, because of her own experience in moving camp, these two men riding behind the entire party were the procession's rearguard.

There were five women with the party, two of them wearing white, beaded buckskin dresses, while the other three wore different shades of beautifully beaded and tanned buckskin dresses. Three of the five women were sitting astride horses that were each pulling a travois, while the two other women—one carrying a baby in a cradleboard upon her back—walked along at the side of the ponies. These two women who were afoot were deep in conversation, though every now and again they laughed.

There were also many children running about in all different directions, and Czanna, who had been trying to count them, soon lost track of exactly how many youngsters were a part of the troupe. Several of the younger boys were engaged in playing games, one of the sports appearing to be much like tag. All of the girls—except for the very youngest of them—were carrying dolls and were quietly talking to one another, which made them easier for Czanna to count. There was one very young girl who appeared to be about the same age as Briella; she was riding upon one of the travois which was latched to a horse, and Czanna conjectured the woman riding this pony was the child's mother. Three of the women were clearly white women, though their pale skin looked to be a light shade of tan. But, these women each had a different hue of blonde hair, which clearly boasted their heritage.

Czanna speculated these three had to be the white women Stands Strong had often spoken of. One of them was his almost-mother; but which one?

There were two other women in the procession who were Indian, having the lovely and permanent reddish-tanned skin color. Both were quite beautiful.

Because the entire troupe was slowly coming in closer to her, Czanna could clearly see two boys—perhaps adolescent boys— who were riding alongside the caravan, one on each side of it. And, Czanna, upon more careful observation of the two youths, knew their task was to guard their families also, though from the two opposite sides of the middle of the group.

One of the two men at the front of the procession rode ahead of the other, and Czanna thought this man might be a chief, not only because his dignity boasted the position, but also because of the unusual horned headdress he wore. Gazing at it, she saw at the top of the headdress were two horns, and, because of their size, the horns could be no other than those of the buffalo bull. It was unusually decorated, also. In front were several long white furry skins that hung down both sides of the man's face, falling clearly down to his chest, each skin being little more than a centimeter wide. The same, though shorter, strips of fur decorated the top of the headdress, as well as some brown fur, there at its top. What looked to be eagles' feathers attached to the headdress hung down from it all the way to the man's waist.

His clothing was white, but whether it was from an animal with a white-colored skin or was from an animal of a darker skin bleached white, Czanna could not be certain, being as she was still somewhat distant from him. Decorated with beading down each sleeve and a beaded strip of leather falling inward from the shoulder, this man's tunic made the sight of him at once dignified. A blue-beaded shell necklace hung down the man's chest in loops, and he looked so elegant she dared to think he might have appeared even more regal than many of the "best people" in Hungary.

As he rode a black prancing stallion, Czanna knew this man had to be a chief.

Following him at a short distance was another handsome man, dressed similarly, but without the horned headdress. This man appeared to be the younger of the two men, though their facial features were similar. However, instead of a horned headdress, this man wore a more typical war bonnet, but it was made in such a way as to cause the feathers to stand straight up, while a cascade of similar feathers hung down from the headdress at the man's back and reached even past his horse's flanks. This man, too, wore all white clothing, his tunic likewise being beaded and decorated in row after row of blue, red and green colors. Both men were mightily armed with bow and arrows, lance, shield, tomahawk and knives. Both carried shotguns upon their laps.

Woe it would be to anyone who might dare to attack them.

Gazing down at her own best light-blue cloth dress, she felt almost drab by comparison. But, it was her best American-bought dress, and it would have to do.

Looking around her own camp, Czanna saw there was no one else but her and her young sister, whom she held by her hand, to greet these people. Where was everybody else? Liliann would be with her father at the springs, of course, but the numerous bushes and tall grasses surrounding the pool hid them from Czanna's view.

Where were the others? Were she and Briella to be the only ones here to greet these people?

Running her free hand down her dress, she pressed the front of her skirt, then took a moment to draw her free hand through her hair, and, for a moment, she wished she looked as elegant as this troupe of people. But, how could she appear to be anything else but wilted? She who, while being afraid of encountering enemies, and who, though being unfamiliar with this country, had yet navigated a prairie wagon single-handedly over the rough prairie terrain and had brought the schooner to this spot safely.

How did these people do it? How did they look so refreshed and so happy despite all the difficulties and dangers of this country?

She was staring at the black-and-white spotted pony of the younger of the two men when it happened: one minute Czanna was holding Briella's hand; the next, her sister twisted her hand, forcing it away from Czanna's grip, then ran forward at the same time toward the chief leading the procession.

"Pretty horsey!" Briella cried, then she laughed gleefully as she sprinted toward it.

Czanna, startled, was not fast enough to respond. And, though she took flight and ran forward as quickly as she could, and though she was shouting "Briella! Stop!" as loudly as she could, she wasn't going to be on time to save her sister from being trampled by the black stallion, which, spooked by the excited youngster, was rearing.

To the man in the lead's credit, he immediately tried to swerve away from the child and control his steed, but even he couldn't make the horse respond quickly enough to prevent its harming Briella. The second man in the lead ran his own horse toward the stallion to try to control it, also.

But, it was impossible. Even now, the horse was bucking and kicking its rear legs, and the two men couldn't quiet it.

As though she were watching the scene from above herself, Czanna realized she was going to be too late to save Briella unless she could sprint even faster. She tried to pick up her speed, then realized they would both be trampled if she could even get to Briella in time.

*No! No! This cannot happen! I must save my sister! I must!*

"Briella, no! Stop now!" Czanna was shouting with all her might while running with as much speed as she could muster toward the child. "Come back! Please, come back! Please, Briella!"

All of a sudden, the image of Stands Strong sprang into view; he was coming upon them from the side and speeding his own mount in a line directly toward Briella. Guiding his pony with only one hand, he was hanging on to one side of the horse, and, as though he were part eagle honing in on its prey, as soon as his mount brought him in close to the child, he picked Briella up and brought her firmly into his arm at the exact moment his pony made a sharp turn away from the danger, the pony avoiding a collision with the uncontrolled horse, which was still rearing. It wasn't until he and the child were safely away from both Czanna and the others in the procession when she saw Stands Strong at last straighten back up into his seat, the child still held firmly within his arm.

Czanna was running toward them and was crying out at the same time, "Briella! Stands Strong! Thank God you are both safe! I could not bear it if I had lost you both!"

Crying, she sped right up to Stands Strong and his pony, halting beside them and reaching up to take hold of her sister. In an instant, she brought Briella into her arms.

Looking up at Stands Strong, Czanna cried, "I am so sorry she escaped me! It is my fault, but it happened so fast! She was gone before I could catch her! What would I have done if you hadn't been there for her, for me?" She gazed up at Stands Strong with what she felt must be a look of her utter admiration for him, this man who always seemed to be there when she needed him.

He didn't answer. Indeed, he appeared to be as alarmed as she felt. But, instead of scolding her—as Czanna felt she deserved—he simply gazed down at her from where he sat upon his mount, and at last, taking a deep breath, he said, "It is not your fault. What could you have done? I only feared I would not be fast enough to save her. Much of the credit is due to my buffalo pony, who carried me safely to your sister and then safely away."

Then he dismounted, coming to stand before her, and, reaching out, he brought both her and Briella into his arms. He didn't speak. Neither did she.

Briella, however, was not to be silenced, and, looking up at Stands Strong, she wiggled in Czanna's arms and said to him, "Love you, Stan Song. Love horsey, too."

After a moment, Stands Strong answered Briella and said, "I love you, too. Both of you." Then, kissing Czanna's cheek, he murmured, "I fear there is now no manner by which we can hide our love for each other. I fear it is there for all to see."

And, though what he said was true, still, Czanna cried.

****

Supper had come and gone. It had been a wonderful affair, filled with the best Pikuni food, stories and laughter.

Yet,…

Because it was almost summertime, the days were getting longer, and, although the evening meal was over, the sun was only now starting to set in the west. All of the families were seated on blankets set in a circle around a fire pitched in front of the most beautiful tepee Czanna had ever seen. Painted in blue, green and white patterns of stripes, triangles and round circles, it was large enough so that they all could have easily and comfortably gone inside. But, the evening was warm and the sunset too beautiful for the people to be so soon shunted inside.

Czanna took note of the seating arrangements at once: the men sat on one side of the circle; the women on the other. All of the children were included in the circle, although the younger ones, playing their games, ran around the adults but never did they come between their elders and the fire.

Thinking back, Czanna had to admit to never seeing a people so quick in making camp, and she considered the Hungarian Army might be shamed by how soon the women had set up the camp.

Indeed, once the chief had announced where they would pitch their encampment—which was on the prairie close to the springs—the women had gone to work.

Amazed at how quickly all of the women—including the young girls, except for the babies—had joined in to raise up each of the lodges, Czanna had watched in awe. The entire task had been done in minutes rather than hours.

Each family's possessions had then been taken off the backs of the ponies and placed within the lodges, while the older boys had led the animals out to the best pasture, two of those boys being stationed there to watch the herd.

At present, Liliann and a few of the older girls were watching the two young ones, one of them being Briella, while Stands Strong's almost-mother held her newborn baby in her arms.

All through supper, and even now with the warmth and buzz of conversations happening all about her, Czanna had done little more than look at Stands Strong where he sat across from her, the evening fire between them. He, too, seeming to be immune to all the laughing and talking, gazed back at her.

Czanna knew she was in moral trouble, if only in her own mind. At present, her every thought was about and centered around Stands Strong. She saw again and again his acts of bravery: Stands Strong coming to help her and her family; Stands Strong teaching her to scout; Stands Strong telling her he loved her. Stands Strong kissing her. Stands Strong saving her sister. But, most of all, he was Stands Strong, the man whom she craved to keep near to her.

Indeed, she had never felt more in love with another human being, not in all her days upon this earth. Her heart and her mind—indeed, all her senses—were begging her to acknowledge one true fact: she should marry this man. Perhaps then, and only then, could she achieve the feeling of closeness she sought with him.

Oh, how she wished she could marry him. But, she dared not. She was charged with a duty to her family, and she couldn't let go of her obligation.

If only their two worlds were more alike…

Their lifestyles, however, were not similar in any manner, and, like a magnet, Czanna felt pulled by both of their culture's opposing poles. Yes, she felt charged with the duty she'd known was hers from her first breath upon this earth. But, she also knew this: never in this entire world would she ever find a man she loved more than Stands Strong. Never. Stands Strong had somehow taken his place within her heart, now and forever.

But, to become an Indian like these three white women, who were now seated beside her and who were chatting happily back and forth, was not in her plans. Two of these women Stands Strong referred to as his almost-aunties. The other was his almost-mother.

Earlier this day, Czanna had met his lovely and charming almost-mother, Sharon, who, holding her baby, was now sitting beside Czanna on her left. Both of his equally fine-looking aunties were seated on Czanna's right. And so, the three women talked to one another back and forth and around Czanna, and while they included her in their conversations, she knew she dare not join in with them.

She supposed it was as Stands Strong had said it would be: there was no way to hide their love for one another from his family. Not now.

And yet, they were not married, nor were they lovers, though they would have been had Stands Strong not possessed the strength to pull away from her that one time when they had been scouting.

Should she give in to him and marry him? His heroism today on her own and her sister's behalf inclined her to believe she should. And, she would certainly marry him if only she didn't have to change who she was in order to become his woman. She could never be an American Indian.

Still, there was a hidden and deep knowledge within her, soothing her fears and pleading with her to listen to her heart, begging her to hear its words:

"*He is the one,*" it whispered. "*He is the one man, indeed, who has always been meant to be yours.*"

As she gazed wistfully at Stands Strong across the fire, meeting his gaze because he was also staring back at her, she knew he, too, was ignoring everything else around him except her, even while she could hear the other men congratulating him on his quick action today.

It was then when, without warning, she was struck by a voice coming straight from her heart.

"*It is time,*" it said. "*It is time for you to say goodbye to what once was.*"

She almost sobbed, recognizing her heart's wisdom. But, was it really true?

It very well could be true, she admitted to herself at last. The past was now gone, to be no more. She was here now. He was here now. And, she loved him.

She sighed, if only to quiet the tingling in her body, for she had, at last, recognized a very basic truth. Even if she were to return to Hungary, she would, indeed, be going back to a different country from the one she had previously known.

True, though her brother had charged her to carry a family treasure to deliver to her cousin, he had also directed her to make a new life here in the American West. Would he be shocked, were he still upon this earth, to find she had changed so completely? That she had gone from being part of the Hungarian gentry to now considering she should embrace a new life—a life as Stands Strong's Indian wife?

Then again, would her brother's supposed shock, were he alive, really matter? Neither her parents nor her brother were here to guide her, and her life in Hungary was gone forever. And, if this were so, why then was she still seeking to garner approval from her former culture and from a society she would never again be part of?

Undeniably, today's events had done much: they had changed her. No longer did she feel the need for approval from a people she didn't even know anymore. In truth, this man was hers; he had said as much to her. She might try to ignore it, but perhaps refusing to acknowledge what was in her heart, here, right now, was not wise, nor was it good for her or for him. She loved Stands Strong, and, with complete honesty, she realized she was as much his as he was hers.

Yes, the time had come at last for her to say goodbye to the past, and, to herself, she whispered, "Goodbye."

Catching Stands Strong's eye, she took courage from her newly found understanding, and, gazing directly at him, she mouthed the simple word "Yes."

He seemed to understand her at once, and she looked on as he briefly closed his eyes while several emotions flitted over his features. When he opened his eyes, he sent her a radiant smile and gave her a tiny, yet distinguishable nod. Indeed, he understood.

Looking away, she smiled. She had uttered no more than the one straightforward word, yet she knew Stands Strong had understood this and more. She was no longer confused about her duty being more important than what he was to her. She wanted him to be a permanent part of her life, and she to always be a part of his.

Sometimes, she decided, it was good to say a fond farewell to a time now passed. It was here and now where she would make a new life…with Stands Strong, and she by his side.

She watched him as he came up to his feet and stepped around the circle of people to come to her. Silently, treading up behind her, he placed his hand on her shoulder, and, reaching up, she laid her hand over his. Then she smiled up at him.

Meanwhile, the entire camp—even the children's voices as well as the air around them—had become quiet, and she knew every eye was upon them, though no one looked at them overtly.

She came up to her feet. And, though she knew she was openly declaring her feelings for this man, what the others might be thinking about her little mattered; she couldn't help the happy pleasure rushing through her, practically bursting to be released. And, as she and Stands Strong paced away from the others, they shared a smile with one another, and then they both laughed, sounding as though they were small happy children.

"Come," he said. "I sought out your brother's approval to marry you this day, hoping you might have a change of heart. But, it will not be until tomorrow when I will seek him out again and bring him horses. Tomorrow we will go with the others to the white man's fort, but tonight I know of a private place where we may pledge ourselves to each other."

She laughed and murmured, "Yes, please."

****

He led her out into the balmy warmth of evening, the cloudless night hosting the few stars beginning to shine in the dark-blue sky in the east, although pinks, purples and reds were still lighting up the sky in the west. As they stepped toward the pony herd, Stands Strong held Czanna's hand in a tight grip as though he had no intention of letting it go.

However, once within the herd, he let go of her hand to separate out two ponies, and, leading them toward the western side of the herd, he paced a little away, bending down to pick up some blankets. These he threw over the ponies' backs, one of those mounts the "star" of today's adventure.

She asked, "Are we not going to ride only one pony? I have a need, it seems, to be as close to you as possible tonight, and I had hoped..."

He turned toward her, smiling slyly before he said, "I promise we will be very close this night, if only because I do not intend to let you out of my arms, even in sleep. But, there are boys watching the pony herd, and because our families have brought with them no more than thirty horses to care for, those boys will see all we do, though they will turn their backs to give us privacy. Also, although where we are going is not far, we will still be out of the hearing range of my people should we encounter a war party. It is for this reason why we must take precautions to remain safe. And, since each one of us riding a single pony gives us more of an advantage, I think it best if our horses carry only one rider."

As he was settling the buckskin reins into the mouth of each mount, she said, "Oh, all right." But, then she asked, "Where did the blankets and the reins come from?"

Again, he gave her a sexy, yet shrewd grin, saying, "I had set them here earlier...in hopes."

She laughed, then chortled, "I am glad."

"As I am, also," he answered.

He helped her up into her seating on the horse, and sassily she commented, "I thought it was against an Indian man's nature to assist a woman when she is attempting to gain her seat upon her steed."

Again she was treated to his grin. He said, "You forget. My almost-mother is white. She sometimes requires help in getting onto her horse, and my almost-father seems to be more than happy to aid her, stealing kisses from her all the while...that is, when no one is looking."

She laughed. "But, you must have seen them do it in order to be able to tell me about it."

"Of course I have watched them, although I was always well hidden when I looked." They both chuckled before he added, "A boy has to be clever if he is to learn about love, after all."

"Then, I must admire your ingenuity, especially since I am to be the recipient of this knowledge. Are your almost-parents deeply in love, then?"

"They have five children, including me, though they have only been married for fifteen snows. My almost-mother wishes to have a large family, and my almost-father is happy to accommodate her. I believe he would deny her nothing. Yes, they are deeply in love."

"As much as us?" she asked.

"I think so," he answered, "although we are only beginning our life together. Perhaps our love might shine as much or more than theirs, if there were to be such a contest."

"It would be a silly contest."

"*Aa*, so it would be." He easily found his seat upon his mount.

Observing him and the pony together, she was caught up by an observation: this horse and rider seemed to be of one mind. She said, "This is the same animal you were riding when you rescued my sister today, is it not?"

"It is," he replied. "This stallion is the best buffalo pony in all the tribe. He is not only smart, he knows exactly what I require of him when we ride together. I rarely have to guide him. These kinds of ponies require some training, but they are as excited as its rider when we go to hunt buffalo. He sometimes knows my thoughts before I have the chance to say any words to him." He paused, then added, "He knew we had to save your sister. He was honored and excited to bring me in close to her so I could grab her. He knew, also, the moment when I had her clutched in my arm, and he took a sharp turn away to avoid a collision with the frightened horse Chief Chases-the-enemy was riding. The chief's horse is a recent acquisition and is not yet properly trained. My buffalo pony knew this and was able to speed away without my even having to guide him."

"My goodness. What a beautiful animal he is. I, too, love horses very much. But, I had no idea they could be trained in this way. Is his name Buffalo Horse?"

"*Saa*, it is not. His name has roots in both the Pikuni and the Lakota languages, since I am both. *Naato Omitaa* is the Pikuni name for 'Holy Dog' in English."

"Holy Dog?"

"*Aá*. When these animals first came to the Lakota, my people were quick to see the horse could do the jobs of our dogs, only better. They could carry more of a load and could be trained to help a man in war or in the running of buffalo. They were often smart and have been known to save their masters from harm. And so, the Lakota called this new acquisition 'Holy Dog.' *Naato Omitaa* is the Blackfeet translation for *Suŋka Wakaŋ'*, which is Lakota."

"How do you say them both?"

"Naa-to Omit-aa is Pikuni. Sun-ka Wa-kan is Lakota."

"I think I have it. *Naato Omitaa* is Pikuni, and *Suŋka Wakaŋ'* is Lakota."

He smiled. "I like to hear you speak my language."

She grinned in return. "Is this your own personal name for him, then?"

"It is."

"Good. What name do you use the most when you call to him?"

"I have given him both names, and he knows them both, also. He probably would even come to you if you called him 'Holy Dog.'"

"Perhaps I might," she answered. "But, I think I shall address him by his Indian names. Both of them have a lovely sound to them, and since I am now your woman and you are my man, I should learn to speak your language, though it may take me a while to do so."

"It is good," he said as he guided his pony, *Naato Omitaa*, to where Czanna sat upon her mount. He brought the animal up on her side, his own horse facing the same direction as her pony. Reaching out, he took her hand in his and brought it up to his lips where he kissed each of her fingers. He said, "I care not what language we speak when we are together. I care only to make you happy with me."

Dropping her hand, he narrowed his eyes and looked away from her to gaze directly in front of him, and, turning around, he looked to his rear, then to each side, his gaze away from her and out into the environment.

She sighed, her fingers still tingling from his caress. But, it appeared he had other matters on his mind.

At last, he looked back her and said, "I neither see nor feel the presence of an enemy. And so, we go. Follow me. The way is not far, but it is enough distant from here to give us privacy."

"I shall," she said, and, bringing her own fingers up to her lips, she kissed them, then blew the kiss to him. As though she had smacked him by the simple gesture, he slipped from his seat and fell to the side of his pony, away from her.

To the sound of her giggle, he regained his seat and said, "*Áa*, my new wife has power in her kiss. I greatly anticipate the night ahead of us, so I might experience more of her power. Do you think I might?"

"Sir, I think you are well aware you will, and I think, too, you are flirting with me."

"Do you only think it?"

Leaning over and reaching out, he caught her around the waist and, lifting her up, brought her into position before him, she sitting sidesaddle. And, as one of his arms came around her, he gathered the reins of both his pony and hers in his other hand and said, "I think you were right. We should be close. But, be warned. All the way to our marriage camp, I intend to show you what I do when I really mean to flirt!"

She giggled and he laughed. But, she stayed right where she was, directly before him on his smart and handsome pony, Holy Dog.

## CHAPTER TWELVE

Once they were out of sight of the pony herd, Stands Strong repositioned Czanna until she was seated facing him, her skirt pulled up to her knees and her legs around him. Presently, she was hugging him, her breasts against his chest, her head nestled into the crook of his neck.

Bending his head, he whispered in her ear, "Is this close enough?"

She sighed before murmuring, "This is good, yes, but I'd like to be even nearer to you, though I know it's impossible. I do not understand it. I feel as though I would like nothing more than to crawl under your skin. Sounds silly, I know, but this is how I feel."

He chuckled. "I think I cannot grant you this wish. However, should I disrobe you and make love to you here, now, as we speed over the prairie? Do you think we might be joined together enough, then?"

"Could you?"

"Perhaps," he said, leaning down to kiss the top of her head. "I have never tried to do it, nor do I know of a man who has done it. But, if it can be accomplished, I am certain there are men and women who have engaged in it and who have liked it very much. Such is the power of love between a man and his woman."

"Hmmm," she groaned.

"But, we must wait, I think," he said. "You are not yet accustomed to the act that unites a man and his woman, and I think if we were to attempt to make love in this way now, it would be hard on you and maybe not enjoyable for you, either. And, I would have you like the act which makes you my woman.

"Also," he continued, "we are not far from camp. Do you see the hill?" He pointed.

"You mean the mountain? Isn't it a mountain?"

She felt him smile. "On the side of the hillish 'mountain' in that direction"—again he pointed—"is a coulee where there is water and grass for our horses and many cottonwood and willow trees to hide them...and us. This is where we will make our camp for this night."

"Oh," she said. "But, sir, then we will have to set up camp, which takes some physical work, and we might be exhausted after, and—"

His laugh was hearty and spontaneous. "Had I known how greatly you wish to become a part of me—"

"Oh, stop it," she interrupted. "You know very well you have caused it. Every day you have been teasing me...rubbing my shoulders and my chest, as well as running your fingers through my hair...rubbing my back...kissing me as though you would make love to me...making comments about wishing to see me naked...but then you have always walked away from me. Have you really thought all these acts, these words, have had no effect upon me?"

"I have hoped. But, you now know why I have had to walk away, as you say. *Niitá'p*, if you think back to it, have you not seen I have been experiencing the same as you?"

"I do not know. Have you? Do you?"

Again, he bent down slightly to kiss the top of her head. "Of course, I have. I do. Why do you think I have been teasing you? If I didn't wish to have you close to me also, I would have said no to your pact and walked away, never to touch you again."

She bit her lip. "Never to touch me again? Oh, please, do not even say it. Are we almost there?"

"We are.  As you can see, we have only to climb down into this coulee.  It is not too steep.  We will hobble the horses once we get to the bottom of it and will let them graze while we get to know one another a little better."

"I am glad."  She breathed in deeply.  "I love you very deeply, Mr. Stands Strong.  I love you, I think, more than I have loved another living soul.  I know it took me a little while to realize I should leave my past behind me.  But, I have done so.  I wish now only to be happy and to create my life with you.  I hope to make you as happy with me as I am with you."

"It will be my honor to do the same.  *Niitá'pt,* it is my honor."

\*\*\*\*

She wasn't really aware of how far down they had climbed into the coulee until he brought his buffalo pony to a halt, the other horse still following behind them stopping, also.  This part of the canyon was wooded across the floor of the coulee to where the land extended out into the sparkling, babbling stream.  The timber was thick here, consisting of many willow trees and tall majestic cottonwoods, and reached out in a line both east and west up to and against the north end of the canyon.  And, the scatterings of numerous bushes and tree limbs from windfalls caused the ponies to have to step over or around them.

Czanna breathed in deeply, and at once her lungs were filled with the woodsy scent of the grasses and timber, whose green-colored leaves flickered in the warm breeze and showed off a reflection of the reds, pinks and purples of the late evening sunset.  It was odd, this northwestern territory, in that the sky darkened so slowly and the sunset seemed to go on and on, well into the very late hours of the night.

However, once inside the timber, it wasn't long before they stopped again, and, after sliding down from his seating, Stands Strong reached up to help Czanna dismount.  But, instead of letting her feet touch the ground as she came off the horse, he held her up against him and hugged her, her face on a level with his.

And, then he kissed her lips, her eyes, her cheeks, and, holding her up and against him with only one hand, he reached up to massage her ears, her neck, her breasts.

She closed her eyes, reminding herself to breathe. For a moment, it seemed her body had forgotten.

He whispered, "If you have ever had any doubts of my love for you, let me show you tonight how much I adore you. Ease your mind, my beautiful woman, about my having to keep some distance between us. It, too, is now in our past. I take you for my wife now, for all my life and perhaps forever. Should I tell you more? Should I say to you how taken I was with you from the start, from the first moment I heard you singing, there upon the *pisskan*? So much was I charmed, I had to know more about you. I had to see this woman. And so, I climbed up the *pisskan's* cliff to see you. And, when I beheld the beauty of the woman who matched the allure of her voice, this was when I started to love you. And, though you wished me not to follow you, I could not let you go. I had to ensure your safety.

"And, why did I do this, you might ask?" he continued. "Because I loved you from that moment on. Come with me now to a shelter I have built. I set up this camp earlier today, hoping you might change your mind about becoming my woman. But if, by my earlier actions, you have thought I have not loved you enough, let me tell you the truth of my passion so you do not doubt it. It was and is my love for you which has led me. Though I have said this to you before, let me repeat it now: I would not ruin you. If you have wished to be close to me, I might tease you about it, true, yet I think your desire mirrors the yearning in my own heart. I, too, want you close to me…always. I do not ever wish to let you go, and I promise to not let you out of my arms this night, except perhaps only for the call of nature.

"And now, as the wise men of my tribe have often counselled to a new couple, let me tell you what I vow to you as my woman," he said, letting her feet fall to the ground. And, bringing his forehead to hers, he began again, the baritone timbre of his voice soft as he said, "I promise you now before my God and yours to take care of you, and to keep you and any children we may have always in my thoughts. I promise to protect you and our children to the best I can so you might feel secure in your daily lives. As your God decrees, I promise there will be no other woman I will take into my life as a wife. And, I promise to never use a harsh word against you, but if we do disagree and I feel I cannot speak to you without bad words, I will leave so I might cool my temper. But, never fear I would go away never to return. I promise to come back to you so we might talk with our minds not influenced by anger. I am yours. I have been yours since the moment I first saw you. Whatever we must face, whatever comes, do not ever doubt my love for you"—he kissed her forehead gently—"and these are my promises to you."

As Czanna stared up at this man, she became aware of each tiny line around his eyes, of the beauty of his deep dark eyes which, passion-filled, were looking back at her. There was a soft look in his gaze, also, when he stared back at her, reminding her of this man's heroism in her defense and his devotion to helping her. But, until now, she hadn't really seen his actions for what they were.

As she continued to gaze up into his eyes, she looked at him as perhaps she never had before, and with only a few evening stars overhead to light the evening's sky, she was dazzled by his utterly handsome countenance, the oval shape of his face, his dark, almost-black eyes, his perfectly straight nose, his full lips and firm jawline. The deepening sunset and the few stars overhead silhouetted each of his strong features as though it, too, embraced him. Yes, he was the handsomest of men, but he was also a man capable of great compassion and care, though it seemed to her he tried to conceal this particular quality, projecting instead a tough warrior's image.

She reached up to run her hands through his long hair, which was currently unbraided and falling about and over his shoulders. She whispered, "Thank you, my dearest husband. Thank you for what you have pledged to me. And now, I believe it is my turn, since I think I, too, should abide by the counsel of your wise men. And so, let me tell you what I promise you."

Stands Strong simply nodded, but he didn't utter a word. And, gaining comfort from the warmth of his embrace, she murmured, "I admit I was a little frightened of you when we first met. Yet, upon talking with you, I realized I had nothing to fear. It was then when I beheld the goodness of your heart. Yes, I could clearly see how handsome you were from the start, but a pretty face and handsome figure are not necessarily a woman's first concerns with a man.

"It was when you came to help us, bringing us food and staying with us to help guide us back to the fort when it happened: I was devastated when you bluntly inferred my kiss against your cheek was less than satisfactory. I felt as though I had been thrust into a world of an unknown quality. Yes, my reaction to you was partly because of the potential danger in the environment, but it was also due to my body's reaction to you—as though I would like nothing more than to kiss you over and over again until you agreed to make love to me. I was shocked at myself.

"And yet, you seemed unmoved by me. It seemed so unfair. How could you be unmoved by me when I felt on fire from merely being close to you? And then, the next morning when you came to awaken me and kissed me and massaged my back, I knew then that it was only a matter of time before I would come to love you much more than a friend.

"But, it has been hard for me because I am entrusted with a duty to my brother, my parents and the rest of my family, and we, you and I, were, and we still are, so different because we have been raised with conflicting views of life.

"And yet, every day thereafter, your kindness toward me, my brother and even Mr. Henrik has caused me to love you, as I have already told you. My husband—I like calling you my husband..." She sighed. "Loving you, however, has been difficult because I have wanted you to touch me, to kiss me and to love me. And yet, as you know, I couldn't envision my life with you. Only as a lover, I thought, could I ever allow you into my life.

"But, I have changed my mind about it all. I cannot, indeed, envision my life without you. And so, let me tell you what I promise you. Like you, I vow to take a moment before I say harsh words to you. Only when we both have let time cool our tempers, as you say, will we talk, and only then will I speak to you, with no anger left in my heart. This is wise. But, because I have no conception of what is yet before me as your wife, I can little give you promises about it. But, this I can promise: I will love you and no other, and for all my life. The idea of taking on a lover other than you, as I have believed is my right, is, from this moment forward, forever gone from my heart. Further, I will love any children we might make as much as I love you, and I will do all I can to raise them always with their good in mind, promising to shower them with the same love I hold for you. I will try not to interfere with important duties you may have in your life, but beyond this, I do not know what is expected of me, so I cannot say more about it.

"I can only give you this: I am yours, and I will try to bring you happiness in the life we will share together."

He didn't speak for several moments, and when she looked up at him, she saw his eyes were tear-stained. At length, he cleared his throat and whispered, "You have promised me more than I ever hoped to hear you say. And so, now let us look around us and see where we are so we may remember this moment at some time in the future when youth has fled from our bodies—let us look at the heavens above, the stars seen through the trees, the sound of the rushing stream, the smells of the forest, the trees, the grasses and the firmness of the earth at our feet.  Let us set to mind all these we sense so we can keep this moment forever in our hearts."

When she nodded but didn't also look around the environment, he continued and said, "I will direct you.  Do you see the stars overhead?"

She nodded.  "I do."

"Their light is strong in the east and weak in the west.  Do you see this?"

"I do."

"*Soka'pii*.  Now, take a look around again.  We are here in my country, at Sacagawea Springs.  It is spring, almost summer.  The grass is green and soft.  In the air is the scent of flowers, trees and bushes.  The night sky is becoming dark, and there is a wind from the south, bringing us its warmth.  Always, let us remember this time when we became one."

"Yes," she whispered.

Something was happening to her; oddly, as he spoke, she felt her senses expand out beyond herself and into the environment.  In awe of the new feeling, she felt herself grow so close to him it was as though she became him, though she little understood how this could be.  She was still who she was.

Looking up at him, she asked, "Do you feel it?'

He nodded.

And she murmured, "For a moment just now, it was as though I were you, though I was still very much myself.  Oh, my darling, I do not know how to say this in words.  I can only tell you this: you are now a part of me and I a part of you."

Standing on her tiptoes, she placed her arms around his neck.  Then, with a soft giggle, she said, "Perhaps now I can find the closeness I have been craving with you for some time.  Do you think we will be as close to one another as we truly desire?"

"We will try," he murmured. "But, it might take us a lifetime to fully realize it." He grinned down at her. "Yes," he said, then repeated, "it may take us a lifetime."

****

After hobbling the two horses and seeing to their comfort, Stands Strong led her to a shelter nestled in a deep wooded grove a little away from the noise of the rippling stream that ran through the bottom of the coulee. At first, she didn't even see the lodging, so closely did it resemble the environment. But, eventually, as they came in closer to it, she began to understand it was a structure and not simply more of the woods.

It was shaped somewhat like a tepee but made of tall wooden slabs of logs placed closely together, the limbs obviously being gathered from the many windfalls in these woods. There were also interlocking slabs of tree bark placed over the upright poles, and around the bottom of the structure were even more tree limbs arranged to about a two-foot height.

It was like nothing she had ever seen. At one of its sides was what looked to be a smaller, yet similar structure perhaps a little more than one meter in height and extending outward for what looked to be about seven meters. Made of smaller logs, it looked like an upside-down "V", and it appeared to be the only entrance into the larger structure.

As they stood together looking at it, he said, "This is a war lodge."

"What? A war lodge? My husband, I thought we were going to make love. Are we, instead, going to war?"

He chuckled, then answered, "Only if you wish there to be war between us. This is for our first night together. I wanted to build a structure where we might feel secure enough to relax. A war lodge is what Blackfeet men make when they come in close to an enemy encampment. Within this lodge, the smoke from a fire is not easily sensed by an enemy, and its light cannot be seen. It is a sturdy shelter. It was my wish for us to be able to be together this night and to be comfortable with a good fire, and without the fear of an enemy seeing its light or smelling its smoke."

"Oh my," she said. "Imagine, a war lodge. How is it used when you go to war?"

"In this way," he answered. "We make these lodges when we come in close to an enemy camp; this is why they are built carefully so they are not readily seen and where all those within it can smoke the pipe, make dried meat and sleep without fear of it being detected. Also, we can leave food in the war lodge in case we lose the dried meat we carry with us. Here, too, we can gather together after the fight or leave messages to each other. Often we store extra weapons in case we lose them in battle. It is good for sleeping, too.

"In hopes of you changing your mind about becoming my woman," he continued, "I wished to make a lodge which is hard for an enemy to perceive and would give us cover well enough so we would have little fear in being disturbed."

Czanna cast this man a curious glance, then asked, "You built this all by yourself? Today?"

"I did. They are easy to make and take little time. This war lodge is smaller around than the ones we usually build, and so it was done easily and quickly."

"Easily? It doesn't look easy to me."

He turned toward her and grinned. "Do you wish to flatter me? It is my duty to ensure we will have a lodge where we can come to know one another without fear."

"I do not flatter you," she said. "I am truly in awe of you having put this together today, and yet you were there when I needed you most."

"As I always hope to be. Now come, let us go inside. Step this way… I fear you will have to come down on hands and knees to enter. Here, follow me and do as I do."

She complied and followed him into the war lodge, crawling behind him and through the long entrance, coming at last to stand up behind him, scooting in close to him. Immediately, she smelled the strong scent of pine needles within the lodge, and except the dim starlight filtering in through the very top of the structure, she saw there were no other openings within the lodge. Indeed, it was quite dark within it.

As she glanced around the one room, she came to understand the reason for the strong scent of pine: bows of balsam were scattered over the ground within the lodge. As her eyes adjusted to the darkness within, she saw two blankets to her left neatly set together, as well as a soft robe at the head of the blankets, its use most likely being that of a pillow.

She must have been staring at it intensely, because Stands Strong seemed attuned to her thoughts, and, gesturing toward the blankets, he said, "Our bed."

Oddly, she wasn't embarrassed by the obvious, yet suggestive statement. Indeed, she was thrilled, and, looking more closely at their "bed," a rather wanton excitement washed through her system.

Turning, Stands Strong put his arms around her, and she fell forward, at last gaining a hint of the intimacy she craved. She whispered, "I like it."

Gazing up at him within the softness of the darkened interior, she watched as his head descended toward hers, his lips unerringly finding hers. At the contact, she felt her body melt into his until she doubted even the width of a pin could have been inserted between them. And, as she thought she might at last be near enough to him, she realized it was still not enough.

But, at last it appeared he was ready to do all he could to grant her wish.

Breaking off the kiss, he picked her up and strode toward their bed of soft blankets. He didn't let her go, though; instead, he drew her down onto her knees, he also kneeling before her. Meanwhile his hands were working over her clothing as though her garments were nothing more than an encumbrance. It didn't even occur to her to wonder how he knew how to undress her, since, if she were to have given it better consideration, she would have realized that most Indians were unfamiliar with the layers of clothing a white woman was required to wear.

But, the clothing gave him no reason for hesitation. Still kissing her, his hands worked over the snaps, buttons and other fastenings holding her dress together.

Then, at last, she was kneeling in front of him, completely adorned in nothing more than the manner in which she had come into this world. But, she was to be disappointed momentarily because she soon became aware she was the only one naked. As near as she could tell, he was still wearing his shirt, leggings, breechcloth and moccasins.

She whispered against his lips, "Am I the only one to be undressed, then?"

She felt his lips rise up into a grin. Then he said, "I promise I will disrobe, but in a little while. Let me enjoy the feel of you and the look of you without the need to commit to the act of love. I fear that if I also undress, I would think only of fulfillment. Instead, I would savor this moment."

"Yes," she agreed.

And, then he pressed her backward, enveloping her body within his arms until she was lying down beside him. But, he wasn't reclining. Instead, he was kneeling by her side, and, looking up at him, she saw his gaze was everywhere upon her.

He whispered, "You are more beautiful without your clothing."

And, with no more said, he felt her everywhere, from her head to her chest, downward over her arms to her stomach and lower still toward her femininity, and there he massaged her briefly before he brought his hands down to caress each of her legs, then felt down farther toward her feet, and these he massaged.

Then he came back up over her body, caressing and kissing her everywhere until he reached the top of her head, which he massaged, while she whimpered and groaned.

She whispered, "It feels so good."

He lay down beside her, and then kissed her deeply, his tongue reaching into the recesses of her mouth and toying with hers. Meanwhile, his hands were rubbing her, massaging her everywhere, his hands lingering over her breasts. One of his hands remained where it was over one of her breasts while his other hand journeyed over her body until it reached her core.

"Open your legs," he whispered.

She complied, there being no thought of resistance within her.

And, then his fingers found the moist place most sensitive to his touch, and she thought she might swoon, so good did it feel.

With the age-old instinct of love, she wiggled a little, immediately rewarded by a thousand points of pleasure washing over her. Again she groaned, and she murmured, "What you are doing feels so intimate and so soul-stirring, it's as though what you are doing has taken my breath. Is it always to be this pleasurable?"

"I hope it will always be so," he whispered.

The massage there at her core continued on and on, and still he remained fully dressed. But, she was now barely aware of it. All she knew at this moment was the love she felt for this man who was giving her body these millions of carnal, amorous pinpoints of feeling that stretched from the top of her head all the way down to her toes.

The sensations went on and on, building there where he was touching, and, within moments, she felt the passion of their crescendo, becoming fuller and fuller until bliss became all she knew.

It happened then. A fury of arousing sensation encompassed her, it seeming to have no time, yet was so full of seductive pleasure she could barely breathe. She shut her eyes to more fully experience its heat. Never in all her life's teachings about her place in life had she been told about the sense of joy she could attain because of the act of love.

Perhaps this was the reason she had been startled the first time when she had come in close to Stands Strong and had so innocently placed her lips upon his cheek. She hadn't, until then, ever known the utter desire a woman could experience by simply coming in close to a man she especially liked; she had only known the facts of lovemaking, not the pull of attraction. At the time, hers had been an unexpected response, especially because her first kiss upon his cheek had been so tiny a gesture.

At last, a feeling similar to falling through space encompassed Czanna, and she felt the full force of her love for this man. Her heart beat so quickly within her chest that she could only compare its speed to the act of running; to wit, it was similar to it if the race were one of flying, because this was how she felt…free and above herself. And, when she at last came back to the earth and gazed up at Stands Strong, she found him still beside her, grinning down at her.

She was beyond words. Truly. Completely.

But, no words were needed. Quickly disrobing, Stands Strong brought his naked body down to hers, and he whispered, "It might hurt you at first. But, fear not, it soon will go away. Are you ready?"

She nodded.

And, then he truly and physically became a part of her, and, innocently, she would have never suspected she would have rejoiced in the feeling. At last, she felt she had come to be as near to him as she could possibly be.

He hesitated once they were as one together; he didn't, indeed, move at all. It seemed to her as though in this way he thought he might take away the pain. But, when she didn't seem to object to the feel of him, he began to move.

And, this was when she realized the truth of what he had told her: at first it hurt, but it went away after a while. Besides, she wasn't about to stop. It felt too good to be so entangled with him.

And, then he began the dance of love, and she met him with every move. Never could she recall feeling as though she were a part of another human being. And this, she realized, was what she had been craving from him for some time now.

Gradually, as they danced and they danced together, the same pleasure she had experienced only moments before began to build within her again, and it wasn't long before she was experiencing the same exquisite pleasure he had bought to her earlier.

As she met his moves and added her own gyrations to his, she was aware she was reaching toward the same peak of sensation a second time, and when it at last encompassed her, she felt the final momentum of his dance before he joined her there.

*Oh my. To be so close to him is as though I've found a bit of heaven.*

And, when she felt him gift his seed to her, her senses exploded. But, something else happened, also.

Somehow, in some way, she had become so attuned to him in this brief moment, she sensed she was he. Indeed, she was feeling what he felt, knew his thoughts, too—easily, as if they were her own. And, it was in this moment, set out of this world's time stream, when she at last knew she had attained what she had been seeking since she had first come to know this man. This was the intimacy she had been yearning for, little knowing that, while being completely herself, she would become him, too.

How this was possible, she didn't know; she only knew it was.

She placed her arms around Stands Strong and hugged him, and, as she did so, she felt peace settle over her. She didn't want him to ever move away from her, though she realized the utter impossibility of it. Oh, if only she could make this moment last.

As she massaged his shoulders, his back and his head, she whispered, "I, indeed, do love you, my husband."

"And I, you."

And so, their lovemaking continued in a like manner throughout the entirety of the night. Over and over they gave to one another, loving one another and deepening their commitment to each other. Indeed, within this night they didn't even come apart long enough to build a fire.

After all, what need had they of a fire? They were making their own warmth and heat.

And, when the first rays of morning could be seen through the top of their war lodge, they awoke and made love all over again.

## CHAPTER THIRTEEN

The sun was high in the sky and the wind was calm, meekly carrying the scent of sage in the air when Stands Strong and Czanna set out upon the trail back to camp. As the sun shone down its warmth upon them, Czanna couldn't remember a time when she had ever felt as happy as she did now. And, although she and Stands Strong weren't riding the same horse—as they had done on the previous evening—in some ways, it was almost as good as it might have been had she been sitting so closely to him. Because custom, as well as safety, demanded she ride behind Stands Strong, she was presented with the handsome image of Stands Strong as he rode out ahead of her.

Tall in his seat, his shoulders were broad, his back straight, showing off his weapons of many arrows as well as his bow, all of which were stored in what he called the skin of the *áámmóniisí*, the otter. He had strapped his rifle over one of his shoulders, and upon his other shoulder he carried his shield. She had seen his shield hung from one of the posts in the war lodge the previous evening, but she hadn't thought too much about it, her attention at the time on other matters.

Because his breechcloth was moving up and down as well as swinging with the wind as he rode his pony, she could see the wide band of this clothing upon his waist. On this belt and upon his right side, he had hung a knife, encased in a beautifully beaded sheath. And, on the left side of his belt was a tomahawk with a stone head at one end of it, which looked to be a large stone, chiseled until it had formed a sharp point. The weapon was decorated with beadwork on its handle, as well as feathers attached to it that fluttered with his movements.

His long loose hair fell down his back over his quiver and reached almost to his waist. But, what Czanna was finding so fascinating about him at this present moment was the manner by which his leggings and breechcloth accentuated the upper part of his thighs and the outline of his buttocks, since his leggings and his breechcloth were only hung together by rawhide strings.

Why she was only now noticing these little nuances of his figure and clothing was probably due to his habit of wearing his long shirt almost continually, and since it hung down to about his mid-thigh, it completely covered this area of his body. But, not so now.

His shirt was now placed within a bag she had seen him tie to his pony, thus leaving his upper chest bare, and she was thus presented with a good view of the extent of his handsome figure. It brought back, indeed, many delightful memories of the previous night.

However, she was only allowed a moment to reflect upon their time together because, looking ahead, she could see they were quickly coming in close to Sacagawea Springs. A wave of disappointment swept over her; she wished very much to keep this man near to her for a few more days.

But, it was not to be.

Earlier in the day and before they had set out upon the trail, he had told her about their families joining the main Pikuni tribe who were on their way to trade at Fort Benton. He had said, "The entirety of my tribe is only a half-day's ride from the springs."

"How do you know this?" she had asked.

He had gone on to explain, saying only, "The scout told it to me this morning."

"There was a scout here? This morning?"

He had grinned at her. "Did you not see him on the hill, there to the north of us?" He had pointed toward the place. "He saw us when we came out from the woods, and, gaining my attention, he waved his blanket so I would know the location of our people. He charged me with the duty to relay this message to our families so we all might join them by evening."

Czanna had stared at him with what must have been amazement, as well as a little doubt. "He said all that—and with only a blanket?"

"Of course. Did you not see me answer him by holding up my arm and waving to him?"

"No," she had answered, "I did not."

He had grinned at her. "It will be my pleasure, I think, to instruct you on many of our customs, including…" He had left the rest unsaid as he had leered at her, scanning her form from the top of her head to the very bottom of her feet.

She had giggled, his suggestion unspoken, but understood. She had responded back to him, however, saying, "I wish we could have a little more time with each other before we have to join the others."

"I, too, wish this. But, even though we have only recently become united, I have a duty to report what I have observed to my family. But, do not fear. There will be time enough to again come to know one another intimately…and soon. I will ensure it."

She had smiled then and had nodded. "Do you promise?"

"I do," he had responded at once. "Now, I will tell you before we return to our family what you might expect. Perhaps it will help a little to ease you into this life you might, at first, find strange."

"I would, indeed, like this very much."

He had squeezed her hand then and had kissed her deeply with a kiss that would have to substitute for additional lovemaking, though it made her ache for more.

And then, with a long hug, they had started out upon their journey back to the springs.

****

A warm wind from the west pushed strands of hair into her face. Reaching up, Czanna brushed the dark wisps away and looked forward as, enchanted, she looked on with awe at the brilliant colors set out before her: blue sky with green-dotted brown and gray bluffs, green prairie stretching out in all directions, the blue-green pool of Sacagawea Springs and the vivid and rainbow colors of the painted tepees surrounding it. Combined, it did help to take her attention off so short a honeymoon.

She looked carefully at each lodge, noticing they all had positioned their entrances to face east. Why? Was it a custom? Or perhaps a necessity, since the west winds in this land could be strong? She would have to ask Stands Strong about it.

But, for now, she was captivated by their beauty. Indeed, these lodges appeared to decorate instead of mar the landscape around them, appearing to not only be in harmony with and a part of God's natural environment, but more.

Looking outward at them, she sighed. Over to the east was a lodge painted with circles of orange and blue, a little distance away was another tepee painted with both blue and white triangles at its bottom edge, another displayed the image of a buffalo painted upon the lodge's white hide. A few more of the conical tepees were decorated in colors of red and white stripes, another with blue circles on the bottom edge of the tepee, and one was painted completely in a light blue.

Taking a deep breath, Czanna felt her spirits relax…at least a little. Obviously, she was worried, wondering how her new relatives might greet her after having run away with Stands Strong last evening. Would they condemn her? Or would they welcome her?

And, although she fretted over it, the beauty of their camp gave her to believe these people might be naturally tolerant. She hoped they would be.

Why hadn't she thought to ask Stands Strong about what his people's attitudes might be toward her? But, would he have answered her without more teasing?

Perhaps it was best she hadn't asked.

However, her nervousness returned forthwith when, riding in closer toward the camp, she saw some of the older boys sitting around the camp in front of the lodges. What would they think of her? Had a few of them seen her and Stands Strong within the pony herd last night?

At the thought, even more questions came to mind: did American Indian women experience the same kind of passion she had known the previous night? And, even if they did, would they have acted as she had, utterly surrendering to her husband?

However, when both she and Stands Strong rode slowly back into camp, no one looked at them oddly nor even expectantly. Indeed, no one appeared to notice them at all. Were these people simply being polite, or was it an everyday occurrence for a woman to run away to marry the man she loved?

Well, perhaps it little mattered. What had happened, and was happening even now between herself and Stands Strong, was not an everyday occurrence. It was love, it was passion, it was all this, but more. Both of them had a great deal to learn about the other, especially since he was marrying a woman from outside his tribe and she was allying herself into a society she had no knowledge of. In truth, she was leaving all she had ever known to become this man's woman.

Surely, this was not an everyday occurrence. Still, she had to admit it felt good to not be gawked at or looked at sternly or even excitedly.

Soon she and Stands Strong dismounted, and, taking hold of each pony's buckskin reins, they led their animals back into the pony herd, and, whisking away the blankets from their mounts' backs, which had served as saddles, they left their precious animal friends within the herd, there to enjoy a meal of the abundant prairie grass. But, before they stepped farther into the encampment, Stands Strong reached out to take her hand, then squeezed it.

He said, "I see you are worried. Do not be. All will be well. There are, within my family, three other white women who have experienced what I think might be the cause of your distress. These women, too, had doubts about becoming a part of a tribe they had no knowledge of and could little understand. I will take you to my almost-mother who will help you. She will love you. You also have two aunties within the tribe who have gone through much the same. They, too, will be of great aid to you."

Czanna nodded, then said, "Yes. Good. But, how did you know I was worried?"

He grinned at her and winked. "We are as one now."

"Yes, true. Still…"

"Come," he said. "There is little to fear."

She nodded once more, then took a deep breath to calm herself as they paced farther into camp. But, looking around, she was even more confused because only a few moments ago all had been quiet and peaceful.

But, now the entire camp was in disarray with everyone in motion; the women and young girls were busily engaged in taking the encampment down. Indeed, there was activity everywhere as, one by one, the rawhide skins of the lodges were taken down and folded, then the lodge poles disassembled and set aside, although some of these were being strapped into place by ropes upon a waiting pony. Even the dogs were being loaded with bags full of each family's possessions.

Czanna turned to Stands Strong and asked, "What is happening here? Where is everybody going? And, so quickly?"

"We are moving camp. As I mentioned earlier, we will join the rest of my people who are going to Fort Benton for trade. You will come, too. You can either drive your wagon or allow one of the older boys to do it for you while you take your place with my almost-mother and almost-aunties."

"But…but how did they know to take down the camp? Didn't you say you were charged with asking them to break camp to join the main procession? I thought when we returned here you would calmly tell the others what the scout had said, and then little by little we would make the journey to join the others."

"I have already told them what the scout related to me. And, the way we break camp might appear to be sudden, but for my people, it is leisurely done," he replied.

"I see…I think. But, we have only now returned to camp. How did you tell them the message so quickly?"

His smile at her was tolerant. "Do you remember," he said, "my telling you our marriage site was not far from my relative's encampment?"

"Well, yes, but I have no memory of seeing you on a hill and waving a blanket, which I am assuming is what you did."

He grinned. "And yet, I did so. I did tell them, and you are right. I did this by using my blanket."

"But…I did not see you do it. And, I have been with you most every moment."

"Áa, again you are right. It was when you had returned briefly to the war lodge, having forgotten your comb, when I sent the message."

"Oh. Yes, that's right. And, are we, too, required to go with them and find the entire troop of your people?"

"Áa. But, not required. We could remain here if we choose."

"We could?"

He nodded.

"Then, I think we should stay here. After all, we must be considerate of Mr. Henrik's condition, as well as his daughter,

Liliann. Truly, I had thought we would stay here—you, me and my brother and sister, as well as Liliann and your friend. It was my understanding your people would go on, but we would remain here, still doing all we can to save Mr. Henrik's life. After all, we cannot simply leave Mr. Henrik alone, with only his daughter to hold his hand."

Again he grinned at her before saying, "And, so we should be required to stay here, if what you say were true. But, did you not see the happiness of your friends when we first entered camp?"

"Ah, no. What happiness?"

Stands Strong pointed toward the pool, then replied, "Our medicine men have been praying and using their own individual medicine to help your Mr. Henrik. When we came back into camp, did you not see your father's man is now awake? He was even sitting up. *Niitá'p,* so much better is he, any weakness he had will be gone within a few weeks. He lives."

"Oh my." Czanna gulped. "He lives. And, here I thought he might… Oh, this is a happy day. A happy day, indeed!"

Looking up, she smiled at Stands Strong. But, he merely nodded and turned away, motioning to her to follow.

However, after a moment, he turned back toward her and said, "I will have to teach you how to look and see what is there to be seen. It will be my honor to do so. Come, now. I will take you to my almost-mother."

And so, she followed him, hoping what Stands Strong said about being welcomed into his family were true. Still, she worried…

## CHAPTER FOURTEEN

Sharon watched as the two families formed into several lines spread out upon the prairie to ride or to walk toward the established rendezvous point with the rest of the tribe. Remembering again how each member of the family—even the children—had touched her shoulder as they had left, and had each said to her, "*Ákáá,*" which she had later discovered meant, "perfect, complete," had so greatly affected her, she had been struck again by the incongruity of what she had been led to believe about these people.

*Ill-mannered? Ungodly? Nothing is further from the truth.*

Yet, she worried, not knowing what her place would be amongst these people. What would be expected of her? And, what would happen to her if she were to fail to meet their expectations?

Would she become the object of gossip? Would they shun her?

Oh, where was Stands Strong?

Though she knew Stands Strong had been rushed a little earlier when he had left her, as well as her little sister and Liliann, alone, she wished she had asked him more about what was expected of her today. He had said only, "Stay here until I return."

But, he had taken off so quickly that she hadn't thought to inquire about when he planned to return nor what she should do in his absence.

*Stay here until I return…*

Standing here so close to Sacagawea Springs and watching the families move away from her, Czanna studied each person closely, hoping to catch a glimpse of Stands Strong. But, when she could not pick out his image in the long line of people, she worried even more.

*Where was he?*

Surely, he had not already joined the Pikuni scouts from the main column of the Pikuni people without telling her, had he? Recalling that earlier, after they had returned to camp, Stands Strong had told her about his chiefs calling upon him to scout for the tribe, she now wondered if he had been given a moment to find his almost-mother and ask for her help.

Were his duties as a scout so great that he might have forgotten?

Still, he had told her he would return, and, so far, she had never known him to say he would do a thing and then not do it. Also, in all this time she had known him, though short, he had made it a point to stay close to her.

Her thoughts were weighing more and more heavily upon her, when, in the distance, she saw him coming toward her; he was leading two ponies by their reins, while his almost-mother, whom she had already met, rode astride one of those mounts. Czanna's brother, George, also accompanied him.

All of her apprehensions faded as soon as Stands Strong came within hearing distance, and she had greeted him with a warm smile. He returned the gesture, then turned to help his almost-mother—who was carrying the baby on her back—from her horse. Only then did he step toward Czanna.

Drawing in close to her, he reached out to take her hand in his own and he whispered, "Amongst my people, it is not done to show too much affection where all can see. But, I fear I have left you waiting too long."

"It is true what you say," Czanna had answered. "I admit I was a little nervous of your return, but now you are back, it is forgotten."

He nodded, then said, "As I told you earlier, George and I will help the others to scout—"

"You will? You are taking George? But, I thought it is I who is always to be the one to help you scout. Why do you not let George stay here with the others, while I come with you?"

When he frowned at her, she explained, "How else am I to learn if you do not take me with you?"

Reaching out to her, he took hold of a lock of her hair and twirled it around his fingers before he replied, "There will be much time to teach you to scout once we return to our people and camp next to the fort. For now, you are needed here, and I hope you will honor me by remaining with my almost-mother, who is anxious to know you better. George and I have come here, also, to help First Rider carry your father's man to the wagon. My almost-cousin, Howling Wolf, has returned from his successful pony raid and has agreed to drive the wagon. This will help to give you the time to be able to talk to my almost-mother, whose heart is joyous at the prospect of speaking to you."

"Oh, I see. I thank you, and of course I will stay here with your almost-mother. I am as anxious to talk with her, and perhaps as you say she is wishing to speak to me. But, if I had a choice in the matter, I would be with you, my husband."

"And I, you. However, the time to do this is not now." Letting go of the lock of her hair, he reached out for her hand and brought it up to his lips, where he proceeded to kiss first her fingers, then her palm. "We must be on our way. The others are already well ahead of us. Once we settle your father's man into the wagon, we will move out quickly; the three of us will stay with you until you reach the other members of my family, and then all three of us— George, First Rider and I—will join the other scouts. You are now with my family. They will ensure your safety."

What could she say? She didn't know, and so she simply smiled. But, deep within her was still a worry. The losses of her brother and her parents were too great to easily sustain losing another one so very beloved; and she experienced again the desire to not let this man out of her sight.

If it meant she would have to learn how to scout, then she would do it. If only he would let her do it, and now, which he didn't seem inclined to allow her to do.

*If only…*

The distant laughing of several children, who were passing by her, caused Czanna to remember where she was and that this man had never failed her. Besides, she was not the only person this man loved. His love for his family, his tribe and his close friends, which included her brother, George, was heart-felt and was an undeniable strength of his nature.

She realized she would do well to add the power of her own spirit to his.

With her hand held firmly within Stands Strong's, and, with him positioned so closely to her, she was aware her worries were dissipating. And then, realizing how much George would benefit from Stands Strong's guidance, she felt her objections evaporate as water does to the warmth of the sun.

She said, "You are wise, my husband. I will welcome speaking with my almost mother and I know George will benefit from being with you."

He squeezed her hand and grinned at her, and, as she gazed up into his dark eyes, she said, "I am so glad I was, at last, wise enough to marry you. I love you so much!"

"And, I, you." And then, despite the others looking on, he kissed her.

****

"I cannot begin to tell you how happy we are, all of us, to welcome you and the rest of your family to ours."

## She Brings Beauty To Me

"Thank you," said Czanna, then smiled at Stands Strong's almost-mother, Sharon.

"There are many of us, I fear," said Sharon. "The other women in our family would also like to be walking with us, since they are all curious to know you better. But, we have decided all five of us might overwhelm you, and it is our wish to comfort you and allow you to come to know us gradually."

"This is, indeed, very kind of you all," replied Czanna. "And, I thank you for the consideration."

Sharon smiled. "Although I know we have only just met, I am hoping you might permit me to tell you a little about our family."

"This would, indeed, be favorable," replied Czanna.

"Good. I thank you, and I will try not to bore you with too many familial details—only enough so you will feel welcome. I suppose the best way to start is to begin with us, the women in the family. There are five of us in the immediate family, and now six, including you. Four of the women in our family married into the Pikuni tribe, having come from another tribe or other cultures. And now, with you, there are five of us."

"Oh my. Are you speaking of the family of Chief Chases-the-enemy?"

"Indeed, I am. There are many people in the entire family: grandfathers and grandmothers, as well as cousins, aunties, uncles, nieces and nephews. But, I think it wise to keep my story to your more immediate relatives, and these are: my husband, Strikes Fast, who is Crow; myself and our children—we have five children including the baby girl you see on my back. The oldest of our children is Stands Strong, who is Lakota by birth."

"Yes, my husband told me about his heritage, and about you, too, when we first met."

"Did he, now?"

"Indeed, he did. Because I am obviously not Indian, he asked me if I were your friend and if I was looking for you. I think he could not understand what I—a white woman—was doing all alone, and on a bluff overlooking the prairie."

"Yes," said Sharon. "I can imagine you took him by surprise."

"I think I did. But, I am very glad we met as we did, if only because later we were to need his help very much. I will never forget how he came to our aid, and to the support of my father's manservant, Mr. Henrik."

"I am happy to hear this," said Sharon. "I did not realize how the two of you came to know one another. But, I can only imagine how you must have felt at first; he probably scared you."

Czanna laughed. "That he did. Quite so. But, my fear of him lasted only a little while. As we spoke, he set me at my ease. But, please, tell me more about my new family. I fear I have dominated our conversation when I very much wish to come to know more about Stands Strong's family."

"It is your right to dominate the conversation," said Sharon, and she smiled. "It is your family now, also. In truth, I would like to ask more, but I do not wish to pry. I love my almost-son as though he were of my own blood, and so of course I like to hear him spoken about in such a loving way."

"I, too, like to speak of him. He does tend to tease me a great deal."

Sharon laughed. "And, so it has been his way for as long as I have known him. He has a good heart. I only wish…"

After a long pause, Czanna asked, "Yes? You only wish…?"

"I am sorry. I do not wish to burden you with my own problem. We have much time to get to know one another. And, I think it best if I tell you about us and about how excited we all are to welcome you into our family."

"Indeed, I would like to hear this…very much."

"Good, then let me tell you about all your new relatives—at least those who are closely related to you now. Well, I have told you about myself and my husband, Strikes Fast. So, let me continue with my dear friend Amelia and her husband, Gray

Falcon, who is a medicine man. They have three children, who are very excited to meet you," continued Sharon. "Next, we come to Amelia's sister, Laylah, who is married to the well-respected medicine man, Eagle Heart, and they have four children. Eagle Heart is also Chief Chases-the-enemy's younger brother, and it is Chief Chases-the-enemy who is the head of our family's clan.

"Now, as for Chief Chases-the-enemy's intimate family, he has two wives, and between his two wives, he has eight children. As you have probably become aware, some Indian men take more than one wife."

"Yes, I know, although Stands Strong has promised me he will not marry another woman. As you know, it is against our religion, and I could never marry a man who believes he could take another wife."

Sharon grinned. "Yes, I had a similar objection. And so, my husband has also promised this to me, as have Amelia's and Laylah's husbands. Indeed, Stands Strong knows well our beliefs—I have ensured this—so I am certain this came as no surprise to my almost-son.

"But, in truth," continued Sharon, "most Pikuni men take only one wife. Chiefs, however, who are duty bound to entertain guests and many other people from various different tribes, require a great deal of work from their women...too much work usually. Most women, who then are married to a chief, appreciate her man marrying another woman, if only to have another to share in the tremendous work imposed upon them. But, sometimes other men take a second or third wife because our men are prone to go to war, and so we lose many of our men in battles.

"Someone, you see," said Sharon, "must take care of the widows. Also, the brother of a man is oftentimes responsible to marry his deceased brother's wife and to provide for her, unless the woman marries another."

"Really?"

"Yes," said Sharon. "There are no servants and no slaves here. This is the reason for the custom. And so, sometimes it is the wife of a man who will ask her husband to marry another, often her own sister, so as to get help with the workload."

"But," asked Czanna, "if there are no servants or slaves, and if our husbands can only marry once, who is there to help us with the work expected of us?"

Sharon grinned. "All the people know of our religious beliefs and honor them. So, do not fear. There are many who will help. After all, all of our men have sisters, aunties, mothers, grandmothers and nieces. And, there are some widows who do not ever wish to marry again. All these might offer to help, and if they do, our husbands ensure they have good lodges to live in and meat enough so they do not go hungry. And, we women tend to help each other even if not related by blood. It is, after all, a time for us to get together and gossip or talk about many different matters...many of which are our men or the boys who go courting."

Sharon laughed, and Czanna giggled, saying, "It sounds like fun."

"It is," admitted Sharon. "But, don't tell our husbands. They think we are so overworked, they often volunteer to help us, also."

Czanna chuckled and said, "I will remember this."

"Yes, I know this may all seem confusing, but after a while, I think you will be very happy here," Sharon said. "Most usually the Pikuni men love their wives deeply and devote themselves to pleasing them, and so life here can be very pleasant, indeed."

Czanna gazed at her almost-mother-in-law and grinned. "I am very happy to hear it," she said.

In response, Sharon laughed. "But, returning to our most intimate family, I should probably first tell you about the man who is already known to you, First Rider. Although his mother is one of Chief Chases-the-enemy's wives, she is not Pikuni. She is Crow, and her son's father was also Crow."

"Really? They are Crow?"

"Indeed, they are. And, even though the Crow, as a tribe, are traditional enemies, they are still welcomed here. It was Chief Chases-the enemy, Eagle Heart and Gray Falcon who welcomed my husband, his sister and his sister's son into the family. It is a long and exciting story of what took place to bring them here, but this tale is for another time."

"Ah, I understand. But, what about Chief Chases-the-enemy's first wife?" asked Czanna. "Did she not object to her husband taking another wife?"

"Indeed, it is not so," answered Sharon. "You see, Little Dove, who is my husband's sister, was in a bad way when she came here, her own husband having been killed. And then, having almost lost her son, as well as then being required to come and live in what is considered by the Crow people to be a hostile tribe... Well, as you can imagine, it was not easy. My husband, her brother, accompanied her here to ensure she would be well taken care of.

"But, his concern was for naught. All was well, you see," continued Sharon. "Morning Sun Woman, the chief's first wife, is one of the sweetest and the kindest of all the people in our band of the tribe, and she welcomed Little Dove and her son into their family with an open heart. It is said she has cared for Little Dove as though she were her own sister."

"Goodness! It seems incredible," said Czanna. "And so, if I understand this correctly, First Rider is by blood Crow, but by tradition is now Pikuni?"

"Yes, this is true. But, let me tell you a little more so it does not seem to be too unusual. Little Dove is my husband's only living Crow relative. It is he who told me about his sister's first coming to the Pikuni tribe. Apparently, she was afraid to meet her new husband's first wife. This is because both she and the chief became united together for many months following the trail of her son's abductor."

"Abductor?"

"Yes.  As a babe, First Rider had been stolen by an enemy tribe.  And, it is this story I wish to tell you at some length once we have, ourselves, become more acquainted.  But, as it happened, the chief's first wife had no knowledge of why her husband was missing, and so she was in mourning, fearing her husband had been killed.  This is why Little Dove—my husband's sister—expected the chief's first wife, Morning Sun Woman, to hate her on sight.  But, it was simply not to be."

"I am glad," replied Czanna.  "However, I can understand why Little Dove might have thought this."

"Yes, to be sure.  But, those fears were quickly put to rest.  Truly, Morning Sun Woman was so happy to see her husband again, alive and well, she barely took notice of Little Dove.  And then, upon learning of her husband's and Little Dove's plight in rescuing the baby—the young man you know as First Rider—Morning Sun Woman took pity on Little Dove and welcomed her into the family with a full and loving heart.  She and her husband's kindness helped Little Dove through many trials in the beginning."

"This is very good," said Czanna.  "Yet, it still seems incredible to me.  But, my, what a story this is.  First Rider was abducted as a baby.  I did not know this, but then I have seldom had cause to speak to him.  Might I please ask who abducted him?"

"Of course you can, although we seldom speak of it."

"Really?  Why is this?"

"I fear it is because his captor was from an unusual tribe."

"Oh?" asked Czanna.

"Indeed it is true," said Sharon.  "His captor was a female from the tribe of Big People."

"Big People?  I have never heard them."

"Yes, this doesn't surprise me," Sharon replied.  "They are different from us in many ways, and they tend to keep to themselves.  But, she did take Little Dove's son."

"And, the chief helped her to regain the boy?"

"Yes," answered Sharon.

"And, did you not say Little Dove's first husband was no longer alive when this happened? Is this why the chief had to come to her aid?"

"Yes, it is so. As the story goes, when Little Dove's son was taken, no one else except the chief was near enough to hear her pleas. This is why he came to her defense. But, the task to rescue the boy took many months, and, as you might imagine, being forced into one another's company, the chief and Little Dove came to be closely united. In the end, they married, the chief adopting First Rider as his own son.

"Now, continuing on with our family, the chief already had one son with his first wife, Morning Sun Woman. This son is not much older than First Rider, and his name is Medicine Fox. One might suppose there might have been great animosity between the two boys, since they are not related at all by blood.

"But, it is not so. Medicine Fox seems to have inherited his mother's kind heart as well as his father's empathy for others, and so the two boys grew up as almost-brothers and have remained closely knit to one another even to this day."

"My goodness. It seems as if there are many adventures to be had in this country. Indeed, listening to this, it puts my own plight into proper perspective. Please allow me to tell you how happy I am for enlightening me with a little of the history of my new family."

"It is my pleasure to do so. Little Dove is one of your almost-aunties. And, because she is married to Chief Chases-the-enemy, both he and his first wife, Morning Sun Woman, are part of your family now, too. I think you might come to love them all as much as I do."

"Oh my," declared Czanna. "I admit it is quite a good feeling to have so much family, even if they are only related by adoption. But, please tell me about the two other women who are white and who have also been adopted into the tribe."

"Indeed, I will. Also, I think you might find that family, even if only by adoption, is still thought of as a relation, regardless of being a blood relative or not. And, the relationship is just as loving.

"But, let me now begin my story about Amelia and Laylah," Sharon went on to say. "Laylah," continued Sharon, "is the wife of the medicine man, Eagle Heart, who, again, is the chief's younger brother. Laylah was the first white woman to marry into the tribe, and not only was she welcomed with kindness into Eagle Heart's entire family, she has since gone on to become a medicine woman and is almost as well-known as her husband.

"And, then there is Amelia, Laylah's sister," Sharon carried on. "She met her husband, Gray Falcon, when they were little more than youngsters in their teens. Although Gray Falcon's family welcomed her into the fold of their lives, it was Gray Falcon, himself, who was not convinced Amelia would make him the kind of wife he thought he was expected to marry. You see, his family has a long lineage of medicine men. And so, Gray Falcon was uncertain Amelia would be welcomed. However, love will have its way, and Amelia was accepted wholeheartedly by his family. In truth, they are one of the happiest married couples in the tribe.

"As for me, I met Amelia when she was living in St. Louis, and I remember how determined she was to return to Indian Territory. Because I looked upon her as a sister—though we are unrelated by blood—I could not let her endure the journey back into Blackfeet Country unattended. I had thought in the beginning of the journey that I would return to St. Louis once she was settled, but it was not to be. I met my husband, Strikes Fast, through his heroic deeds on my behalf; he saved my life several times. And, I fear I love him so dearly, I would brave any calamity to keep him with me. It was hard for my husband at first to live amongst the Pikuni, since he is Crow and the Pikuni and the Crow tribes are at war. But, there are some friendships that rise above all feelings of hostility. Such is the friendship of your almost-father-in-law, Strikes Fast, with the medicine men, Eagle Heart and Gray Falcon. It is they who adopted Strikes Fast into their family. And, it is because of his friendship with these two medicine men that my husband came into his own power as a medicine man.

"And, so you see," Sharon went on to say, "the family you can now call your own is a diverse, yet a kind and powerful people. Now, I admit it is probably a little too much to take in all at once because our family is large, but it is my wish for you to find as much happiness with my almost-son, Stands Strong, as I have found with my husband. Please know this: we love you already, and we will do all we can to make your life amongst us as joyful as we are able."

Czanna, listening to her almost-mother-in-law, felt a little overwhelmed, it is true. But, Sharon's kind and calming ways made it a little easier to understand how similar their families were to her own.

In truth, they set her so much at her ease, she found she was unable to speak for a moment. And, with this knowledge came another thought: although she had so recently lost most of her family, she now had attained a new one, and apparently a good-hearted one.

For several moments, Czanna hesitated to say anything more. Instead, she found it easier to merely nod, while also trying her best to smile. Such graciousness and generosity was hardly what she had expected of these people.

Into the silence between them, her almost-mother murmured, "We are very close, you know."

Czanna didn't reply at once, but in due time she asked, "Are you speaking of Stands Strong and yourself?"

"I am," replied Sharon. "If you will bear with me, I'd like to tell you a little about how Stands Strong came to live with us, since he is a Lakota man living amongst the Pikuni. Have I overwhelmed you with all our history, or would you like to hear a little about my almost-son, your husband?"

"Oh, yes, please," Czanna was quick to say. "I would very much like to hear what you have to say. You see, Stands Strong has told me a little about his heritage, but I would be pleased, indeed, if you would tell me more."

"*Soka'pii*, good, very good," said Sharon. "It is what I had hoped you might say, and I am glad. Please allow me to tell you yet another story, a very important one about how Stands Strong came into our lives. It is about how we first came to know one another and how he became our almost-son. It is important to me because...well..."

"Yes?" asked Czanna. "You mentioned before about there being a problem. Won't you please tell me about it now? I promise I will do no more than listen."

Sharon glanced away and sighed before saying, "I should not be bringing it up to you now. I can only hope you will forgive me. This is all so new to you, and I should not have even mentioned it."

"But," answered Czanna, "since I am married to him now, perhaps it is best for you to tell me. Won't you, please?"

Again Sharon sighed. "Yes, there is a problem, and I think it weighs on my almost-son, although I doubt Stands Strong has told you about it. He tends to speak little of it. It is not his way to do so. Yet, I am aware of it and know it troubles him."

"He did tell me about him asking for the hand of Good Shield Woman. Is it about this?"

"I fear it is not," answered Sharon, "although I believe God has ways of bringing people together whom He knows will lift up the spirits of both people. And, although I knew well how brokenhearted my almost-son was when Good Shield Woman married another, I thought then that perhaps God knew there was another yet to come, one who might be able to bring my almost-son closer to finding what he has always sought. I think you are the one."

"Oh my. Me? The one? Thank you for your so-gracious compliment. And, although I am appreciative of your praise, I

## She Brings Beauty To Me

think, perhaps, I am not the one. After all, I am only a woman who loves your son, and with all my heart. I have no power other than this."

Czanna's almost-mother looked askance at her and smiled. She said, "And yet, love, itself, is a healing power. Love, it is said, can heal any breach."

"Oh? There is a breach?" asked Czanna.

"There is, I fear," answered Sharon. "But, I go before myself. Let me first tell you — if you would like to hear — about how Stands Strong and I came to know one another, for it is this which causes us to be devoted to one another."

"Yes," said Czanna. "Please."

"*Soka'pii*. This means 'good' in the Blackfoot tongue, by the way. Well, the story starts out in perhaps a bad way, but please do hear me out. It is not bad. Although I think God tries to bring people together smoothly, sometimes it simply isn't possible to do so without a little 'bad' to season the relationship. But, I also believe He knows the injury experienced at first will turn to good, and I have often thought that perhaps the ways in which we find one another might be the only manner He can bring us to know one another."

Czanna felt she was close to tears, so kind and gentle was Stands Strong's almost-mother's voice. Was it any wonder why Stands Strong spoke so highly of her?

Breathing in deeply as though to collect her thoughts, Sharon began, "My story with your husband starts when he was only seven years of age. At the time, I saved Stands Strong's life, and, many days later, he saved mine," said Sharon. "In those days, he was known as Rising Bear. But, this was before he had earned a strong warrior's name. Here, let me dig through my pouch and show you this gift he made for me when he was only seven years old. He fashioned it with my husband's help, I am told, because he wished to give me what the Indians call 'medicine,' and also he thought it would bring me the blessings of his god."

Czanna nodded, looking sideways at this pretty woman. Indeed, she, being about Czanna's height, was unusually beautiful, with her tawny, reddish-blonde hair caught in braids at both sides of her face. She appeared to be in her early thirties, and she was also slim in figure—a feat, considering she had birthed four children within the last fifteen years.

But, Czanna didn't wish to stare—it being the height of bad manners—and she returned her gaze to the front, squinting and staring ahead of her, seeing without really seeing the colorful parade this family made as they rode, skipped or paced forward in this, their journey to connect back to the main branch of the Pikuni tribe.

Gazing back toward her almost-mother-in-law's back, Czanna caught the eye of the babe Sharon was carrying in a cradleboard; this way of carrying a baby left her almost-mother's hands free to look into her parfleche bag. Still looking at the baby as the little girl gazed out upon the world from the safety of her mother's back, Czanna saw a child who appeared to be quite happy. Catching the babe's eye, Czanna smiled and received a grin in return.

"Excuse me, Czanna," said Sharon. "I seem to have left the statue made by Stands Strong with my other things. Please allow me to retrieve it. For a reason I do not quite understand, I think it is important to show it to you. I should be only a moment or two."

Czanna smiled. "Yes, of course. I do hope you will find it; I would like to see it. It must be very precious."

"Indeed, it is," said Sharon. "Excuse me, please." And, with these few words, Czanna's almost-mother-in-law hurried away, her pace quick as she made a path toward her friends and family.

## CHAPTER FIFTEEN

Czanna was watching her almost-mother when she became aware of the laughing of several children who were passing by her. Smiling, she watched them for a while. Then, she looked forward, espying Liliann, who was carrying Briella in a cradleboard—a gift from First Rider—on her back. Czanna couldn't help but notice Liliann was keeping her pace close to the speed of the wagon, and, since Czanna was walking behind the girl, she studied her almost-sister, noting Liliann's wavy, pale blonde hair was loose and was blowing in the slight wind.

How pretty, she thought, was her almost-sister. It was odd. Once, Stands Strong had commented upon Liliann's youthful beauty, and Czanna had felt a tinge of jealousy at the time.

She no longer thought this way. Basking in Stands Strong's love had brought about many pleasant changes within Czanna's nature, and she felt very much richer because of it.

Czanna wondered if Howling Wolf—one of the older Pikuni boys and a son of Eagle Heart and his wife, Laylah—was enjoying the task of driving the wagon. He had recently returned from a successful raid to regain stolen horses. But, at present, he appeared to be happy to assume the duty of driving the wagon, thus allowing Mr. Henrik to sit as comfortably as possible within the back of it.

Despite her earlier worries, Czanna had to admit the day had turned into a beautiful, sunshiny afternoon, the sun being bright and warm even though it was now the latter part of the afternoon.

But, oh, how she yearned to have Stands Strong here beside her, and—

"Mistress, where be ye a goin'?"

Czanna looked up at Mr. Henrik, who was sitting upright in the back of the wagon. She smiled at him before replying, "We are accompanying the Indians to the main procession of the Blackfeet, where we hope to join them as they journey to Fort Benton. And, let me say again how happy I am to see you on the mend. I fear you have given us quite a scare."

"'Tis true, Mistress. 'Tis true. Me own daughter, who be walkin' there next to thee, was tellin' me how close I was to death's door, right enough. But, these here Indians…I owe me life to them and to thee. Ye did well to join up with 'em, Mistress. Ye did well. Thy father would be proud of thee, if'n he knew."

"Thank you, Mr. Henrik."

"It be true, Mistress," said Liliann as she kept pace beside Czanna. "Thine own father would be proud of thee."

"Proud!" shouted Briella, and then she giggled.

"Czanna! Almost-daughter! I have it!"

Czanna looked up to see her almost-mother hurrying toward them, the baby on her back laughing, perhaps because of all the jostling movement caused by the quickness of her mother's pace.

Czanna continued to watch as her almost-mother fell into step beside them and caught her breath. After a short pause, Sharon said, "I found it. I had placed the statue for safekeeping into a different bag because the bag contained a blanket which I thought would keep it from breaking."

"I am glad you have found it," said Czanna as she observed her almost-mother reach into the parfleche pouch over her shoulder, there to draw out a wooden object. The statue was painted white and was perhaps ten centimeters in height. Looking at it closely, Czanna could see it was the carved image of a white bear.

Czanna smiled. "My goodness! It is beautiful! If Stands Strong made this when he was only seven years old, he was then, and is still, an artist."

"Yes," agreed his almost-mother, Sharon. "He is an artist as well as being the best scout within our tribe."

"Yes," said Czanna. "I am aware he is a scout; it is good to know he is the best. He is trying to teach me how to do it, actually. And, though I think I understand a little of what a scout is, perhaps you might enlighten me about what the duties of a scout are?"

"Of course," answered Sharon. "But, did I hear you correctly? He is teaching you to scout?"

"Well, yes, but only because I have insisted on accompanying him when he goes on any of his excursions."

"You have? Really?"

Czanna cleared her throat. "Yes, but... It is a little complicated," she said. "I...I and my brother and sister are the last of our family, you see. We are fleeing from oppression in our homeland, and after I was informed of my mother's, my father's and my brother's deaths back in Hungary—and then there was Mr. Henrik, too, whom we thought might die... And then I met Stands Strong and he decided to help us because we would have obviously perished without his aid. You see, we come from an entirely different world than this one, and we found this land to be filled with all kinds of dangers we didn't understand, and I...well, after sustaining so many losses, I didn't wish to have Stands Strong leave us and perhaps to never come back. I...ah...I insisted on accompanying him wherever he were to go, to...ah...guard him, if you will."

Sharon laughed wholeheartedly before saying, "This must be a first for my almost-son, I am sure. No wonder he is so much in love with you."

Czanna felt the blood rushing to her face, and she looked away.

But, Sharon was continuing to speak and said, "Do not be embarrassed, please. I am sorry if I have caused you to feel uncomfortable. But, I thought you knew. When we saw him rescue your sister and when he looked at you across camp and was not able to take his eyes from you, and you were looking back at him, well, his love for you and yours for him was obvious to us all. And then, when you both left together, there was great happiness in our camp because, you see, he is very beloved to us all. And, we already love you as much as we do him."

Czanna's eyes teared as she gazed at her almost-mother. For a moment, she couldn't speak. But, in time she said, "Thank you. But, I should tell you I have never sewed a garment in my life, nor have I ever cooked a meal, nor kept house. I feel I should tell you I am quite ill-qualified for whatever is expected of an Indian man's wife. When I was growing up we had…we had…"

"Servants?"

"Yes, Almost-mother. Oh, is this correct? Should I call you Almost-mother?"

"Of course you can," said Sharon. "But, also addressing me as Sharon is very good, too. We women — we three who married into the tribe — call each other by name, although the Indians never do this. They address each other by whatever their relationship is, be it a cousin or a sister or some other relation. But, we three who knew the European world before this one address each other as we always have. It makes it easier."

"Wonderful. This is good to know, and thank you."

Sharon nodded, then said, "But, if you would be so kind as to permit me, I would like to tell you a little about this statue and why it is a treasure and why I am anxious to tell you its story."

"Certainly," said Czanna.

Sharon caught hold of Czanna's arm and said, "Please, let us fall behind the others so I might speak to you privately."

Czanna nodded. "Yes, of course. I would welcome this."

As soon as they were well to the rear of and out of the others' hearing, Czanna's almost-mother began, "What happened took place about fifteen or sixteen years ago. The man you now call Stands Strong was only a boy of seven then, and his name at the time was Rising Bear, as I have already told you. My husband, Strikes Fast, and I had only been recently married, and we were escaping a war party of eight Cree warriors, who were determined to find us and kill us. We took refuge in the Bears Paw Mountain range.

"One day, while my husband was away from camp hunting, I heard a scream. There were no other people around us, but when it came again and it sounded like a human cry, I went to investigate. This was when I saw your husband, who, as a child, had been left by a war party to die. He was trying to return to his people, the Lakota, and had asked God, the Creator, for help. When in trouble, one must ask for His help and must pray.

"Well, help was given him in the form of a female white bear, who stayed with him, giving him warmth when he slept and hunting roots and berries for food to give him. They had come to a river crossing and the river looked frozen from one shore to the other, but once he walked about halfway across the ice, it broke, and when I saw the child, he was desperately trying to hold on to the sharp edges of some floating ice.

"I swam to him and brought him back to shore, for the way was not far and I knew I could save him. But, as soon as we came ashore, some ice that had been hanging from a tall tree above us suddenly broke loose and fell upon me.

"I am told I almost died. I do not remember. All I know is when I awoke, I saw first my husband and then my almost-son, the Lakota boy, Rising Bear."

"Oh my," said Czanna. "There is little wonder the both of you are so close."

"Yes," replied Sharon. "My husband and I decided to ask Rising Bear if he would like to become our almost-son. He cried, as did I too, for, you see, he was without family, his mother and father having been killed by those who had left him to fend for himself or to die. But, there is more to the story."

Czanna nodded and remained silent.

"Your husband, then only seven, saved my life a little later. He did this in two ways. When we were finally tracked by the Cree warriors and confronted by them hostilely, one member of the war party came on to kill me. Rising Bear, though only seven, came to my rescue, confronted the man and shot his tiny arrows at him. But, though his arrows did little harm to the warrior, Rising Bear had also sent out a silent cry for help, which was shortly answered by the white bear. I, with my gun, and Rising Bear, with his bow and arrows, had tried to hold the man back, but when the white bear came in answer to my almost-son's plea, the Cree warrior fled, while the white bear ran quickly after him.

"And so, you see, after these encounters, we became very close. Sometimes I think we are closer knit than we might have been were we even blood related."

Czanna paused, unknowing of exactly what to say. At last, however, she murmured, "As I mentioned earlier, when I first met your almost-son, he told me about you, his almost-mother, because he thought, being white myself, I knew you and so was perhaps trying to find you. He offered to take me to you."

"He has always been kind, though sometimes a little mischievous."

"Yes." Czanna smiled. "I know," she agreed, then laughed. "When I first met him, I asked him how he had received his name, and, reluctantly, he told me. But, he told me little more than his standing up to a warrior, full grown, in order to try to save you. I am glad you have related the entire story to me."

"Yes. Thank you. But, I fear there is more."

"There is?"

"Yes, indeed. But, perhaps now is not the time to tell you the rest since I see in the distance we are about to meet up with the others of the tribe. If you would be so kind as to join me this evening, after camp has been set up and the others are visiting each other's lodges, I would be honored if I could tell you the rest."

"Yes, of course," said Czanna. "I admit I would like to hear it all, but I also understand this is impossible to do now. I would be honored, indeed, if we might get together a little later tonight."

"And, so it will be. Later tonight, when the others are visiting, let us speak again."

"Yes," answered Czanna. "Shall I come to your lodge?"

"I think," said Sharon, "you might stay with us until we women can raise up a marriage lodge for you and my almost-son. Perhaps you and I might even encourage our men to go visiting once the children are asleep so we can speak without having to hide our talk from them."

"This, indeed, sounds to me to be a perfect plan. I shall look forward to it. Tonight, then."

Sharon nodded.

## CHAPTER SIXTEEN

Overwhelmed, Czanna looked on as their wagon stopped briefly before joining the main body of the Pikuni procession. Though she had wished to remain as unnoticed as possible, it was not possible to do so—not when her wagon claimed her to be what she was: a white woman.

What would her reception be?

It was an accomplishment to be accepted by Stands Strong's family, who would be somewhat inclined to like her. It was another to realize how alien she felt from the rest of these people.

Still, did she have a choice?

Sooner or later she was going to have come to know these Pikuni people. Perhaps her new family might shelter her in the beginning, but it was for her to make her place beside Stands Strong. And she, who had never washed a dish in her life nor ever placed a stitch into a piece of cloth, was now an Indian man's wife.

What would they think of her? Would they laugh at her? Spurn her?

Czanna set her shoulders back and raised her head as she made a determination: whatever was to come, she would learn it well and she would become good at whatever was required of her…very good, indeed.

Looking forward, she gasped. Why, what was this?

Happy laughter filled the air as she gained sight of the Pikuni's procession moving on toward Fort Benton. My goodness, how many of these people were there?

So long were the lines of the people's movement, Czanna could not see the beginnings of it, nor its ending. Indeed, it looked to be many kilometers long.

And, she and her family were going to join them?

Unfortunately for her, there wasn't another covered wagon in sight. Would she be looked upon as an oddity?

Gradually, their wagon came to a stop outside of one of the moving lines of people who were directly in front of them. And, almost immediately upon stopping, several children came running toward them, surrounding them. The children, though not openly rude, were yet staring at her and at the wagon as though they had never before seen a pioneer's wagon. Only the girls came to surround Czanna, while the boys crowded around Howling Wolf, who was sitting up front on the wagon's seat.

Excited young voices from the head of the wagon were speaking in Blackfeet, their unfamiliar words floating back to Czanna where she stood at the wagon's rear. Unfortunately, the children's foreign-sounding voices had the effect of causing her to feel further alien from them.

Her natural reaction was not to shrink back from them, but rather to lift her head. Soon the young man, Howling Wolf, jumped down from his seat up front and strode to the back. Speaking kindly to the children, whatever it was he said to them had the effect of sending them scattering across the prairie and back to their families.

Turning to Czanna, the young man grinned before saying in English, "They have never seen a covered wagon before and are excited to touch it and find out more about it. I have asked them to return to their mothers."

"Yes," Czanna answered. "Thank you. You speak English?"

"My mother is white, and so, yes, I speak her language, as well as Blackfeet."

When the young man started to turn away, Czanna asked, "Excuse me, but have you seen my husband?"

"We spoke to one another earlier this morning," the young man answered. "But, fear not. He is performing scouting duty. He has tasked me to drive you alongside the procession of our people and to bring you to his almost-mother as soon as we make camp."

"Oh, yes, yes, of course," said Czanna.

He nodded, then turned away to pace back to the head of the wagon. Dimly, she heard the squeak from the front seat as he climbed up into it.

It was with some relief when she espied her almost-mother hurrying back toward them. And, as soon as she paced to within hearing distance, she called out, "I have come back, as you can see. Our people probably make a fearsome sight to you, but I have come here to you now since we have reunited with the main Pikuni line. I hope you will allow me to join you."

Czanna smiled. "I welcome it very much, and I thank you."

Slightly out of breath, her almost-mother smiled, then said, "Perhaps we might finish our talk before the evening fires are lit within our lodges. All my almost-sisters have agreed upon the plan to put up a lodge for you and my almost-son before we attend to our own."

"You have agreed to do this? You will?"

"Indeed, we will. It is only right. You are newly married and should have a lodge of your own; nor should you be required to sleep within the tepee of my almost-son's family…my own lodge. And so, you see, there is a happy night yet to come."

A tremendous feeling of relief flooded through Czanna, for this was very welcome news. She had worried, knowing his almost-mother's lodge also housed several young children.

In response, Czanna heaved in a deep breath before saying, "You are all most kind."

"Thank you. We also decided we must erect a lodge for your father's servant and his daughter. Your young brother will stay in my lodge, if this is agreeable to you."

"It is, indeed, agreeable. It is more than I had hoped for, believing as I did that my father's servant and his daughter would be required to sleep within the wagon. Perhaps my brother would have been required to make his bed within the wagon too, although he seems to have become quite independent of late."

Sharon smiled. "This is good. He is, after all, male and will enjoy many companions of his own age here in camp."

"Indeed, I think he will."

"Ah, at last, my almost-sister's son, Howling Wolf, is turning the wagon in a direction to join in with the rest of the people. We should reach the fort by afternoon, and there we will set up camp. Come, let us follow along behind the wagon as we did before."

"Yes," said Czanna. "I do very much wish to hear the rest of your story about my husband and the white bear, especially since you say there is more to the story. I would like to hear the rest, since there has been mention of it troubling my husband, even to this day. If this be true, will you tell me about it?"

"I will," said Sharon, dropping back out of hearing distance from the wagon. "But, first let me ask if you have knowledge of an Indian boy's adventure into manhood?"

Czanna shook her head. "I do not, I fear," she said.

"Then, please let me tell you about it...even if briefly. You see, Indian boys, after a certain age, endeavor to fast and to dream, so they might obtain an animal protector. This they require as a means of helping them to keep alive when they are confronted by an enemy. Animals have many powers. And, although they are spiritual powers, sometimes their medicine can manifest into the physical realm. Often, animals are called upon by Sun, the

Creator, to help one of the people. And, sometimes a person might call for help, and the help is answered by an animal."

"I admit, this is all so very strange to me," confessed Czanna. "But, I am fascinated. I did not know animals had this kind of power. Although, if I am to be truthful, I have often talked to my horses, and they back to me. Even plants and flowers sometimes speak to me."

"*Soka'pii.* This is good. Perhaps what I am about to tell you will not seem too astonishing, then. But, to return to how a boy obtains his power, it goes like this: when old enough, a boy, along with his father's help, sets up a place where he will not be disturbed and where he can fast and can dream.

"We women and men bring the boy the water he needs to continue his fasting and his prayers, but this water is all he is allowed to have. He prays to the Creator, or Sun—or Old Man, as the Indians here sometimes call the Creator. He tries to sleep and to dream. After several days of fasting, the boy lies down to sleep, hoping his shadow will venture forth into the shadow land where animals and men can still converse. But, I should perhaps tell you what is meant by this kind of dream, for it was strange to me when I first heard of it."

"Yes, please," encouraged Czanna.

"Very well. Now, in this kind of dream state, the shadow of the boy—this is what you or I might call the 'soul'—ventures forth into the shadow world and asks for the help of an animal to be his spirit protector. He sometimes has many adventures in this world, which is the same world we all live in, but different. As a spirit, he can talk freely to all the animals, and they can talk back to him. Even the trees, water and plants can speak to him and he to them.

"Sometimes, even while awake, our medicine men talk to the animals, and they speak back to him. And, always a medicine man talks to a medicine plant, explaining he will not uproot all of its children, so the plant may yet live on. But, for a boy, this is not common to speak to these animals or plants aloud. And so, in his "dreams," a boy's shadow ventures forth, seeking an animal helper without fear, for the boy will not be damaged in this shadow world.

"Always the boy prays to Sun, the Creator, and begs an animal to hear him and become his protector."

When Sharon paused, Czanna asked, "And, has my husband done this?"

"He has," Sharon answered, but didn't say another word further.

After a slight pause, Czanna asked, "And…?"

"There is some trouble about it, and it concerns the white bear, I fear."

Again, Sharon said nothing further, causing Czanna to ask, "What is this trouble?"

"My almost-son has said nothing to you about it?"

"I fear he has not," answered Czanna.

Sharon sighed, but spoke nothing more…until, at last, she murmured, "He believes the white bear is his spirit protector, and yet in none of the wanderings of his shadow has he been able to contact the white bear again."

"Oh?" asked Czanna. "What does this mean?"

"To my almost-son it means that he has lost his medicine helper, the white bear. We know not what happened to the white bear fifteen years ago after our fight with the Cree. We saw her, the bear, only once after the fight was over, and we counselled together, and then never again."

Czanna frowned, but then a thought occurred to her, and she asked, "But, even if the white bear were no longer alive, couldn't my husband find a different animal protector?"

"We, too, thought this way. But, it has not come to be. There is a little more to it also, which I should relate to you, if you would like to hear it."

"I do. Please do tell me all of it."

"Well, as you know, my almost-son is natively Lakota. What we did not have knowledge of for a long while was about his lineage."

"His lineage? Pray, what do you mean?"

"It is simply this: he comes from a long line of Lakota medicine men. But, when his father was killed on that day, fifteen years ago, my almost-son was certain this inheritance, passed down from father to son, was killed, also."

Czanna frowned. "But, wait," she uttered. "Did you not tell me your husband is a medicine man?"

"Yes, it is true. But, they are not related by blood, and sometimes the inheritance passes down from the bloodline alone. In truth," continued Sharon, "I do not fully understand it, and so I have been of little help to my almost-son. All I can tell you is this: in his own mind, Stands Strong has lost the power, and he has lost it twice, once by the killing of his father and once because of the desertion of the white bear, his spirit protector. He does not believe he will ever regain what was once his."

Czanna thought she understood the problem, strange though it seemed to her. However, its oddity brought a question to mind, and she asked, "But, he is still so young. Surely, he could gain it back, can he not?"

"Young, he is. But, when a man believes he cannot master the pain within his soul, he cannot then, in his own mind, do it."

Ah, so this was it; at last she understood. However, Czanna barely knew how to respond to this revelation or what to say. Yes, it was all so foreign sounding to her, and yet this she knew: her dearly beloved, kind and handsome husband was, so he thought, without hope of attaining what should have been his by inheritance. And, coming from a lineage of medicine men, it would naturally follow for him to aspire to the position of medicine man, as well.

At last, Czanna said, "Thank you for telling me about this, Almost-mother. I wish I knew how to help him. But, I do not."

"Nor do I," replied Sharon. "I have tried to change his mind for many years, but it has been in vain, I fear. In truth, I think he now believes all aspects of what should have been his, by rights, is now in his past. As he might say, it is as it is. And, he appears to be happy enough to have the reputation of being the best scout within all our camps.

"Yet, some of his many cousins have their feet upon the medicine path. And, there are many times when I have espied a wistful look within my almost-son's eyes when one of his kin is called upon to heal another. I have sometimes sensed it was his witnessing the fight that killed his mother and his father that is at the root of this.

"Perhaps he felt inadequate because he could not prevent their deaths, even though he was a lad of only seven winters. But, then when he became lost in the Bears Paw Mountains during a blizzard, he found his medicine animal—the white bear—only to be deserted by it...or at least it seems to him as if the bear has deserted him."

Czanna stared out into the vast stretch of prairie extending out before her. Softly, she said, "Yes, I can see the problem, and although I would like to help him with this, I, who have no knowledge of the Indian myths or religious beliefs, would be of little assistance to him, if any at all. Though, of course, I would like to be. Thank you for telling me this and also for taking your time to help me transition into your tribe. I will not forget your kindness."

"And I, yours."

"My kindness?" asked Czanna. "It is your kindness I find special. I have done nothing."

"This is not true. You, with your God-given beauty and your kind ways, have captured the heart of my almost-son. I have truly never witnessed him to be so happy nor so carefree. This is because of your influence. Yours, you see, is a rare heart. I recognized it from the start. Yes, yours is a very rare heart, indeed."

****

Wafting in the warm breeze was the distinctive aroma of perhaps thousands of lodge fires, as well as the delicious fragrance of buffalo ribs roasting over what must have been hundreds of fires. Additionally, the beat of many drums—perhaps hundreds of them—could have been heard miles away. But, it was the sound of both masculine and feminine singing that welcomed Czanna and the others in the Pikuni procession into the encampment of the Blackfoot Confederation.

It was late afternoon when their procession proceeded into the Indian camp surrounding Fort Benton. Looking forward, Czanna espied hundreds, perhaps thousands, of lodges spread out in every direction. So many of them there were, she thought she would be hard-pressed to count them all.

Graceful tepees painted in different colors of red, blue, white, yellow, orange and tan caused the entire plain to appear as though a rainbow had descended to earth. In truth, on all sides of Fort Benton—save its southern edge where the Missouri River flowed—the plains were alit with color from every tepee, and these lodges were stretched out as far as the eye could see.

All at once, the procession's movement stopped at this, the western side of the fort. Then began a different kind of activity, where the women quickly unpacked their horses and began setting up their family's lodges. Meanwhile the younger girls were unpacking and bringing their possessions into the tepees.

Looking back toward the southwest, Czanna could see their encampment would stretch all the way up to the steep and rocky shoreline of the Missouri River, as well as butting up to the hills, buttes and plateaus rising up quite impressively in the west. What was astonishing to Czanna was how many thousands of these lodges were already here encamped. This sight, she thought, of the rainbow-like image of the Indian campsite would forever be engrained upon her memory.

Also, farther out from the lodges, both north and east, were herds of what must have been thousands upon thousands of ponies. And, what seemed incredible to her was how the herd seemed distinctly divided into little groups of ponies, from perhaps a few hundred to maybe thousands.

Indeed, their familial procession, which had seemed so large only a short while ago, looked small now in comparison to the sight of the entire encampment. How many people did the Blackfeet boast?

As though her almost-mother were attuned to her thoughts, she came to stand beside Czanna and said, "There are three different bands of the Blackfeet camped here. There are the Pikuni, divided up into the southern and northern Pikuni; the Blackfoot proper, or *Siksiká;* and the Blood Tribe, or the *Káínaa.* Some of the tribes have been encamped here for several weeks already, awaiting the return of the steamship, which they anticipate will be carrying many items of trade goods. This year, we will make our campsite on the western side of the fort, as you can see. Long before we set out upon the journey to come to the fort, the chiefs of the tribes had counselled together and had established the sites for each of the bands of Blackfeet. These locations change often. The western side of the fort, where we will be this year, is my favorite."

"I can understand why you would say this. What a beautiful stretch of prairie this is. Might I ask if you know if our wagon will remain out here where we camp, along with the rest of the lodges?" asked Czanna. "Or do you think we might be required to bring it into the inner sanction of the fort? And, if I should bring it into the fort, should I do so now?"

"I wish I knew how to answer your questions, but I really do not know," said Sharon. "These matters are determined by the chiefs, and because we have only arrived here, I am uncertain where your wagon should be parked. Perhaps my husband,

Strikes Fast, or Stands Strong will know what has been decided. We shall ask them the first chance we get.

"Meanwhile," continued her almost-mother, "would you like to see how we women erect a tepee?  Several within our tribe have offered to let you and Stands Strong use one of their own lodges because some families have many…for their married children, you see, or perhaps for visitors.  And so, we will not be required to make one now, although I am certain you will wish to have one of your own once you are settled.  I am happy so many of the people offered you the loan of a tepee. In this way, you shall have more of a proper honeymoon."

"Yes, and I thank you and the others.  And, in answer to your question, I would very much like to be involved in setting up the lodge, although I fear I may be of little help.  But, I will try.  What say you, Liliann?  Would you like to help in the setting up of our lodge, as well as your own?  Because, if I understand this correctly, you and your father are to have your own lodge while we are here encamped."

"Yes, Mistress," said Liliann, who had been standing silently beside her.    "I would like to join in with thee.  Very much.  And, are we to really have our own lodging?"

"Yes," answered both Sharon and Czanna, and almost at the same time.

"'Tis most wonderful, is it not, Mistress?  There we were with no one all those weeks ago, and fearful we were, too.  And, now we have so much. I thank thee."

"It is the least we can do," said Czanna's almost-mother. "After all, you and your father are now to be part of our family, too.  It has been so decided."

"Part of your family?"

"Because my almost-son addresses you as his wife's almost-sister, then so it is. Welcome."

Czanna looked on as Liliann burst into tears.  As she stood there, with Briella carried upon her hip, at last she said, though her voice caught on each word, "I thank thee.  I thank thee very much."

Sharon and Czanna smiled.

# CHAPTER SEVENTEEN

"*Be* ye willin', now, ta sell this here wagon, miss?"

To this question, Stands Strong heard his wife correct the man, saying, "I am not selling it, and I am a missus, not a miss. Please understand, I have no intention of selling the wagon at all."

"But, I be willin' ta give ye five hundred fer it."

Stands Strong frowned, recalling only moments ago when, with great enthusiasm, he had been anticipating being with his wife again and the possibility of sharing more lovemaking with her. She was now especially on his mind after having spent several days in scouting. But, what was happening here? Where had all these white men come from? There were at least ten, perhaps twelve of them. Certainly, the steamship had arrived, but why were there so many of these white men here in his people's encampment—and why were they crowding around his wife?

Admittedly, he was accustomed to seeing the French engagées and voyageurs depart from the steamship to be quartered within the fort. But, a quick glance at these men showed each one of them to be neither an employee of the company, nor a trapper or trader.

For one, as a group, they smelled bad, as though they hadn't bathed for perhaps many months. For another, they were an unkempt bunch of men, with long greasy and stringy beards, unwashed and greasy hair and clothing scented with perhaps unmentionable body fluids.

All of them appeared to be of questionable grooming standards, except a few of the younger men who were clean-shaven and were perhaps even handsome. But, why were there so many of them here? And, why were they crowding around his wife?

At first Stands Strong had thought to stand aside from them, if only to escape their stench. But, then he had spotted his wife within their midst.

And, though the words from this noxious crew appeared to reflect that their reason for coming into their camp was the wagon they each one seemed determined to purchase, no one was examining the object in question. Obviously, the attraction was not the wagon, but *his* woman.

One of the younger and better looking of the men said something to his wife to which she laughed, but whatever had been said remained a mystery to Stands Strong. All of his attention was centered upon one concern and one concern only: why was his woman speaking to these men and even laughing with them when she was married to him?

When one of these odorous men stepped forward and placed a hand upon his wife's shoulder, Stands Strong stepped quickly forward and planted himself firmly in front of her, his arms holding his shotgun clutched against his chest. He said in perfect English, "The woman said she does not wish to sell the wagon."

"So? What's it to you, Injun?" The foul-looking man who had asked this question fingered a gun hung down within his belt, and slowly the man lifted the weapon up from its holster.

With the swift and sure reflexes of a trained warrior, Stands Strong thrust his rifle straight up, and, pointing it into the air, fired off a loud and explosive shot. The fact that his action brought several warriors racing in his direction didn't at first register with him. He was only aware of this: he would make a stand here and now. He would not allow his woman to be manhandled by any of these lowlifes.

After all, these men had come into the Indian camp where all men, Indian and white, were equally armed. But, Stands Strong had no time to overly reflect upon this. All he knew was simply this: no one was going to lay a hand on his woman.

"Hey, we's only askin'," uttered one lowlife.

"No need ta go ta war over it," said another.

With several mumbles and grumbles, the stinky newcomers began to retreat, and it was only then, once they had turned their backs upon him, when Stands Strong took note of the Blackfoot warriors who had gathered in back of him and who had taken a stand along with him. Some of these warriors were still aiming their shotguns toward the whites; some had affixed an arrow to a bow pointed directly at these unwelcome men.

Who were these white men? Certainly they weren't traders, nor were they engagées. To his knowledge, no white trader had ever laid a hand on an Indian woman, unless that woman was his wife.

Again he asked himself: who were these detestable men?

But, perhaps a more important question to him at this moment was: why had his wife laughed at some statement made by one of them? One of the youngest and handsomest of them?

Still, although these thoughts were gathering storm clouds within Stands Strong's mind, neither he nor any other warrior made a move to let down his guard until every single one of the offensive and stinky men had returned into the inner sanctum of the fort. But, as soon as the last one was admitted there and the gate was closed, the warriors—who had crowded around him and had given him their support—slowly backed away, many of them grinning.

One of them, Howling Wolf, placed his hand on Stands Strong's shoulder and said, "I should have driven the wagon into the fort. Then, there would have been no trouble."

"It is not your fault. Think no more about it," replied Stands Strong, and, turning around to confront his woman, he said to

Czanna, "Come with me. My relatives have erected a tepee for us. I will show it to you."

When his wife did nothing more than nod, this pleased him very much, and, calmly, with each step deliberate, he led the way to their new lodge. There would be time enough to talk to her without others hearing what he had to say to her.

And, perhaps in the time it took to pace through the camp and out toward the western side of the encampment, his temper would have cooled.

\*\*\*\*

"You are angry with me, are you not?"

"*Saa*, I am not angry with you," answered Stands Strong.

Czanna looked over at her husband with a critical eye. "But," she said, "you are angry."

He grinned at her. "Have I done a deed to make you believe I am angry?"

"Well, for one," said Czanna, "you shot your gun into the air."

"What I used to fire off the shot was my rifle. Not a gun."

"Rifle, then," agreed Czanna. "What did I do? I know instinctively that you are angry with me, though you try to hide it."

Czanna looked on as her new husband sighed, then he grunted in his throat, the sound low, much like a growl. She waited for his response, and as she did so, she glanced around their newly loaned lodge. It was beautiful. Absolutely beautiful.

It was much roomier than she would have ever imagined one of these tepees might be. It was probably eight to nine meters across or, as the Americans might say, about twenty-six feet. And, both she and Stands Strong could stand up straight within it with a good deal of room above their heads.

Long and slender, though sturdy poles made the shape of the lodge, and a buffalo hide—which was none too light and consisted of about twenty-eight hides sewn together—kept the interior of the lodge cool. "Ear flaps" at the tops of the poles could be adjusted in order to allow the smoke to rise.

Also, today Czanna had asked and had learned why the outer part of the tepee was slightly raised up from the ground. The reason was because the inner tepee liner—their own being colorfully decorated in shapes of triangles and circles—fell completely to the ground, which allowed air to come in between the outer buffalo hide and the liner, which in turn allowed the people inside to adjust the temperature within the structure.

It was a simple style of architecture, but highly efficient and portable. And, were she to think more deeply about it, she would have to admit it was quite ingenious.

But, at last it appeared Stands Strong was going to answer her, and she gave him her full attention.

"I am not angry with you," he said. "However, I admit I am disappointed."

"What? What have I done to disappoint you?" she asked.

Again, he didn't speak to her at once. Instead, he turned and stepped toward the "men's" side of the tepee; then he sat down, and, gesturing toward her, he invited her to do the same.

When she had at last settled down with her legs together and to the left, he began, and he said, "You allowed these men to speak to you and even laughed with one of the better-looking of them. This is what disappoints me."

"He was not so very good-looking. Not as handsome as you are."

Stands Strong nodded, but not even a hint of a teasing smile crossed over his countenance. At some length, he said, "His pleasant looks are not what causes me to be disappointed. It is your speaking to him at all, and also to the others. When I sought you out, I did not anticipate finding you to be the center of attraction for those men."

"Oh, I see," she said at once. "But, my husband, I have every right to laugh if someone—male or female—makes a joke. It was an honest reaction and quite a good response, I should say."

"Not if the one making the joke is a man when you are a woman," he countered at once.

"Oh, please." She made a face. "It was nothing."

Stands Strong shook his head. "It is not...nothing. Consider this: our tribe is small. Only in the summer do we gather together like we are now in a large group. No one wishes there to be jealousy or fighting between the men of the tribe because of a woman's flirtation with another man." Suggestively, he pointed to his nose. "There could be consequences."

"Flirtation? Are you telling me you think I was flirting with that man simply because I laughed at his joke?"

"Were you not?" he answered with the question.

"This is ridiculous," she uttered, pouring deliberate disdain into her tone. "Are you telling me I am not 'allowed' to talk to the other fifty-percent of the human race simply because I am female and the other fifty-percent is male?"

"I do not know what this 'fifty-percent' is, but this I do know: when we are encamped, yes, you are not to talk to a man unless he is related to you."

She sat unmoving for many moments. At last, she asked, "Are you serious?"

He nodded.

She paused, letting this information seep into her mind, along with other pertinent facts. After a while, she frowned, then said, "Well, I won't do it."

Her husband said nothing at first. And, he sat so still he could have been a rock instead a living being. At last, he said, "My woman, try to understand. You are beautiful. You are white. Many men, Indian and white, would enjoy talking to you, and occasionally they will try to touch you, as one of those men did today. The impulse to do so would be irresistible. And so, if you insist upon this path and speak to any man you please, I think you will bring me much trouble."

Czanna was stunned, and again she found it difficult to speak…but only for a moment. After the slight pause, she said, "Then, I guess you'd better get used to having a lot of trouble in your life, because I will not let you forbid me from speaking to the other half of the human race whenever I please. Further, I would like to point out that women, like men, were endowed by their Creator with the right and the gift to speak to whomever they wish to talk to and about any subject they wish to speak about. What you are asking me to do is against how the Creator made each one of us. And, I will have no part in it."

Again he touched his nose, but it served to only irritate her further, and she asked, "Are you threatening me?"

"I am not," he said. "I am informing you again of our ways."

"Yes, well, they are not *my* ways, and I will not do as you are suggesting. I am a human being, and I have a right to speak to whomever I want, whenever I want and on any subject that I choose."

"Not in this camp."

"Yes, in this camp. Now, let me ask you a similar question: are you allowed to speak to women…to any woman you might choose to speak to?"

"Yes, of course. But, a man, after he is married, does this very rarely, since he does not wish his wife to become jealous."

"All right," she said. "But, let's say he does talk to a woman and makes a joke, and by this, as you have suggested, he creates some trouble. Does he also have to endure the same penalty as the woman?"

"No. We have already spoken about this."

"Then, let me say this to you, Mr. Stands Strong. If a woman is to suffer such a terrible consequence for such a minor error, then the man should also suffer a similar punishment. Indeed, I think this man should have to have something done to him of a comparable nature…perhaps cutting off the end of his nose, too."

The look upon Stands Strong's countenance was not only surprised, it was angry at the same time. And, his voice was suspiciously soft when he asked, "Are you telling me this is what you would wish for me if I were to act as you were today?"

"Of course not," she answered at once. "But, can you not see how silly it would be for me to even bring up such a punishment into our conversation, and all because of the simple act of laughing at a man's joke?"

He frowned at her. "It is not 'silly,' as you call it. Your actions, were you to continue in this manner, could cause both you and me to face much danger. My wife, perhaps you do not understand the nature of a man, and so I will tell you: a man is empowered by your laughter and your conversation, and this could lead to upsets between us, as well as causing me to have to fight men away from you so as to ensure your good reputation."

Once again, Czanna sat mute, stunned into silence. At length, however, she asked, "And so, what you are telling me is a woman, who speaks to a man or who laughs at his jokes, can have the tip of her nose cut off?"

"*Saa*, no, it is not so. It could happen only when a woman makes love to a man who is not her husband."

"Well, I can tell you honestly, this is not going to occur with me."

"Think you not?" he asked. "A man is stronger than you are, and he could force you to do his will, and then he could lie about the woman's struggles to the tribe."

Czanna thrust out her chin and said, "Tell me this: do your people allow the woman involved to have a say in the matter?"

"Not usually, because it is thought the punishment is so severe, she might lie."

"And, the man? Do they not realize the man might lie, as you have suggested?"

Stands Strong didn't answer.

"And so, she has the punishment enforced upon her, while the man walks free to perhaps do the same to another woman."

"I did not say I agree with the custom; I only tell you it is still done to this day."

Czanna sucked in her breath before saying, "I can hardly believe we are having this conversation because one of those men said something funny and I laughed."

"You were not talking to simply one man. You were surrounded by them."

"Not at my choosing," she countered.

"You could have walked away," he quickly uttered.

"And, they would have followed me," she said, defending herself. Then, frowning, she went on to say, "I do not agree with you about this 'custom' done to a woman only and not to a man. If she gets the punishment, then so should he, since he is as guilty as she. Perhaps I might suggest this to the other women in camp and thus bring about its abolishment."

"You will n—" He stopped short of saying whatever had been in his mind to say. Instead, he looked at her across the unlit fireplace, his mouth still open. But, he shut his mouth both quickly and firmly, then stared at her, she back at him.

And so, they glared at one another from over the perimeter of the campfire where no fire had yet been lit. They glowered at each other, and they stared and they stared, neither saying a word. It was as though each one of them had hit an impasse; there would be no compromise between them upon this issue.

At last, he opened his mouth again as though he would say a few more words, but instead of speaking, he jumped up suddenly and, stepping quickly toward the tepee's entrance, bent at the waist and stepped over the entrance flap.

Then, without another word, he trod away.

For several moments, Czanna sat staring at the place where he had left, utterly shocked.

*Dear Lord, what have I done? What have I gotten myself and my entire family into? If I or any of my family should dare to act or speak in a manner unsuitable to the men of this tribe, we could be...*

*Please help me, dear God. Please help me.*

She hadn't really meant what she'd said: she wouldn't really try to organize a women's protest against the custom.

But then, why not? This punishment for women was cruel. It went against all the laws of Nature. How could an Indian man say he lived so closely knit with Nature and not know this simple fact?

Did he not realize she was only trying to cause him to consider what it might feel like if there were a similar punishment for a man?

But, she feared her analogy hadn't worked.

She could only wonder if, indeed, she had come all this way and endured all she had in the name of remaining free only to find she now lacked the right to say what she believed, and to say it to whomever she chose, simply because a man might take it into his head to punish her.

She would not back down. She couldn't.

*Dear Lord, what am I to do?*

****

*Are we going for a run? I'm ready when you are!*

In the silent world of mind-speak, Stands Strong heard his pony's question and answered in the same manner, *No, we are not going scouting or upon the war path today. Be at your ease, Naato Omitaa.*

His pony answered with a light nicker and rubbed his head against Stands Strong's chest. And, Stands Strong, in reaction, petted this, his most treasured friend.

Keeping with the typical warrior mode, Stands Strong had tied his favorite buffalo pony next to his lodge. Standing as he was, so close to the animal, he came to be aware of his pony's wish to be loosed and led into the horse herd, there to enjoy the fresh grass of the prairie as well as the company of the other horses.

Knowing the walk away from the encampment to where the horses were grazing would do him good as well, Stands Strong reached toward the ropes where the pony was tied and began to undo the knots.  But, before he could complete the task, he was approached by a young lad.

Looking up, Stands Strong said, "*Óki napí*, Hello, friend."

"*Óki napí*," returned the youngster.  "I have been sent to bring you to council.  You are needed again in the council of the chiefs, which is still ongoing in the lodge of the chief of the Small Robes band.  I will take you there."

"*Soka'pii*," said Stands Strong.  "I will go with you at once."

"*Soka'pii*," acknowledged the boy, who then turned away to lead the way to the chief's lodge.

"I am sorry, my friend," Stands Strong said in Blackfeet to his pony.  "Perhaps later we will go there."

Naato Omitaa answered with a soft whinny.

And, pushing his own troubles aside temporarily, Stands Strong followed the lad.

Moments later, Stands Strong entered the lodge of the head chief of the Small Robes band of the Blackfoot tribe, and the chief gestured toward a place where Stands Strong should sit.  Oddly, it was at the very back of the lodge—a place of honor.

Pacing to the back of the other seated members of the council, Stands Strong came to the place suggested and sat.  He said not a word, as was the custom, and he looked neither right nor left, as council manners dictated.

What was this about?  He had already given the chiefs his report on what he had seen and what he had discovered while scouting.  And, although the urge to ask this very question was deep within him, he asked no questions and waited patiently for the chief to speak, knowing the inquiries would come soon enough.

It couldn't be about his encounter with the whites this very day, could it? Nothing really out of the ordinary had occurred. The scum had made trouble and had been forced to retreat.

Well, he would wait patiently. He would know soon enough.

After the pipe was passed to him and he had smoked it, taking the oath to Sun to speak truly, he waited. And, as soon as the pipe was passed back to the chief, so began the chief's inquiry.

Said the chief, "Almost-son of the medicine man Strikes Fast, and the first and best scout within our nation, we have further questions we wish to ask you; thus, we have bid you to return to our council so we might ask them of you. I will begin."

Stands Strong barely nodded.

"These gold seekers you mentioned, what did they look like and what did they say?"

As was tradition, Stands Strong waited a moment before replying. In due time, he said, "I did not see the gold seekers; I only know the results of what they did. By my oath to Sun, I will tell you what I know, although some of it was related to me by my newly married wife and her brother. The gold seekers came upon my wife's caravan in the night and convinced a scout, whom we know by the name of Hanson, to betray those who had hired him. This scout, Hanson, drank too much of the white man's poison and, throwing his lot in with the gold seekers, stole all of the gold and silver given to him for his services by the manservant, Henrik, whose duty it was and still is to take my woman's family into the Backbone-of-the-World Mountains to meet with her cousin, whom we all know as Old Tom Johnson.

"This man, Henrik, left my woman and her family alone because he decided it was important to go after Hanson and regain the treasure stolen from him. But, he was shot at several times and was badly wounded; he almost lost his life. He is, however, recovered now, and from this man, Henrik, I learned the gold seekers are heading south and west toward a place known as the "gold fields" to the whites. We know this place to be within

Blackfoot territory, but it is used by all the tribes, and with our consent, for hunting.

"This is all I know of these whites. The man, Henrik, is, as you know, now mostly recovered and could be asked to this council if there is further knowledge required about these men who chase the evil golden rock."

No one spoke, and it was at some length before the chief replied, "You are to be honored for your role in saving the life of the man, Henrik, and for bringing him here. It is as we have all feared since the Stevens Treaty with the whites of only one winter ago. As you all know, we were told by the interpreters that the whites only wished to make a road through our country; that they would not stay nor take anything from us, save their need to hunt for food. As you all know, it was at the place we call *O-to-kwi-tuk-tai*, Yellow River, where this treaty was made.

"But, we were not told all of the parts of the Stevens Treaty. Because the whites chose the interpreters, we were informed only of the part of the treaty that favored us, not the part of it which favored the Blue Coats. I have since asked three of the white women in our camp, who are all married to medicine men, to obtain a copy of this treaty and to read it to us in all its parts. We asked for this because of people like these gold seekers who are swarming into our country and who seem to have no god or morals to prevent them from killing or stealing. As we all have discussed, we have trouble now with these men, since they often come into our camp as though they are friends, only to molest some of our women and young girls. It is because of their actions that we have learned of the deception of the treaty, which I fear many of our chiefs signed.

"It is not right because we were not told about the treaty giving the 'right' for these strangers to enter into our country and to settle upon our lands, taking as much land as they need for their cattle. They were also given the 'right' to make towns upon our lands and to take from it whatever they would need.

"We did not know this at the treaty signing. We trusted our interpreters. Perhaps they, too, were deceived," continued the chief. "We do not know. But now, because of this deception within the treaty, and without our knowledge, we have much trouble. We must now decide what we are to do about this, because, as you know, our warriors now believe it is the whites who have broken the treaty, causing many of our warriors to go on the warpath against their coming onto our hunting grounds and settling down. Some white men have already claimed a part of our land, and some of our warriors have now sworn to go on the warpath against these whites.

"Almost-son of the medicine man Strikes Fast, because of this trouble, we might require your skills again in the future, since you and a few others speak the white man's tongue. For now, we will have to think well on this, and we will need to counsel together again in the near future about what we are to do. As you know, the killing of a white man — regardless of his wrongs against us — could bring us much grief."

Looking directly at Stands Strong, the chief went on to say, "Since you told us of your duty toward your woman, we inquired of the other bands of our tribe about your woman's cousin, Old Tom Johnson. We have now discovered this man's whereabouts from our relatives in the north. This is how we know he is no longer to be found in the Backbone-of-the-World Mountains. Because the beaver are all trapped out where he made his home in the Backbone-of-the-World Mountains, and he has moved to another place. You will now find him in the Bears Paw Mountains. You are free now to take your woman and her family there, and we will speak again when you return, since we may yet need your skills in the near future."

Stands Strong nodded and signed, "Good. It is good."

The chief then brought the council to a close, and Stands Strong, along with the others, filtered out from the chief's lodge.

Stands Strong's first thought was to return to his lodge and let his wife know where they would now find her cousin, but upon realizing he was not yet calm enough to speak to her with good words, he left to visit with his almost-mother and -father.

*Áa, this is a better plan than letting the slip of my tongue further estrange me from my woman.*

## CHAPTER EIGHTEEN

*C*zanna had originally considered waiting until Stands Strong returned, knowing he would come home sooner or later. However, although she was well aware of his "disappointment" in her, she, too, was disillusioned with him.

Was she honestly expected to never again speak to a member of the other gender? And, this was so because of a "custom" a man could use to his own advantage?

No, she would not do it. It wasn't right.

Yes, all creatures should use discretion in a matter concerning jealousy; this she could agree to. But, to have to follow a general rule of never again being able to talk to another man or boy…?

She couldn't, she wouldn't agree to it.

But, on the other hand, she was married to Stands Strong—a man she loved with all her heart. And, if he believed this custom held legitimacy…

*Oh, what am I to do?*

It was the asking of this question that caused her to know what her path must be: she had to leave, if only to gain a few hours of peace. She would walk out of camp and go somewhere away from here; she would find a place where she could come to peace with her own thoughts and fears. Perhaps, she might even envision a resolution between her and Stands Strong.

Yes, this was a good plan, and this was right, but she shouldn't go too far away. However, it needed to be distant enough so the drums and the singing within the camp wouldn't interfere with her own personal soul-searching.

Upon stepping out from their lodge, she beheld Stands Strong's favorite pony tied up next to the tepee.

She was about to turn away when she heard the silent talk from the animal, and it said, "I will go with you. I see you are grieving, and I wish to go with you."

Czanna almost cried, and she felt for a moment as though the animal understood her dilemma. Stepping toward the pony, she placed her head against its own.

And, she said to it silently, "I cannot take you with me. You do not belong to me. Rather, you are my husband's favorite mount. But, your empathy for me brightens my heart."

Naato Omitaa answered her thoughts, saying in the mind-talk, "You should not leave here alone. I will go with you. Your man, my master, will understand. If he does not, I will tell him."

Czanna couldn't help what she did next: she broke into tears. She said, "I…I…"

"Take me with you," the pony insisted.

Czanna nodded, and, reaching out for the knots tying the animal, she quickly untied its bindings; then, taking hold of its reins, she led the pony out of the camp.

****

The sun was only beginning to set in the west, sending up its orange, golden and even red streaks into the sky when Stands Strong at last felt himself able to return to his lodge, there to speak with his wife without being in the throes of anger or resentment. Upon stepping closer to their lodge, he saw his pony was missing.

Gazing at the ground, he could discern at once what had happened: here was the trail of his wife, as well as his pony's, the animal following along behind her. Still, he threw back the tepee flap and glanced inside, confirming what the prints in the earth told him: his wife was gone and she had taken Naato Omitaa with her.

The tracks left upon the earth showed him that she wasn't riding the animal.  Instead, she was guiding it, and his pony appeared to be following her meekly enough.  It was all there to be read upon the earth.

*Soka'pii*, good.  His pony would serve to protect her as well as it could.

He followed their trail easily, her boots alone leaving a distinct impression upon the ground, they being so different from the many other moccasin imprints of the others.  This made following them so easily done he could do it almost without thought.

She was heading in the direction of the western hills, and leisurely he kept pacing along where their path led.  He did not worry about her possible abduction.  No war party would dare come into a Blackfoot encampment where all the people could easily thwart them.

That's when he heard it: his wife's voice, rising up into the air and filling the atmosphere for a good distance around her.  The song she sang was sad; it was consuming also, yet the lyrical notes of the song were so beautiful, they wrenched at his heart.

*Have my words to her provoked this?*

Indeed, it had to be.  How could he think otherwise?

Gently, and without willing it, tears stung his eyes, and he paused, listening to her voice and the melody of her song, so ethereal.  She was singing in English rather than a language he didn't understand, and he lingered there, hidden from her, listening to her words:

*Dear God, help me to understand what I must do.*
*Do I stay?*
*Do I go?*
*I love him so; I must stay with him.*
*But, to stay means I must again change who I am.*
*And, I cannot.  I will not.*
*Dear God, help me to understand what I must do.*

*Do I stay?*
*Do I go?*
*I love him so, and yet to stay requires of me to change who I am.*
*Dear God, help me to understand what I must do...*

The song continued on in a like manner; the timbre of her voice was clear, yet so sad, so exquisite, Stands Strong felt his own heart was breaking by simply listening to her. Again he wondered: was he really the cause of so much sadness within her?

Yes, he admitted; his words, though not unkind, had been laced with the fervor of jealousy. Seeing his wife laugh so merrily with a white—and handsome—man had truly stirred up his vehemence.

But, conversely, there had been some truth in his words. She couldn't go about doing as she had most likely done in her life before coming here. This environment did not allow a woman to speak to a man with such obvious delight, since a man, both Indian and white, would look upon her as a prize to be won, not someone to speak with in mere conversation.

Even considering she did not wish to be such a prize and so would need his protection, he could not be with her every moment of every day. Honor bid him to help his tribe by scouting. Duty caused him to leave every day on the hunt.

If she continued to talk to any man as she wished, and with nary a thought to the consequences, she could be taken over by a man's superior strength and forced into servitude to the man or worse. If only she could defend herself like a man.

He paused, frowning. *Defend herself like a man...*

Was this a possible means to resolve this matter between them? When he was required to be away from camp, either hunting or scouting, could he demand she carry a rifle, a gun and several knives...maybe even a hatchet?

Perhaps. But, she would have to know how to use those weapons without hesitation, and, being female, her nature might make her hesitate to damage another, allowing the stronger power of a man to take her weapons from her and use them against her.

Yes, he could demand she arm herself, but if she were to be safe in carrying this kind of equipment, he would have to teach her how to use the weapons, as well as educate her into the mindset where she would not hesitate to use them. If he could do this, and if she would allow him to teach her, perhaps then she could talk to another man without injury to herself and without him personally and constantly being worried about her, or worse, having to defend her honor.

Still, though he wished to bring comfort to her now, he didn't disturb her nor her song. Instead, he continued to linger out of her sight, watching over her, guarding her. And, his heart broke each time he heard her cries. But, still he didn't disrupt her, realizing she needed this time to be alone.

He watched as she stood away from the overlooking cliff where she had been perched and then reached out for his pony, who stood at her side. Gathering up the pony's reins, she began the trek back toward their camp. Still Stands Strong didn't announce himself, although he followed her at a distance and kept to a much slower stride.

Once back in the encampment, she didn't at once return to their shared lodge. Instead, as she came in sight of his almost-parents' tepee, she stopped, announced herself, and, leaving his pony outside their lodge, she entered it. When he heard the welcome greetings from within, he knew it was only a matter of time before she would return to their own lodge.

Good. It was good.

He stepped slowly forward toward his almost-parents' tepee to ensure his pony was tied up securely there; then, with this done, he trod toward his own home. And, upon entering into their lodge, he began to think of various ways he might present this idea of carrying arms to her until, at a loss to broach the subject, he gave up his wondering. He would have to let their love for one another dictate what would be and what should be said.

Reaching into one of his parfleche bags, he withdrew his flute which he had fashioned by hand. A Lakota man, since time out of mind, was well known to play the sad notes of the flute when he went courting the woman of his heart. Hence, Stands Strong had carved out this flute many years ago, knowing there might come a time when he would need its strength.

Perhaps its magic might work its wonders yet this night.

\*\*\*\*

The sad notes of a flute reached out to Czanna, and she stared around the Indian camp. Where was it coming from? And, who was playing it? Its scale was in a minor key, and its sad, beautiful and forlorn notes tugged at her heart.

So strange. The sound vibrations of the flute seemed to mimic the lyrical refrains of the European instrument, with which she was familiar.

*But, a flute? Here? In an Indian camp?*

For a moment, the music stopped, and she stepped in closer to the lodge she shared with Stands Strong, where she petted and bound Naato Omitaa to his post, kissing the pony on his head. It was then when the music started again, and she recognized it was coming from within her own lodge.

Obviously, Stands Strong had to be within. Inhaling deeply for strength of mind, she pushed back the entrance flap and stepped inside.

It wasn't long before she recognized the sad, ethereal melody her husband was playing. Oddly, it was her own song—one she had composed this very day. But, for a reason she didn't know, his playing it on his flute sounded even more sorrowful than her own song had been.

But, surely he hadn't been there with her today. And, if not, how did he know this melody?

Coming a little farther into their tepee, she stepped toward her quarters within their lodge and sat directly across from Stands Strong. She didn't look up at him. Gazing down, she simply listened.

The song went on and on, and when at last the melody stopped, she glanced up to find her husband gazing back at her, his countenance serious. She sighed; was he going to lecture her again?

But, he said not a word. Instead, as he sat before her, he looked at her wistfully as though he would like nothing better than to take her into his arms.

He did not do it, however. Instead, they sat there together, merely staring at each other in silence—and for what appeared to be a very long while, indeed.

At last, he said, "I have saddened you, and it was not in my heart to do this to you when we spoke earlier. I wish I could take back my words and my anger, but I cannot. What was done is done. All I can do now is to try to make it better for you."

She looked away from him, and she felt her lips shaking as she said, "I, too, am saddened by our talk, and I realize now I, too, should not have said what I said to you. I apologize. You should know, though, that I meant what I said then. But still, I am deeply grieved to have caused you to become disappointed in me. My husband, I do not know what to do. I still feel as I did then, though it greatly grieves me."

"I know," he uttered softly. "I admit part of my anger was because of jealousy, and this is not right. But, part of it was also concern for your safety. Because of the manner in which you have been raised, I fear there is a danger for you here."

"You mean, do you not, because of my belief in my right to seek love outside of marriage?"

He nodded.

She sat forward a little. "But, my husband, this is no longer how I think or what I feel. When I said my vows to you, this notion fled from me forever. I love you, my husband, and only you — and with all my heart. There is no place in my heart for any other man but you."

He nodded. "So it is with me, also. I, too, feel this way about you. But, hear me on this," he said when she began to speak again. "Men are stronger than women. The Creator has made it so. And, when a man wants a woman, he is inclined to take her regardless of her wishes, because, my wife, to the men of these plains, white or red, you are sought after much like the white men seek gold. Many will lust after a woman so beautiful as you, and they will wish to take what is not theirs to take. Your talking with them can reinforce this lust within a man and give him cause to think you favor him. And, this is the danger."

"But, I never had this problem in the land where I was raised," she countered. "I was free to speak to whomever I wished. Not all men wish to take what is not theirs."

Again he nodded, then said, "This may be, but you are no longer in the land where you were raised. I do not lie to you about a man's nature in this place where you now find yourself. My problem is this: I cannot always be here with you. There are times when I have duties elsewhere.

"Now, Indian mothers know this about the nature of men," he continued, "and they shelter their daughters until they marry. But, once she is married, it is the duty of her husband to protect her, and this I cannot do if I am not here. And yet, though I know your speaking to a man tempts him, I also understand your right to talk to whomever you choose. This is the way in which you have been raised, and you are right about this. The Creator gives you this right."

Czanna sat in silence. She understood and yet…

"But," he continued, "perhaps there is a way to make us both happy about your speaking to other men, even when I am not here to protect you."

"Yes? There is?"

"I have given this much thought," he said as he laid down his flute, the instrument, she noted, fashioned much like a recorder instead of a flute. It looked very much like a long bird with a red plume on its head at the end of the flute and its mouth open. It was also decorated with feathers and beads, and it was an instrument like no other she had ever seen.

Stands Strong, having placed his flute aside, came up to his feet and trod around the fireplace, which now contained a fire happily burning, crackling and spitting out sparks that were contained by the stones placed around it.

Sitting down beside her, Stands Strong took her hand in his own and said, "I begin to think this way: if you were equipped to go about your duties well-armed with shotgun, pistol and knives, and if you knew how to use those weapons like a man, I would perhaps not worry about your safety so much.

"It would require an effort for us both," he went on to say. "I would be required to train you on your weapon's use, but more. I would have need to ensure you would be of a mindset to use those firearms against another if there were to be a need of having to defend yourself. You see, a woman's heart can be soft, and she might hesitate to act instead of presenting a solid force against a man's intention. Because he is stronger and trained for war, if a woman would hesitate to use her weapons against him, he could take these from her and use them against her."

"Really? You would do this for me?"

He nodded, then continued, "I do not wish to enforce rules upon you which are strange to you and are about matters you do not agree are right. But, be warned: what I am suggesting would require your having to follow me each day out on the hunt so I could ensure your aim is good and your spirit is set to do what must be done to survive against a man's lust if necessary, but—"

"I would have to follow you to hunt and learn how to kill an animal for food, and I would also need to be with you day in and day out while I would be learning to shoot?"

"I fear it is the only way."

"Well, my husband, I do not understand why this seems to sadden you. I think it is a very good idea. Indeed, it is so good, I am wondering if we might start now…tonight?"

When she glanced up at him, she espied surprise in his eyes. But, all he asked was, "You would agree to this so easily?"

"Without even another thought," she answered. "From the moment I first met you, I have wanted to learn what you do and how you do it. Partly this is because I do not want to let you out of my sight, but also I have wished this because it is the only way I believe I will feel secure in this new environment."

He nodded before saying, "But, the women's work… You would not be learning what you must know in order to care for a family."

"Well," she said, "I guess we would have to plan out how we — and I do mean *we* — would be able to do both."

He stared at her as though he could not believe what she said. But, suddenly he laughed, and she joined in with him before she said, "I recognized the melody you were playing. How did you know it?"

"I followed you today," he said.

"You did? But, I did not see you or hear you."

"This is because I am a scout and can become invisible when I choose to make it so."

"Then, you weren't upset with me because I had taken your pony with me?"

"Never," he said at once.

"Naato Omitaa asked to come with me, you know."

"He is a good pony, and I am glad he was there for you."

"Oh my!" she said, turning fully toward him, and then she flung herself against him and into his arms, which caused him to fall backward. It was exactly the way she wanted him, and she settled herself suggestively on top of him, murmuring, "My dear husband, if this is the way in which any of our future arguments are going to end, I shall not flinch from them. But, perhaps we should make a pledge to always end our arguments in such a pleasant way as this. When do we start our training?"

He grinned at her, then said, "As soon as I have trapped enough beaver to purchase a shotgun for you."

"But, I have enough money to buy—"

He shook his head and said, "I will not let you obtain the gun with the evil golden rock. Perhaps we will need to have more discussion on this rock and the consequences of its use. But, for now, I will trap the beaver or other animals whose fur and skins are favored by the trader, and I will acquire the rifle for you. Meanwhile, we will prepare to leave here to go to find your cousin. I now know where he is. As soon as we have the weapons for you and enough food to start our journey, we will go."

Easily changing their positions so he was now lying atop her, he leaned down over her and kissed her once, then once more before he whispered against her lips, "Let us end our argument in the only way a newly married couple should."

"Oh?" she murmured. "What is in your mind, my husband?"

"You shall see, my wife. You shall see." And, he proceeded to show her exactly what he had in mind. Indeed, it was well into the night before they at last found contentment in sleep.

## CHAPTER NINETEEN

"River people," said Stands Strong, tracing the track made upon the ground.

"How do you know this?" asked George.

"It is easy when you know what to look for. Do you see how the moccasin that made these prints is put together with soft leather?"

George shook his head.

"Here," said Stands Strong, "I will leave a print from my own moccasin next to this one."

Getting up to his feet, Stands Strong placed his foot close to the print left behind in the soil, then he lifted his foot. "Do you see the difference?" he asked. "Because the Pikuni moccasins are made with parfleche, which is a stronger rawhide than a simple leather, there is a more distinct print left behind from my moccasins. But also, do you see this print was made yesterday morning?"

"I do not see this at all, my husband," said Czanna.

Stands Strong smiled at her, his look tolerant and loving as he squatted back down to run a finger over the print. Then, he looked up at her and asked, "When was the last time there was moisture in the air?"

"Why, yesterday morning," answered George.

"Yes, you are right. I remember it now," added Czanna.

"*Soka'pii*, good. Now look closely at this print."

Both she and George did so.

"Do you see the edges of the tracks hold together more solidly than the rest, as though they were made when the ground was wet?"

"Yes."

He nodded. "This tells a man the enemy came by here yesterday morning when it was last wet and misty in the morning. It is all revealed here in the earth. But, how many of the enemy were here? And, where are they going?"

Both Czanna and her brother looked back at Stands Strong, dumbfounded.

When no information was forthcoming, Stands Strong said confidently, "There were four of this enemy. It is all here for anyone to see. Look. Can you tell the differences in the prints of the same people? Some of these tracks show the feet to be larger, some are wider. *Áa*, there were four of them who came through here, and their tracks lead into the forest at the base of the cut ridge over there to the west."

He pointed to the western outcrop of mountains.

"They are heading home as quickly as they can after stealing some of the Pikuni buffalo meat from our plains. They hurry because they do not wish to be confronted by a Pikuni war party defending what is ours. Were we not on our own scouting expedition, we would follow them and take from them what they stole from us. But, we must push forward instead."

Czanna, listening to Stands Strong, couldn't help observing, "Perhaps their people are hungry. Maybe this is the reason they would dare to invade your country."

"Then, they should come in peace to our chiefs and ask to hunt in our territory," said Stands Strong. "Our chiefs are not without heart and would hear their pleas without interruption. The Gros Ventre made peace with us long ago for this reason, and it lasts even into the present. They are under our protection.

"But, know this, my woman," continued Stands Strong. "Were we to fail to defend our country from these aggressors who come here only to take what is ours, we would soon be overrun by many tribes, and it is then when we might go hungry instead of our enemies. It is because of the love of our people that we, the men of our tribe, must defend our country from those who would take it from us."

She nodded. "All right," she murmured. "You make a good argument."

Stands Strong smiled at her. "It is not my wish to argue at all; it is my desire to—"

"I think I'll leave you two alone and get myself back to camp now," said George, interrupting.

Stands Strong grinned, while Czanna felt her face flush.

"*Póóhsapoot*, come, we will join you," he said. "Let us all return to the others and continue our journey northeast and to the Bears Paw Mountains. They are now in sight. Our path there should not be long."

Czanna trailed along behind George, who was leading the way down into the deep coulee where they had made their day camp. Stands Strong followed her, his position one of protection, not subservience.

They had been on their way toward the Bears Paw Mountain range for several days now, traveling only at night and resting during the day. Their party consisted of seven people: Stands Strong and George, along with First Rider, Liliann, Mr. Henrik, Black Beaver—a brother of Tom Johnson's wife—and, of course, herself.

At Stands Strong's suggestion, Czanna had left Briella in the care of her almost-aunties, Laylah, Amelia, Sharon, Morning Sun Woman and Little Dove. Between all five of Briella's new aunties, she would be well cared for. Though Czanna had fretted over leaving her young sister behind, she had also realized Stands Strong's wisdom in suggesting it: Briella would be safer with her aunties than she would be were she to accompany the rest of her family into the mountains, where there was always the risk of encountering war parties.

Because it was late morning, the Bears Paw Mountains, which had looked black against the early morning's silver sky, were now beginning to show off their colors of green and brown as the sun climbed higher into the sky. For a moment, Czanna paused while Stands Strong paced up beside her.

He said, "Our country is beautiful. What a rich land this is, and we will fight to keep it."

"It is, indeed, beautiful, with its rolling green and brown prairies, its steep mountains and buttes, cut by clear streams, lakes and rivers. I have never seen a country so diverse nor so grandly beautiful. Nor one so rich in game. You truly want for nothing…and all this without the need of the evil golden rock."

"My heart is happy to hear you call this golden rock evil," said Stands Strong. "The stone is evil and perhaps worse than evil, if this is possible. It makes the white man's heart forget he is part of all things living upon this earth; he forgets he is also human, as are all those he loves, and it causes him to kill men of his own kind and to steal from them, not for his family or tribe, but for the rock, only. Does he not know that if he does this, he becomes enslaved by all manner of physical ills? Crueler still, does he not know his spiritual nature is at war with the physical? Always, the physical lures a man to become more like the solid earth beneath his feet. If he heeds the physical only, he will, without doubt, be made to be less spiritual, and he can come to be uncaring and unaware of the plights of others. This will always cause his divine degradation.

"*Niitá'p*," Stands Strong continued. "I fear a time might come when the evil golden rock could make slaves of men, white and red, and if this time ever comes to be, it will be a sad day, indeed, for my people, a people who are now your tribe, too. They might forget their God, who gives life to all creatures, and because the spirit of life is not physical, the people could become enslaved.

"I, for one, will not live as a slave," Stands Strong went on to say. "I would rather stand and die than be forced to do another man's bidding."

Czanna stood mute for several moments, recognizing the profound wisdom of Stands Strong's words. But, though her heart expanded at his astute observations, she wondered how he could have become so sensible about the world at so young an age? Perhaps he had learned it from his parents or maybe from others in the tribe…mayhap their medicine men?

And, when had she changed? So gradually had her views started to shift, she had barely noticed when she had begun to value friendship, family and marriage more than any show of outward material wealth. Only these — friendship, honor, courage, tribe and family — were important. Only these made a person "rich" in God's Creation.

She felt Stands Strong's arm about her shoulders, when he murmured, "This beauty I see all around us reminds me of you, who have brought so much grace into my life. Indeed, the softness of your voice lifted up in song, as well as your sweet spirit, makes my heart soar. Every day when I pray, I thank Sun, the Creator, for bringing you into my life."

Hearing these words, so dear to her heart, caused Czanna to cry, though she tried to not show it. Had she ever adored anyone more than Stands Strong? If she had, she didn't remember it.

All she could say in response was, "I, too, my husband. I, too, feel as you do. I have never loved another as I do you. Perhaps I shall tell this to you every day of my life so if and when we ever argue again we will be reminded of how dearly we love one another."

Turning toward her and bringing her closer into his arms, he bent down, bringing his forehead to hers, and he whispered, "I will pray it will always be so. But, perhaps we should use a trick if we ever feel we must argue."

"Oh?" asked Czanna. "What is this trick?"

"It is merely this: perhaps we should disrobe before we say bad words to each other. I think, then, our arguments could be less, or, if not less, they would be short."

She giggled, and then he kissed her.

****

As soon as they had returned to their temporary camp, George immediately flung back the entrance to the shelter he shared with Black Beaver and First Rider, while Stands Strong and Czanna continued toward their own small hut. While on the trail, there were three shelters the men erected each day, putting them up quickly after their nightly trek. The third refuge was shared by Liliann and her father.

As Czanna and Stands Strong crawled into their own tiny dwelling, they each disrobed, since they slept in only their underthings—he wearing his breechcloth alone, and she being clothed in only her chemise. As they fell onto their sleeping robes, it became obvious they were not, either one of them, exhausted enough to immediately fall to sleep.

Instead, as Stands Strong took her into his arms and brought her in close to him, he leaned over her to place a kiss against her lips, her nose, her cheeks and even her eyes. And, when he came down farther upon her, while his kisses ranged lower toward her breasts, he caressed first one and then the other of her feminine mounds. As a rush of pleasure washed over her, she wiggled a little; she couldn't help it, the pleasure was so powerful.

He whispered, "I love you more this day than even yesterday. How do you think this is possible?"

"I do not know, my husband," she murmured softly. "But I, too, feel the same. I had thought once we married, my wish to be close to you might fade. Instead, I find my yearning to keep you as near to me as I might becomes stronger."

He laughed a little, and as he looked up to her, he uttered, "It is good, I think."

And, then he kissed her a little lower still toward her femininity, and he said, "Perhaps this might help to ease this need of yours." And, then without any warning at all, he kissed her there at her core.

At once, a feeling not unlike a lightning strike cascaded through her body, and she jerked upward. But, he calmed her and said, "Lie still. You will like it."

And, he went about proving his words to be true.

Czanna had never known nor had been told about this kind of lovemaking by any of her nannies, and as the pleasure surged through her, she understood his words more exactly. If she had felt herself to be, at last, as one with him when they made love, it was nothing compared with what he was doing to her now. Indeed, she felt herself opening up to him spiritually, while physically she begged him to continue.

The ultimate pleasure went on and on, and when at last she met her release, she felt the essence of who she was again merge with him, and she wondered which was more pleasurable, the physical or the ethereal experience of meeting him on this plane, soul-to-soul.

And, then he scooted up over her, his face coming in close to hers as he kissed her ears, her neck, her cheeks, her nose and eyes, and then her lips, his tongue opening her lips and playing with her tongue as he became physically one with her.

They danced then—the dance of love. And, as their love blossomed between them and expanded into a beautiful movement, he caught her gaze and kept it, their look at one another not wavering until, at last, they both met their pleasure. And, still they gazed at one another.

It was as though, for a moment, they had both stepped outside of time, becoming one in body as well as in spirit.

He didn't move away from her at once. However, when at last he rolled to the side of her, he murmured, "I will love you always."

"Always," she repeated in a whisper. It was like a sacred vow between them. Regardless of what the future might bring to them, it was their own pledge, willingly given, willingly taken.

Forever.

\*\*\*\*

*Help me! Please help me!*

The words came to Czanna in her mind.

Czanna sat straight up in her bed where she had been cuddling up so cozily next to Stands Strong. Should she awaken him? Had he heard the cry for help?

No, he was sound asleep.

What was she to do?

*Please, I need help!*

Czanna took a deep breath. She could not do nothing. She at least had to investigate, if only to discover who needed help and why.

Slowly, so as not to awaken Stands Strong, she came up onto her knees, and, grabbing ahold of her dress, she quickly threw it on, then crawled toward their little shelter's entrance. Pulling back the lodge flap, she crept over it and rose up to her feet, seeing the morning had turned into the afternoon.

*Help me!*

The plea came again, but from where? Since she was hearing the appeal within her mind, she responded in the same manner and asked, *Where are you? Tell me where you are, and I will come there.*

*At the water, by the stream. Hurry!*

Czanna didn't know why she wasn't frightened to do as asked, but she wasn't. Instead, she was afraid only to be too late to help.

*I see you. Do you see me?*

Looking outward, Czanna saw nothing at first. And, then she beheld a movement. What was it? Was it human?

"Ah-h-h!" She inhaled on a breath and gulped. She didn't scream. It was as though the ability to make a sound was beyond her.

In front of her, at only a little distance away, was a large white bear. It was not standing upright, but rather was down on all fours.

*Please hurry. We need your help.*

It was the bear who was "speaking" to her.

*We?* asked Czanna silently.

*Please, yes. My baby needs your help. Please hurry!*

Why she didn't hesitate to do as asked, Czanna didn't know. She only felt as though the Creator, Himself, were directing her steps, and she paced slowly toward the animal, keeping some distance between them, yet unable to turn away from the animal's cries.

And, then she saw it and heard the baby's scream; it was a brown and white bear cub, caught in the sticky mud of the stream, the mud perhaps having been created from the flow of the snow melting and crashing down from the mountains. Realizing what was at stake, her steps turned immediately into a run, and she came right up to the shore where the animal was struggling farther out.

With no fear for herself, she waded into the water toward the cub, feeling, herself, the sticky substance of the mud. Still, she plodded on toward the creature until she was right next to it. Then, she reached out to try to pull the small bear out of the muck without herself also getting caught in the sludge.

But, it was too late. She was already caught in the swamp-like mire, too.

Still reaching out for the animal, she positioned herself so she could keep its head above water, and then, before her strength gave out, she screamed, "Stands Strong! Help! Stands Strong, wake up! Help me!"

In what seemed like much too long, yet was probably no longer than several seconds, she saw Stands Strong running toward the edge of the water. Wearing only what he'd worn to bed—his breechcloth—he waded into the water, though he was careful not to come in too close so as to become stuck himself.

Together, they tried pull the cub out. But, the animal was too greatly stuck. Still, both she and Stands Strong kept its head above water.

"Here!" came another masculine voice. "I have a rope! Grab hold of it!" It was First Rider, who was now standing on the stream's shoreline. He was soon joined there by Henrik, George, Black Beaver and Liliann.

Stands Strong missed the first throw of the rope, but caught hold of it on the second try and quickly tied the rope to the bear cub.

"Grab hold of the baby!" Stands Strong told his wife while he bent toward her, keeping an arm around her. "My friends will pull the cub from the water, and you shall come out of the mud along with it."

"Get...horse!" Czanna heard First Rider's cry to Liliann.

While Henrik, Black Beaver, George and First Rider tugged on the rope, and as Stands Strong fought to free the cub from the mud, while keeping its head above water, Liliann ran toward them, leading Stands Strong's pony behind her.

At once, the men took possession of the horse and tied the rope to it, then all—the pony, Liliann and the four men—joined in pulling the bear cub and Czanna out of the mud. With the aid of the pony, Holy Dog, it took only a few seconds longer to free the baby bear, as well as Czanna.

As the cub came to lie upon the shoreline, Stands Strong bent over it, turning it onto its back, before saying to Czanna, "Quick, get me one of our parfleche bags from our shelter."

She didn't hesitate. Running swiftly to their lodge, she grabbed one of the parfleches, dumped its contents on the ground and then ran back to Stands Strong.

"Quickly, fill the bag with water and bring it here to me!" Stands Strong said to her as First Rider knelt down next to the small bear, whereupon both he and Stands Strong took turns performing the lifesaving task of ridding the water that had accumulated in the little bear's lungs. And, as the two men worked over the bear, Stands Strong instructed Czanna to wash the mud from its fur.

With a loud, gurgling noise, water gushed from the cub's mouth, and the baby began to cry and to breathe. For a moment, it lay still as precious oxygen filled its lungs, then it came up onto its legs, and, looking around at the men and the two girls, it gave a gentle roar as though it were thanking its rescuers. Looking around, it finally spotted its mother.

Still, the cub didn't leave at once. Instead, it stared at the group of men and women as though it would memorize who these people were. With a few slow steps at first, but then gaining its strength, it hurried toward its mother, who had, up until this moment, hidden herself behind a few trees farther upstream.

It was when the white bear stepped out from behind its cover that Czanna heard Stands Strong's indrawn breath. She chanced a glance at him, only to witness a look of disbelief upon his countenance.

Then, at some length, she heard him say "*Oki Napi*" in the Blackfeet language. And, then in English, he continued, "It is good to see my old friend again."

The bear roared, although Czanna heard the bear say silently in mind-speak, "I have looked for you, my friend. I know you have been calling me, but I have been unable to find you, even in the shadow land. It caused great sadness in my heart. But then, the Creator spoke to me, comforting me and telling me He was awaiting your wife to join with you. I am happy to see you again and to look upon your wife's beauty. Expect me later tonight. I will come to you to teach you the medicine ways of the bear, the ones you have been seeking these many years. Look for me."

And then, she and her baby turned and walked slowly away until they both disappeared into the woods, a few beams of the afternoon sunlight seeming to lead them.

As Stands Strong stood watching the white bear, First Rider, George, Black Beaver and Mr. Henrik joined him. Many congratulations were exchanged between each one of them. And then, First Rider placed his hand upon Stands Strong's shoulder.

"You heard?" asked Stands Strong in the Blackfeet tongue, then in English.

"I did, my friend," answered First Rider in Blackfeet and sign language so as to include Czanna. "It is well known the bear medicine is the strongest medicine of all the other animals. She, this white bear, has at last returned to you, and she will teach you well, and you shall become a great medicine man, as I think Sun has always intended you to be. It is a great day!"

"*Áa*, it is a great day!"

Turning, First Rider, as well as Black Beaver, George and Mr. Henrik stepped away, which left only Czanna standing at her husband's side.

It was after several moments had passed when Stands Strong murmured softly to her, "It is the Creator and you whom I must thank."

"Me?"

"*Áa*, it is so. It is because of you and your love; your love has empowered me enough so as to bring the white bear back into my life. I thought it wasn't possible to ever see her again. I thought…I thought… Come here," he uttered, turning her into his arms where they hugged, neither of them making a move to leave one another's embrace.

"Do you know the story of the white bear?" Stands Strong asked.

"Only recently have I learned of it. Your almost-mother told me a little about it and how it saved your life when you were only seven. And now, you have saved her cub's life. Forever, I think, she will be in your life...perhaps her baby, too."

"*Áa*, she has always been in my life, though distant from me all these many years. Your love, my wife, has given me the strength to bring her back into my life."

"I am unsure I was the one to bring her to you again, but it little matters. I am glad she is once again in your life where she belongs," she said. "I am so very, very glad."

How long they stood there in the warmth of the early afternoon's sunlight, she did not know.

She only knew that neither of them returned to their shelter to sleep. They waited through the rest of the daylight and well into the night until at last the white bear returned. And, once she had come back to them, there at the shoreline of the stream running down within the sheltered coulee, she sat down on her haunches and began to tell them both about the deeply coveted bear medicine and how it was to be used.

Czanna stood away from them and was beginning to pace back toward their little hut when she heard the bear say silently, "This is for you, too, wife of Stands Strong—you, who first heard my call. Come closer. I wish you to have this bear's healing knowledge, too."

And, so it came to be that Czanna retraced her steps and sat next to Stands Strong where she learned, there alongside her husband, about the sacred bear medicine. Never, she realized, never would she ever be the same again. This wild country had changed her forever.

And, it was so very, very good.

## CHAPTER TWENTY

"Well now, folks, are you lost or are you comin' up the mountain to see me and the missus?"

Early in the morning on their twenty-second day into the Bears Paw Mountains, they were met by these words from a man who looked more bearlike than human being. Czanna stared at the man in awe, but with misgivings. Was he friend or foe?

As her husband had been teaching her, if the man made a move against them, should she shoot to kill? She didn't move, though she was ready for action if it were to come, and she brought her rifle up against her breast, ready to use.

Looking outward at the man, it was difficult to determine his height since the hat he wore looked to be more wolf-like than hat and it stood perhaps twelve centimeters—about four inches— above his head. A long white beard covered his lower face, the sides of his face and his upper lip. However, what she saw was not a well-groomed beard, and she feared there might be creatures living within it. Bushy gray eyebrows completed his "look," and his shirt appeared to be made from tanned buckskin. The sleeves of it were fringed with buckskin, and all down each sleeve were rows of white, red, blue and yellow beads as well as equally colorful triangles.

Surely, this had been done in the style of the Plains Indian. But, was he friend or foe?

The man wore trousers made of buckskin, and these were fringed, as well, and beaded much like his shirt. His moccasins came well up to his knees and were perhaps made in two parts.

"*Oki Isstamo*, Hello, brother-in-law," said Black Beaver to the man. Then, continuing in Blackfeet, he said, "As you can see, I have brought friends of yours to visit with you."

"*Oki napi*," said Stands Strong, and then in English, "We have, indeed, come visiting."

"Have you, now? Good to see you, Black Beaver, and it's Stands Strong, isn't it?"

Stands Strong nodded.

"Women. White women," said the oldster. "You've brought white women up into these mountains? And, here I thought my woman was lying when she told me there were two white women in your party."

Could this be her cousin? If it were her cousin, he didn't look the Hungarian aristocrat at all. He appeared to be quite rugged, old and unkempt.

"Cousin Alfred, is that you?" asked Czanna in the Hungarian tongue.

The man turned his attention onto Czanna and stared at her as though he were looking at a ghost.

"Who are you?" he asked in English. "We don't speak Hungarian around these parts."

"I think I am your cousin, Czanna Fehér, and this"—she pointed to George—"is cousin György Fehér, although we call him, George."

George, doing as Stands Strong had done, merely nodded.

Meanwhile, Czanna continued to speak to the man, and she said in English, "Cousin Alfred, we bring you greetings from home."

"Well, I'll be tongue-tied to a bear's tooth. Cousin Czanna, I haven't seen you since you were only this high." He indicated the height with his hand next to his waist. Cousin György, you were a mere baby last time I saw you. And, here was I unbelievin' of my woman. Well, come this way. All of you. Come this way. We aren't far from my homestead. Just over the next ridge. Won't my woman be happy to see you all, and especially you, Black Beaver. I was planning to come a visitin' next summer. But, now's as good a time as any."

The way to his home was not long and was an easy trip for both Czanna and Liliann, if only because the snow had all melted and the land was dry at present. Peeping up here and there from the soft ground were beautiful wild flowers of purple, blue and yellow, and the short grass was as green as any she'd ever seen. Indeed, it was spring even up here in the mountains.

The trail to her cousin's cabin cut through a heavy and perhaps overgrown pine tree forest. It was a narrow trail, and it was dark because the trees, reaching upward to the sky, hid the sun. But, Czanna felt safe, if only because the men—and there were now six of them—were all heavily armed with shotgun and bow and arrows, as well as knives of all different sorts and shapes. And, her cousin carried an axe as well as shotgun.

As they neared the end of the forest, Czanna saw what looked to be a small cabin in a clearing directly in front of them. Somewhat surprised to be looking at a white man's log cabin instead of a tepee, she yet felt pleasantly inclined toward it. The small house, looking as though it were made from logs plastered together with mud or river clay, gave her the impression of it being a haven against the wildness of the mountain landscape. There was smoke shooting upward from a chimney, and the scent of the fire and smoke was quite pleasing and welcoming, making the end of their long trek akin to coming home.

Standing in front of the cabin was an Indian woman dressed in a mix of cotton clothing as well as buckskin. Her hair was braided, and even from this distance Czanna could see the woman's features were agreeable.

Czanna drew in a deep breath. She had accomplished what had seemed impossible; she had found her cousin. Now it only remained for her to take Cousin Alfred aside and present him with the family treasure, as well as the letter from her brother.

No sooner had they all dismounted than Cousin Alfred was introducing them, one and all, to his wife, Pretty Ribbon Woman, who, smiling at each one in turn, invited them to come into her home. All accepted the invitation except Stands Strong and First Rider, who both graciously volunteered to see to the care of their horses. But first, without saying a word to Stands Strong, Czanna untied a bag she had earlier fastened to her mount.

When Stands Strong looked at her curiously, she gave him a smile, hoping he would understand: she had a gift and a message for her cousin, but it was for her cousin, alone. The promise she had given to her brother forbade her, despite Stands Strong being her husband, from telling him the entire purpose of her mission.

In open Pikuni hospitality, they were all treated to food and drink, consisting of fire-roasted buffalo ribs as well as the delicacy of tongue. Berry soup completed the meal. And, while Black Beaver and his sister traded stories with one another, and with Stands Strong and First Rider engaged in speaking to one another, Cousin Alfred sought out Czanna and regaled her with tales of his adventures in the Backbone-of-the-World Mountains, and why he and his woman had moved their home to the Bears Paw Mountains.

"But," he said, "I reckon you haven't come all this way to listen to me talk. I figure you have some news for me from home."

"I do," said Czanna. "Although I am hoping to speak to you privately. You see, we — my brother, myself and my baby sister — have, like you, fled from Hungary. Both my mother and father, as well as my older brother, stayed behind to try to clear my father's name and his part in the revolution. Is there a place where I might speak to you privately? You see, I have a message and a letter to give to you from my brother, as well as a gift."

Cousin Alfred nodded. "Come with me outside. I fear it is the only place where we might speak privately."

"Yes. Please," replied Czanna.

As both she and her cousin came to stand to their feet, Stands Strong sent her another inquisitive glance, and she, in turn, smiled at him. How she would like to invite him to join them outside, but she could not do it. Frederic had, after all, solicited her promise to give this message and the gifts to no one else but her cousin.

As soon as they stepped foot outside, Alfred led her to a place next to the corral where he kept his animals. Placing a foot atop the bottom log of the corral, he asked, "Is this private enough for you?"

"It is, indeed," said Czanna. "Let me begin by telling you how honored I am to give to you a gift my brother bid me to bring to you, and you alone. This"—Czanna reached into the bag she had taken off her horse earlier and took out an object from it, then presented it to her cousin—"is part of the treasure our family holds. I am to give it to you."

Alfred—or Old Tom Johnson, as he was known to the Blackfeet—stared at the object as though it were more of an encumbrance than what it was: their family's coat of arms. Red, white, green and blue colors of the sky, as well as the bright-brown stone of a castle glittered from their highly polished golden setting upon a rectangular wooden bed.

"Then, this means…"

"I fear it is true, Cousin. My father and mother, along with my brother, were arrested, tried and hung. Before my brother's death, he bade me to find you and give this to you, along with this letter."

Reaching once more into her bag, she pulled out the letter she had carried between sheets of wood for safekeeping all this time; it was tied with ribbons. For well over a year, she had bore these treasures somewhere on her person or in their wagon. Truly, it was with a great deal of relief to at last turn them over into the safekeeping of Cousin Alfred.

"Come here, gal," said Cousin Alfred as he brought her into his arms to hug her. "Bless you for bringing them to me."

As they stood there embraced, Czanna said, "It has been my pleasure, as well as my duty, to do so."

At last, Alfred took her by the shoulders and said, "Do you know what is in this letter?"

"Some of it, I think," she answered. "My brother told me to give it to you and said, also, that you would help me and the rest of our family to find a safe place in this western frontier…to perhaps purchase land, if possible."

"It does, indeed, say this. Are you married to that young fella back in the cabin? The one who is watchin' over you?"

She nodded. "I am," she answered. "I would never have found you if not for his ready assistance to me and to the rest of our family."

"And, do you love him?"

"I do," Czanna answered. "Very much."

"Then," said Alfred, "you are as well set as any to survive in this country. But, things, they are changin'. It would be well if I keep an eye out for land being placed on sale. It would be pure thievery of Blackfeet land, mind you, but times, they are changin', and there be those who will take what is not theirs to take. In the last year, since the treaty with the Blackfeet and the other northern tribes, we are seein' more and more of the white man come into this land, and he is of a kin we have never seen here before. He is a man who would steal and kill without nary a thought. Yep, things, they are changin', and so I will do as your brother has bid me to do. I will keep an ear and an eye out for property goin' on sale for you and the rest of your family."

"I…I thank you, Cousin Alfred. I thank you very much."

He nodded, and, placing an arm around her shoulders, he led her back to the cabin.

****

Most of the tribe had already moved away from Fort Benton, heading in a northerly direction toward a beautiful plain, there to perform their ceremonies to Sun for the renewal of their life upon these plains. When Stands Strong's small party—which now included his wife's cousin, Old Tom Johnson, and Tom's woman—arrived back at the fort, all that remained of the large Pikuni encampment was a small band consisting of only ten tepees.

How barren the plains looked without the thousands of his people's beautifully painted tepees encamped around the fort. And, how dull was the fort without the colorful camps of his people to brighten it.

His woman, Matsowá'p, said, "I miss the thousands of lodges all set up and surrounding the fort. It does not look the same. Indeed, it appears to me as though the fort, without the Indian villages, is little more than a blot upon the land."

"*Áa*, it does," agreed Stands Strong. "Without my people here, the land is barren. Yet, it is not all bad. The steamship brings many items to trade. Did you see there is another steamboat arrived here? It will be bringing more guns, blankets and other necessary things we will need before we join our relatives in the north. I only hope it will not be carrying more of the gold seekers. Come, your cousin and I have decided to go into the fort to see what supplies the boat brings. Your cousin has many furs to trade."

And, so it was that their party made their bid to enter the fort on this balmy day in early summer.

****

The trading room was not crowded on this day. In truth, there were only a few other people within the trading room when their party—the six men and two women—stepped foot into its chambers. Since this was the first time Stands Strong had brought his woman inside the fort and its trading room, he wondered how she might look at the place after being within the Pikuni camp.

Would she compare it to the graceful Pikuni lodges? And, if she did, which would be the prettier of the two?

As he looked around the room, Stands Strong saw the many buffalo robes which were thrown over the trading table, and, gazing beyond it to the shelves behind the counter, he glanced over the many different items of trade: the striped woolen blankets, the rugs and cooking utensils, as well as the pots and pans. There were several different buckskin jackets hung on antlers at the corners of the room. At one far end of the small room was a fireplace, and, at present, a cheery fire was lit within it. Guns, knives, ammunition and paints were also amply displayed on the shelves behind the trading table, and at the corner of the table were beads of all colors, awls, needles and thread.

While he and the other men bartered for guns and ammunition, the women crowded around the sparkling colors of the beads, as well as the cups and saucers, and the pots and kettles.

"I think this is the fort they were to come to."

Stands Strong heard a male voice say these words in English, the sound of the words used similar to the manner in which his wife spoke, but he thought little of it until his wife grabbed hold of his arm and whispered, "Did you hear that man's accent?"

"A little," he replied.

"Well, it sounds…it sounds a lot like—"

"A lot like?"

"No, never mind. It couldn't be."

But, when the man continued to speak, her grip upon his sleeve increased, and she said, "It sounds…it sounds like…no it couldn't be."

Stands Strong frowned and looked toward the three white people—two men and one woman. But, seeing nothing out of the ordinary, he turned away while Matsowá'p again caught hold of his sleeve. She said, "I…I…have heard that voice before, and yet…."

Suddenly, the woman laughed and turned toward one of the men, her profile showing her to be an older woman, but not too elderly. It was then when he heard his wife gasp.

"What is it?" he asked.

"I...I..." Matsowá'p's eyes were wide, and her face turned suddenly white as though she were staring at a ghost.

Matsowá'p's voice was a mere whisper when she asked one of the men, "Frederic? Is it you? Mother? Father?"

*Mother? Father?* thought Stands Strong. *But, weren't they dead?*

As though in complete unison, all three people turned to glance at his wife, and, looking down upon her, Stands Strong could see she could barely speak. Yet, she managed to ask, "Is it you, truly? Frederic? Mother? Father?"

"Czanna!"

Then, all at once, Stands Strong's world seemed to spin as Czanna and the three strangers ran toward each other. And, as he looked on, he saw his wife collapse into the three strangers' embraces. George, he noticed, joined the foursome with a wide grin upon his countenance. And, as Stands Strong stepped back to give the five people more room to talk, he heard the one woman with the group say, "Czanna! György! I cannot believe it is really you. We have looked for you everywhere!"

"But, I thought you were... I thought you were... I received a letter... I was given to believe you were no longer alive!" Matsowá'p said. "But, here you are! I cannot believe what I am seeing! You are here! You are here!"

By this time, not one of them, not even George nor Matsowá'p's father's eyes, were dry.

"But, here I am, forgetting my manners." Turning, Matsowá'p reached out to Stands Strong. Taking his hand into her own, she brought him forward to stand beside her. She said, "Frederic, Mother, Father, let me introduce you to my husband, Stands Strong."

Matsowá'p's father reached out his hand to shake Stands Strong's, and, at his woman's urging, Stands Strong took the man's hand, feeling a firm grip there.

"Oh my, Czanna! You have married!" It was his woman's mother speaking. "Welcome to our family, young man. Welcome!"

Stands Strong nodded.

"Oh, you're not getting away with that. Come here!"

And, Stands Strong allowed himself to be pulled into the older woman's embrace while she planted a kiss on each of his cheeks. He wasn't certain he was supposed to return the same, but he found himself kissing both of her cheeks anyway.

"And, that man over there," Matsowá'p said as she gestured toward a corner of the room, "is my husband's friend, First Rider."

First Rider nodded.

"And, this mountain man you see here is our own Cousin Alfred. Do you see? I found him, Frederic! I found Alfred, our cousin."

"You did it, Czanna! You have done what I thought was impossible!"

"Yes, but it was not I who found him; it was my husband who discovered where he was and brought all of us there. But, please let me continue. Beside our cousin Alfred is his Pikuni wife, Pretty Ribbon Woman, and standing there beside her is her brother, Black Beaver. You know, of course, Mr. Henrik and Miss Liliann, who are standing next to First Rider. First Rider is the man who saved Mr. Henrik's life with his medicine man's treatment, when Mr. Henrik had suffered an injury that would have otherwise taken his life."

"I thank you, Mr. First Rider," said the elder man. "Mr. Henrik has been with our family for so many years, he is almost like one of us."

When Stands Strong translated what his father-in-law had said, First Rider smiled, but only a little.

"Oh my, you are here!" Matsowá'p said. "You are alive, and you are here! Oh, I am so happy!" Matsowá'p then turned to Stands Strong. "Oh, what am I to do, my husband? I did not know this kind of happiness would ever be mine. Oh, what am I to do?"

Leaning down toward his wife, Stands Strong whispered, "Perhaps you could invite them to our lodge. We should have a great celebration, and then there should be much talk."

"Yes, yes, of course," she replied. Then, turning toward Frederic and her parents, she asked, "Won't you all please come to our lodge, where we may speak of the many stories we have to share? Come, follow us. Oh, what a grand night this will be."

## CHAPTER TWENTY-ONE

It was much later in the evening when they all gathered together within Czanna and Stands Strong's lodge. A fire blazed happily and lit up the tepee as though the lodge were a lantern. And, although there were no formal seating arrangements this night, it mattered not. Each married couple sat happily next to one another while Pretty Ribbon Woman, as well as Liliann, Czanna and her mother, served the hot, roasted buffalo ribs to the men, which was the custom.

When it was at last done and the women had also enjoyed their part of the meal, Czanna took her place beside Stands Strong, then began her story, and she said, "I had received a letter from Sebestyn, your manservant, Frederic. He wrote to me to tell me about you as well as our mother and father being hanged. He begged me in his letter to come back to Hungary, but I could not do it, as you know, since you were quite strict about making me pledge to never return to Hungary."

Said Frederic, "It was Sebestyn who betrayed our family to the authorities. It does not surprise me that he would try to persuade you to come back to Hungary. You see, the three of us had escaped with some help of other freedom fighters, and we were in hiding. In truth, if he could have convinced you to return there, he could have held you ransom, which of course would have forced us out of hiding, and had it happened, we would all have been imprisoned. Do you still have the letter?"

"I do," answered Czanna as she came to her feet and trod toward the back of the lodge, the place where she kept her possessions. Digging into a parfleche bag, she pulled out the letter and gave it to Frederic. "Oh, how happy I am that you had the foresight to make me vow to never return to Hungary."

"I, too, Czanna. I, too."

"By the way, where is Béla?" It was Stands Strong's mother-in-law who asked the question.

"We now call her Briella," said Czanna. "We decided—all of us—to change our names so they would sound more American. We now call Béla, Briella, and György we call George. But, our younger sister, Briella, is not here at present. She is in the care of five of our almost-aunties."

"Almost-aunties?" asked Czanna's mother. "What is an almost-auntie?"

"They are aunts, but they are not bound to us by blood. We did not wish to bring Briella with us into the mountains in search of Cousin Alfred. And, since she would be quite happy to stay with her aunties, we left her with them for her own safety."

"I am glad you did not take her on such a long journey," replied her mother. "And, where are the aunties now?"

"They are gone into the Sun Dance camp. You see, the Pikuni people move around their land, going from one place to another. They are not far away, and we hope to join them soon. I think we should all go to their encampment as soon as possible. What say you?"

It was agreed by them all to join the Pikuni as soon as they were all packed and ready to set out upon the trail. And so, it was settled: they would leave to go to the Sun Dance encampment within the next few days.

But, at last, the night wore on, and soon Frederic as well as Czanna's mother and father left them to go to their own quarters within the fort. Meanwhile, Mr. Henrik and Liliann bid them a good night as well and returned to their lodge, while First Rider and George set up their own tepee, as did Czanna's cousin, Alfred, and his woman, Pretty Ribbon Woman.

At last, Czanna was alone with Stands Strong, who had been curiously quiet during the entire proceeding.

Turning toward him, she said, "My husband, I fear I have not included you in much of my conversation. I fear I have not been very attentive to you this evening. And, now I worry I might have displeased you."

"Displeased me? Why should you have worried over me? Being reunited with your family after you had thought them forever lost to you was at first shocking for you, I admit, but I could see the happiness bursting within you all through this evening. I would have not detracted from it by bringing attention onto myself. After all, your happiness is my own, too."

"Oh, my husband, you are so very kind. I love you very much."

"And I, you."

"I admit my life might change a little since my parents and Frederic are now here. But, one aspect of my life will not change, and this is my love for you and our path together through this life. I do not wish to go back to the way I was before I met you. I have changed my mind about being an Indian man's wife. I am your woman, now and always. Besides, we have many obligations to fulfill now that we have been taught how to use the bear medicine. I wish to be a part of this very much."

"Áa, we have much to do, because one of our duties will be to perform the bear ritual before our people. Only then will our bear medicine enrich our people's lives. Together we will do this. Always together."

"Áa," Czanna said. "Together always.

And, then they kissed, it being their seal to a pledge they freely gifted to one another.

Indeed, it would come to pass. Although their road through life might have its pleasures and its bumps, it mattered little; always they would meet each new experience together.

And, so it came to be.

# EPILOGUE

"Good shot!" praised Stands Strong. "Come, let us pray over our kill before we cut up its meat."

With both of them bending down toward the buffalo cow, Stands Strong took up some dirt and some sage from his pouch and sprinkled it over the animal. Then he prayed, "We thank you for the life you have lived and for your part in keeping our people from becoming hungry. Go now. You are free to live again in another place and time."

He motioned the spirit of the animal toward the sky, then turned to Matsowá'p and said, "She is free to go elsewhere now."

Czanna nodded.

"Come, where she is going, her spirit will be welcomed. Let us now look closely at your shot. Do you see how, if you place your aim below the ribs, its speed goes directly into the animal's lungs and heart, killing it at once? You did this well!"

"Why, thank you, husband." Czanna laughed. "I killed almost as many as you today."

Stands Strong grinned at his woman, then said, "Almost. Our people will not go hungry. Come, let us cut up this meat and pack it onto our horses. There will be much joy in our camp tonight."

"It is good," said Matsowá'p. "It is very good, indeed."

"And now, my wife, do you see you have no need of the evil gold coin?"

"I do, indeed."

"Then, perhaps you should throw it away?"

"Oh, husband, please! Throw it away?"

"Can you not?"

"I admit I cannot."

"And, why is this?"

"Because, my husband, I gave it to my brother. I no longer have the gold, nor any coin. As you said, I no longer require it. Besides, the gold was really Frederic's. He gave it to me, after all. And, perhaps he and my parents might need it in the future. Especially if they are to buy the land they have been talking about." She sighed. "I fear, my husband, you have made me so happy I have no need to pretend an outward show of my pleasure."

He smiled at her. "And, I am pleased to hear you have given the evil gold rock away. It might save us from arguing about the evil it would bring into our lives."

"Perhaps. But, I also think I should tell you, husband mine, that I dread having any more arguments with you, though I know it is impossible to agree with one another on all things. However, the truth is, I do not like being upset with you or to have you upset with me."

"Then, as I said to you once before, you should take off all your clothing before you bring your argument to me."

"What?" his wife asked. "Are you asking me to disrobe? Here? Now?"

"If you wish to do so, I would greatly encourage you to do it, although we are not yet arguing."

"I do not understand."

He sighed. "Very well. I will tell this to you again so you might remember its importance. I only ask you to not repeat the manner by which we settle our arguments to anyone. It is to be a secret between only us."

She looked directly at him and frowned. At length, she said, "All right. But, I do not remember your telling me anything about my stripping naked in order to prevent an argument."

"Then, I will tell it to you again," he said. "This is how to make all our disagreements very short, and also how you might win most all of our arguments."

She didn't answer; instead, she treated him to a doubting glance. "You are not teasing me now, are you?"

"I?" he asked. "Tease you?"

"Oh, please!"

"I tell you true. Before you begin any disagreement with me, disrobe. Take off all your clothes."

"All of them?"

"*Áa*, all of them." He grinned at her. "If you do this, I think I would be very happy to end our quarrel quickly, and I would probably do as you wish without further argument."

She giggled. "Be serious."

"Think you I am not serious? Are we to argue about this now? If so, take off your clothes now and see if I am being honest with you."

She laughed. "Well, perhaps I will," she agreed. "Although before I strip off every bit of my clothing, maybe I should tell you my own secret."

He frowned at her. "You have a secret from me?"

"I do, indeed," she said, although there was a joyful note in her voice. Then, a little more seriously, she added, "My dear husband, my secret is this: you are to soon be a father."

Stands Strong couldn't move for a moment, nor could he speak. But then, all at once, he began to laugh. And, without another word being spoken between them, he picked up his beloved Matsowá'p and swung her around and around, his laughter joining hers.

"You have made me a very happy man," he told her at last.

"And, you have made me a very contented and blissful Indian man's woman. I love you!"

"As I love you, my sweet, strong and beautiful woman."

He kissed her, and then he kissed her again, only this time, the kiss was long and quite sensual.

It is said they lived long and joyful lives, blessed with many children who would remember the happiness of their home and who would carry on in their ways.  Always.

# THE END

# GLOSSARY

Because I use some foreign words in this story—both Lakota and Blackfeet— I'm including a glossary. Many of these words are defined within the text, but some are not. And so, I am hoping the glossary will serve to assist one to read the story more easily.

*Áa* – Blackfeet, meaning yes.

*Aakíí* – Woman

*Ákáá* – Perfect

*Ánniayi* – That's enough

*Hau, hau* – Yes in Lakota, men only. Women say, "*Han.*"

**Everywhere Water** – The Ocean. In this story, it is the Pacific Ocean.

**Go Before Myself** – A phrase meaning "thinking" or "being" ahead.

*Ha'* – Expression meaning to show scorn.

*Ha'ayaa* – Male expression meaning, "Oh, Oh! as in being caught.

*Hánnia* – Really! Is that right!

*Isskán iimat* – Blackfeet, meaning almost sister

*Kitsikákomimmo* - Blackfoot phrase, meaning "I love you."

*Móókaakin* – Pemmican

*Niitá'p* – Truly or really or indeed

*Pikuni* - This is the Blackfoot people's name for their tribe. They are sometimes called the Piegan, although Pikuni is the name the Blackfeet people, themselves, more commonly use. At the time of this story, there were three bands of the Blackfeet that, together, comprised the Blackfeet or Blackfoot Nation: the Pikuni, Southern and Northern; the Káínaa or the Blood band, Northern; the Blackfoot or Siksiká, Northern.

All three of these of these bands were independent at this time period and were known to the early trappers by their own individual tribal names. But, because the three shared the same language, intermarried and went to war with the same enemies, it became more common to call these people Blackfoot/Blackfeet or Siksiká.

Today the word, "Blackfeet," refers to the southern Pikuni people living in northwestern Montana. Whereas, the word, "Blackfoot," refers to the Blackfoot people in the north. But, because at the time of this story, these people were known as the Blackfoot or Blackfeet interchangeably, I have chosen to use the word "Blackfeet" as a noun and the word, "Blackfoot," as an adjective. I did this for no other reason than consistency.

*Piit* – Come in

*Saa* – Blackfeet, meaning no.

*Tsa Aamista'piiwa* – What is it?

## About the Author
### KAREN KAY/GEN BAILEY/GENNY COTHERN

Bestselling author of Native American Historical Romance, KAREN KAY is a multi-published author of romance and adventure in the Old West. She has been praised by reviewers and fans alike for bringing insights into the everyday life of the American Indian culture of the past.

As Reviewer, Suzanne Tucker, once wrote, "Ms. Kay never fails to capture the pride, the passion and the spirit of the American Indian..."

KAREN KAY's great grandmother was Choctaw, and she is adopted Blackfeet. Ms. Kay is honored to be able to write about the rich culture of a people who gave this country so much.

"With the power of romance, I hope to bring about an awareness of the American Indian's concept of honor, and what it meant to live as free men and free women. There are some things that should never be forgotten."

Stay in touch with Karen Kay by signing up for her newsletter;
https://signup.ymlp.com/xgbqjbebgmgj
Find Karen Kay online at: https://www.novels-by-karenkay.com

Please enjoy this sneak peek at Book Five in the Medicine Man Series

# SHE BELONGS WITH ME
## Prologue

### Northwest Indian Country
### Territory of the Blackfeet
### The Month When Geese Come (May) 1857

**Cherokee Proverb**

"A woman's highest calling is to lead a man to his soul to unite him with source.

"A Man's highest calling is to protect the woman so she is free to walk the earth unharmed."

In rhythm to the drums beating in the Pikuni camp, came *Tsistsaakii*, Bird Woman, daughter of Chief Flying Hawk. In her hands, she carried a bowl of what must have been broiled buffalo meat, and she looked neither right nor left, though she passed by many of the people who must have been speaking teasing words to her, because, as Liliann Varga looked on, she saw the people laugh or giggle as Bird Woman passed by them. However, the pretty girl said not a word back to them, nor did she even share a grin with them.

Liliann knew Bird Woman was performing the strict law of the Blackfeet wedding ceremony; she had come into this knowledge because her almost-sister—as the Blackfeet called her former mistress, Czanna—had informed her of this. First Rider, a young man Liliann knew as the man who had saved her father's life, was the about-to-take-a-woman man, or the groom.

For three days Liliann had looked on as Bird Woman had performed this same ritual both morning and evening. Today was the fourth day, and it was on this day when First Rider, who had gone out hunting with his friend, Stands Strong, would return to his lodge, where Bird Woman would be awaiting him.

She would cry out, "My man!" to which First Rider would reply, "My Woman!" Thus, they would begin their life together.

Tears flowed down Liliann's cheeks as she watched Bird Woman's procession toward the large lodge which had been erected by Bird Woman's powerful family. At last, looking away, Liliann wiped the tears from her cheeks, and, standing up, bent over to throw open the flap of her almost-sister's lodge, stepping inside. Her almost-sister, Czanna, greeted her with a worried look, and asked, "Has Tsistsaakii reached First Rider's lodge yet?"

"Yes," answered Liliann. "They are now man and wife."

Barely looking around the lodge of Czanna and Stands Strong, where she, her brother and her father were residing, a tear found its way down Liliann's face. Luckily for her, no one except Czanna was, at present, within the lodge.

Not bothering to wipe the tear away, Liliann took her place to the left of the tepee flap and sat down, bringing her legs, Indian fashion, together and to her right. Looking up, she caught Czanna's eye, then hurriedly looked away.

"They were promised to marry each other before we ever came to know First Rider," said Czanna, the empathy in her voice, calm and soothing, yet had the opposite effect to what Czanna had perhaps intended. In reaction, another tear fell down over Liliann's countenance.

Liliann nodded, though she didn't look at her almost-sister, glancing down instead. At last, however, she replied to her friend in a shaky voice, "This be known to me."

Czanna seemed to pause before she spoke, but after a moment, she said, "Tsistsaakii is a good woman, having been brought up under the strict Blackfeet laws for women. She will make him a good wife."

"This be known to me, too. She is also very beautiful."

"*Áa*," said Liliann's almost-sister, the word meaning "yes" in the Blackfeet language.

Silence ensued between the two friends, until at last Czaana uttered, "Beautiful she is, indeed. I am sorry. If it makes any difference to you, my dearest friend, I believe he does not know how much you admire him."

Liliann nodded.

"Come sit before me, Liliann, where I shall endeavor to brush and re-braid your hair."

Liliann nodded, and arising, she trod around the fire to sit down in front of her friend. As Czanna undid the clasps holding Liliann's braids in place and set to pulling a brush through Liliann's long, pale-blond hair, Liliann inhaled on a deep sigh. At last, she said, "He be too old for me, right enough, he being eight years beyond me own age."

"It's not so much older than you. And, I know he cares for you. Indeed, I think you hold a special place in his heart, since he tells the story of how you added your spirit to his song last year when he was in the act of saving your father's life. Often, as we sit around the fire, he tells the tale of how you sang the strange words of the Bigfoot song with him, as though you, too, knew it. I know he admires you; after all, he gave you the bullet he had pulled from your father's chest. I have learned from Stands Strong that this is a rare honor he bestowed upon you. But, you are only a girl of fifteen now, having recently had a birthday, and he is a man full-grown."

Liliann nodded, looking down.

"Please, my friend," continued Czanna as she whispered her next words, saying, "there will be many other men who will come to admire and love you. Your beauty, alone, will attract many hearts of eligible young men, both Indian and white, I am sure. And, when they come to know and experience your sweet nature, you will be able to pick your forever love from amongst them."

Liliann didn't respond except to nod, and, as she looked away, another tear raced down her cheek. She murmured, "Aye, I be sure ye are right about this, Mistress—"

"Almost-sister, please. I am no longer your mistress."

"I be a knowin' this, almost-sister. 'Tis only that I was bein' so certain there be somethin' special a-tween us…somethin' worth holdin' onto."

"And, so there is. Even my husband noticed there was an uncommon bond between you and First Rider. Once forged, it will never go away, though you will go on to find another who will love and adore you. But, always, the attachment between you and First Rider will remain. Mark my words, almost-sister: always, the two of you will share the moment when you both came to realize how special you are to one another. It will not die, though you both might be destined to live apart."

Liliann nodded. Indeed, it was all she could do. Even now, tears fell down her over cheeks and onto her breast as her lips quivered.

But, her almost-sister was right. She would go on to live her own life, though it would needs be apart from First Rider.

At least, through the years ahead of her, she would keep within her the knowledge that once, she and First Rider had touched each others' hearts. It would have to be enough.

Her voice soft and barely audible, she whispered, "Though this be a sad day for me, it be a glad time for First Rider and for Bird Woman. So, I be now makin' a wish for them both, that life be always good to them, and I hope them to be always happy. I would not be havin' it any other way. I be wishin' also that I might be forever a special friend for First Rider and his wife." Then sighing, she looked up at the tepee's entrance, and asked aloud, "Almost sister, may I be helpin' ye with supper?"

"Of course," answered Czanna. "I cannot think of anything more pleasant at this moment than to have your help."

Liliann nodded and, turning around to gaze at her friend, bestowed Czanna with the biggest and best smile she was able to give, though she feared her lips still quivered. Mechanically picking up the fat ribs to be roasted over the fire, she steadied her hands as she placed them over the coals.

*Soon, I shall be leavin' the Pikuni village with my father to go and live with my almost-sister's parents at Fort Benton. And, once there, I shall be tryin' to forget that I once hoped to be First Rider's bride, right enough. Instead, I shall be wishin' to be his friend now and forever.*

Printed in Great Britain
by Amazon